There was so much blood.

Macey stilled when she saw the subject of the spotlight. *Grady*. He wasn't looking at her. He sagged between two undead who held him with their sharp-nailed hands. There was a lot of blood.

No.

It took every bit of control she owned to keep from moving to him.

No. Wayren, you promised he'd be safe. You promised.

Macey was paralyzed, and she could do *nothing* as Iscariot cast a knowing smile at her and moved to Grady.

A cry lodged in her throat, but she couldn't reveal her terror. She couldn't let them know. Couldn't expose herself, couldn't do a thing to save him…

"The rings, Macey. Give me the rings."

No. I can't…Oh, God, don't make me choose…

"Give me the rings…and he will live," Iscariot said.

As if on cue, Grady lifted his face and looked right at her.

His lake-blue eyes. They were filled with pain and terror, pleading…but no recognition flared in them when he looked at Macey.

Nothing.

He didn't know her.

He was going to die, and he didn't even know why.

Praise for The Gardella Vampire Hunters

The Rest Falls Away, *Gleason's publishing debut...turns vampire stories--and romances--on their ear with a decidedly dark, decidedly unsentimental Regency heroine who stakes the undead with the best of them.*

-- Detroit Free Press

The undead rise to great heights through Gleason's phenomenal storytelling. She creates a chilling world with the perfect atmosphere of fear and sexual tension.

-- Romantic Times

Gleason keeps upping the ante with each novel, weaving the characters around her readers with each engaging conversation and narrative, every stage set of all the appropriate gothic gloom and melting beauty.

-- Book Fetish

A promising, enthusiastic beginning to a new paranormal historical series, Gleason's major label debut follows the adventures of a conflicted young vampire hunter in Regency England.

– Publishers Weekly

Sophisticated, sexy, surprising! With its vampire lore and Regency graces, this book grabs you and holds you tight till the very last page!

– J R Ward, best-selling author, Lover Revealed

Witty, intriguing, and addictive.

– Publishers Weekly

A paranormal for smart girls who like historicals. Buffy in a bonnet takes on the forces of darkness in Regency-era London.

– Janet Mullany, award-winning author of Dedication

The paranormal world should rejoice, for a new Queen has emerged!

– MyShelf.com

...Above all, the writing is what recommends this book most. Gleason's writing is sharp and taut, which makes for excellent action sequences, and a plot that travels quickly from the start. The writing strength alone gives me ample reassurance that this potentially plot-heavy series is in the right hands. I'm definitely looking forward to the next installment.

– Smart Bitches Love Trashy Books

…Victoria is the perfect heroine. Smart, sexy, and tough while remaining vulnerable, she is the reason I love this book. Secretly I'm dying to be her, including wearing the fancy dresses and kicking undead butt. Even though Victoria is a very modern heroine for the time period, she works well with the rest of the storyline. Max is another great character, with brooding good looks and full of mystery; there is a lot in his past that I will enjoy reading about in future novels. Then there is Sebastian, but trust me you will want to read about him for yourself....

– Blogcritics Magazine

… The paranormal world should rejoice for a new Queen has emerged! Colleen Gleason has written an explosive debut novel that is assured to please paranormal fans for a long time to come. This is the first in a series that is destined to be one that will go down in history. Very highly recommended.

– MyShelf.com

With its wonderfully witty writing, action-infused plot and sharply defined characters, "Rises the Night," the second in Colleen Gleason's irresistible Regency historical paranormal series, is deliciously dark and delightfully entertaining.

– The Chicago Tribune

A tense plot line and refreshingly diverse supporting characters complete the package, giving series fans plenty to sink their teeth into--and plenty more to look forward to.

– Publishers Weekly

...Heart-stopping scenes and sexual tension. With numerous twists, [Gleason] leaves you hanging, eagerly awaiting the next installment.

– Kathe Robin, Romantic Times

Other Books by Colleen Gleason

The Gardella Vampire Chronicles
Victoria Gardella
The Rest Falls Away
Rises the Night
The Bleeding Dusk
When Twilight Burns
As Shadows Fade

Macey Gardella & Max Denton
Roaring Midnight
Raging Dawn
Roaring Shadows
Raging Winter
Roaring Dawn

The Envy Chronicles
Beyond the Night
Embrace the Night
Abandon the Night
Night Betrayed
Night Forbidden
Night Resurrected

The Draculia Trilogy
Dark Rogue
Dark Saint
Dark Vixen

The Medieval Herb Garden Series
Lavender Vows
A Whisper of Rosemary
Sanctuary of Roses
A Lily on the Heath

The Unexpected Love Series
The Shop of Shades & Secrets
The Cards of Life & Death
The Gems of Vice and Greed

The Stoker & Holmes Series
(for teens and adults)
The Clockwork Scarab
The Spiritglass Charade
The Chess Queen Enigma

THE GARDELLA VAMPIRE HUNTERS

ROARING DAWN

MACEY BOOK 3

COLLEEN GLEASON

AVID PRESS

Cover Illustration: Ravven
Cover & interior design: Dan Keilen
ISBN: 978-1-931419-91-8

Prologue

A Secret Mission

1840
In the shadow of Muntii Făgăras

I F VICTORIA KNEW ABOUT THIS, she'd have your bloody head."

Sebastian Vioget glanced at his companion in the moonlight and quelled the ever-present surge of emotion—or, more accurately, emotions, *plural*—the man evoked. Even though eighteen years had gone by since things had—well, ended the way they had…Max Pesaro still made him want to dust the floor with his arrogant face. And then hang him by his thumbs over a hot pit and watch him suffer.

But at the same time, after what the two of them had done together—what they'd each sacrificed for the women they both loved, what they'd lived through in a hideaway in this very mountain where Lilith the Dark had once resided—there was immeasurable respect and trust between them.

One could say it was an incredibly warped relationship that had settled between Sebastian Vioget and Max Pesaro.

"More precisely," Sebastian replied as he lifted his lantern to see ahead of them, "if Victoria knew you'd agreed to go with me—and, more importantly, *without* her—she'd have *your* bloody head." He smiled humorlessly at the man who had everything he once thought he'd wanted. "But that would only be after she made your life miserable for several days."

"You're assuming she doesn't already make my life miserable." Pesaro grimaced. "In her own unique way."

Then his expression—a dark one of haughtiness and arrogance—softened. "I had to get the bloody hell away from London. The girls…Christ, if it isn't one damned ball or fête or theater or musicale, it's something else. Not to mention the gowns and the damned shoes. Gloves. Ribbons. And the *hats*. There aren't enough bloody hat racks in all of London to hold their millinery acquisitions. Feathers exploding every-damned-where, fake flowers on the landing—even lace in my study."

Sebastian couldn't contain a snort of laughter, despite the fact that they were approaching a very dangerous place during the middle of the night. The moon was full and the swath of stars broad, making it nearly as bright as day.

He was certain they were being watched by more than one set of eyes lurking deep in the harsh crevices or behind clumps of brush. Though Lilith was long gone, that didn't mean all of her minions and relatives were as well.

Nevertheless, together he and Pesaro were well prepared and could handle anything—despite the fact that Victoria wasn't there with them, though she would certainly disagree—and that was why he'd asked the arrogant bastard to accompany him.

"Ahh…the travails of being the father of debutantes," he said with mock sympathy. "And taking into account your own severe lack of fashion sense, one can only imagine the pain it must cause you to be inundated with that particular matter."

Max cast him another glance, and to Sebastian's continued delight, it was filled with chagrin. "I never imagined one could spend so much money on bloody damned *ribbons*."

"Isn't Isabella's coming out this year? You needing to outfit her as well as the twins—not to mention your lovely wife—well, one can only imagine the cost. Not that you can't afford it, being richer than the Vatican." Sebastian didn't feel one iota of sympathy for the man. At least *he* wasn't going to live forever.

Or at least live for a very long time—which was the case with Sebastian. *He* would be existing forever…or until he completed his "long promise." Whatever it was, and whenever the hell that might be.

"It's not the damned money so much as it is the bloody *time* spent on it, and the incessant *chatter* and squeals and *sighs*—and the sheer *number* of gowns and fripperies," Max grumbled, and scanned the craggy brush that grew up along the side of the moonlit trail on which they road. Always on guard, always watching. He stiffened almost imperceptibly, and Sebastian noticed, meeting his eyes in a brief confirmation.

Just as they'd suspected. They were not alone. Undead, for certain. Tutela members? Just as possible.

"And you've got it wrong, Vioget. Bella won't be out for another three years. Eighteen is apparently the magic age. Probably just as well for society, though my hair might be completely silver by then."

"So she's a hellion, is she?" Sebastian asked with relish. It was one of his favorite pastimes, imagining Max Pesaro with an entire herd of females in his house—and being utterly overrun and overruled by them. Sebastian would have loved every minute of it, but Pesaro…he should stick to the undead, for he was simply not equipped to handle the female race.

"Worse than her mother, if you can believe it. Stacia and Juliette raised hell enough when they were younger, but Bella… good God, I have no idea what I did to deserve that red-headed termagant."

Sebastian lifted a brow. Pesaro might not have any idea, but Sebastian sure as hell did. The man was insufferable, autocratic, and cold. It sounded as if his youngest daughter was precisely his opposite.

And just like her mother.

He grinned to himself. He couldn't wait to meet her—Isabella Sebastiana, as she'd been named; a decision that had surely been made despite Pesaro's certain vociferous arguments.

"And then there are the blasted *suitors*," the father in question muttered. "Underfoot all the bloody damned time. Lining up at the door on social call days, and lurking about on other ones. Flowers and bouquets and blasted notes *every*-bloody-where. Those boys turning up in the parlor, the library—one of them even walked into the *kalari* when Victoria and I were—er—training." The slight, unconscious curve of his lips confirmed Sebastian's suspicions about the type of training they'd been doing, and he couldn't help but smile himself.

Ah, those had been the days.

"Much more comfortable than a carriage," Sebastian said lightly, relieved that he could do so with hardly a pang in the vicinity of his undead heart.

"Naturally." Pesaro cast him a sidewise look noticeably devoid of apology, and also intended to covertly signal the presence of yet another watcher among the craggy mountainside. A slight twitch of his brow, barely noticeable in the faulty light, confirmed for Sebastian that his companion sensed undead—something more difficult for him to do himself.

"But no weddings yet? I presume I would have been invited if there was one on the horizon." Sebastian's pulse skipped a beat when he saw the large, hulking tree that grew in a skeletal black canopy as broad as a house. Its branches were dark veins against the starry sky.

The pool was there—just beyond the Tree of Masidies. The last time—the *only* time—he'd been here was eighteen years ago, with Victoria and another Venator named Brim.

"Not yet, but it appears inevitable that we will soon be relinquishing Juliette's future wardrobe bills to a bloke named Denton. But only if he promises never to touch her." Pesaro's voice was filled with flat determination.

"And only after you've paid for the trousseau, of course." Sebastian grinned, feeling a twinge of sympathy for Denton, the poor sot. Then he sobered. The time was at hand.

"Naturally." Max's voice remained even, but his dark eyes were sharp. His body emanated readiness like the sun radiated heat.

They rode beneath the Tree of Masidies and its spectral-hand black branches. Pesaro had to duck to avoid the lower-hanging ones, and Sebastian saw his hand move down as he did so, pulling a weapon from inside his boot.

Sebastian casually withdrew a stake from beneath his cloak as well, keeping it hidden among the folds. He had a pistol within reach on the other side as well.

The Pool of Samung hadn't changed in the last two decades. It was hardly larger than a puddle in the center of a London street, and was surrounded by an outcropping of rocks, apathetic grass, and scrawny bushes. Reflected beneath the night sky, it looked like a perfect mirror.

He and Pesaro alighted from their mounts, both on alert even as the other man continued to gripe about his three adored—but expensive—daughters. Anyone who actually knew Max Pesaro would have figured out by now that he was much more verbose and forthcoming than usual, but the conversation was a necessity to obscure their actions.

"And there's an *Irish* devil named Stoker," Pesaro continued grimly. "And I have to bloody look *up* at him when I talk to the bloke."

"Surely he's not interested in Isabella," Sebastian said, setting his lantern on a tall rock.

He walked near the edge of the pool, looking for the right place. Where had he been when he felt that angular, pointed object in the water? Though it had been almost two decades, the events of that day were imprinted on his mind.

"Devil take it, Vioget. Bella's only *fifteen*. It's Stacia that Stoker's sniffing around. I see the way he looks at her—though he hasn't had the stones to do more than cast puppy eyes at her. She's been leading a trio of rakes on a merry chase this year," Pesaro said. "I'll almost feel sorry for the damned fools when she drops them like a hot potato." There was definite relish in his voice.

"I think this is the spot," Sebastian said, kneeling next to the glass-still pool. The air was filled with a strange, subtle scent wafting from whatever it was that filled the indentation in the earth.

Pesaro walked up next to him, his shadow long and ominous as he clumsily knocked two stones into the pool near Sebastian's feet. Sebastian watched three concentric ripples disappear into the flat, smooth water as quickly as they'd come. One of them, a plop he'd caused when he knelt, was much closer to the shore than the others.

His companion jabbed a stick into the cursed liquid. The branch immediately vibrated, fried, and disintegrated. "Good God, Vioget. Are you certain you mean to put your hand in there?"

He looked up at his longtime friend and rival, whose face was completely in shadow. "We've got to get the stone. Now that Nicholas Iscariot is free from whatever curse in which Lilith imprisoned him, you know he'll be after it."

"Better you than me," Pesaro said dismissively, but Sebastian read the underlying edge in his tone.

And by now, he too felt the subtle, eerie chill at the back of his neck—more difficult to discern, as he himself was undead—but there, and familiar, nevertheless.

They were being monitored until just the right moment. So it was up to Sebastian to make it good.

"Here I go," he said, kneeling at the edge of the pool. And damned if he didn't feel a little stab of trepidation as he prepared to lower his beringed hand into the flat, silvery water.

The five copper Rings of Jubai had been fused to his digits ever since he'd thrust his hand into the pool eighteen years ago. Wearing all of them was the only way to safely insert anything into the water—appendage, stick, metal sword…

As he looked down at the mirrorlike surface, Sebastian couldn't help but wonder whether the protection might have worn off since his last visit, or whether this second immersion might somehow reverse the fusion of copper to flesh.

If the protection had worn off, he'd be less a few fingers before he realized it, for he assumed the evil fury of the mercury-like pool worked instantly on flesh as well as wood.

Without looking at Pesaro, he plunged his hand into the silvery substance that wasn't precisely water, but wasn't really anything else. Sebastian breathed a mental sigh of relief when he didn't feel the searing, shocking pain he feared.

Now that his lingering uncertainty was gone, Sebastian was able to focus on the task at hand, which included scrabbling around the bottom of the pool. When he brushed against the hard, angular sides of the small pyramid he'd encountered during his last visit, a rush of relief flooded him. It was still here.

"Any luck?" Pesaro asked, as if reading his mind. He sounded supremely bored, but Sebastian wasn't fooled.

"Not…yet," he replied, still putting on a show of feeling around with his hand. All the while, he felt the increased intensity of the chill at the back of his neck. Still crouched, he withdrew his hand covertly. Little droplets of liquid formed and bounced like tiny opalescent moons, then disintegrated with individual puffs of ash during his movement. Sebastian scooted a short distance around the pool to search another area of its bottom.

"Ah!" he exclaimed, becoming still except for the hand moving beneath the surface. "I think…" He made a sound of satisfaction and dragged his arm from the thick, clinging substance.

"Did you find it?" Pesaro's voice was unusually enthusiastic.

"I did." Sebastian rose with great alacrity, displaying his prize in a great flourish. The large emerald stone glinted in the lantern light. It was a square, about the size of two female thumbs side by side, and he made certain whoever was watching could see it.

"Excellent. Now let us take our—" Pesaro broke off, spinning around as the first attacker appeared as if from nowhere, launching himself from behind a large boulder.

No sooner had he landed, flatfooted and lashing out at Pesaro with a long-nailed hand, than five others emerged from behind various bushes and stones.

Sebastian flew into action, his greatcoat swirling as he flung it aside—the better to keep from being grabbed by the hem and tossed into the pool—and slammed his stake into the heart of the first undead who got close to him.

The attacker froze, his eyes wide and shocked, then his entire being exploded into silvery ash that fluttered to the ground like moonlit confetti as Sebastian turned to meet his next threat.

As he did, the green stone flew from his hand in a great, shining arc and tumbled to the ground. Cursing, Sebastian lunged for it, lost his balance, and was knocked to his knees.

He scrambled toward the stone, but the vampire had already snatched it up with a great cry of triumph.

"Max!" Sebastian shouted, pulling to his feet much more slowly than usual as the undead bolted away. "Stop him!"

Pesaro spun and whipped his stake, sending it spinning through the air. It lodged not in the heart of the escaping vampire, but harmlessly in the back of his shoulder.

Pesaro cursed and dug a second stake from his boot as he turned to meet the attack of two more undead, just as Sebastian whirled and caught a fifth one with his shoulder, sending him flying toward—and into—the pool.

The result was not a pretty sight. And it didn't smell very pleasant either.

By the time Sebastian made his complete circle and turned back around, the space was quiet and empty. Undead dust wafted prettily to the ground—all that was left of the vampires except the one who stole the emerald.

Pesaro stood there holding a stake, looking grimmer than usual despite the fact that everything had gone as planned. "Bloody *damned* hell," he groused.

Sebastian checked his pocket to make certain the black pyramidal stone he'd slipped from the pool was still safely in place. "You missed."

Pesaro cast him a withering glance. "Me? *Miss?* Don't be ridiculous—" Then he caught himself, and a flicker of humor twitched his lips when he realized his companion was merely playing the role. "But that was my favorite stake."

Sebastian climbed on his horse and reached over to take up the lantern, but Pesaro had already grabbed it. "All set?" he asked, for his companion hadn't yet gathered up his reins to mount.

Max seemed to be searching the ground, using the lantern's glow as assistant. "Thought he might have dropped it," he muttered, kicking a stone aside as if to look under it, then starting along the path the escapee had taken. "Damn it to hell. What does a bloody vampire want with a damned stake embedded in his shoulder?"

"Blast it, Pesaro, you can get another silver-tipped stake," Sebastian told him, shaking his head. Sometimes the man was utterly incomprehensible.

"I know that," Pesaro said, still looking around, his expression growing darker. "But that was the one Victoria gave me, and if I don't get it back, she'll notice. That woman notices *every* damn thing. And if *she* doesn't notice, Bella will. Christ." His voice was unusually tense.

"So the biggest problem is not that you've lost the stake she gave you, but that you're going to have to tell her *how* you lost it." Sebastian howled with delight, feeling free for the first time in years.

Pesaro looked up at him, something like apprehension in his eyes. "When she finds out we didn't bring her, there'll be hell to pay. For both of us."

Sebastian couldn't stop laughing. It was so very rare that Max Pesaro was off his game. "You're the one who married her, *mon ami*. The spoils of war are all yours."

"Go to the devil, Vioget."

One

A Dark New World

May 1926
Chicago

THE TUNNEL WAS PITCH BLACK AND ENDLESS. Macey Denton couldn't see anything, including the stake in her hand. She felt her way blindly, the back of her neck cold as an iceberg. The brick beneath her fingertips was damp and rough, and the air smelled like rot, bodily functions, and unadulterated evil.

She crept along, silent and steady, the rhythm of her pulse thudding solidly through her limbs. Her sturdy boots crunched fine pieces of stone, and knocked into heavier, larger ones. Something scuttled in the darkness, and something else dripped ominously.

Malevolence radiated, quiet and pervasive, through the air.

"I've been waiting for you."

Nicholas Iscariot's rasping voice filled Macey's ears as she fought to control her heartbeat—to keep it her own, instead of allowing it to be absorbed by the power he wielded. She knew what it was like to have her heartbeat connected to his.

"I knew you'd come, Macey," he said, his voice closer, somewhere in the dark. "You couldn't stay away." There was a lick of satisfaction in his tones as they filled the blackness.

Suddenly there was a small circle of light. It surrounded a tall, skeletal-slim figure and cast a shape on the rough ground the size of Al Capone's dinner plate. Iscariot was dressed in a pinstriped suit with a blood-red handkerchief in his breast pocket and a matching tie. In the center of the tie, something glowed, sickly green and malevolent.

His dark hair was slicked back, gleaming as if it was wet, and only one half of his face was out of complete shadow. Those fine features—handsome in a stark, elegant way—were a chiaroscuro of shadow and light. His eyes blazed red. They were rimmed with a bold blue ring, as were all of Judas Iscariot's children, and Macey was careful to keep her gaze slightly averted from his powerful one.

Iscariot turned his head slightly, and now she saw his other cheek: marred by a burn in the shape of a thick cross. She allowed a grim, satisfied smile to curve her lips, for she'd been the one to put that scar on his face.

"Of course I came," she replied. "I couldn't resist looking at your handsome face." She braced herself, expecting him to launch toward her in fury.

She would end this now. Tonight. The stake was firm in her grip. She was ready.

Her heartbeat was her own.

Instead, he showed her his fangs and, to her surprise, became very still. His eyes burned brighter.

He seemed to wait…to concentrate. Something shifted in the air, and she felt the space between them change. It thickened. Shimmered darkly. Her breathing clogged a little, and her pulse began to thud a trifle slower. He was fighting to capture her heartbeat, to make it his own. To get into her very blood, to control the depths of her heart.

To control *her.*

As she fought the tug, Iscariot recognized it and smiled lasciviously. He displayed a mouthful of wicked fangs, and his tongue slipped out, red and glistening. As the air between them pulsed with power, stretching and shimmering with malevolence, he licked his lips as if tasting something delicious. His eyes burned on her with lust and hatred.

"We are well matched, Macey Gardella," he told her, his gaze resting heavily on her as the energy pull eased. Nevertheless, she continued to avoid his eyes and forced back the desire of her heart to meet the pulsing beats of his. "You've marked me, but I too have marked you." His white hand moved sharply.

A searing pain streaked down the front of her torso, tracing her sternum from the hollow of her throat to the bottom of her ribcage.

She felt a sudden rush of blood springing from the scar that had healed over months ago, striping the front of her shirt. And then a second hot pain, around the nipple of her left breast.

Iscariot's eyes blazed with fever, but he still didn't move toward her. Instead, he made a sharp gesture with his hand and another light popped on—somehow, someway in this primitive tunnel, he created a small spotlight with the flick of a finger.

Macey stilled when she saw the subject of the spotlight. *Grady.*

Her former lover wasn't looking at her. He sagged between two undead who held him with their sharp-nailed hands. There was a lot of blood.

No.

It took every bit of control she owned to keep from moving to him.

No. Wayren, you promised he'd be safe. You promised.

Macey was paralyzed, and she could do nothing…*nothing*… as Iscariot cast a knowing smile at her and moved to Grady.

A cry lodged in her throat, but she couldn't reveal her terror. She couldn't let them know. Couldn't expose herself, couldn't do a thing to save him…

"The rings, Macey. Give me the rings."

No. I can't…Oh, God, don't make me choose…

"Give me the rings…and he will live," Iscariot said.

As if on cue, Grady lifted his face and looked right at her.

His lake-blue eyes. They were filled with pain and terror, pleading…but no recognition flared in them when he looked at Macey.

Nothing.

He didn't know her.

He was going to die, and he didn't even know why.

"So be it." Iscariot cast her a triumphant smile as he swirled toward Grady in a flutter of black cloak, wide and heavy, and as enveloping as the darkness in the tunnel.

Macey screamed inside, horror rushing through her as the cloak wrapped around her, heavy as death, tight as bindings. She raged and twisted, fighting to free herself, to go to Grady as Iscariot tore into him with fangs and sharp nails.

Blood, everywhere, blood…

Blood…darkness, binding her, smothering her…

Macey woke suddenly, bolting upright amid twisted blankets. Her face was wet, and her chest heaved as if she'd run miles. She was shaking.

Oh God, oh God, no.

It was just a dream. *Just a dream.*

She looked around, straining into the dim light that filtered from beneath her bedroom door. She forced herself to see the shape of familiar objects in the room: a glint from the mirrored dressing table holding her pocketbook, combs, and jewelry, the tall, odd hat stand with the new pink confection from Aunt Cookie, the bulky chair where she'd tossed her dress and stockings hours ago.

Panting but no longer disoriented, Macey flung back her covers and got out of bed. The very action of putting her feet on solid ground helped bring her back to now, to reality.

Just a dream.

Her heart still hammered, and her knees were trembling… but it was just a dream.

Yet it was a dream that could very well come true.

Clammy with cold sweat, she made her way in the dark to wash her face. By the time she drank a large glass of water and dried her hands, the trembling had stopped and she was breathing normally.

But she wasn't going back to sleep.

Macey glanced at the bed, a mountain of lumps in the strained light. She could make out the hills of its cyclonic mess of sheets and coverlet, and was incredibly grateful Chas hadn't been there to witness such a display.

But then again, he had his own demons.

What a pair they were, she and Chas Woodmore.

Her pulse still a little off balance, Macey shrugged into an ivory chenille robe that comforted her with its soft, fluffy embrace.

She slipped out of her bedroom, padding down the silent corridor lit by a single sconce. Temple's room was at the end—she'd been encouraged to take over the one that had belonged to Sebastian, as it was the largest and most comfortable.

Now that she was no longer allowing Al Capone to blackmail her, Macey had moved into another of the small apartments connected to The Silver Chalice. There were several rooms and hallways, plus a kitchen and living space that spanned the underground area between the pub and Cookie's Smart Millinery—a hat shop located down the block and behind The Silver Chalice.

When Macey opened the silver-gilded, cross-encrusted door that separated those back rooms from the pub, she expected to find the bar silent and empty. After all, it was well past dawn. Sebastian—and now Temple—had always closed up just before sunrise because he slept during much of the day, as most vampires were wont to do, and opened at sundown.

But damn, the place wasn't empty. Chas was there. He sat at the long, scarred counter, nursing a glass of something considered illegal, thanks to the U.S. government.

Macey hesitated. The last thing she wanted was to be drawn into conversation with anyone—let alone one as perceptive and blunt as Chas.

But it was too late. As careful as she'd been, he'd obviously heard the soft sweep of the door, and turned to look. Macey saw hard weariness and irritation on his face. That was nothing new—those emotions were usually etched there, except in rare moments of levity or passion…both of which she'd experienced firsthand.

"You all right?" he asked in a rough voice. "You're up early for having been out all night on the streets. At least, that's where I assume you were. What happened?"

She wanted to turn back around and retreat to the sanctuary of her room before he saw the fear and discomfort lingering in her eyes…or before she did something else equally foolish.

But at the same time, as much as she wanted escape, she was drawn to him. He was magnetic and powerful in an unsettling way. And one thing Chas did well was help her forget. Help her clear her mind—or empty it, depending how one looked at it.

And Macey was in desperate need of clearing her mind. So she sat on a stool at the corner of the bar as she tightened the belt of her robe.

"Couldn't sleep," was all she said.

He looked up at her from beneath a thick lock of blue-black hair without moving his head. Just his eyes: dark, bloodshot, heavy-lidded. Nevertheless, they were lit with something that made her pulse leap and her mouth go dry again. "I know a remedy for that." His lips quirked up a little on one side.

"And so you do," she replied, holding his gaze while her insides flipped and dove, and a sizzle of heat shot through her. But it was ruined by a pang of sadness.

She looked away. "When did you get back?" He'd gone off somewhere for a few days without warning. But at least he'd left a note, so she didn't wonder whether he too was gone for good.

"A while ago. Did you miss me?"

No. Yes. A little. Maybe. More than I should've, you arrogant, frustrating bastard.

After all, it was just he and Macey now left to face Nicholas Iscariot. To find a way to destroy the powerful vampire lord. And unless one of them turned out to be the so-called "dauntless one,"

Macey wasn't certain of their chances at success, as foretold in Lady Rosamunde's prophecy:

"Upon its unleashing, a root of malevolence shall marshal such power as never before known. It shall permeate far and deep, and only the dauntless one and his peer shall rise up to it."

Thus, without Chas…she was on her own. So he'd better stick around.

And without the dauntless one and his peer—who Al Capone, at least, had believed was Macey herself—what were their chances of stopping the "root of malevolence," which could only be Nicholas Iscariot? Perhaps not enough.

But *no.* She hadn't missed Chas. Not in the way he implied.

Macey chose not to respond, and the question sat there between them, seeming to pulse in the silence.

He set his empty glass back on the counter. "Christ—it's not like I asked if you loved me."

"That'd be a hell of a lot easier to answer," she muttered, casting him a sidewise look.

Chas's grin flashed, then was buried as he reached for the bottle and refilled his drink. His hand was steady. "Want some?"

"It's seven o'clock in the morning."

He shrugged. "You look as if you had a rough night."

"Maybe I did."

"The question is—was it a rough night *out*, or was it a rough night *in*?"

He really was too perceptive. Just another reason to find him annoying. But she could turn that around, poke him back. "So where were you for three days?"

"I had things to attend to," he replied.

Silence settled there, taut and tense and fraught with too many unspoken words.

"Well this is a fine conversation," she said, suddenly impatient. "Neither of us giving anything up." She used one hand to vault herself over the counter, landing easily in Sebastian's old spot behind it. She bent to dig out a short, heavy glass.

"It's morning here, but somewhere else in the world, where there are no bloody vampires, it's seven at night," she said, and slammed the vessel onto the counter. "So I'm in."

"Best way I know to forget things you're better off forgetting," he said, and tipped the bottle to fill her glass with a thin gold stream. "Well…second best way." He gave her that look again—and this time, the shot of heat went right to the pit of her belly and below. And stayed there.

Macey considered him, considered the offer, and lifted her glass to drink. He was right, dammit. And the way she was feeling—the way she'd been feeling the last few weeks—maybe a good, hard roll in the proverbial hay would be just the ticket she needed.

Because if she was going to keep having those nightmares—

"Ugh!" She pulled the glass away from her mouth and glared down at it. "What the hell *is* this?" Sharp and bitter and flat was what it was.

Chas's mouth twitched again. "Hardly a level above rotgut, if you ask me, but I don't know where Temple is putting the good stuff anymore."

Macey dumped the thin liquid down the sink and slammed her glass back onto the counter. "I know where she keeps the really good stuff—the bottle Sebastian had been hiding from… Well, hiding. Turn around, if you please."

He rolled his eyes, but to her surprise, he complied, swiveling on the stool so his back was to her.

Once she was certain he wasn't watching, she pulled a narrow rack of glasses aside beneath the counter, revealing the thick metal door of a safe. A little twist of the knob and she opened it to reveal the inside, which contained three bottles of the most unusual liqueur she'd ever tasted—not that she was any expert. None were labeled, but one of them had been opened and was corked with a pyramid-shaped onyx stopper.

She pulled it out as Chas turned around. "So that's where she keeps it."

They—she, Chas, Temple, and even Wayren—had offered a toast to Sebastian from that very bottle on the night he died.

Macey lifted a brow as she poured the rosy-gold liqueur into her glass. "I think you'd best forget whatever you might think you know, Chas."

He shoved his empty—again—glass toward her, then—

"What the *hell?*" Chas fairly knocked over the precious bottle, he moved so abruptly, lashing out to grab her by the arm. "Macey, what the hell is *that?*"

She was so shocked, she couldn't form a reply—but then she saw he was staring down at the opening of her robe-, at the red line seeping down the front of her nightshirt. Down the center, along her sternum.

Fresh blood.

From Iscariot.

Her head went light and dizzy. "But it was a dream," she whispered, pulling out of his grip, dragging the robe away. She brushed wildly at it like Lady Macbeth. *Out, out, damned spot…* "It was a *dream.*"

There was another stripe of blood, around the front of her left breast. Her heart began to thud wildly, deep and heavy.

"What the hell are you talking about, a dream? I know that's from Iscariot. Did you see him? *When did you see him?*"

"It was a dream," she said once more, numb and cold. The cotton was damp—the blood was *real*—and the red lines were growing thicker.

"But you're bleeding. From your old scars." Any trace of inebriation in Chas's voice was gone.

"In the dream, he made me bleed like this. I-I didn't realize…" Her hands were ice cold. *How?* Her heart thudded as she stared down at the impossible sight.

"You didn't see him except in your dream?" Chas repeated. "Iscariot made it happen…from a dream? Good Christ." His eyes were filled with shock.

Macey had already begun to unbutton her nightshirt—just to make sure. She had to make certain…she had to see it with her own eyes.

"My God," he whispered when she pulled apart the top of her shirt.

She looked down and saw the line of blood, somehow—*impossibly* somehow—erupting from her skin.

"It's real," she whispered. The realization made her cold with terror. "It's *real.*" She looked up at Chas to see the same emotions reflected in his eyes.

"He wants the rings," she said, putting into words what they both knew.

"Yes. And until he gets them, or we destroy him…" He shook his head, his lips flat and grim.

Neither needed to put it into words. Iscariot would bring hell to Chicago, hell to them all, in order to get those rings.

And it was only the two of them to stop him.

Two

Solitude in the Sanctuary

BUT THE RINGS OF JUBAI were as safe as they possibly could be.

Nicholas Iscariot had no hope of retrieving them on his own, for at Wayren's suggestion, the five copper bands had been secreted in the sacristy of St. Patrick's, a very small, unremarkable church Sebastian had visited on a regular basis.

It was into this church that Macey stepped, two evenings after she had the nightmare, cutting off the symphony of Chicago by night. The distant echo of gunshots, accompanied by the sounds of automobile horns and squealing tires, was left behind as she moved into the silent space.

She eased the heavy wooden doors closed—denying them even their normal soft thump as the solid walnut panels settled into place. Inside, the place was quiet and dim, filled with flickering candles and traces of the essence of frankincense. The Easter lilies were gone, and a large red banner had taken their place.

This evening, the church was empty but for a solitary figure near the front.

Her heart squeezed, for the person who knelt in prayer was not the elderly woman whom she'd come to know—and who'd given her the rosary that saved her life twice. No, that wise woman was gone, and Macey had lost yet another guiding mentor in her life.

Now all she had was Chas—and much as she cared for him, Macey knew he was just as damaged as she herself was. He was searching in the same way, too—and was just as lonely, just as solitary.

Just as angry.

And he didn't even belong here, in Chicago or in 1926. He'd been "transferred" to this time and place several years ago with the help of Wayren. So his very presence here felt frighteningly transitory.

Macey wasn't Catholic, but she genuflected nevertheless—because that felt like the right thing to do—then settled in a pew about a third of the way from the back.

She looked around aimlessly and realized she was waiting for something to happen. At the same time, she fought the sense of bewilderment and fear that had come over her since her dream two nights ago. Every time she thought about that nightmare-turned-real, her hands went cold and her stomach churned.

How could Iscariot have such a hold over her? How could he have drawn blood in a *dream*?

Months ago, during their first encounter, he'd fed on her in an automobile—rough and violent—while his goons held her down by the wrists and ankles in the back seat of the car. That was when he sliced into her skin with his dagger: tearing through her dress, her undergarments, and her flesh, and circling one breast as well. But those scars had healed, as had his bites, thanks in part to Chas's application of salted holy water.

When Macey faced Iscariot again a few weeks ago in the city morgue and seared him with her cross, he'd somehow managed to make her bleed again from the same healed scars…but he'd been *there*, in person. That alone had been frightening.

But now he'd done it again, *in a dream*.

How? And what did it mean?

She wasn't certain she really wanted to know. She was a Venator, a vampire hunter descended from the most powerful ones who ever lived. She was skilled, strong, smart—and had been *chosen* for this life. It was her vocation. She was *made* for this.

Yet the slick, evil Nicholas Iscariot terrified her—mainly because no one seemed to comprehend the depths of his power.

His abilities seemed to be beyond what other vampires had ever been capable.

And more importantly, more frightening of all, was how he would use that power to get the rings.

How many innocent people—ones she knew and loved, ones she had never met—would die or be mauled before this was resolved?

What perhaps concerned her the most was that, other than his appearance in her dream, as of late, Iscariot had been all but invisible in Chicago. If she didn't know better, she might have thought he'd left.

There'd been no major vampire attacks—there were always random ones, of course, like there were muggings on dark street corners, but in this case with blood and fangs, but nothing terribly newsworthy. Nothing that gave her a clue what to expect next, or even anything to focus on.

Macey felt as if she were simply *waiting* for Iscariot to make the next move—just as she was *waiting* in this church for something to happen.

Neither thought sat well with her at all.

That had to change.

She would make it change.

She would *do* something.

She would turn the battle into one *she* controlled.

Macey was drawn sharply from her thoughts at the sound of a kneeler being raised into place with a soft thump. The other person in the church rose and walked along the pew, clearly ready to take his leave.

It wasn't until he'd turned down the aisle and was nearly to her pew that she recognized him in the dimness.

"Chas. What are you doing here?" She met her friend in the aisle.

"What do you think I'm doing?" he replied with a sting of irony that told her he probably *had* been praying. He was such an oxymoron of a man.

"I thought you might be here to check on the rings. Maybe try them on?" She was only half teasing. No one had tried on the five rings since Sebastian left them, for there was the chance the bands would seal to their fingers as they'd done to Sebastian's for a century.

"Right. I offered to do it previously, you recall. To wear them, and to go to the pool at Munţii Făgăraş."

"But Wayren declined your offer." She looked up at him, trying to read his expression. "So maybe you were tempted to try it anyway." It wasn't as if the thought hadn't occurred to her as well.

He inclined his head. "I wouldn't presume to argue with Wayren. I mean that," he added when she lifted her brow to give him a sardonic look. "Wayren is…" He trailed off, and Macey was struck by the bald sincerity in his voice. It was in his eyes as well. "She's the closest thing we have to perfection."

She couldn't argue with that, but it didn't mean she had a lack of questions for the mysterious woman.

"We need to find a way into Iscariot's den," Macey said, formulating into words her most terrifying and determined thoughts. She started to walk down the aisle, to the back of the church. "Because that's the only way to catch him by surprise and destroy him."

Chas lifted a brow as he walked along with her. "Bold and brassy. I like it. But never say you think you'll just waltz right in and stake the bastard."

She rolled her eyes. "First we have to find where said bastard is hiding before I can waltz right in and then stake him."

"This might help." He produced a folded newspaper, and it smelled of fresh ink.

The evening edition of the *Chicago Tribune*. And on the front page, dominating half above the fold, was a huge photograph of Nicholas Iscariot.

Three

The Gauntlet is Thrown

FOR THE MOST PART, Macey had come to avoid reading the *Tribune*. Every time she saw the byline *J. Grady* next to a story—and there had been more and more of them lately as he became more and more successful—her heart hurt.

The last piece she'd read with his name on it was a front-page report of Harry Houdini's funeral. The escape artist and magician, who died in a Detroit hospital after a show, had been a friend and mentor to Grady. The sorrow and grief over the loss of his friend had come through in the prose, despite the fact that it was a journalistic piece.

At least he wasn't also feeling sorrow and grief over losing Macey—because he didn't even remember her, thanks to Wayren and the small golden disk Macey had asked her to employ.

Now, she looked down at the folded paper Chas thrust at her, stepping under one of the sconces in the church to better examine the story. The front page was dominated by a huge photograph of the beaming Nicholas Iscariot shaking hands with Mayor Dever, and flanked on the other side by Colonel McCormick, the *Trib*'s editor in chief. Macey automatically glanced at the byline. Her heart sank.

J. Grady.

So her favorite newshawk had been there. He'd seen, spoken to, and interviewed Iscariot.

And Iscariot knew who he was.

While Grady, though he'd been imprisoned by the vampires and tortured by Iscariot only weeks ago, would have no idea who the other man was.

All because of her.

Trepidation stabbed her as she looked down at the photo, at Iscariot's arch, patrician features. He was looking out at the camera, staring straight at the viewer with a modest smile. But she saw the truth through it and read the underlying evil and satisfaction burning in the curl of his lips and the glint in his eyes. It was as if he were looking directly at Macey, tossing the challenge at her feet.

Waiting for her to figure out his plan.

Italian Baron Graces Chicago, read the headline. The subhead gave more information: *Nicholas, the Baron Politano, newly arrived from Rome, debuts into society at Cardinal Ball.*

She let her arm fall, allowing the paper to drop away, and looked up at Chas. He was watching her with eyes that were too intuitive for her comfort.

She gritted her teeth and collected her thoughts. She focused on fury, duty, and determination—and immediately felt powerful. "Well, at least he should be easier to find, now that he's debuted into society. Aren't young ladies supposed to be debutantes—not barons?" she sneered.

"That's the way it used to be, back in my day," Chas replied. But he was still watching her carefully.

Macey shoved the paper back at him and pulled out the stake she'd tucked into a garter beneath her frock. "Let's go. I'm in the mood for a fight."

"That's the best thing I've heard you say in a while." His eyes lit with appreciation. "Let's dust some vamps."

"Tie it like you mean it," Grady said. "Even *you* could get out of these. They have to be tighter."

Detective Jameson Linwood, who was still eternally grateful for the fact that he'd somehow recovered from a near-death attack a few weeks ago, frowned at the insult. Nevertheless, he tugged at the ropes digging into his nephew's wrists. The daft kid's fingers were already starting to turn grayish white. "It's already cutting off your blood, you damned fool."

"Be that as it may, but Houdini never complained about that. I tell you, make them tighter." Grady, who was facing him, lifted his bound wrists impatiently toward Linwood. "Come on. You're a cop—pretend I'm one of your most dangerous perpetrators and you don't want me slipping off into the night like an eel."

"You're no damned Houdini, and if you don't be taking care, you're gonna get yourself killed, Grady m'boy," he grumbled. Nonetheless, he did as he'd been told and retied the ropes with every bit of strength he owned, rolling his eyes when the nephew grunted with pain at the new onslaught.

At least he was here to release the fool when it became necessary.

"If I can live through the dirty, murderous streets of Dublin, I can live through a few tight ropes. Besides, Harry taught me a lot—and once you learn the techniques and obtain the tools, it's just practice. A lot of…practice. And…mastery of the…body." Grady's words were uneven, due to the pain and discomfort that was surely throbbing in his arms and numbing his hands.

"So you say. I hope you ain't planning on taking this act on the road, boyo. Is that tight enough for you, y'foolish mick?"

"It'll do," was the reply.

"And now you want me to do what?" Linwood asked, looking balefully at the coffin-sized box in the center of Grady's living room. It had arrived not long after Harry Houdini died—a bequest from the escape artist for his protégé. That, and *seven crates* of books from Houdini's personal library.

"Stuff me in there, tie my ankles the same way—then lock it up."

"Next thing, you'll be wanting me to throw it in the river," Linwood mumbled, helping his nephew to climb inside. "With you inside."

"And then chain it closed with that padlock over there."

"What in the bloody hell are you talking about? You're never going to get out of there." He examined the box. "Hell. At least you've got yourself air holes."

"That'll be the next phase." Grady grunted as the ropes were yanked tight around his ankles. "Filling those in so I can do it underwater. Once I get—this—down."

Muttering curse words alternated with prayers for the improvement of his nephew's mental capacity, Linwood did as directed. At least he'd be able to relax and have a nice spot of whiskey while his blarney-brained boy thrashed around inside a coffin for a bit.

Jesus, Mary, and Joseph, he didn't know what was wrong with the kid lately. Well, he wasn't actually a kid, Linwood admitted as he fit the top over the coffin. Grady was coming on to thirty years of age, and had lived a more harrowing life than even Linwood had done since becoming a cop in gangster-infested Chicago. No doubt about it: the boy was lucky to be alive, no thanks to Linwood's miserable sister.

"Remember to time me," came the muffled voice from inside, followed by a thump. "Use the stopwatch."

"Right." Linwood looked down at his handiwork—at the padlock hanging near the edge of the coffin, of the chains wrapping it like a Christmas present. (That thought brought back to mind the memory of his wife, Camilla, and the way she'd make him use his finger to hold the ribbon in place as she tied them in this very room. Ah, Lord, he missed her.)

"Did you start the timer?"

"Yes, yes, I did," Linwood said. That was a little white lie, for he'd glanced at the clock on the fireplace mantel after he set the coffin lid in place. He didn't see any need to start the stopwatch. Even if Grady did manage the impossible, who cared whether it took twenty minutes and five seconds or twenty minutes and fifteen seconds?

He turned and wandered into the kitchen where he knew his nephew, like the good Irish Catholic boy he was, kept a fine bottle of whiskey beneath a loose floorboard.

Linwood poured two fingers of the liquid amber, then splashed in a third one to help wash away the memory of Camilla, and looked out the window.

The house—the one he'd lived in with his wife until she was gunned down in the crossfire of two feuding gangsters and he realized he needed a change of scenery—overlooked a small park. As it was May, even though it was nearly eight o'clock, the sun still cast a welcome light over the swings and climbing bars below. All were in use, and he felt a twinge of sorrow that he and Camilla had never had children. Grady was as close as they'd come, and they hadn't even met him until he came to Chicago after the war.

That in itself had been Divine Providence if it ever was, and Linwood gave thanks every day for bringing the boy—who had never even been a boy as long as he'd known him—into his life. It was miraculous, truly, for, thanks to his mad, deeply disturbed sister's elopement and disappearance, Linwood hadn't even realized Grady existed until the boy looked him up in Chicago.

He didn't know what he'd do without him.

He rested his glass on the windowsill so he could take out his handkerchief and blow his nose. Boy needed to dust his damned house once in a while.

When he looked down to pick up his drink again, he noticed something most curious. Crosses, carved into the wood, there on the sill. Three of them. They were filled with something metallic, something shiny. Like silver?

Linwood frowned. They certainly hadn't been there when he'd lived here. What a strange thing to do.

His attention strayed to the kitchen counter, where Grady had set his pocket watch along with the signet ring he'd been wearing. The ring was silver. And come to think of it, it was a relatively recent addition to his nephew's wardrobe. A silver ring. And silver crosses set in the windowsill.

What was the boy up to?

He heard a rattle and a thump from the other room and grinned to himself, picturing the blarney-brain kicking ineffectively at the coffin from inside. A glance at the kitchen clock told him Grady'd been messing around in there for less than four minutes. *I'll give him another five or so before I check on him.*

"Got some of that for me?"

Linwood nearly dropped his glass—which would have been a waste—and whirled. He couldn't believe his eyes when he saw his nephew standing there, rubbing his wrists, wearing a very smug expression.

"Holy Mother of God," was all he could say.

By now, Grady's smugness had exploded into a delighted grin as he held out a tangle of ropes.

To be honest, Linwood was happy to see such a carefree expression on the man's face, for the last few weeks had been dark ones. It was as if something had happened to change the easygoing yet determined Grady into someone withdrawn, irritable, and frustrated. He'd been the kind of man who could charm the knickers off a nun and have her apologize for taking so long to pull 'em down, but lately, things had been different.

Ever since Linwood had come home from the hospital, in fact.

Part of Grady's change was due to his uncle's near-fatal injuries, he knew, as well as the shocking death of Harry Houdini. But Linwood sensed something else was wrong with his nephew.

He'd tried to ask about it, even probed a little about the sweet little colleen he'd been seeing—Macey was her name, he *thought*, and she had beautiful, dark eyes—but Grady had simply acted as if he didn't know what Linwood was talking about. He looked at his uncle as if he'd lost a few marbles, to be honest.

Maybe he had been confused himself.

After all, that attack—some of the details of which were still murky in his mind—had really set him back. They'd given him a lot of medication in the hospital, and everything before and during his recovery was fuzzy.

Linwood still wasn't completely back to normal—though he'd gone back on the beat—and his scars had been slow to heal. Grady wouldn't talk much about what happened either, even when Linwood tried to resurrect their theory that vampires had been involved.

Both he and his nephew had long shared a belief in the existence of vampires, for they'd seen evidence in attacks occurring in Chicago for years. And even if they hadn't, after Linwood's near-death at the hands of red-eyed men with fangs, he, at least, had no choice but to believe in the undead.

But Grady had become reticent about it. He didn't actually deny their discussions, but he didn't engage in them as he had done in the past.

Still. There *were* the silver crosses embedded in the windowsill. And Linwood sure as hell hadn't put them there.

"How long did I take?" Grady demanded, dragging Linwood's attention back to him. He picked up the ring on the counter and replaced it on his finger.

"Uh…" Linwood scrambled around in his brain, looking at the clock and calculating.

"You didn't use the stopwatch," his nephew accused, picking it up. "Why not?"

Linwood shrugged. "I figured I'd be unlocking the bleeding thing and it wouldn't matter."

Grady shook his head. "Oh ye of little faith. Now how am I going to know if I'm faster next time?"

"You're going to do it again?" Linwood asked.

Someone knocked on the door, and they both turned. It was eight at night, and Grady—being a top investigative reporter—had a telephone installed so he could be called for any urgent stories instead of wasting time for a courier to arrive. So the visitor probably wasn't from the *Trib*.

"Expecting anyone?" Linwood asked as his nephew went to answer it.

"No."

Moments later, Grady was back in the kitchen, looking at a piece of paper that had been folded. His eyes were filled with surprise and wariness—and enthusiasm.

"Well, this is quite unexpected. Linwood, I'm going out."

He handed the message to his uncle.

Meet me at Clancy's Gold Coast at nine o'clock. Come alone.

"What the hell is this? One of your sources? And what's that little squiggle on the bottom there? Is that supposed to be a signature?"

"In fact, it is. As Conan Doyle wrote: 'The game is afoot.'" He already had his hat in hand. "Don't wait up, uncle."

Four

Of Cobras and their Comparison to Dangerous Men

A PHOTOGRAPHY EXHIBIT?" Macey repeated as she dropped her stake onto the counter of The Silver Chalice. As it was approaching dawn, the place was silent and empty. "You want to go to a *photography* exhibit?"

There were undead to hunt, an immortal lord to track down and assassinate, plus a city to keep safe…and Temple wanted to go to a picture display.

The woman in question was replacing clean glasses neatly on their shelves, and she gave the stake on her counter a dark look. The pub had just closed, and Macey had wandered in from a night of searching out vampires.

"Look out, I just cleaned the counter," Temple said, giving the stake a little shove to send it rolling onto the floor. She snatched up a rag to wipe off the bar again, putting as much elbow grease into that task as she did taking Macey through her paces practicing in the *kalari*. The shellacked bar shone like a mirror, and Macey was often bruised and sore when she was finished with her work. Temple was very good at what she did. *Whatever* she did, and that included getting her way.

"Don't knock it, sister. The exhibit looks interesting."

Temple was tall and lithe, with long, sleek muscles. Her age was near thirty, and she resembled the singer Josephine Baker, with her smooth, coffee-with-cream skin and shiny blue-black hair crimped into waves that just covered her ears. In fact, the first time Macey had seen her, she'd been singing in a cabaret called The Gyro.

Temple had come from New Orleans more than a year ago—not long before Macey learned about her calling as a vampire hunter—ostensibly to assist her Aunt Cookie in the hat shop she owned. But in reality, Temple had been assigned to Macey as her hand-to-hand combat trainer, or *comitator*. She was also well versed in the history of the Venators, as well as the prophecies of the Venator Lady Rosamunde Gardella, which had been written in the twelfth century. Additionally, Temple had recently taken over the ownership of Sebastian Vioget's pub.

She was not, however, a Venator like Macey, Chas, and Sebastian.

"The article was in the *Tribune*," Temple went on. "They're exotic photographs from all over the world, and some of them are from a female adventure photographer. She's taken photographs in some of the most dangerous and unique places—like from the top of Notre Dame in Paris. The article said she climbed up one of the spires to get the shot."

"When is the exhibit?"

"Tonight. Mayor Dever is opening the exhibition, so it'll be a very high-society reception. Tickets are hard to come by, but I've managed to snag three of them—don't ask me how. I have my ways. I know it's Saturday, but I can close up for one night. You should go to bed and rest up. You look like you could use a night out without the undead, sister—and the Good Lord knows I could. Aunt Cookie wants to come, and you know she'll make sure we look our best. Be at her shop by five, and she'll take care of everything." Temple seemed almost giddy at the thought. "Who knows—there might even be a vampire or two lurking about, and you can kill two birds with one stake."

Her eyes danced with unusual levity, causing Macey to wonder if the woman had secretly been hitting the gin. Though blunt as a dull knife, Temple was usually more dry and pragmatic.

"All right, I'll go," Macey said. Mayor Dever was going to be there. Perhaps she could talk with him and see what she could find out about "Baron Politano." "There's just as likely to be undead there as anywhere else." Maybe even the so-called Italian baron himself. She suppressed a little shiver.

"How many vamps did you find tonight?" Temple was well aware of the current dearth of vampires lurking about the city and that this apparent lack of undead could only be the calm before the storm.

"Not enough. I got five, and so did Chas."

"You and Chas?" Temple gave her a speculative glance and looked like she was about to speak again.

Macey forestalled the curiosity lighting her friend's eyes by gesturing toward the stack of glasses yet to be put away. "How about pouring me a little something to help me sleep? I liked that stuff we had the night—the rosy-gold stuff Sebastian kept in the safe," Macey said.

The liqueur was so thick it was just about like syrup, but it burned along with its unique sweetness. There was also a spiciness as well.

Temple didn't comment, but pulled out the bottle in question. "Never saw this when he was still around," she muttered, working off the fancy triangular stopper. "Sebastian was holding out the best stuff on us, sister. Wish I knew why he kept it locked up in a lead box. And wish I knew where to get more of it." She filled a glass and slid it across the counter, then held up the bottle and squinted at it. "Looks like *someone's* been helping themselves." She eyed Macey balefully, and that seemed to bring her back to the previous topic. Unfortunately.

"So…you were with Chas last night," Temple said. "He hasn't come back yet. Do you know where he is?"

Macey shrugged, feeling the weight of her friend's interest settling on her. "It's not my job to keep track of him." She couldn't control the soft heat in her cheeks.

Temple didn't look away. "You're playing with fire there, sister. You know that, don't you? Chas Woodmore's not like other men."

I'll say. But Macey declined to speak. She wasn't giving Temple any more ammunition for a lecture. It was none of her business what Macey and Chas had done in the back alley tonight after slaying six vampires in five minutes flat.

Temple had no reason to know how they'd turned to each other, panting and exhilarated after the wild battle that had ended much too soon, chests heaving, eyes glinting with satisfaction and yet still looking for something more. How Chas's dark Gypsy gaze clashed with hers, hot and wild. How Macey grabbed him by the front of the shirt and spun him, then threw herself at him so forcefully he stumbled back into the brick wall.

There in the dark alley, amid broken crates and soggy cardboard boxes, the stench of rotting waste mingling with the scent of undead ash that still clung to their hair and shoulders, they'd devoured each other. Mouth to mouth, hot and sleek, tongues clashing, hands everywhere. The abrasive alley wall was behind him as she tore at the fastening of his trousers, plunging her hand down into the heat, closing around him as she groaned against the moist, warm skin of his neck—then suddenly, Macey found herself lifted. He gathered her up, pivoted, and shoved her against the wall, holding her with one powerful hand at her throat as he yanked up the skirt of her dress.

The fresh night air brushed her bare thighs as Chas lifted her over him, settling her with her legs around his waist. Her fingers were deep in the thick, wavy hair on his head as she kissed and licked and nipped at his throat, yanking his shirt wide open.

So needy. She needed, *needed.*

Needed *something.*

The beads on her dress caught and scrubbed against damp, rough bricks as he found the slit in her knickers, then slipped his fingers inside to feel how hot and ready she was. He moaned against her temple when he found she was, and with one quick shift then thrust, he was inside her.

Macey tightened her legs around his waist and moved with him—fast, hard, wild—the back of her head scraping against the wall, until finally she found her peak. She made no effort to stifle her cry of release, and felt another roaring sweep of pleasure when his deep, heartfelt sigh reverberated against her hair.

She sagged back against the wall, balanced on his hips as he leaned forward, braced by one hand against the bricks, while the other held her up at the waist. Panting, gasping, at last he eased her to her feet. She landed there, unsteady for a moment as her loose shift slinked back into place over her thighs, then was suddenly shocked back to reality when she saw a figure pass by at the end of the alley.

What was I thinking?

She looked at Chas as she straightened her frock, pulled up her sagging, twisted stockings. Still weak-kneed, still reeling from the flood of lust and passion, she saw that he was studiously putting himself to rights as well. Without looking at her.

Dammit.

"Well that was…unexpected," she managed to say, wondering how many beads were left on the back of her dress.

"You'll get no complaints from me, lulu," he said in a rough, rumbly voice. "Sure as hell beats the way I…used to do it."

"In a bed, you mean?" she teased, trying to break the awkwardness.

"With fangs," he said curtly.

Macey snapped her mouth shut. There was nothing she could say to that, for she well knew what it had cost Chas to admit such a thing.

She wasn't clear on the details, but she knew Chas had fallen deeply in love with a vampire woman. He'd lost her—Narcise was her name—to another man. Then Chas had spent the last decade trying to forget her—and at the same time, battling his need to be fed upon by an undead while having sex.

It was an untenable condition: to be a vampire hunter addicted to the bite of an undead, to be attracted to that enthralling loss of blood and control while in the throes of passion. To *need* it.

Macey shivered, and her last bit of warmth and pleasure evaporated. She'd been fed upon by Nicholas Iscariot, and though she feared and loathed the vampire, she'd felt the base stirrings of lust mingling with the evil and darkness that came along with being enthralled.

She couldn't imagine how difficult it was for Chas.

"That must've been some memory."

Temple's voice jolted Macey back to The Silver Chalice and the glass sitting in front of her with the rosy-gold liqueur.

She looked up to find her companion's eyes on her, far too shrewd and knowing, and Macey took the opportunity to lift her glass and place a barrier between them while she sipped. Somehow the liqueur didn't feel quite as warm and soothing as she remembered.

"We got trapped in an alley with six vampires," she explained. "It was a very intense few moments."

"That explains the mortar crumbles in your hair and the—er—condition of the back of your dress," Temple said blandly.

"Like I said…it was intense."

"You're going to get hurt," Temple told her, slamming her hand onto the pointy bottle stopper a little harder than necessary to shove it home. "Ouch." She looked at her palm, then up at Macey. "Or he is."

"I'm already hurt," Macey said flatly, and slid off her stool. Now she didn't feel much of anything but weariness and apprehension. And cold. Empty cold.

Even the hot, wild moments in the alley hadn't changed that. The thing that frightened Macey the most was the fear that nothing ever would.

She changed the subject again. "Did you see the paper last night? The evening edition?"

Temple sobered. "Yes. Iscariot right on the damned front page. Have you been in touch with Wayren?"

"No," Macey said, then continued in a burst of frustration, "No, I haven't heard a thing from her since that night…the first night we had this." She lifted her glass with the special liqueur, then set it back down without drinking.

"I've been studying the prophecies a bit more," Temple said. "Going back further, and ahead a little more too. A bit of light reading, shall we say, before bedtime." Her voice was flat and ironic. And maybe a little lonely.

"And…?" Macey was hoping she'd say something finite and specific, like: *And Chas is the dauntless one.* Or, *We were wrong— the root of malevolence doesn't refer to Iscariot after all.*

Not that Macey thought for one minute there could be anyone more malevolent at the root than Judas Iscariot's vampiric son.

"And…I've come to no further conclusions. But I think it's a mistake to rely too heavily on what the damned prophecies say, anyway, sister."

Macey nodded grimly. "I agree. The only reason we even know about it is because of Al Capone, and he was wrong anyway."

"It still tickles me, in a laughable way, that *Capone* thought he was the dauntless one's other half."

Macey's smile was grim. "But not that he thought I was the dauntless one." She sighed. "Could he be right after all? About me?"

"We've been through this. The dauntless one is a man, but either way, you don't fit the description. You did not root from 'the deepest bowels of madness and grief,' sister. Your parents loved you and cared for you—"

"Until Max Denton left me." She found it difficult to refer to her father by anything but his formal name. "After my mother was mauled and torn to shreds. He sent me away."

Temple gave her a sympathetic look. "And look what you've done to Grady as well."

Macey gritted her teeth and sent her friend and mentor a very dark look. "At least he doesn't remember me. I still remember my father." She watched Temple, who was once again industriously drying glasses. "Regardless, I'm going to forget about the damned prophecy. I want to find out where Iscariot's lair is, and then I'm going to figure out how to get in there and take him. I'm not waiting for him to make the next move. This is *my* game. Not his."

Temple nodded in approval, and lifted her glass in a sharp toast. "Damn right. Time we women took charge and showed those men what we can do."

Macey grinned and clinked her glass against the other. "You said it, sister."

✝

The weather was brewing what looked like an ugly storm when Macey and Temple left Aunt Cookie's hat shop, dressed in their finery.

"Hope the storms hold off until we get home," Temple said, looking at the dark clouds with a jaundiced eye.

Thunder rumbled in the distance, and Macey shook her head. "I doubt it. But it'll keep any vampires off the streets tonight—or at least, their victims off the street," she added as they drove along in what had been Sebastian's automobile.

The photography exhibit that had Temple—and, it appeared, a good portion of the wealthy and powerful of Chicago—over the moon was being held in the Preston Bradley Hall of the stunning Chicago Library.

The building boasted two domes and several grand staircases with elegant archways. Macey, who'd been living in Chicago for less than two years, had never been inside the ornate structure, and she couldn't help but gawk as she and Temple alighted from the car at the entrance on Washington Street.

"This is one of the reasons I wanted to come tonight," Temple said, looking up as they passed through the arched portal and doors framed in bronze. "I needed an excuse to see the place."

The lobby off Washington was three stories tall, with a vaulted ceiling. The walls were constructed of white marble and finished with mosaics in intricate organic designs. The glass, mother-of-pearl, and stone mosaic pieces were all the colors of the rainbow, yet the white marble overruled their colorfulness and made the lobby feel light, open, and airy despite the number of people crowding within.

"It's a shame Aunt Cookie couldn't attend after all," Macey said as they handed their tickets to the doorman who stood at the base of grand staircase made of pristine white marble. It was studded with green marble medallions and more mosaics all the way up its broad flight. "After she spent all that time and effort getting us dressed, it's too bad her hip began to act up."

Macey's mid-thigh red frock glittered and burned from the swirling scarlet, orange, and gold beading that shimmered with every movement. She looked like the blaze in a fireplace, Cookie had told her as she adjusted a three-inch-wide crimson headband around Macey's forehead. On one side was a hand-sized rose, each red petal edged with scarlet glitter so it too sparkled as her dark head bobbed. A flowing evening jacket of gossamer fabric the shade of honey and shot with gold thread covered her shoulders, which were bare except for two skinny straps. She also wore blood-red gloves that reached past her elbows and were embroidered with black and gold sequins.

With a getup like that, Macey didn't even need any jewelry, but she did wear two large black studs that glinted at her earlobes.

"When Aunt Cookie's hip goes out, there isn't much for it but to put that stinky old Cajun poultice on it and let 'er set," Temple replied as they started up the grand staircase. The Tiffany glass dome, the focal point of the hall, loomed above, and the sparkle of stars and moonlight filtered through the glass. "Maybe a voodoo charm to help, but I let her handle that part of it." She flashed a bright white smile. "Anyway, I promised her we'd hand out her business cards if anyone asked about our costumes."

Temple wore a stunning shift of honey, gold, and amber, which fairly glowed against her rich cocoa skin. A slender headband studded with palm-sized peonies and an elegant arch of matching feathers completed her look, along with chunky black shoes sporting glittering gold sunburst buckles.

Preston Bradley Hall was crowded with people and tall round tables that echoed the curved walls of the room, as well as freestanding easels and temporary dividers that had been constructed to display the photography.

The exhibition was an elegant affair, with white-gloved waiters weaving through the maze of people and stationary objects, holding trays at the ready. In the corner, a string quartet played something more classical than jazzy.

Temple snagged a tall flute of something that sparkled like pale sunshine, and Macey looked at it in astonishment.

"Surely that isn't what I think it is," she murmured as Temple lifted the glass to drink. "Mayor Dever wouldn't allow alcohol to be served so blatantly, would he?"

Dever was known in the press as "Decent Dever," because although he was a "wet" person—he didn't support the Volstead Act—he did his best to enforce Prohibition because it was his job to uphold the law. Much as many of the Alcohol, Tobacco, and Firearms team of the government did.

Unfortunately, the same could not be said for more than half of the Chicago Police Department, and this conflict made the city a hotbed of violence, crime, and danger. Not to mention rife with bribery and much looking-of-the-other-way.

"It's only carbonated cider," said Temple, her slender, arched brows lifting. "Although I wouldn't be surprised if the real thing was around here somewhere. Even Dever…well, I expect if you said the right thing to the right pers—Well, hello there, darling." Her voice dropped to a purr, causing Macey to look over in surprise.

A handsome, broad-shouldered man, dressed smartly in a pinstriped suit, snowy-white shirt, and spats, had taken Temple's hand. He bowed, lifted her hand to press a kiss to the back of it, then raised his face—still holding her slender fingers in his darker ones.

"Miss Temple," he said, his brown eyes warm and liquid from behind round spectacles, "I don't believe I've ever seen anything so ravishing in my life as you tonight." His voice, like his skin, was deep and dark as molasses, and tinged with a bit of Southern. His wiry hair was close-cropped and held a light sheen from scented pomade. Something like pine. "You are indeed a sight for sore eyes."

"You're looking mighty fine yourself, Joseph," replied Temple in a low, throaty voice. "Apparently you managed to slip away from your patients tonight, after all."

"No one seemed to need a puncture sewn up or an appendix removed, so I felt it was safe to leave on time. And I had a compelling reason to make it here." He smiled warmly. "I'm delighted you were able to use the tickets."

Macey gaped while the two looked at each other as if they were about to devour the other, and all at once things began to fall into place. It was no wonder Temple had been so insistent about attending the exhibition.

She stood for a moment, feeling the absolutely palpable sizzle of tension between the two, before her friend seemed to recall her presence.

"I'm sorry, darling," Temple said, taking Macey's hand and pulling it toward her as she slipped her arm around Macey's waist. "This is an old friend of the family's, who has recently moved to Chicago. N'Awlins' loss is our gain. Please meet Dr. Joseph Sevin, the new chief of surgery at Provident Hospital. Joseph, this is my dear chum, Miss Macey Denton."

Macey noticed her friend's voice had slipped into more of a Southern lilt since she'd found her old friend, and she smiled. Clearly "friend of the family" was a euphemism for something much more interesting. She beamed at Dr. Sevin, who was just as charming and gallant when he bent over her hand—though Macey noticed he released her fingers more quickly than he'd done Temple's.

"I'll let you two get caught up on all of the news back in New Orleans," she said, giving Temple a sly look. "The exhibit looks fascinating."

"I'll find you later," Temple said with a discreet wink.

Macey wandered off in the wake of a delighted, low-throated laugh from her friend, and saw no reason to hold back a smile of her own. Dr. Sevin was surely the reason Temple had been in such a good mood lately. Even with the loss of Sebastian and dark threats on the horizon, she had something to be happy about.

Macey's smile faded as the reality of her own life set in. Hell. All she had was a vampire lord who was out to get her and seemed able to make her bleed at will, and the realization that she'd probably not live to see her twenty-second birthday.

Oh, and a father who might still be alive—if one could believe the likes of Nicholas Iscariot—and, by the way, hadn't bothered to get in touch for more than thirteen years.

Macey's life was just a meadow full of daisies.

But sulking, she told herself firmly as she paused in front of one of the photographs, was *not* the way to spend an evening when Cookie had worked so hard to fix her dress and do her hair all pretty for the occasion. She was here to have fun, and to be a walking display for the older woman's fashion creations. And, if the opportunity arose, to shove her stake in a few undead hearts.

Macey had had her choice, and she'd made it—signed her life away to the Venators and the fight against immortal evil. She'd made the decision to be alone and never marry, to give up the chance of happiness and a "normal" life…to live in the world of difficult decisions and too much knowledge about the insidious evils on this earth.

And so perhaps she should focus her attention on saving the world instead of…other things. She should find Mayor Dever and attempt to speak with him, to see what she could discover about Nicholas and hope for clues of what he might be up to, and where he might be hiding.

She was about to turn from the photograph when the hair on the back of her neck stood up and she felt a swift rush of awareness.

And then she heard his voice.

The bottom dropped out of her belly and her heart kicked off beat, too fast and hard. Macey stilled, staring at the photograph with unseeing eyes as the air stirred, and she sensed him moving toward her from the left side of the exhibit hall. Everything prickled and went hot and warm and cold, and back again.

It took every ounce of control not to sneak a peek at him from out of the corner of her eye as he walked closer, speaking to someone—a female, it sounded like. Of course it would be a female. A man like Grady, with all that thick walnut hair, Irish charm, and expressive blue eyes, was irresistible to women.

Macey mentally lifted her chin and squared her shoulders. Then she blocked him out, waiting for him to pass by, and concentrated on the photo, really seeing it for the first time.

It was the stark image of a street, many stories below, shot with automobiles cruising along, pedestrians on the sidewalk, street lamps, benches…and when she realized how the photograph had to have been shot, her heart clutched again—but for the cameraman this time.

For the image was taken straight on, directly downward, as if the artist was suspended over the center of the street—not from a building or a balcony, but something that allowed—she checked the photographer's name—S. Ellison to look directly over the middle of the street.

The sides of the buildings stretched down, down, down along the periphery of the photograph, neither side close enough for the picture to have been taken from either of them.

"And this one. Paris, I think?" The subtle Irish in a familiar voice slipped over her like a warm blanket.

Macey closed her eyes against the wave of grief and regret, then gritted her teeth.

Of course Grady and his companion had paused at the very place she stood. Out of all the images in the whole damned exhibit, they had to stop at the one she'd found. Because her life wasn't interesting enough as it was. Fate had to stir the damned pot. *Stir, stir, stir. Double, double, toil and trouble.*

She tried to remember the rest of the verse as a distraction, but her traitorous mind focused instead on the conversation Macey didn't want to hear. The bitch.

"Yes, it is indeed Paris. Not so far from Notre Dame, where I shot that triptych from behind the gargoyle."

Macey edged to the side, but she couldn't force herself to walk away. She remained, torturing herself—no, *testing* herself. It was a test.

Hell. If she couldn't get through this moment, how did she think she could face down Iscariot—in his own lair?

Grady's feet came into view next to hers; she didn't dare look over to see anything higher than his polished black shoes (no spats) and about knee height of the loose gabardine trousers that were in fashion. They were midnight blue, the color of his eyes when he was sleepy and relaxed. The back of her throat burned.

He was close enough that his arm moved alongside hers, a mere three inches away. Close enough that she smelled him—his unique essence of musky aftershave balm, hair pomade, and simply Grady.

She moistened her lips, aware that her heart was thudding about as hard as it did when she was faced with the likes of Nicholas Iscariot. She wondered crazily which one was more dangerous to her: Grady or Iscariot. Because at the moment, she didn't know.

"Oh, excuse me, miss," he said, when he bent forward to get a closer look at the photo and nudged her with his elbow.

"Not at all," Macey replied.

He straightened up, and as he did so, he looked at her for the first time. His eyes widened with what was probably appreciation—for she did look great tonight, and Grady certainly appreciated a fine set of legs, among other female attributes. And there was a flash of something else there—something hard or irritated. But not recognition.

No, there was nothing in those blue eyes that indicated he had any idea they'd once known each other—and in the most intimate of ways.

Her heart broke then, with the finality of it all—in a way it hadn't on the night she asked Wayren to use the special golden disk to wipe Macey from Grady's memory.

It really had happened. It really was done.

Over.

"I don't know how she did it," Grady said, still speaking impersonally to Macey, but clearly referencing the woman standing next to him—who, Macey suddenly realized, must be S.

Ellison. "But it had to have been an extremely delicate maneuver, getting into position like that."

Now he glanced at the photographer, and Macey's attention followed him. Her mind went utterly still, for though S. Ellison was more than a decade older than Macey herself, the photographer was the most stunning woman she'd ever seen. And they were standing very close together, very companionably. Grady was even holding her arm.

In her late thirties, perhaps even forty, the photographer was tall, with true black hair and an air of worldly sophistication. She possessed olive skin and exotic features, and she looked the way Macey had always imagined Cleopatra would. The woman even wore eye makeup, dark kohl lining her almond-shaped eyes with a short, subtle curl at the outside corners—similar to the images in the recently discovered tombs of Egypt.

However, she was dressed in a very modern column of shimmering black beads and sequins with blinding white evening gloves fastened along the wrist with onyx beads. A small, diamond-shaped fascinator of dazzling white trimmed with ethereal black feathers was anchored over the left side of her head, its lower point just above an arched brow.

S. Ellison laughed, her eyes flickering over Macey, and replied, "That shot was certainly a challenge. But the most difficult part of it all was keeping the people on the street below from gawking while I was framing the photograph. I didn't want a crowd looking up or people stopped on the walk. I wanted a shot that showed an everyday street." She extended a hand to Macey as she continued in her slightly accented voice, as if English wasn't her native language but she'd been schooled in England. "I'm Sabrina Ellison, one of the photographers—as you've no doubt guessed. Thank you for braving the threatening weather and attending the exhibit."

Macey shook her hand, aware, *so* aware, of Grady's attention sliding back and forth between them. The other woman's grip was firm and confident, and Macey matched it with her own. "I've just arrived and this is the only picture I've seen, but I'm looking forward to enjoying more of them. Thank you so much for the background information on that one. Now, if you'll excuse me, I'll let you finish your conversation, and I'll move on to the next display."

Macey was relieved to make her escape. *That wasn't too bad.* Her pulse was still a little fast, and her belly a little nauseated, but that would soon settle. She'd leave Grady to his stunning, *older* lady photographer and go off to find the mayor.

At least his *older* lady photographer wouldn't get him mauled by a vampire. Or worse.

And with that thought, Macey realized with a mixture of relief and disappointment that she didn't feel any indication the undead were present tonight.

She turned to take a flute of carbonated cider from the tray of a passing waiter—desperately wishing for something stronger—when she caught sight of another familiar figure.

Al Capone appeared to notice her at the same moment, for their eyes met and she recognized a flare of surprise in his gaze. He looked away quickly, then turned to speak to someone next to him without even nodding in her direction.

Macey wasn't particularly fond of Capone for several reasons that included his business ethics—or lack thereof—as well as the fact that he'd fairly kept her on house arrest for six months, manipulating her into being his personal bodyguard against the undead. Why he'd felt the need to have her watching his back when he was a Venator himself had been a source of anger for her, but he'd made it clear if she didn't help him, he'd use his power to disrupt the lives of her friends and colleagues…"disrupt" being a euphemism for much stronger actions that likely would have involved Tommy guns or the like.

After a particular crisis, Macey had finally realized how foolish she was being, allowing him to have such influence on her life, and told him to take a hike. Ever since then, she'd been admittedly concerned that Capone might not have gone very quietly into that good night—to quote the old poem—and was somehow planning his revenge, and would turn up at a most inopportune time.

But instead of approaching her with his haughty ways, Capone seemed unwilling to even acknowledge her. Considering the fact that there'd been photographs of the two of them together splashed over the front page of the *Tribune*, Macey found that disturbing as well as curious.

So she made her way through the strolling exhibit attendees directly to Capone's side.

"Good evening, Snorky," she said with a broad smile, though she kept her gaze hard. "You're looking fine tonight. Carbonara on the menu tonight at the Lexington, was it?"

Capone actually glanced down at his tie to see if there was a spot to which she'd been referring, then snapped his face back up to look at her. "Evenin', doll," he said. His beady, dark eyes were darting around the room behind her, as if watching for something. "I hear your friend Vioget has…er…gone on to greener pastures."

"That's right," she replied. "You missed all of the excitement."

"That's just the way I like it nowadays," he said, easing back from her. "Nice seeing you, doll," he added. "I got some biz-ness to attend to over there."

"I left a few things at the Lexington," she told him, wondering why he was in such a hurry to make off. Usually Capone took every opportunity to flaunt his wealth, clothing, or the weapon beneath his coat—not to mention the fact that he virtually controlled half the city—to anyone with whom he spoke. "I hope you kept them for me."

"Yes, yes, of course, doll. You send for 'em any time you want. The clothes and stuff are all dere. Enjoy the exhibit," he said, then slipped off into the crowd.

Macey watched him go, more than a little disconcerted at his abrupt departure. Yet whatever had gotten into him, she didn't mind. At least it appeared she wouldn't have to worry about Al Capone any longer.

As she wove through the displays, Macey barely glanced at the photos. Nevertheless, she noticed a close-up of a tiger among the grasses of a savannah, the portrait of a cobra, sitting up with its "wings" spread and vampire-like fangs bared so that one could actually see *inside* its gullet, and a particularly breathtaking shot that framed Westminster Abbey on a moonlit night, taken from what appeared to be the crow's nest of a ship on the Thames. There were African villages, a stormy Mediterranean crashing against a ruined shipwreck, and a group of chubby, naked children playing in a mud puddle.

But there was one photograph that caught her notice—a picture she found herself stopping to give a full examination.

In contrast to the other dangerous and exciting images, the subject of this one bordered on the mundane. It was also tucked into a corner of the exhibit, as if it were an afterthought. Definitely not one meant to attract attention.

The frame was dominated by a man, sitting at a desk. He was looking down at a paper on which he was writing, one hand holding the stationery in place. Tension emanated from his body. The man had thick, dark hair, and strong but elegant hands with well-tended fingernails. Those were the only visible features, other than the hint of dark brows, nose, and mouth. He was wearing a shirt, sleeves rolled halfway up a muscular forearm, and a button was loose at the neck. He didn't look like a simple clerk, or even a businessman. He looked powerful, despite an everyday pose with his face averted in something like submission.

Or determination.

Macey didn't know what it was about the photograph that caught her attention, but something about it was utterly compelling. The man seemed strangely familiar to her, and the entire, simple scene was nevertheless fraught with emotion. It was a juxtaposition of power, determination, and regret—and it all came through, somehow, via the composition, the lighting, and the way his hands held the paper and pen. Perhaps he was writing a difficult letter.

She didn't know why that crossed her mind, but when she saw the title of the photograph, printed on a card beneath, her brows lifted. *A Letter Long Due*. And the photographer was none other than S. Ellison again.

She looked closely at the paper, trying to discern the words scrawled on it. Of course, they were upside down and shadowy from the viewpoint of the camera, but the first line looked as if it read "Dear…" something with a capital M, and a descender at the end. Mary? Macey frowned, and her pulse gave a little jump when she looked closer. Huh. It could…geesh, it could just as easily be Macey as Mary. Which would be utterly unbelievable. Fanciful, really. She was reading too much into—

"I see you've found my favorite of the bunch."

Macey nearly leaped out of her skin when the soft, accented voice spoke so close to her. For a Venator, she certainly was off her game tonight. She sure as hell hoped she wouldn't be so jumpy if an undead showed up…

Macey turned to find Sabrina Ellison—sans Grady, thank you, God—looking at her with those exotic dark eyes.

"It's… It looks very emotional. And yet it's such a simple, everyday image," Macey managed to say. "Nevertheless, I found it quite moving."

"You appear to be the only one to have noticed him among the pyramids, cobras, tigers, and the aerial views." The woman gave a little laugh. "Forgive me, but I've already forgotten your name, and we met just moments ago."

Macey hadn't actually given her name, and surely that was merely the woman's polite way of asking. "Macey Denton. It's a pleasure to meet you. You're very talented…and very courageous."

Sabrina Ellison's eyes glinted with something like satisfaction. "Thank you, Macey. Oh, dear." She seemed to catch herself. "I hope you don't mind the informality—please, do call me Sabrina."

"Thank you, I will," Macey replied politely, but she felt strange that a woman she'd just met and would never see again should be so eager to talk to her as if they were chums.

Maybe it was simply because they were both women—surely it couldn't be easy being a woman in a vocation that was obviously dominated by men. Her smile became more genuine. The two of them had that in common, at least, though Sabrina Ellison would have no way of knowing it.

"It really is one of my favorites, and taking it was very nearly as life-threatening as shooting the one of the cobra," Sabrina said, her eyes focused on the photograph.

"Why was that?" Macey asked in surprise.

Sabrina smiled sadly, still watching the man in the picture. "Because the subject is far more dangerous, and he didn't know I was taking the shot. If he had…I fear I would have been better off facing a stirred-up cobra than that man when he was truly angry."

There was something in her voice that was almost wistful. Sad and strained; Macey felt a sudden and unusual affinity with this woman she didn't know.

"Have you ever loved a man it was safer not to?" Sabrina asked.

Macey blinked. Did this woman somehow *know* what was inside her mind? But she heard herself responding, nonetheless— and honestly, too. "Yes."

Still staring at the photograph, its creator gave a brief nod. Then she looked over at Macey with a short, chagrined laugh. "I apologize. I don't know why I even said that—I don't usually pry into other people's business, especially their private business."

"Don't mention it." Macey wasn't sure whether she should flee from the side of this unusual, rawly honest yet magnetic woman, or reach out to pat her arm in comfort.

She might have continued the conversation, but at that moment, a light, eerie chill scuttled across the back of her neck, fingering lightly along her shoulders, lifting the fine hair that grew there.

The undead were here.

At last.

Five

Stained Dresses and Hasty Exits

Please excuse me, Miss—er, Sabrina," Macey said, even as she turned to walk away. "I need to attend to something."

"Of course."

Macey felt Sabrina's curious eyes on her as she slipped off, making her way through the crowd. Tonight she had a stake slipped in each garter, both high on her thighs, as well as the same silver cross that had burned Nicholas Iscariot tucked beneath her gown. She considered it her good-luck charm, even though it was bulky and the size of her palm.

It would give her great pleasure to inflict a matching scar on Iscariot's other cheek.

Macey measured and followed the unpleasant sensation that settled over the back of her neck, and it led her toward the opposite side of the hall, the chill growing stronger and eerier as she made her way there. It occurred to her that perhaps that was part of the reason Capone had drifted off so quickly. Could he have somehow aligned himself with the undead, now that Macey had rid herself of him?

Galvanized by the thought, she moved swiftly between the people, dodging waiters and navigating around tables, all the while looking through the crowd to see if she could determine where or who was the undead…and if she could locate Capone.

She wasn't paying attention, and all of a sudden, Macey walked into a solid figure. One with which she was intimately familiar.

Startled, she looked up at Grady for a frozen moment, then removed her hand from where it had accidentally landed on his jacket and muttered an apology before ducking off into the crowd.

"Miss?" she heard him call after her. "Miss, is everything all right?"

She ignored him, ignored the pounding of her heart, and the way that silly incident had put her off, and made a beeline toward a cluster of distinguished-looking gentlemen standing in a tight group.

There. The vampire was there, among the men.

And so, Macey realized, was Mayor Dever. But not Al Capone.

As far as she could tell, Iscariot wasn't there either. She felt a little shimmer of relief that the slick-haired "baron" hadn't deigned to attend a photography exhibit.

And that she wouldn't have to face him, at least today.

Then her jaw set, and she felt her lips stretch into a grim smile. She'd have a chat with whatever undead *had* attended tonight. She knew how to be persuasive—thanks in part to Chas—and surely she would be able to find out where the baron was staying.

As Macey approached, she considered several ways to interrupt the close-knit group. Blunt and direct, ingenue-ish and confused, or coquettish and charming—any of the three would likely work.

But as it turned out, she was saved from having to make the decision. For when she was only a few steps away, the group parted like a theater curtain to reveal a tall, slender woman sitting on a chair among the men.

She had carrot-colored hair and dead-white skin, except for the freckles sprinkled over it. Her frock was a shimmering display of sunny yellow, gold, and clear crystal beads in large diamond-shaped patterns.

"Macey, darling," said the woman as one of the fawning gentlemen helped her to her feet. "What a pleasant surprise."

She smiled, and her eyes glowed red for a moment before her vampirism was quickly banked.

"Flora," Macey said, successfully hiding the shock at seeing her former best friend. "What are you doing here?"

"Why, the same as you, I assume—looking at a photography exhibit." Flora cast a sly glance around the circle of her admirers—including Mayor Dever—and smiled *very* warmly at them. "It's a very enjoyable event, I must say."

When Flora's admirers grinned back giddily, Macey realized the gentlemen companions were under Flora's thrall. Hanging on her every word, and she was controlling them with such ease.

The woman had become surprisingly powerful and confident in the last year.

Apprehension skittered through Macey like cat claws on a wooden floor. What was Flora up to? Any answer that came to mind was definitely not pleasant.

"It is a wonderful exhibit," Macey replied casually. "Do you have a moment? I'd like to speak with you, privately."

Flora smiled like Lewis Carroll's Cheshire Cat. "I'm afraid I'm a little busy here right now, darling Macey. Perhaps we can catch up some other time?" Once again, she turned her attention to the men clustered around her, sweeping her gaze over one after the other. Macey actually saw each give a subtle shiver as the vampiress's thrall connected with his eyes.

"Very well," Macey replied, giving her old friend a hard look—but a brief one; she knew better than to allow Flora to capture her gaze. "We can catch up at another time. But I do have some business with Mayor Dever." She directed this last to the man in question.

"I'm afraid he's rather tied up right now too," Flora said in a smooth voice. Her eyes danced with malicious delight and her lips—painted blood red, perhaps in an effort to hide any evidence of feeding—curled up at the corners.

Because, after all—what could Macey do? She couldn't exactly attack the vampire right here in the middle of a party. Especially when Flora had an entire tribe of men at her beck and call.

She hid her irritation and acquiesced—at least outwardly. "Have a lovely evening then, Flora. Excuse me, gentlemen." She turned and walked away, feeling the weight of her friend's blazing eyes boring into her back.

Macey ground her teeth. Now what? She'd been jilted by Temple; run into the last person she wanted to see; had encountered an astonishingly subdued gangster king; and had found a vampire she couldn't do anything about—and now she had to leave her to whatever devices she had in mind.

But what if there was a distraction? That might free the gentlemen from Flora's thrall—or at least give Macey the opportunity to drag the vampiress away. She needed to stake her, yes, but just as important, she needed information.

So what sort of distraction could she manufacture? Cutting out the lights was an option, if she could figure out how to do it. People might even blame it on the bad weather.

But that was impractical—for even if Macey found the fuse box and pulled the correct fuses, she'd still have to make her way back here to the hall in the dark, and among panicked people, and by then, who knew where Flora would have disappeared to—and whom she would have taken with her. Macey needed an accomplice…but Temple was otherwise occupied. Hmm. What about Capone? Perhaps she could appeal to his Venator side and get him—or better yet, one of his minions—to help. But she didn't see him anywhere in the room.

Another option was for Macey to find a way to lure Flora from her post.

She pursed her lips. What a frustrating situation for a Venator to find herself in. Being held hostage, in a way, by a single female vampire. She doubted Victoria Gardella had ever found herself stymied in such a manner.

By now Macey had walked far enough away that she could still watch the cluster of gentlemen and their vampiress coquette, but Flora couldn't see her. Her arms folded over her middle, Macey leaned against one of the columns that held up the archways at the top of one flight of stairs, looking around for inspiration.

She saw Grady, without his *older* lady photographer, and felt a stab of relief that he seemed to have divested himself of her—or vice versa…and then she felt guilty about the thought.

Dammit. It wasn't as if *she* could be in his life, so why was she hoping for him to be alone? He'd never done anything to warrant what she'd done to him—erasing his mind, indiscriminately taking away memories both good (she hoped) and terrifying. And now here she was, wishing and hoping he'd be alone. To what end? So he'd be as miserable as she—without even knowing *why?*

You're a selfish bitch, Mace.

The thought was sobering in its raw truth, and her heart ached a little more. She'd done the right thing; she *knew* it in her heart. She had loved Grady, and she didn't want him to experience pain or suffering simply because a woman targeted by the undead had fallen for him. He didn't deserve that.

He deserved a woman who could love him, who could have a family and make a home with him. Not someone who had to creep around dark, dangerous streets every night, putting her life at risk every day.

Not someone who was the most wanted woman in the world, according to the undead.

Not someone who had a vampire "baron" that could make her bleed in a *damned dream.*

Grady didn't deserve to be tortured and torn into ribbons as Macey's mother had been, simply because she'd loved Max Denton. Simply because she'd meant something to a Venator.

She tasted sour in the back of her mouth, and Macey swallowed and then stilled. Grady was making his way toward Flora and her cluster of men.

Her heart began to thud harder. Flora not only knew who Grady was—and what he meant to Macey—but she also had helped herself quite liberally to his blood on that horrible night two weeks ago, when Iscariot tried to kill Sebastian.

Macey's palms dampened and she moved away from the wall. *No, Grady, stay away from her,* she thought, sending the mental message as strongly as she could, and fully realizing the huge flaw in her decision to have herself removed from his memory.

The gold disk Wayren used might have erased Macey from Grady's mind, but it couldn't remove *him* from *the vampires'* memory. And she wasn't even certain to what extent the disk worked—did it erase everything about her and their memories together, and leave everything else? Did Grady still believe the undead existed, just as he had done before they'd met?

And as long as the vampires knew—or even suspected—Macey cared about Grady, there was nothing to keep the vampires from using him as they saw fit.

"I can give him something that will help keep him safe."

Wayren's words, the single thread of hope Macey clung to, came to mind. She clenched her fingers tightly into her palms, hoping the woman had done what she promised. Hoping whatever it was whatever she'd given Grady, it was enough.

Macey continued to move closer, feeling for the stake anchored to her thigh beneath the heavy, silky shift. If it came down to staking Flora here, in front of everyone, she'd do it. Let the chips fall where they might.

Grady was still moving purposefully toward the mayor—it made sense for the ace reporter to want a statement from the man—and Macey lingered nearby, watching from the corner of her eye while pretending to admire a photograph of the Parisian catacombs. Gruesome things they were—walls studded with skulls arranged like bricks, and skeletons everywhere.

Just as Grady came within view of the group of men and Flora and hailed them, a waiter passed in front of Macey and paused to offer the items on his tray to a couple strolling by. They all clustered in front of her, effectively blocking her view, and there was little she could do other than push them away to see what was happening as Grady shook hands with the mayor.

"No thank you," Macey snapped when the waiter turned to offer her the tray after the indecisive couple had finally made their choices and strolled on. She dodged around the waiter and nearly knocked over an easel as she began to rush toward her quarry.

Then she came to such an abrupt halt that her shoe made a sharp *smack* on the marble floor.

Flora was gone.

Grady was there, conversing jovially with Mayor Dever, but the tall, slender redhead had disappeared.

Macey paused to send up a prayer of heartfelt thanksgiving, then started off quickly in the direction she knew Flora must have gone. Gauging the sensation at the back of her neck, she determined there was still an ugly, lingering chill. And it was getting stronger, and—

"Looking for someone?"

Macey spun neatly and yanked the stake from beneath her shift as she lunged into the quiet alcove at her elbow. She had her stake raised before she actually saw Flora, and the momentum of her movement had her slamming the taller woman back against the wall.

"I found her." Macey had one hand on her old friend's shoulder, pinning her in place. The other held the stake poised over her heart.

Flora bared her fangs, her eyes burning red. "Really? And now what are you going to do?" Instantly, she faded from feral undead back into the familiar, cheery face of Macey's old friend.

"I'm going to put you out of your misery," Macey told her. Then she lowered the stake slightly. "But first I need some information."

Flora laughed, low and guttural, and her fangs peeked from beneath her upper lip once more. "That's a convenient excuse. You need information, so once again you're going to neglect to 'put me out of my misery,' as you said. There's no reason for you to keep spouting the fairy tale that you're going to stake me, Macey, because we both know you can't do it."

"I've already done it," Macey retorted.

"Oh, yes. Right. But you missed the target, didn't you?" Flora thumped herself in the center of her breastbone, right where her heart was. "So I don't believe that actually counts as staking me.

How many times have you missed when stabbing a vampire, Macey?"

"What are you doing here?" Macey asked, moving the stake back into position again. Flora's taunting was making Macey's vision flush red with anger. She had no qualms about slamming the stake into the vampiress's heart, old friend or no.

"I told you, I'm looking at the photo—"

Macey drilled the stake tip into Flora's sparkling, sunshiny frock, right between the breasts, and held it there with two hands. One good thrust and her childhood friend was dust. "I don't have any patience left tonight, and regardless of what might have happened in the past, it's impossible for me to miss my target tonight. So talk, Flora. If not, I'm sending you to the devil."

"I'm already with the devil," Flora snapped. "I came to you for help, remember, Macey? And now look at us. Two weeks ago, you said you'd try and find a way to help me save my soul."

"And then you immediately went and mauled a man."

"I have to eat." There was a hint of whine in her voice.

"You didn't have to leave him to *die*." Macey had no desire to go over this conversation again. "I want to find Iscariot. How do I find him? Where is he?"

"Why should I tell you that? The minute I do, you'll pin me through the heart and that'll be the end of me. At least if you leave me alive, Macey—Wait a moment, just think about this. If I'm alive, you have someone you can trust who's close to Iscariot."

Macey snorted. "If I could trust you, we wouldn't be in this situation right now."

"Fine. Maybe trust isn't the word. Maybe just someone you *know*. Doesn't our history mean anything to you? We've been friends for thirteen years."

"We were great friends—until you decided you wanted to become immortal."

"Look, Macey, I've never tried to harm you—which is more than I can say about you."

Macey contemplated this excellent point for a moment, then retorted, "But you've hurt others. Without remorse. And you went down this path because you were trying to get back at me."

"I'd never hurt you, Macey. I truly wouldn't. I might have… needs—a gal has to have sustenance—but—"

"It's not me I'm worried about. I can take care of myself. It's all the other innocent people you might decide you need for sustenance, and then leave to die. Look, I'm not going to stand here all night. Tell me how to get to Iscariot, tell me *something* relevant and valuable, and maybe I'll let you walk away tonight. One time. For old times' sake. But you'd better make it worth it." She pushed the stake deeper, and a blossom of red began to seep around the wooden point.

"Now you've stained my frock," Flora said. "All right, just give me a minute," she added when Macey's expression darkened and the stake thrust a hint deeper.

"Thirty seconds. Spill something, or it's over."

"All right. All right. I'll tell you this: he wants the Rings of Jubai." Flora's eyes widened when Macey twisted the stake a little deeper. "All right, you already knew that. But do you know he has the amulet of Rasputin?"

Macey eased up on her weapon. "Rasputin? He was the mystic who served the Romanovs of Russia, just before the Great War. He supposedly saved their son's life."

"That's the one. He's nothing but ash now, but his medallion somehow came into Iscariot's possession."

"Tell me about the amulet. What does it do?"

"From what I understand, it gives the vampire stronger powers, and can help protect him from the sunlight. Rasputin used it to cloak himself and enthrall the tsarina while he was living at the Russian court. There might be other powers. Iscariot wears it all the time now."

Macey felt a sudden shivery spark. "Does it glow green? Like an emerald with a light behind it?"

Flora nodded. "Yes."

Macey kept her attention on the stake and its position, but her mind was reeling and the pit in her stomach was growing deeper. In her dream, Iscariot had been wearing something glowing green. But she'd never seen him in real life with it on. "What else? What's he after with the Rings of Jubai? Tell me that and I'll let you go— this one time. If you promise to leave the premises."

"There's something in the pool—you know about the pool, I assume? The one the rings help access—right, well, there's something in there that had been placed there centuries ago, around the time Vlad the Impaler made his contract with Lucifer. You don't know about that? About the Dracule? Stars, Mace, I thought you were a librarian and knew everything. You always acted like—"

"Enough commentary on my lack of education on the topic of vampire history. What's in the pool?"

Flora shrugged, and the stake shifted slightly. Macey tightened her grip; she wasn't about to be taken off guard by her sly friend. "Rekk's Pyramid is what it's called. It's not very big—that's all I know, I swear it."

"You swear it? On what? The Bible? Don't make me laugh."

Flora's eyes flashed coal-burning red, then her lips twisted ruefully as her fury ebbed. "Guess I can't blame you for speaking the truth. Look, Macey, really, truly...I do want your help. I..."

Her attention had strayed to somewhere behind Macey, and she seemed to catch her breath and almost recoil, backing even further into the corner. "All right, I told you what you wanted to know. You said you'd let me go after I did."

Macey eyed her suspiciously, even as something itched behind her, as if she should turn and look at what caught Flora's attention. Capone, perhaps?

But she didn't trust the woman enough to take the chance of removing her eyes from her, even for a second. And as the back of her neck wasn't any more chilled or prickly than it had been a moment ago, she had no reason to fear an approaching undead.

Unless, she supposed, Iscariot *was* here and he was wearing Rasputin's amulet, safely cloaked from her notice by its power.

Nausea pinched her belly. That sort of freedom made him all the more dangerous.

"I'm going. Now. I really am," Flora said, trying to edge away even as the stake continued to pin her lightly against the wall. "Do you think I'd stick around with this happening?" She gestured to the blossom of crimson in the center of her frock. "Talk about causing a commotion."

Macey was still undecided when she heard a voice—no, two voices—behind her that she recognized. Her cheeks warmed when she recognized Grady and Sabrina, and it sounded as if they were accompanied by others in a group as well.

She glanced at Flora to see the vampire still looking more stricken than an undead had the right to be, considering the circumstances. "What's wrong with you?"

"Nothing. It's just…well… Nothing." Flora tried to edge away. Macey would have none of it, and she gripped her friend's arm, still holding the stake in place.

"What is it?"

"You said you'd let me go if—All right, fine. You might as well know. Your man, that reporter Grady, with the very fine blood and delicious head of hair? Well, I suddenly have a strong aversion to him. So I would very much like to leave, and you can be certain I won't be back as long as he's here." She was actually trembling and very nearly cowering at the same time.

Macey stared at her, trying to determine whether the vampire was lying. But surely she wasn't. "I'll let you go—but listen to this: he's not my man. Not anymore. We aren't together, and he doesn't even remember me anymore. His memory has been altered. He doesn't know me, and *he means nothing to me.* Do you understand that?"

"Right, right—whatever you say. Big mistake on your part, Mace. He's very fine. Now let me *leave.*"

Macey gaped at Flora in astonishment then stepped back to allow the woman to slip away even as she tried to make sense of what the vampiress had said.

Then, for the first time in weeks, she smiled, and felt weak with relief. Whatever Wayren had done, it was working.

Grady didn't remember Macey, and the undead couldn't abide him.

He was safe.

Six

Of Self-Censorship and Propriety

MACEY REALIZED HER OPPORTUNITY almost too late. Just moments after Flora disappeared, slipping away to make her escape from the photography exhibit, it occurred to her that if she followed the vampire there was a good chance Flora would lead her to Iscariot.

She had a heartbeat of hesitation—how would she let Temple know?—then went on, navigating around the warren of exhibit walls in the direction Flora had gone. Temple, of all people, would understand. She knew how the Venators worked. And besides, she was obviously preoccupied with the delightful Dr. Sevin.

Macey measured the sensations at the back of her neck, for the chill from Flora's undead presence lingered. Moments later, she was outside and—to her dismay—discovered that the sun had long set, and Chicago was being covered by a soft rain and a blanket of mist.

The sidewalks were nearly empty of pedestrians, but the boulevard was busy with automobiles crisscrossing in a steady stream.

The doorman was kind enough to tell Macey which way the tall, slender redhead had gone—though he gave her a pitying look when he saw that she had neither an umbrella nor any other protection besides her whisper-thin evening jacket.

"Going to be a bad'un," he said, looking out into the night with a knowing air—though at the moment, the rain seemed fairly benign. He gestured with the whistle he wore on a chain around his neck. "Are you certain you don't want me to call you a taxi, miss? Surely your friend has already gotten her own ride."

Macey declined with some reluctance—she would rather get into a warm taxicab than ruin her shoes and freeze to death in the wet, cooling night air, but…duty called. This was the best chance she'd ever had to learn where to find Iscariot.

So she hurried down the block in the direction indicated by the doorman, for the first time feeling mild regret that she was no longer allied with Al Capone—for he would have had a car waiting for her use, or at least a bodyguard with an umbrella.

To her grim satisfaction, the eerie chill over the back of her neck, which had begun to ebb, grew stronger as she made her way toward the next cross street. That success, however, was balanced by automobiles rumbling by, splashing up a goodly amount of water, and the fact that her shoes were made for indoor wear, not puddles and raindrops. The feathers in her headband were already slumping limply over an ear, and her arms were covered with goosebumps beneath her evening jacket.

But she went on, hurrying down the gray-black street lit with erratic pools of light from restaurants, headlights, and street lamps. Few other pedestrians were out, and those who were carried umbrellas or at least wore fedoras tilted against the rain.

Flora was too far ahead for Macey to see her; she had only the sensation at the back of her neck for direction and the information the doorman had given her.

Then, all at once, the telltale chill became very sharp and strong. Her shoulders and arms prickled, and it wasn't because of the rain.

Macey paused and slowly turned, her heart thudding harder. She looked across the street, beyond the river of automobiles, through a small group of young people walking past, and saw him.

Nicholas Iscariot.

She caught her breath and straightened, automatically sliding her hand down to close over the stake beneath her skirt.

The vampire lord stood there, separated from her only by four lanes of vehicles and a thick, foggy curtain of rain. He wore a long black trench coat buttoned up over his clothing and a top hat that glistened from the rain. She could see the jagged shadow on one side of his sharply cut face, part of the burn she'd inflicted on him.

His eyes glowed bright red, rimmed with ice blue—the only hues in a drab night. The strength of his heartbeat and its desire to control pulsed steadily across the distance.

Macey Gardella. Macey…

She felt his voice, rather than heard it. The syllables hissed softly in the depths of her ear, as if originating from inside her mind, rather than from across the boulevard and carried on the air.

We meet again.

Her heart thudded wildly, yet the solid grip of the stake beneath her fingers helped to steady her. Macey measured the distance, calculating the angle and timing, and the speed she'd need to plant the stake in his heart…and knew he was too far away to strike.

As if reading her mind, he inclined his head, just enough for her to see the arrogant acknowledgment there. Of course he wouldn't take such a chance.

I'll have the rings. They belong to me.

In response, she used her other hand to touch the silver cross hanging beneath her dress, the very one that had burned into the flesh of Iscariot's face. The one that marked him.

She had marked him.

Steadied by that thought, empowered by it, she dragged the pendant out from beneath her dress and allowed it to fall against the front of her bodice, thunking there solidly.

She faced him still, allowing him to see that she had no fear of him—that she dare not show it, at least—and that she had come armed.

The rain poured down, and his red eyes glowed, and the silver cross over her chest gleamed in the filtered light.

Neither of them moved.

Autos zipped by. Water streamed. A laughing couple dashed through the rain, splashing past Macey.

All the while, Iscariot's pulse thudded between them, reverberating like radio waves, tugging, coaxing, *pulling* at her.

She fought it, fought the allure of control. But even as she did so, the blood in her veins stirred, and her own pulse leaped and surged, fighting to match his. She gripped her stake, touched the *vis bulla* though her beaded dress, and kept control of her own heartbeat.

Come and get me, Iscariot.

She didn't open her mouth, but he heard the words—for his head jolted back just enough that she knew she'd surprised him. His eyes blazed like small fires circled with dazzling blue.

I'll destroy everything you love, Macey Gardella. I'll have the rings.

She curved her lips wryly. Little did he know, she had nothing left to love. Now that Grady was safe, now that he had moved on and was protected, now that Sebastian was gone, and the rings were hidden away…

Suddenly, Iscariot blinked—and the two pinpoints of red and blue were extinguished, and the world was back to drab, wet gray again. The sidewalk where he stood was empty.

He was gone.

Macey suddenly felt the cold, not from the outside, but from deep within. Her knees were trembling, and her breath was making rapid white puffs in the gray mist.

And then she felt the warmth seeping into her—no, *from* her…for she was bleeding again from the old scars.

Iscariot had made his point.

Max Denton had never been to Chicago.

He'd generally confined his revenge on the undead to annihilating vampires throughout Western Europe, though he had strayed further when the need was warranted—for example, to Romania and Turkey, once to India, and also once to Russia—

St. Petersburg. In fact, in St. Petersburg, Max had saved the day by staking the infamous Rasputin after a plan to assassinate the creature had been spectacularly botched.

But Sebastian was gone at last, the poor sot, and Max Denton's presence was needed in gangster-infested Chicago. So he had come—despite his desperate desire to never cross the Atlantic.

It wasn't that he feared traveling over the ocean—whether it be by air or ship—and he sure as hell didn't fear Nicholas Iscariot. In fact, he couldn't wait to meet the devil face to face, for it was on the vampire lord's orders that Max's wife Felicia had been attacked and mutilated almost beyond recognition thirteen years ago.

And he'd already delivered to Alphonsus Capone the one and only warning he'd give him about staying out of the business of the Venators—though he was rather hoping the man would ignore it, just so he'd have something fun to do. Max smiled coldly to himself, then the humor faded as he looked around the dark, smelly, dingy pub in which he waited. The place was no better than an armpit, and it was owned by the damned bootlegger himself.

No, it wasn't the gangster or the vampire lord or the travel, or even the fact that it was illegal to order a good whiskey once he crossed into the United States that unsettled him.

It was only a woman.

A merely mortal woman—well, really, *two* women, dammit, now that he actually thought about it—who were even more likely to kill him than Iscariot was. Though Max didn't give Iscariot a very high probability of succeeding anyway.

But the women…well, that was another matter entirely.

He looked up as a cloaked figure—unaccountably dry though it was pouring rain outside—made its way through the dimly lit pub, heading unerringly in his direction.

Another woman, but this one, at least, didn't have it in for him.

"Max." Wayren's lilting voice somehow filtered over all the shouts, guffaws, clangs, and other noise that filled the joint. And with her simple greeting came a wave of peace he desperately needed.

She didn't seem to mind the dinginess of the place, the rough voices and even rougher appearance of the patrons, the thick cloud of smoke that filtered over everything (at least tobacco was still legal in this backward nation), and the stickiness of the table at which he sat.

"Apologies, Wayren. This was the cleanest table I could find," he said, fishing out a handkerchief to wipe off a chair for her. He was probably the only man in the whole buggering place who even owned a handkerchief, let alone used it. He didn't bother to comment on the fact that she wasn't dripping wet like everyone else who'd come into this joint.

She smiled at him from beneath her hood, pale blue eyes calm and filled with acceptance. "Not at all, Max. It reminds me of the place I used to meet Andreas—The Snorting Hare—back in… well, *back*. And as that's neither here nor there—"

"Andreas? I'm afraid I'm not as up on my Venator history as I should be. Who is he?"

Wayren smiled beatifically, but she didn't take the bait.

Of course she didn't. Max knew better.

"And how is Macey?"

He winced at the sudden and direct hit, as if a crossbow bolt had slammed into his shoulder, and tried to think of a response that didn't make him sound like a wanker.

As it turned out, he didn't need to reply. The expression in her eyes told him she already knew the answer.

"How long are you going to hide from her…and from Savina?"

Max smothered a curse, for he'd always sensed it would be blasphemous to swear in Wayren's presence. Though that didn't mean he was always able to hold it back. "How do you know about Savina?"

She gave him a look that had him sighing: one blond eyebrow, lifted just slightly as a small smile curved her lips.

As if she'd answer anyway.

The blasted thing about Wayren was: she knew many things—as she was wont to say—but she didn't know everything. And it was hard to guess what she did and didn't know.

But it always seemed she knew just enough to remind him that he dared not anticipate her, either way.

"Savina's here in Chicago."

"Right," he replied. "A photography display. She's exhibiting under her professional name, Sabrina Ellison. But of course you know that."

Savina sent word she'd put him on the guest list for the event tonight, and he'd almost gone…but things weren't quite… Well, things weren't exactly *right* between them. And he didn't know how the hell to fix it.

Give him a damned crossbow and a stake, and he could slay an entire *tribe* of undead. Arm him with a sword, and he could decapitate a trio of Imperial vampires and not break a sweat. Lock him in handcuffs, and he could break free before his jailer walked out of the room. Slip him a pistol, and he could shoot the ashy tip off a cigarette from across the street without damaging the smoker.

But, by God, how to make Savina look at him with love and trust again…he had no earthly clue.

His belly felt sour and empty, and he really, *really* wished for a bloody whiskey.

Wayren reached across the table and closed her small, slender hands over his large, rough ones. For being so slight, they were incredibly warm and strong. "You'll do the right thing, Max. You always do…even if you do come to it a little later than one might hope."

He looked up at her, shocked to find a glint of humor and reproach in her eyes. Ah yes…the not-so-subtle reminder that he'd ignored his daughter for thirteen years.

Well, not precisely *ignored* her. He knew she was better protected than the bloody Crown Jewels and well taken care of, but he also didn't want there to be any chance someone might trace her through him. So he'd remained firmly out of touch and studiously ignorant of everything about her…until the first letter he wrote. The letter he sweated and *bled* over, dragging every word from deep within.

The letter, which, by the way, was never delivered, thanks to bloody Alphonsus Capone.

"Would you mind if we talked about something else?" he said. "For example, something I might actually know how to damn—er, handle?"

"Such as the dauntless one?"

This had Max sitting up straight. "Yes. Who did Rosamunde mean by the dauntless one? I have my suspicions, of course, but I'd like confirmation."

Wayren lifted her brows, both of them this time. An enigmatic smile touched her lips, but she didn't speak.

He ground his teeth. "You aren't going to tell me anything, are you?"

She shook her head, her eyes dancing at his consternation. Perhaps she *was* the third woman who was out to get him. "The prophecy will be what it will be; it's not for you—or anyone—to try and make it happen."

"Then why do we even have the damn—the blasted things anyway?"

"For guidance and warning. But not for a blueprint. Not for a path on which one insists upon riding, without listening to one's own intuition and intelligence."

"Right." He realized she'd removed her hands from covering his, and had taken with them the innate peace that always flowed through her touch.

"I've seen Chas," she said.

"You didn't tell him I'm here, did you?"

Now Wayren gave him a pitying look. "Really, Max, how long are you going to insist on lurking about Chicago without making yourself known?"

He glowered, then scanned the room over her shoulder again. "It's only right for Macey to be the first to know I'm here."

"I think that's an excellent plan, Max. Quite brave of you, in fact."

His gaze flew to hers, but she merely gave him that benign smile and continued, "You can count on my support in that matter. However, I suggest you don't wait too long to reveal yourself. Someone like you won't remain anonymous in this city for long."

"So you won't let on that I'm here? To anyone?"

"I won't."

"But…?"

Wayren did not seem to be able to contain her sense of humor tonight, for her eyes were glinting again. "You should probably know that Macey attended the photography exhibit tonight."

Max felt the color drain from his face. "She did? She was… at…the same place Savina was?" His lips could hardly form the words. But worse than that, his brain couldn't even handle the implications of what would happen if Macey and Savina should… *meet.*

Oh God.

Meet, and talk to each other, and realize who the other was… *Oh God.*

If that happened, he was well and truly fu—

Blast it. He couldn't even *think* a vulgar word in Wayren's presence.

He looked up to find her watching him. "I really need a drink."

"No," she replied firmly. "You need to find your daughter."

Seven

A Discourse Against the 18th Amendment

CHAS SLOGGED INTO THE SILVER CHALICE two hours before dawn—cold, wet, and grumpy as hell.

Mainly because what he'd hoped would happen—that he'd be struck off the earth by one of the violent bolts of lightning tearing through the city—hadn't occurred.

Damn. *And so I'll live to see another day.*

To his surprise, the pub was dark and still, and it wasn't yet dawn—though the clouds were so thick and heavy, who knew when the sun would be able to shine through anyway. A small lamp burned near the entrance through which he'd come, and there was another light at the door leading to the private apartments in back.

It seemed the place had closed early last night—probably because the weather was abysmal, and the customers had stayed in their warm homes instead of braving the wild thunderstorms for illegal libation.

Fine with him. And even finer with him that Macey and Temple weren't around either. He didn't want to deal with *anyone* tonight. Or, rather, this morning.

Chas peeled off his dripping coat and flung it onto one of the stools, removed his shoes and socks, then unfastened the top button of his shirt—which wasn't as soaked as his outer layers. He gave his head a good shake, spraying droplets everywhere, then found a bar towel to scrub away more of the wet from his hair.

Feeling marginally more comfortable, he turned on a light over the counter and slipped behind to fish out a glass and a bottle of something smooth to warm him from the inside out. He paused with his hand over a decent brandy and frowned at the racks of glasses.

Macey had pulled out that special bottle of Sebastian's from right about this area. She probably thought Chas hadn't noticed, but he'd been listening very carefully to where and how she moved.

Thus, it didn't take him more than a few seconds to locate the secret door behind a shelf of lowballs, and he smirked with satisfaction when he opened it.

Hmm. A lead safe? What the hell was Sebastian hiding in here—other than not one, but three bottles of that unique liqueur? Chas felt around inside the safe and didn't find anything else important enough to be locked away like that.

Still musing, he pulled out the open bottle and removed the fancy blue-black stopper, then sloshed a good two fingers into his glass. Back a hundred years ago, when Chas lived in London and traveled to Paris hunting undead and befriending the (occasionally) redeemable members of the Draculia vampire race, Chas had once mistakenly taken a drink from a bottle of liquor offered by a Dracule.

Unfortunately, it had been blood whiskey, and the memory had never quite left him. He still shuddered at the memory.

But this wasn't blood whiskey, and Sebastian Vioget hadn't been a Dracule—so why had he kept this and two other bottles locked away?

Simply so Chas wouldn't get to it? Or anyone else, for that matter?

Considering the fact that he'd never tasted anything like its soft, floral ambrosia that nevertheless burned in a smooth, heady rush all down the throat and into the belly—then softened the mind in just the right way—Chas supposed it was merely practical to keep the good stuff hidden away. It probably cost a ridiculous amount of money, even for a vampire, and especially during the insult that was Prohibition.

He corked the bottle and stuck it back inside the safe, then enjoyed his solitude and his drink as he leaned into a corner of the bar.

He sure as hell was ready to be done with Chicago, and gangsters, and flapper dresses that made all the female figures look like boys' bodies—and he was especially finished with Prohibition. Not that the Volstead Act kept him from imbibing when he wanted, but it was damned inconvenient.

And everything else…well, he was tired of it all. He understood how Sebastian had felt, ready to finish with whatever had brought him to this place. And Chas, unlike Vioget, had literally been *brought* here. Through time.

What he didn't know, still didn't know, five years later, was *why*.

Yes, he'd wanted an escape from everything that had happened with Narcise. And, unbelievably, Wayren had offered him a unique way out. But why here? Why now?

He shook his head and was just reaching down of the bottle to refill his glass for the third time when someone rattled at the door.

"We're closed!" he called, then frowned. What if it was Macey out there, bedraggled and wet? He wasn't certain she was here; they hadn't gone out together hunting tonight. His frown turned grimmer.

After what had happened in the alley two nights ago…well, she probably was avoiding him as much as he was avoiding her.

The door rattled again, and with a curse he shoved the bottle back into the safe (in case it was Temple) and went to see who the bloody hell was so insistent. As he approached, he realized something he'd somehow ignored or submerged deep in his grumbly consciousness: a vampire was present.

Chas was in just enough of a foul mood to fling the door open regardless of whoever might be on the other side. The drink sloshed over his hand as a result of the effort, and he glowered at the huddled figure standing there.

He couldn't make out a gender, but it was only one person, and his sensation measuring the proximity of undead indicated there weren't anymore other than this one.

"Well, come in," he said, checking to make certain a stake was still present in his pocket. Just in case. "Don't think I've ever heard of a vampire drowning before, but it's raining enough that you just damned well might."

"Didn't they attempt to drown Rasputin?"

It was a woman, with a vaguely familiar voice, and when she drew back the hooded jacket to reveal her face, Chas recognized her immediately.

The tall, skin-and-bones redhead had once been a friend of Macey's. Freda…no, Flora. Flora was her name.

"They did. Unsuccessfully—after, I believe, also trying to shoot him. More than once. Well, come in and take that off. No need to be bloody dripping all over the place."

She gave him a curious glance, but stepped over the threshold as she pulled off her sodden jacket. Then she hung it on a hook near the door and turned to face him. She was wearing a bright yellow dress that glittered, implying she'd come from somewhere fancy. In the center was a rust-colored stain that had Chas's brows lifting. "Thank you. I was hoping Macey was here."

"She's not."

Flora raked her eyes over him from head to toe, and she had the temerity to let a sensual glow light her eyes when she did.

"That'll be enough of that," he said, firmly ignoring a tiny flicker of lust.

She giggled and slid onto a stool without being asked, flashing him a sultry look. "I was just checking to see if you were interested. Your reputation is quite profound."

"My reputation with a stake, you mean."

"Your stake?" Her eyes narrowed with delight, and now they were glowing fully red. She ran the tip of her bold red tongue over her exposed fangs. "That's one way to put it."

"What do you want?" he asked, putting the counter between himself and her. More for her safety than his own.

"How about we start with whatever you're drinking." She glanced at his half-empty glass.

"How about we don't." He pulled out his weapon and showed her. "I should probably just put you out of your misery—save Macey the damned trouble."

"She can't do it herself," Flora said—as if they were discussing whether their mutual acquaintance could pilot a plane. "She's had ample opportunities—including tonight. She can't kill me."

Flora settled back onto the stool, folding her arms beneath her breasts and the stain from Macey's obviously aborted attempt to stake her. "From what I understand, *your* habit is such that you…uh…tend to enjoy a woman like me"—she smiled, showing off her fangs and that slick red tongue again—"with one type of stake…and then employ your *other* stake in a different way."

Chas was feeling a little unsteadier than he liked. Was this supposed to be a seduction? It wasn't working. Not much, anyway. "I'm not interested."

"We could have some fun together, you know, Chas. Don't think I don't know about your *darling* Narcise. The story's legendary. Aren't you ready for a permanent replacement for her?"

It was all he could do to keep from plunging the stake into her breastbone…and later he was to wonder what kept him from doing it. Boredom? Complacency? Curiosity?

"There will never be a replacement for Narcise."

The flat anger in his voice seemed to shock Flora out of her fey mood.

"Fine." She sat straight up and slammed her hands on the counter. "What a stick-in-the-mud. At least pour me a drink, will you?"

"What are you doing here—besides making me want to screw this stake into your heart?"

"Macey said…a while ago…she said she would help me. Find a way to"—she flapped her hand at herself—"change this. Fix me. Save me."

"And so that's why you're here—flashing your fangs and burning your eyes—because you want to be *saved*?" His derisive laughter was directed toward himself as much as Flora…because he hadn't been completely immune to her flirtations and the tug of her thrall. The promise of those fangs and slick tongue combined with soft female curves and rich musk.

Damn, there were days he hated himself as much as he hated the devil.

"Yes. It really is why I'm here. I can't help the way I am," she said earnestly. Her blue eyes opened large and didn't hold a flicker of red glow. "I saw her last night, and we didn't get to finish talking."

Chas sighed and leaned down to pull out the bottle from the safe. "I don't know that there's any way to…well, put you back."

"But it *has* hap…pened." Flora was staring at the bottle of liqueur. Her breathing had changed into something rough and audible.

He paused from pulling out the stopper, his hand tight on the bottle. "What is it?"

She blinked, still staring at the liqueur. Then she lifted her eyes to him. "What?"

"You tell me." He kept a good grip on the bottle. Maybe this was why Sebastian had kept it locked away in the lead-lined safe—for clearly, something about the bottle or its contents was of interest to Flora.

"I was saying…it has happened before. Undead have changed back, haven't they?" She was no longer looking at the bottle, but beseechingly up at him.

"Not those like you, of Judas Iscariot's breed," replied Chas, still watching her carefully. Tension was rolling off her, practically lighting up the air. "I've never known it to happen to one of them."

"So…are you going to pour me a drink or what?" she snapped.

"No, I don't think—"

He was ready when she lunged, throwing herself across the counter toward him with her fangs bared and eyes blazing red, and he dodged out of the way.

But the stake he'd set on the counter—carelessly, *foolishly*— she kicked off as she somersaulted herself over and onto her feet.

The weapon rolled to the floor on the opposite side, utterly out of his reach, as he grabbed her by the front of the dress and yanked her the rest of the way over the counter.

Her lithe, strong body was wild and furious, kicking, scratching, grappling. The force of their battle sent them tumbling to the floor in the narrow space behind the counter.

Chas was handicapped, for he still gripped the bottle, protecting it from smashing as he avoided her thrusting fangs while trying to roll out from beneath her in the restricted space. Plus, he'd had more than his share of whiskey, and that made him a little sluggish.

Glasses and bottles crashed down on them, heavy and unyielding, and Flora helped them by grabbing them off the shelves and throwing them down onto him. One round edge smashed into his temple, sending black spots into his eyes and slicing his skin. Chas roared in pain and fury, twisting and bucking up with a powerful movement. He heaved her off, still holding the precious bottle in one hand, and sent her slamming into the underside of the counter.

But it wasn't the bottle she was after, he realized too late, but the *stopper*.

For when he lifted her by the front of the dress with one strong hand, she grabbed for the onyx stopper, popping it from the inside of the bottle just as he flung her over the counter and out into the room.

She landed on the ground, somersaulting quickly to her feet, and bolted toward the door. But Chas had realized his mistake, and he vaulted over the counter just in time to leap onto her. They crashed to the floor again, this time rolling into and beneath a table and its upended chairs.

"What…is…it," he demanded, grabbing her wrist and squeezing hard, trying to get her to drop the stopper.

She bared her fangs and hissed at him, dragging her sharp nails down over his neck and throat, all the while kicking and writhing like a wild person. His blood flew about like sweat, and her eyes blazed hotter with fury and bloodlust.

He had no stake within reach, and he couldn't release her arm with the stopper, so he concentrated on smashing her head to the floor and rolling around, slamming into the wall and table legs, trying to knock her out of breath.

Then all at once, she went limp and lay beneath him, heaving, her face turned away as if waiting for…something. Some blow, some…something…

"What *is* it?" he demanded again, holding her wrist so tightly he felt her bones move beneath his fingers.

"How did you get it?" she replied, still turned away, still panting beneath him. "It's supposed to be in the enchanted pool—"

"Tell me what it—*Arghh!*" His words were cut off as she lunged up, grabbing one arm and pulling him down as she slammed her fangs into his throat.

Chas arched, tight as a bowstring, unable to fight the flood of pain and pleasure his body craved. He didn't release her wrist, but by now he felt the warm, pulsing release of blood flowing from his wounds, the soft, angular body of a female beneath him, the strong hand that had him by the arm, holding him in place, the two powerful thighs that wrapped around his waist and locked at the ankles behind him.

It was the same effect as if an opium eater or laudanum addict had given up the habit, the pleasure…and then suddenly, it was thrust upon him or her once again—unexpectedly, and unwillingly.

The red haze of lust washed over him in wave after wave even as he fought it back—fought it with every ounce of his strength and mental capacity. But she was touching him in places she had no business touching him, writhing and rolling beneath him, sucking and dragging the hot lifeblood from his veins, grinding and arching up against his crotch as she fed.

Chas focused on one thing: the wrist he gripped in his hand. He couldn't let it go, no matter what. He struggled to train every bit of his consciousness, every particle of his mind on not releasing her hand, on blocking away the hot lick of pleasure, the smell of his blood mingling with the scent of musk and sex, the press of her body against him, the sound of her feeding: the utilitarian *kuh-hn…kuh-hn…*

She pulled away from his pounding veins, and he felt his blood pumping free as she tried a new assault: swooping up to cover his mouth with hers. The taste and scent of his own blood on her lips, a mouth that raped his, a tongue that plunged and stroked, was enough to set him free.

With a roar, he gave a great twist, then smashed her hand sharply to the ground and saw the brief glint of the pyramid as it tumbled out of her fingers into the shadows—free for the taking, but lost in the darkness.

As she cried out in pain, pulling away from his mouth, Chas slammed his forehead down into Flora's face and yanked her hand from where she'd been groping him.

Now her cry was that of fury, and she was scratching and kicking in a frenzy. They rolled around, smashing into chairs and tables—none of which conveniently shattered so he'd have a weapon.

Suddenly, as he twisted away while lifting her over him to throw her to the floor, he felt a sharp, hard pain beneath him. The pyramid.

Chas grappled it into his hand as she snatched him by the hair and whipped his head into the floor.

"Fighting like…a…girl," he managed to taunt, even as his head exploded with pain and flashing lights. Then, with a great heave, he flung her off to the side.

He bolted to his feet just as she rolled to hers, and they faced each other, panting. And then he held up the pyramid so it glinted evilly in the dim light.

"What is it?" he asked one more time.

She didn't answer. Her eyes went lasciviously to the object in his hand, and then she grabbed a large table and threw it at him. He ducked successfully, but it was followed by chair after chair careening through the air as she made her way to the door, keeping him stumbling back and putting more space between them.

She whipped two final chairs at him in quick succession so they spun through the air like wild tops, then ducked through the door.

All at once, it was silent and still but for his panting breaths and the sounds of his blood dripping onto the floor. *Plop…plop…plop.*

He had the black onyx stopper…but he didn't know what the hell it was or why Flora had nearly gotten herself killed over it.

And then he looked around the pub, at the tumbled tables and chairs, the broken glasses and upended stools. The pool of blood on the floor.

Christ. Temple was going to kill him.

Eight

Of Thunderstorms and Dripping Frocks

A MERE SECOND after Chas had that thought, he bolted for the pub door, dashing in Flora's tracks…then immediately thought better of it. Still panting, and with blood streaming from his wounds, he spun around and vaulted one-handed over the top of the bar.

He took the precious time to shove the pyramid inside the safe, then dashed out of the pub. The onyx triangle was secure—for the time being.

But he had to find Flora and stop her before she brought the information to Iscariot.

Water splattered wide with every footstep as he emerged from the subterranean stairs and dashed down the street first one way, then the other. He paused, trying to sense the direction Flora had gone, but the vampiress had made her escape.

He felt nothing at the back of his neck, nothing to indicate her presence.

Damn.

He jogged around a block or two, up and down, cursing himself all the way. Bad enough that the information Sebastian Vioget had protected for who knew how long was now revealed, but just as infuriating and demoralizing was the reality that Chas had fought a single vampire and she'd *escaped* from him.

Christ Jesus, what was he coming to?

Chas walked the streets, combing them for any sign of Flora or any undead, for more than an hour, searching for something that would lead him in the right direction. But the vampire had enough of a start ahead of him, and he wasn't certain which direction she'd gone.

At last, sick at heart and lightheaded, he leaned against a damp brick wall, heedless of the incessant drip from the building's cornice that landed on his shoulder. It actually felt good, the cool dampness drooling over skin that was hot and sore from lust and vampire bites. He looked around one more time, hoping he'd find some way to redeem himself from such a blunder.

If it hadn't been for his weakness when it came to lust and fangs, if Flora hadn't mentioned Narcise in that way, bringing up his heartbreak and seducing him at the same time…if he hadn't been more than half drunk and already tired and bone-weary… taken by surprise…

Damn.

What the hell am I doing here? he demanded again. He pushed the dripping hair from his face. *Why am I even here?*

Not for the first time—and more likely not for the last—he glared in the direction of the heavens and demanded an answer.

Why am I still here?

All he got for an answer was rain on his face.

"Could it really be Rekk's Pyramid?" Macey asked.

She, Temple, and Chas were all gathered around the onyx bottle stopper, which had prompted Macey's question.

Chas had returned to The Silver Chalice after exhausting his search for Flora just as Temple had returned—dripping wet and from the *outside* door, not from the depths of the apartments— from wherever she'd been since who knew when. But from the looks of her, she'd been gone overnight, for even Chas knew the frock she was wearing was for evening.

The proprietor took one look at the destruction in her establishment and said, "I sure as hell hope you've got an explanation for this."

"I do. And it's going to make you even less happy than a few broken bottles and splintered stools." With a grim smile, he flipped one of the chairs upright and shoved it into place at its table. "I suggest you get Macey out here too."

So Macey had been roused from her bed only hours after her own return, and Chas filled them in on his altercation with Flora.

"Rekk's Pyramid?" Temple frowned, still looking at the onyx stone.

It would be more accurate to say she frowned *more*, because the irritation lines between her brows and the grim folds at the corners of her mouth hadn't relaxed since she'd entered the pub and saw the destruction therein.

"When I saw Flora at the photography exhibit, I managed to get some information about it from her. I would have told you earlier," Macey said, sliding a sidewise glance at the other woman, "but...well, we went our separate ways. You must have gotten home very late, despite the thunderstorms." She cast her attention down over the same glittering frock Temple had been wearing when they left for the photography exhibit.

A definite flush colored Temple's cheeks, and now the frown lines eased, turning into something more like a secret smile. "Oh, there was some thunderstormin' all right, sister," she muttered. "In a good way."

Chas cleared his throat and raised his brows. "What else did Flora say last night?"

"She told me Iscariot wanted the Rings of Jubai so he could retrieve Rekk's Pyramid, which was supposedly in the enchanted pool near Muntii Făgăraș...but apparently someone beat him to it."

"Presumably Sebastian Vioget."

"Presumably. I wonder how long he had it. And why he never bothered to tell anyone." Temple's frown lines were back, making a little W between her slender brows.

"The joke's on Iscariot—and whoever else wants the rings. It's just bad luck Flora happened to be here and see it, or he never would have known."

"We might not have known either," Macey said, picking up the object in question for a closer examination. She'd seen it numerous times previously, but never paid it much mind.

The pyramid itself shone black with blue highlights, and it fit easily in the center of her palm. As she held it there, she felt the slightest tremor of *something* emanating from it…very subtle, and perhaps even imagined. The sensation made her want to set the stone far, far away from herself.

Someone had created a setting for it from silver, like that of a gemstone for a ring. But instead of it being attached to a band, the "gem" sat atop a rubber-ringed silver stopper in the shape of a cone.

"If we had known, or if Flora wouldn't have managed to escape, we could easily have fooled Iscariot by giving him the rings and sending him on a fool's errand." Temple had begun to pick up the shattered glass behind the counter.

"Sorry I didn't take the chance to dust her," Chas replied sarcastically, gesturing at his damp, bloody shirt and the fresh scars all over his neck and throat. He was still oozing thick, dark blood, and his hair, though finger-combed away from his face, gleamed with rain. "It wasn't as if I've had multiple opportunities to do so."

Macey bristled. "Your point is made, Chas. But I couldn't exactly poke her with a stake in the middle of the Chicago Library. Someone would have noticed." But when she took a better look and noticed how deep and rough his wounds were, her ire dissipated. Flora had really done a number on him. If he weren't a Venator, he'd be lucky to still be alive.

"My question is…how did she even know it *is* Rekk's Pyramid? Could be she's wrong." Temple was piling thick, curved pieces of glass on a towel spread over the bar.

"Could be. But the minute I brought the bottle out from the safe—"

"Which, by the by, what the hell do you mean snooping around back here?" Temple growled.

"Macey's the one who found it," Chas retorted. "She's been sneaking that drink on the sly for week—"

"Traitor," Macey said. "I knew I shouldn't have let you have any."

"Children, children," Temple mocked them. She paused, standing with her hands on her hips. Her hair was almost dry, and she'd hung up her wet coat. "Do I have to draw circles on the blackboard and make you stand with your noses in them?"

Chas blinked. "What?"

"Never mind," Macey said. "You were starting to say: when you removed the bottle...?"

"Right. As soon as I removed the bottle, Flora reacted. It was as if she'd been stung...or maybe... Hell, maybe she *sensed* it. I can feel the evil when I touch it. Maybe that's why it was locked in a lead safe—we've had undead in here before; there's always that risk—and Vioget couldn't take the chance that one of them might come in and recognize the pyramid's presence—or, at least, the presence of something malevolent. So he put it in a safe to mask it."

"Why even have it in the pub at all?" Macey grumbled. "Why not put the damned thing in the church sacristy like we did with the rings—or somewhere else just as safe?"

Chas shook his head, a small smile playing about his lips. "That's Vioget for you. He probably found it wildly amusing to know the very thing Iscariot and all the other damned vampires are desperate for was right here, under their noses. And ours as well," he added darkly.

"Yes. And ours as well. And he never told anyone. We might never have *known* about it," Macey added, suddenly horrified at the thought. "What if we'd never found out?"

"More importantly, what if Flora had managed to escape with it?"

Their eyes met, the three of them, and Macey shuddered.

"But now she knows, which means Iscariot will soon know," Temple said, dropping another piece of glass onto the pile with a sharp clink, as if to punctuate the proverbial falling of the executioner's blade.

"Right. My question is, what's he going to use it for? What does it do? Why is it valuable to an undead?" Macey was still holding the innocent-looking object.

"That's going to require some time in the research library, or an answer from Wayren. And since no one's heard from her for a while…" Temple said, looking pointedly at them both. "Well, if I didn't have a disaster to take care of here, and a pub to run, I could—"

"Go off with you, then," Chas said with a sharp gesture. "That's more important than opening up the bloody pub—and it's well before noon anyway. No one expects you to open till five. Plus it's Sunday anyway—they don't expect you to open at all. But I sure as hell am not going to hunch over tiny, faded text in languages I don't know." He glanced at Macey. "You like books. You could help."

Obviously, he had a burr in his trunks, but she wasn't certain why. Because Flora had gotten away? Because she'd left him bleeding and mangled? "Thank you for the suggestion, Chas," she replied sweetly. "But I think I'll help out in here."

"You'll both just get in my way," Temple said, sounding like a parent again. "I've got all my notes organized, and I know just where to look. As long as the information is there, I'll find it."

After Temple left, Macey turned her attention on Chas. "You need to get doctored up."

"You offering, lulu?" His dark eyes fastened on her mockingly.

"Sure. I'll be happy to pour salted holy water over your open wounds," she replied evenly. "Pitchers of it. With great relish."

He just cast her a black look, then turned to continue setting the tables and chairs upright—using a little more force than necessary.

"Chas, don't be an ass. Those bites and scratches need to be seen to." She could make out fresh blood pumping gently from a deep gash over his shoulder, a result of his current exertions.

When he kept whipping the chairs back onto their feet, she stepped away from picking up chunks of glass. As she approached, he stiffened.

"Leave me alone."

"What the hell happened when Flora was here?"

He shot her another look; this time, one that was probably supposed to portray confusion over her question, but fell short of doing so. "We fought over the pyramid—as you can plainly see."

Macey put her hand on him. She was strong enough that he couldn't easily shake her off. "Chas." She gave his arm a little yank to get him to look at her.

He spun, eyes glittering. "Leave off, Macey. Unless you want to *really* tend to things." His tone left no doubt as to the meaning of his suggestion.

She didn't back away, for below the lasciviousness there was hurt and anguish in his expression. Clearly whatever was on his mind wasn't the simple matter of a vampire escaping him.

"Chas," she said, forcing him to face her. The fact that he allowed her to do so indicated a lack of true resistance. "Talk to me."

Misery flooded his eyes, then was gone as if he'd snapped his fingers. "No. I'm not interested in talking, lulu." His gaze went flint-hard. "But I'd sure as hell be interested in another kind of activity."

Comprehension dawned at last. Now she understood—his anger, his pain, and the self-loathing that he was doing his best to turn onto her. Flora had either tried to seduce him, or vice versa.

"Come on, lulu," he coaxed, his voice edgy and rough. "You enjoyed it the other night, even in the middle of all that trash in the alley." His smile, though devastating in its beauty, held tension at the corners as he moved closer. "And so did I."

Macey felt the edge of a table behind her, and she flattened a hand against the center of his chest. His heart raced beneath her palm, and the heat of his skin burned through the damp, bloody shirt. She wasn't frightened, or even angry. Far from it. The pain lurking in his eyes and beneath his taunts was palpable and desperate, and she knew that was what fueled his actions.

"Chas—" she began.

"You know how it was…all rough and wild," he said, his voice dropping low. "That's the way we do it, isn't it, lulu? You and me. We're alike in that way, and we—"

He was abrupt and strong, his hands pulling her close, his mouth descending on hers as he arched her back over the top of the table. Macey caught herself up with an elbow, and pulled her face away from his skilled, sensual mouth even as he plucked at the buttons of her shirt.

"Let go of me, Chas," she said, becoming a little annoyed at his insistence—as well as her own reaction to his convincing kiss. "This isn't the ti—"

A door slammed open—the exterior door. The glasses on the shelves rattled.

Chas didn't move other than to cast an annoyed glance over his shoulder, but Macey froze when she saw the man striding toward them.

She couldn't believe her eyes, couldn't even catch her breath, couldn't *speak,* before he was there, grabbing Chas by the back of his collar.

"Who the hell are you?" Chas demanded, finally swinging around to face the newcomer as Macey stared, hardly able to comprehend.

"Max Denton," replied the man. "Now take your damned hands off my daughter."

Nine

A Miscalculation of Great Proportion

WHEN MAX IMAGINED how his reunion with Macey might go, he assumed there would be tears. Tears of joy, perhaps; tears of anger too, and likely a few harsh words as well. He wasn't delusional, and Savina had given him plenty to think about.

But he didn't expect Macey to take one look at him then stalk from the room without a word, slamming the door behind her. Though Savina, devil it, had warned him something like that would probably happen. Why were women always bloody right?

The sound of Macey's wordless but emphatic exit echoed in the otherwise silent room.

"Right, then," he said with a forced chuckle, then turned his attention to the chap who'd been mauling his daughter. He scraped up his anger again—which wasn't difficult to do. He was much more experienced in dealing with that emotion than whatever the other was. "And who the hell are you?"

"Chas Woodmore." Besides having been all over Max's daughter, the man also looked as if he'd just come out of a brawl with a vampire. Classy. He eyed Max warily, but didn't back down.

"So you're Woodmore. I'd shake your hand, but I'm not feeling terribly friendly toward you at the moment." Max didn't even attempt to put any warmth in his smile. He glanced at the door through which Macey had made her dramatic exit, wondering when she was going to return.

If she was going to return.

"I can understand that." Woodmore's demeanor was a balance between abashed and arrogant—which was probably exactly how Max would have reacted in a similar situation.

They each sized the other up for a moment, then Woodmore broke the silence. "Want something to drink?" The other man moved behind the counter and thunked two glasses onto it next to a pile of broken vessels.

"If you mean something hard, then by God, *yes*. What the hell are they thinking, outlawing alcohol in this godforsaken nation?"

"My sentiments exactly," Woodmore said as he slid over a glass filled with a generous amount of whiskey.

Max lifted it, sniffed, and smiled. It appeared to be a suitable vintage. "Praise God." He toasted the heavens then sipped.

Chas raised his glass. "Damned pleased to meet you, Max Denton—though different circumstances would have been preferable."

Max clinked his glass against the other man's and nodded in acknowledgment. Yes, he certainly hadn't anticipated that the first time he saw his daughter in thirteen years she'd be *under* a man in the middle of a destroyed bar. He gestured to the mess. "Vioget always ran a tighter ship than this."

"Temple Devereux runs an even tighter one—as long as there aren't unexpected visits by an undead." Woodmore's mouth flattened grimly.

As they sipped their drinks, he explained what had happened with a vampiress named Flora, and Max's mood soured. By the time Woodmore showed him the onyx pyramid, he was disgusted.

"Damn it to hell. This belongs in Rome, in the Consilium— not here in bloody uncivilized Chicago where it could so easily fall into the wrong hands." Even as he examined the shiny stone, he felt the faint reverberation of malevolence emanating from it. The object was damned powerful. "I thought it was bad enough that Iscariot has Rasputin's amulet—but if he gets this as well…" He muttered a vulgar curse that made Woodmore's brows lift in appreciation.

"What does it do?" asked the other man as he refilled their glasses. "Temple is researching it, but I assume you know, despite the fact that you've been underground for some time."

There it was at last, layered beneath the words. Hints of judgment and disdain from Woodmore—ironic, really, for the bastard himself knew a thing or two about running away from his problems.

"As the *Summas* Gardella, you can be damned certain I know plenty—and more than I'd prefer, to be bloody honest." Max shook his head, thrusting away the nagging twinge of guilt.

He'd avoided the leadership responsibilities of his position as head of the Venators ever since Felicia's death, using Macey's safety and his own blind drive for vengeance as an excuse. A paltry one, as far as Savina and Wayren were concerned. They had made their opinions clear to him—the latter in a subtle way, the former much more vociferously. "Though I must say, Bellitano has done a brilliant job in my stead."

"Brilliant doesn't begin to cover it."

"Right, then." Max paused, holding his gaze just long enough for Woodmore to know he acknowledged and accepted the man's opinion, but that as *summas*—and father of the woman Woodmore had just been mauling (a thought Max kept shoving as far back in his mind as possible)—he wouldn't stand for any disrespect. "Rekk's Pyramid is a nightmare in the making in the hands of a vampire. When its power is harnessed, the pyramid allows its—shall we say 'master' to continue his or her thrall even when the enthralled is not present."

"Do you mean to say, it allows the vampire to control people when they are not with him? When they are away?"

"Precisely."

"People? As in…plural? Multiple ones at a time?"

"Correct."

"Like an army?"

"Exactly."

"Good God."

"Quite."

Woodmore looked down at the stone, appearing stunned. "How does it work?"

"That depth of detail I don't know. Most likely Wayren will, or at least she'll know where to find out. Somewhere in that library she totes around masquerading as a satchel." Max finished the last swallow of whiskey, then glanced over at the door again. "I suppose I should go after her."

Woodmore gave him a sardonic smile. "Best of luck to you."

"Right." He gritted his teeth and stood. "Where do you think I might find her?"

Woodmore shrugged. "Possibly in her bedroom. Through that door and down the hall. Last door on the left."

Max tried not to think about the fact that Woodmore knew the location of Macey's bedroom, but that didn't stop him from giving the man a cold look.

"If she isn't there, she's probably gone out—out into the city to find something to stake." Woodmore took Rekk's Pyramid off the counter. "In the meantime, I believe I'll put this back in the safe."

My father is here.

The words repeated over and over in Macey's mind like the fragment of a song she couldn't quite remember.

My father is alive.

What the *hell* was he doing here? Now? After thirteen years? Here?

After thirteen years of *silence.*

She reached blindly for something—a shoe—and whipped it across the room. It hit the wall of her bedchamber with a sharp thunk, leaving a deep dent from its chunky heel.

The travails of being superhumanly strong.

Like many a daughter upset with her father, she'd fled to her bedroom—though *flee* wasn't perhaps the best word. Flee implied fear and cowardice. And escape.

What she was feeling was *not* fear and cowardice.

Escape? Perhaps. But…

How *dare* he just…show up like that? Without a *word*—after *years*? Especially when she and Chas were…

Macey's cheeks heated, for when she reached the sanctuary of her room, she'd realized her blouse had been unbuttoned far lower than was proper.

Surely her father—No, he was no father to her. He was just *Max*. Max Denton. Legendary vampire hunter.

Cold, violent, solitary.

Like every vampire hunter must be.

Like she and Chas were.

Macey looked down at her gapping blouse. Surely Max Denton wouldn't have noticed the telltale opening of three buttons in the flurry of her shoving Chas away and stalking from the room.

And she'd definitely stalked, not fled.

What the hell *is he doing here?*

Upon first entering her room, she'd flung herself onto the bed and stared blindly at the ceiling, fighting *tears* of all things. *Tears.* From a Venator? Had Victoria Gardella ever cried? Surely not.

By God, if Macey hadn't cried over what happened with Sebastian—and, oh God, Grady—why would she cry over the unexpected, *unwanted* appearance of Max Denton?

Though she was shaky and upset, she couldn't lay all that at Max Denton's feet. No, part of it had been the incident with Chas there in the pub before they were interrupted.

In fact, perhaps it would be better if she gnawed and brooded over *that* interlude instead of her father's arrival. As a topic on which to ruminate, Chas and his moods—along with their mutual yet strained attraction—was far less disconcerting than Max Denton's arrival.

And the man—Chas—certainly had a way with his hands and mouth. He definitely knew how to stir up her heat, even when she wasn't thinking in that direction. Even if she didn't love him.

But he also knew how to use his seductive skills as a barrier, and a weapon. A detour.

Would they have done it right there, right in the middle of the pub? Macey's face heated again. If Max had waited another five, ten, fifteen minutes before making his grand exit, what would he have discovered? More than three undone blouse buttons, she suspected.

Her insides shifted and sank, and, furious with herself, with Chas, and most definitely with Max Denton, she rolled off the bed. Her feet hit the floor with two sharp thumps of finality.

She was getting out of here. Now. Before one of those idiot men decided to come looking for her. She didn't know which one of them she wanted to see least.

She just wanted to get away. To get some air, some space, to clear her thoughts.

Macey swiped a forearm over her eyes. Dammit, she wanted someone to hold her. To gather her close and tell her everything would be all right, to help her pare through these wild, confused thoughts. To tell her she was doing the right thing, had made the right decisions.

She wanted to beat the stuffing out of something. To kick and hit and slice and punch. To break things. To stab. To scream.

Panting with emotion, Macey dragged on a pair of men's trousers and a set of braces to hold them up, tucking her rebuttoned shirt inside the waistband. She shoved a stake and a knife into her pockets, jammed a fedora on her head, and flung a trench coat around her shoulders.

She was going out.

Macey could hear the rain still pouring down in sheets as she made her way through the corridors—some underground, some not—that led from the collection of rooms adjacent to The Silver Chalice with the other side of the block, where Cookie's Smart Millinery was located.

When she first learned of her Venator calling, she'd quit her job at the University of Chicago's Harper Memorial Library and spent day after day with Temple in a large practice room. There,

Temple took her through traditional fighting and self-defense techniques that had been passed down to the Venators through their Comitators for ages. The techniques and weapons used had come from distant corners of the earth—*qinggong, karate, tae kwan do*—and required mastery of the mind as much as the body.

Those days, Macey realized as she passed through the empty practice room in the basement—known as a *kalari*—had been easier. So much easier.

"Macey." Temple looked up in surprise when she opened the door at the top of the stairs to the *kalari*. Temple was sitting at a large table with books spread out around her and sheaves of paper stacked and curling next to her.

Rain pelted a window that emitted a smoky gray light. Thunder rolled in the distance. A car horn bleeped below.

Macey thought maybe she wouldn't go out after all. No one was likely to be on the streets, let alone a vampire. Not that she wouldn't be satisfied with pummeling mortal flesh, but only miserable people with no other choice would be out on a day like this. It was Sunday, after all.

"Any progress on the research about Rekk's Pyramid?" Macey asked. She wasn't quite ready to talk about Max's arrival, even with Temple.

"Some. But I keep falling asleep." A small smile curved Temple's lips.

"Late night last night, hm?" Macey felt a bump of happiness for her friend. At least one of them was pleased about the men in their lives.

"Mm-hm." Temple yawned and glanced out the window. "Maybe I won't open the Chalice again tonight. No one's going to venture out in this mess. I can go to bed early. Did you and Chas finish cleaning up in there?"

Macey hesitated. "I left before it was quite finished. So what have you found about the pyramid?"

"It appears to have the power to control a person through an undead's thrall. Like a sort of powerful hypnosis. But in order for the pyramid to work, it has to have its power connected, I suppose you'd say, to an undead—its master has to be created or defined."

"So the ability to use it as a hypnosis and control tool lies dormant until it receives a master? Like Aladdin's lamp in *A Thousand and One Arabian Nights*—it waits for someone to rub it."

"Right you are, sister. And, fortunately for us, it takes the master more than a bit of rubbing on the pyramid to connect himself to it. There's a whole process, though I've not found the recipe yet."

"Surely Iscariot would know how to do it."

"As sure as the day is long."

"What about vulnerabilities? Any information on how we could destroy the pyramid?"

"That's where I'm having the trouble so far." Temple brushed a slender hand over the aged parchment in front of her. "No information on that yet."

"And once it's been connected to a master, how can we disconnect it?" Macey asked, relieved to have specific questions on which to focus, as unpleasant as their implications were.

"Again…no information on that yet." Temple narrowed her eyes, as if really seeing her for the first time. "Are you planning to go out in this weather?"

Before Macey could respond, they heard footsteps in the hall outside: quick and light, and a soft clink when the footfalls paused at the door opposite the one through which Macey had entered. The knob turned.

"Thought you might be likin' some coffee there, missy," said Aunt Cookie as she pushed her way into the room backward, using an elbow to edge the door open. "And I needed a break from the cloche brim I was stitching. Eyes ain't as good as they used to be."

She was carrying a tray laden with teapot, a cup and saucer, and a plate piled with powdered beignets. Once fully through the entrance, she turned around and her face lit up. "Macey, child, bless your heart. I'm so happy you're here. I was wantin' someone to tell me about the exhibit last night, and Temple, ornery miss she is, won't give me one real gossipy detail about the latest in millinery!"

Aunt Cookie was a tiny, will-o'-the-wisp of a woman, fairy-like in her manner and movements. Her hair was thin as a spider web and puffed out in a soft, dark cloud around her head. Her nose, the most substantial thing about her, was long and broad.

She was a genius when it came to fixing up a chapeau, sewing a cloche, or decorating a headband with just the right amount of frills and furbelows, and she was more than competent in the kitchen. But her head was most often in the clouds—likely imagining her next creation—and her thoughts scattered as easily as an overturned container of pins.

She was, in short, just the sort of superficial diversion of which Macey was in need.

She gladly took the tray, making only a token protest when Aunt Cookie decided she should go get two more cups and saucers—and a pot of jam, too, and some crackers—so they could all have coffee and talk about whether ostrich feathers were coming back and whether the veils were cutting as low as the nose, or ended just over one eye.

Sitting with the only two females in the world—besides Wayren, and Macey had severe doubts whether the blond woman was actually *of* this world—who knew the truth about her life was comforting and relaxing.

But then in the next minute, that comfort and relaxation came crashing down.

"Oh, and did your father find you, Macey, dear? He came around, looking for The Silver Chalice, so I went on and told him how to tell it by the finial on the stair post. Hard to see in this weather, bu—"

"Your *father*?" Temple fairly shrieked, looking from Macey to her aunt and back again. She'd half risen from her seat. "Max Denton is alive? He's *here*?"

Macey could do nothing but nod.

"How? I thought he was dead!"

"Welcome to the club," Macey replied, wishing now that she'd made her escape—rain or no rain. How could her father not be dead…and her not know *because no one told her*? No one except Nicholas Iscariot. Sebastian was gone, but she'd believed him when he told her he didn't know, and so had Chas…but then there was Al Capone. He'd seemed almost frightened when she mentioned her father, come to think of it. Macey gritted her teeth. Maybe a visit to old Scarface was in order.

"Wait—are you sure it was really your father? Not a trick?" Temple's eyes were a little wild, and Macey wasn't certain whether it was from fear or awe that the so-called "great" Max Denton had arrived.

"It's definitely him."

"What's wrong, child? Aren't you happy to see your daddy again?" asked Cookie.

"Am I glad to see the man who's ignored me for thirteen years?" she replied tartly, reaching for a cup of coffee. "Who made me think he was dead? Why should I be?"

Temple stirred milk into her coffee and moved away from the desk, appearing relieved to have a break from her studies. "What did he say? Why is he here?"

"I don't know. I left."

Temple and Aunt Cookie looked at her without speaking.

Macey sighed. "He just showed up here without a word, and expects me to welcome him back into my life? To pretend nothing happened?"

"He is your father," Cookie admonished.

"He's Max Denton. He's not my father." Macey shrugged and reached for a beignet, ignoring the trail of powdered sugar that followed the pastry's path. "He's pretended to be dead for thirteen years."

"I'm sure he had a reason for doing so," Cookie said tentatively.

"We all have reasons for what we do," Temple said quietly. "Or think we have."

Macey looked at her and saw a glint of judgment in the other woman's expression. "To just cut someone you love out of your life without letting them have a chance to…" She hesitated, then looked away. *Damn.*

Temple lifted a knowing brow. "You were saying?"

"What happened with Grady—what I chose to do, what I had to do—was a completely different situation."

"Sounds pretty much the same to me, sister. A person—in this case, you or your father—decides to protect someone they love—that would be Grady or you—by walking out of their life, blocking them off. No choices or explanations given, correct? No chance for the person being left behind to decide whether *they* want to be left or not."

"But—"

"But you were only little, that's true, I'll give you that. So maybe you weren't old enough to make a decision about what was best, at that time. But Grady—he was. He is. He's more of a man than ninety percent of the fellas in this city."

Macey's chest felt tight. "It's not the same. Grady isn't a Gardella, he isn't a Venator—he doesn't know what he'd be getting into."

Temple was shaking her head, and her expression was steely. "He was just as instrumental as you were in getting out of that theater with Sebastian, wasn't he? And he right as rain made a difference when you and a hundred other people almost got blew up at the museum." She leaned forward. "All I'm saying to you, sister, is that you made the same decision about Grady your father made about you. And so you, my dear pot, should not be calling the kettle black."

Macey settled back into her chair, firming her lips. Suddenly the beignet and its sweet dusting of sugar tasted like dirt. It was different with Grady. He wasn't part of a family that had been called to a dangerous duty for centuries. He was an outsider. He wasn't equipped to protect himself from the undead.

"Poor, darling child," Cookie said, patting Macey's hand with her soft, cool one. "And you having to get over the loss of your mama at the same time as your daddy leaving you."

"That's right," Macey said, tears suddenly springing to her eyes. "He left me—when I needed him…the most. He sent me… away. They told me he…died. I grew up thinking I was an… orphan."

"Aw, Macey, I'm not saying your daddy didn't do you no wrong. But he had his reasons, just as you did with Grady, and him being a man… Well, he might not have made the right choices. They hardly ever do. I just think you ought to consider his side of the story, since you've got a similar one yourself," Temple said.

Cookie handed her a lace-edged handkerchief, and Macey wiped her eyes and then her nose. All of a sudden, she was more sad than angry. It was as if all of the grief from when she was a child came rushing back, pushing away her feelings of righteousness.

"I'm sure your daddy loves you very much—and he did what he did for that reason," Temple added.

Just as you did to Grady.

She didn't actually say those words, but Macey heard them as clearly as if she had.

"And now he's come back," Cookie said brightly—as if that solved everything.

And now he's come back. But what did that mean?

Macey rose. "Thank you for the coffee, Aunt Cookie. I'm going to—I was on my way out. I need some air."

"Air? Bless your heart; you're as likely to drown as to breathe out in that soupy mess," Cookie said, looking at the rain-streaked window.

"I don't mind."

The outside air was chilly and damp, and Macey was glad she'd chosen to wear trousers and a hat instead of a dress or skirt, as she had last night. Though it was just approaching noon, the day was as dim and dark as if it were near twilight—and the streets were virtually empty.

Only a single vehicle drove down the road, its tires softly crunching the damp concrete. The rain had eased up a bit, but the mist was thick and drops plopped onto her hat and ran off its brim. Her shoes and the hems of her trousers were damp within a few steps.

Someone was looking out for her, for Macey was able to hail a taxi more quickly than she'd expected. "The Lexington Hotel," she told the driver as she took off her hat and shook off the rain.

Despite her masculine garb, Capone's goons recognized her, and one of them agreed to take her up to the gangster's penthouse—but only after she gave them the pistol and knife she carried.

"Hey, boss," called Tony as he escorted Macey into the room after a fourteen-floor elevator ride. "You got a visitor."

"Well, well, Snorky," she said, walking into the private suite as if she owned it. "Got yourself hidden away today, do you? Afraid you might melt in the pouring rain?"

"What da hell are you doing here?" Capone had fairly bolted out of his chair, the ash from his cigar flying everywhere and the wine glass on his desk wobbling alarmingly. He looked behind her as if waiting for someone else to appear, yet at the same time, trying to appear unconcerned. "Tony, I thought I told you I didn't wanna see her no more."

"But she ain't packing nothing—I checked myself—and your wife's not here," Tony replied, looking from his boss to Macey as if he couldn't understand why Capone would be so nervous about a slip of a woman like Macey—especially if she was unarmed. "Besides, she said she left some of her things here, and—"

"Get outta here," Capone told his goon, looking somewhere between furious and mortified—neither of which boded well for poor Tony. "And don't let no one else in. You hear me? *No one.*"

"Right, boss."

"Thank you, Tony." Macey gave him a sweet smile.

Still wearing a confused expression, Tony left the penthouse.

Capone turned to Macey. "Whaddaya want, doll? I thought our bizness was done."

"I've discovered something since I left your employ, Scarface." He hated that nickname, and therefore Macey used it with relish.

"Don't fucking call me dat, you bit—doll." Capone was clearly reining himself in. "Tell me what you want, then get da hell outta here. I ain't got time for you."

"My father is still alive."

He pursed his mouth and tried to look surprised, but Macey realized immediately that wasn't the case. "You *knew* he was alive?" She started across the room, ready to yank him up by the jacket and slam the bastard against the wall—but she thought better of it at the last minute, for she'd probably make a hole in the dry wall. "He's here in Chicago."

"Yeah. I'm aware of that."

"You are, are you—*Wait.*" Macey suddenly went cold and angry herself. "When did you see him?"

Capone shrugged. "He came for a visit a week or so ago. We had a nice chat."

"A nice *chat?*"

Capone looked supremely uncomfortable. "Look, doll, the last thing I need is Max Denton breathing down my neck. So get your stuff and get outta here. I ain't got nothing to do with you Venators anymore anyway."

Macey stared at him with dawning comprehension. "Do you mean my father came here and told you to *stay away from me?*" Her head felt as if it were about to explode. She was going to be an orphan after all, because *she was going to kill her father.* How dare he? She'd handled everything all on her own. She'd rid herself of Capone on her own terms, not because her *daddy* had come and set things straight…hadn't she?

Capone seemed to realize he'd set off a powder keg, and he held up his hands. "We had other bizness, there, doll, and we come to an agreement. I gave up my *vis bulla* and he promised to let me alone. We were both happy with dat."

"What do you mean, you gave it up? You can't just give it up—can you?" She glared at him, and his eyes shifted away.

"He took it. All right? The asshole took it from me, and since he did dat, it means I ain't got nothing to do with you all anymore."

"He can do that?"

"He's the *summas*, ain't he? He and dat Wayren broad can do whatever da fuck dey want," Capone replied, no longer attempting to hide his fury. "At least I already got my reputation built up solid. Most'a da city's terrified of me. I don't need that damned—er—that *blessed* thing stuck through my skin anyway. Always kept getting caught on my shirt and all."

"Do you mean to say you lost your Venator powers when Max took away your *vis bulla*?" She didn't think that was possible. Victoria Gardella lost her *vis*—but that hadn't changed her abilities, had it? Maybe slowed her down a little? Macey was a little fuzzy on some of the details of her family history, to be sure, but she was certain the loss of a *vis* didn't cause Venator powers to go away.

"It ain't just the *vis bulla* being gone, all right? It's just—I dunno—something he did or they did. Him and dat dame in the long dress. Dey made me normal again."

"So you can't sense the undead anymore? You don't have extra strength and fast healing?" Macey stepped toward him. "Let's test that out, shall we?" She was mad enough, frustrated enough, to try it out.

"I ain't no lightweight, doll," he said, his eyes glinting. "I can't sense the undead, but I sure as hell can take you down if I want."

Macey was sorely tempted. The thought of a good fight was right up there with having a few choice words with the almighty Max Denton.

But she thought better of it—this time. Any sort of altercation would send Capone's goons running, armed with Tommy guns and pistols. They might shoot and ask questions later.

"Not tonight, Scarface. Maybe another time. I've got other things to do." She gave him a long look. "But before I go…do you know where Iscariot has been holed up?"

Capone shook his head, fat lips pursed. "No. Believe me, if I did, I'd tell you. He's already causing problems with my—arrangements. The sooner you get rid of that bastard, the happier

I'll be. So get on it, doll. And don't forget your things. They're still in your room downstairs."

"One more thing," she said, hand on the doorknob. "Leave Tony alone. Or I'll be back. And I won't come alone." She gave him a cold smile.

Capone muttered something unflattering, but she was already closing the door when he spoke. Probably just as well.

After Macey left Capone, carrying a single suitcase with the few items she'd retrieved from her apartment, she had no other destination in mind. But she wasn't ready to go back to The Silver Chalice.

And so she walked—trudging through puddles and along the wet sidewalks, alongside shops closed because it was Sunday, churches that were empty because it was past noon, restaurants that were shuttered in favor of family dinners.

It wasn't until she'd walked for a long while—more than an hour, perhaps closer to two—that she realized where her feet had taken her.

She paused, bringing herself up short, surprised—and yet not surprised—when she looked around with suddenly comprehending eyes. There was O'Brien's Hardware, Shillelagh Market, and Garrick's Butcher Shop. And down the street sat St. Martin's Catholic Church, with another church steeple visible only a block away.

And there—overlooking a small park that was deserted now because of the weather, its swings empty and dangling lightly in the breeze—sat Grady's tall, narrow townhouse.

Macey's heart squeezed as she studied the familiar building from across the street. The largest window had its lace curtains pulled haphazardly wide, and the opening was a warm yellow rectangle in contrast to the dreary gray of rain and mist. From her vantage point, she looked into the house, hoping to see a figure moving inside. And though she knew it was inadvisable, she couldn't keep from walking across the street, just to get closer.

Seeking some shelter from the rain, she stood beneath a broad oak in the park, its branches stretching nearly to the brick wall of Grady's house. The window facing her was the one on the side of the deep, narrow building that offered a view from the living room. Now she was in closer proximity to the beckoning window, and when she saw the figure moving around, her heart skittered a little.

He was there. Wearing only a white shirt unbuttoned at the throat and, she assumed, trousers—though she couldn't see below the waist from her angle. She couldn't make out much of his face, but she knew how thick and soft his hair was, how beautiful and changing his blue-gray eyes were… How he'd cock his head and look at her with warmth and call her "lass."

How when she demonstrated her superhuman strength in an effort to show him why he *couldn't* understand her life, why she was different from every other woman in the world, and lifted him up to shove him against the wall…his reaction was to kiss her with passion and love. Acceptance, and even joy.

Her vision blurred and she blinked hard, dashing a hand over her eyes.

He was safe from the undead when inside his home—and not only because of whatever it was that had upset Flora so strangely last night. Macey knew Grady had silver crosses set into the threshold of every window and doorway in the house. And he probably had wooden stakes somewhere as well, knowing him…

All at once, the memory flashed through her mind, so sharply and strongly that she actually gasped in a breath of mist. The night Grady had spent in her apartment in Mrs. Gutchinson's house—or, rather, the morning afterward—Macey awoke to find him half asleep in a chair, holding a stake in his hand.

A stake he'd brought with him. A stake with which he'd come prepared.

He'd known even then about the undead, somehow. But *how* had he known?

Yes, he'd borrowed her book *The Venators*, which would have given him quite a bit of information about her family legacy—

though much of its contents were inaccurate. But even from the beginning, from the very first time they met, he seemed to have known about the existence of the undead.

The first time they'd spoken it was on a street corner, where he showed her a posted sign about a young woman who'd gone missing and her body was found. Jennie Fallon was her name. Some people wondered if it had been dogs or some animal who'd done the horrific mauling, and Macey never knew why she'd made that illogical, murmured comment about vampires. But she had.

Instead of looking at her as if she were loony, Grady had looked at her with comprehension…and curiosity.

Even then, he'd somehow known about vampires. Or, at least, he'd suspected their existence.

And after that first conversation, he'd never given up—on her, on learning more about the undead, on fighting them, on supporting her as she took on her dangerous vocation. On being part of her life.

I'd be there with you till the end, Macey, lass.

Some of his last words to her, before she'd asked Wayren to obliterate his memory. That simple statement hung in her mind, making her woozy and warm and sad all at the same time.

She hardly realized what she was doing until her feet were mounting the steps to his front door. And there it was in front of her: smooth oak, stained a dark toffee color, with a small window and a knocker in a Celtic knot design. Embedded in the threshold floor was, she knew, three silver crosses.

Macey didn't know what she was doing. Why she was here.

But she lifted her hand, grasped the Celtic knot, and raised it and rapped three times.

Knock. Knock. Knock.

Ten

SAVINA ELEIASA, known professionally as Sabrina Ellison, adventure photographer, had just finished a bath. Her hair was damp, and she'd donned a voluminous, warm housecoat and slippers. It was that kind of ugly, dreary day.

She was just coming down from the second floor when she heard a knock.

Grady was already on his way to answer the front door—it was his house, after all—as she made her way down the steps.

"Who on earth would be out on a day like today?" she said as he looked through the window.

He opened the door, and Savina glanced over as she walked by and saw nothing but a slight man holding a small suitcase, the rain pouring off his fedora. A salesman? Surely not on a Sunday. But he looked harmless enough—unless he was a vampire, of course; but even then, Grady would have to invite him in for any threat to be made—and the undead wouldn't be able to cross over the silver crosses in the threshold anyway. Maybe it was someone from the *Tribune*.

Savina hadn't even taken a seat on the sofa in the living room when Grady returned, more quickly than she had expected.

"Who was that?" she asked, moving a jumble of handcuffs and padlocks in order to sit down. Not pillows or even newspapers on Jameson Grady's divan, but locks and cuffs. She shook her head in amusement. The assortment reminded her of Liam Stoker, a brilliant inventor who designed weapons and gadgets for some of the Venators. He was always carrying an assortment of mechanical parts around with him. They clinked and rattled in his pockets.

"I'm not quite certain," Grady replied as he passed through into the kitchen.

Savina shrugged and curled up into a corner of the sofa, trying not to think about Max. It was good of Grady—beyond good—to offer his hospitality while they were here.

And even though Grady had given up his larger bedroom on the second floor to both of them, Max had hardly been here to share it with her since they'd arrived.

She shivered, suddenly miserable and lonely. And perhaps a little apprehensive. It wasn't because of Grady; he was such a nice man, so accommodating and charming, and not the least bit awkward about the amount of time Savina was spending at his home—safely tucked away, as Max put it—while he was…doing what he had to do.

Perhaps she shouldn't have come to Chicago after all. But Max had been deliciously persuasive, and she, like a lovelorn fool, had acquiesced.

Of course, Savina was partly at fault for the tension in their relationship, but things simply hadn't been the same between them since the events of last Christmas. Or, rather, since he'd *left* her, three Christmases ago, and fate had thrown them back together just this past December at a secluded estate in England.

Neither of them had expected to see the other there—hell, as far as Savina knew, Max could have been dead, for all she'd heard from the man with whom she'd been lovers for more than a year.

And that, my friend, is the cause for your entire emotional turmoil. She couldn't trust him with her heart any more.

True, their unexpected reunion had been emotional, and Max had groveled—as well he should have—*but.*

Savina wasn't certain anything had changed: whether he'd gotten over the reason he'd run away from her—no, he'd run from their *relationship*, not Savina. That was a point he'd at least been clear on: it wasn't her, it was him.

Right.

"Do you want some tea?" Grady called from the kitchen. His voice drew Savina from the thoughts she'd been cycling through over and over for months. "Or something else?"

"Do you have coffee? Maybe with a shot of something strong in it to warm me up on such a nasty day?" Savina had been raised in Italy, in the midst of the Venators and their subterranean hideaway in Rome, so she'd never quite warmed up to the English preference of tea.

If only she could find someone in Chicago to make a good cappuccino, she'd be much happier.

As she waited for Grady to bring their drinks, Savina's attention wandered, as it had several times before, over his vast collection of books—a miniature library in and of itself, considering the wide and varied topics they covered. Chemistry, biology, Latin, zoology, history, physics, religion and philosophy—not to mention fiction and biography. And others. There were more shelves and stacks in his bedroom as well.

And then there was the Houdini-type equipment, from the handcuffs and padlocks to a coffin-sized box from which Grady swore he could escape, even if tied or chained.

"I saw Houdini once," she commented as Grady walked in with—thank God, coffee. Two mismatched cups on their own saucers, clinking on a tray along with a few crackers and a small tub of butter. "In London. He was amazing."

"Amazing is an understatement," Grady replied with a smile, taking a seat in an armchair near the dormant fireplace. He glanced at it, then at her. "Should I set a fire?"

"Oh, no, you needn't go through the trouble. I'm sure you have work to do. Don't you have a story to turn in, about the exhibit?" Savina already felt guilty that he'd been the one to escort her to the show last night, and that she'd been here all day with nothing to do.

"Oh, I've already done that one and turned it in. While you were sleeping last night—to make the Sunday edition. So, like

God, today is my day off," Grady replied with a grin. "Unless something big comes up, of course."

Grady had been a good sport about taking her to the exhibit, for he was doing a story on it anyway. And fortunately, Savina hadn't felt one iota of attraction between herself and Grady—and his manner made it clear he didn't either. Of course, she was a good ten years or more older than he was, so it wasn't the least bit surprising. Still, it would have been awkward had that not been the case.

Max had insisted it was safer that he not be seen in public until he got a better understanding of what was happening with the undead in Chicago. He was the most recognizable Venator in the world, and if a vampire noticed him prematurely, it could set their plans awry. It was best for Savina to play her role as Sabrina Ellison, and to keep secret her connection with Max Denton.

Of course, that didn't stop him from slipping into bed with her very early this morning, and gathering her up against his sleek, muscular body—his hair cool and damp from the storm, a fresh aura like the rain itself emanating from his skin, his mouth hot and soft. They hadn't talked, no, he knew better than that, for he knew she'd ask the questions he didn't want to answer. But they did other things, and though he left her warm and smiling, her body loose and humming, inside she had a knot of fear for the future. About how much longer she could do this.

She knew he was in contact with Wayren, and hopefully, by now—Savina *dearly* hoped, for that would go a long way in easing her tension—with his own daughter.

"It's no bother to make a fire," Grady said. "You shivered a minute ago."

Savina smiled at his mistake, but made no move to correct him. "In that case, a fire would be lovely. Thank you."

"When did you see Houdini? Was he doing his underwater escape act yet?"

"It was before the war—in '13, in London. The things he did were miraculous, really. Yes, he did the underwater escape—what did he call it? The Chinese Water Torture Trick. They chained him up, then lowered him *upside down* into a glass-sided container of water. And he got out in less than *forty seconds*." Savina had seen it with her own eyes, and yet she still couldn't believe it. "And I heard he broke out of the most secure jail cell at Scotland Yard. How did he do it? You must know. Max says you were close friends."

Grady was half turned away from her as he worked at the fireplace, but she could see the rounding of his cheek as he grinned. "I know some of his secrets, yes. In general, it's a combination of strength and flexibility—did you know he ran at least seven miles a day, every day, from the time he was fourteen? He did stretches and lifted weights, too. And he ate well and slept well. He kept himself in extremely good physical shape."

Savina was nodding, a smile on her face. Oh, yes, she remembered seeing the Great Houdini remove his robe to reveal a blue bathing suit before being chained up and lowered into the water. The man had been pure, taut muscle. The smooth shape of his pectorals and shoulders had even showed beneath the material of the swimming suit. The women in the audience had swooned privately at the sight of such a masculine specimen while they worried publicly over the dangerous escape he was attempting.

"Being able to dislocate a shoulder helps too, as well as being double-jointed," Grady said, flashing her a look from over his shoulder. "And he was as flexible as a Far Eastern yogi. But there were other…let's say techniques…that he employed. Secreting tiny tools on his person, for example, in his hair or mouth. Sometimes his wife Bess"—he laughed softly, shaking his head—"would even pass him a tiny lock pick when she kissed him for good luck. They're not secrets—any good escape artist knows the basics. But Houdini was the best because he always tried for more, he was in perfect physical condition, he was creative, and above all, he knew how to be a showman. An entertainer." His shoulders slumped a little, then he reached for another piece of wood. "It's simply unbelievable that he's dead, and so suddenly too."

"It's a great loss for the world," Savina agreed.

"Most people don't know that he wasn't just an illusionist and escape artist, but that he helped law enforcement in many ways—along with British intelligence and the United States military."

"That's how you and Max met, isn't it? When he was working with the British army." Max hadn't been enlisted, of course, for he had his own enemy to fight, but he'd done his patriotic duty in other ways and was allowed to be part of the training.

"Yes, that's right. We got to be quite good friends during a week-long training with Houdini." Grady paused in his task of lighting the fire to look at her again. "Max and I would go to the pub after, have a few ales, talk about some of the things Houdini said. Sometimes Harry would even go with us—that was the beginning of how I got to know him so well.

"One time, the two of us were in one of the pubs and Max got up suddenly. He'd been watching this couple sitting at the bar, and he had a sort of intense look on his face. 'I'll be right back,' he told me.

"He walked out the door and I realized he was going after the couple who'd been drinking at the counter. I'd watched the bloke sit down next to a pretty blond woman, and saw how he was getting a little fresh with her. She didn't seem to mind—in fact, she was flirting right back—but she'd also had plenty to drink. They left together, the woman hardly able to walk except with the man's arm around her waist." Grady had a bit of a chagrined look on his face. "I suppose I should have thought to go after them myself, but the way I saw it, she wasn't protesting and the bloke didn't seem threatening. Those things happen every night in a pub like that. But something about them obviously bothered Max.

"I paid for our drinks and followed him—he'd left his hat, anyway—and though I was a block behind, I saw the couple shambling along and Max turn into an alley behind them. He looked like he was holding a pointy stick—though where he'd found that, I couldn't imagine." Grady laughed a little, then turned to poke at the fire. Savina was grinning, for she knew where the story was going.

"I got to the alley and found something inexplicable. I'd seen the man and the woman walk in there, and Max follow—but when I got there, the woman was gone. It was as if she'd disappeared, and it was a blind alley. There was bloody nowhere for her to go. Believe me, I *looked*. The man seemed stunned and confused, and he was bleeding from what I thought was a scratch on the neck. And there was a disgusting film of dust all over Max's coat."

"I suppose Max didn't answer many questions afterward, did he?" Savina asked drily.

"Not a one. He insisted I'd had too many ales at the pub, and that the woman had slipped out of the alley and I must have missed seeing her." Grady shook his head. "But what Max didn't know was how familiar I was with literature. I didn't learn to read until I was fifteen," he added nonchalantly. "But once I did, I devoured a book a day. Quite literally. I worked in a bookshop when I first arrived in London from Dublin." He grinned.

"And since you were familiar with literature, you'd surely read *Dracula*."

"Among other stories too, like *Varney the Vampire*." He sobered, turning back to the hesitant fire for a few moments, coaxing it into something more relevant.

"And so you put the pieces together." Savina's coffee had cooled enough by now for her to sip it, and she tasted the slug of whiskey he'd added. And some honey as well, she thought, for it was deliciously sweet. *Nice touch.*

"I did. He never admitted it, not really, but he didn't really deny it either. And until he contacted me to meet him at Clancy's Gold Coast after he arrived here in Chicago, I never did get confirmation of what I'd seen." He was poking the fire with an iron implement. "He and I have kept in touch since London, though not as much after I moved here—even though I invited him often enough to visit. I was always curious as to whether what I'd seen was what I thought I'd seen."

"Max is a very secretive, closed-off person," Savina said—more to herself than to Grady. "You surely know he lost his wife to the vampires thirteen years ago. That changed him, completely and utterly. I knew him from when he was younger. He's older than me by seven years, but we grew up in the Con—the same environment. He was always very much a rogue and a charmer, someone who bordered on arrogant with his skills and abilities—but he had a right to be arrogant and self-assured. Then after Felicia was murdered, he became a different person. He ran away. From everything. Everyone and everything. He still does."

There was silence for a moment, filled only by the soft rustling and rolling noises as Grady stoked the blazing fire into something that could sustain itself.

"You're not a Venator," he said after a while of staring into the dancing flames. "But Max Denton is."

"He is *the* Venator of Venators," she told him, figuring at this point there was no reason to be reticent. Max had brought them here, he'd admitted what he did, and Grady had the right to know everything she knew. If Max didn't like it, then he shouldn't have abandoned her here for hours and days on end. "The *Summas Gardella*. The leader of the Gardella vampire hunters, descended on a direct bloodline from the first of them all."

"Gardeleus of Rome."

"That's right." Savina was mildly surprised he knew this bit of information, but Grady had proven already how resourceful and enlightened he was about many things.

"Was his wife a Venator too?"

"No. She wasn't—female Venators are extremely rare—and truth be told, Felicia wasn't particularly… Well, she wasn't on the front lines, so to speak. She knew about the undead, of course, and what Max's vocation was, and the legacy of the Gardellas, but she wasn't part of it. Max did his best to keep those two parts of his life separate, while at the same time, protecting her as much as he could. Rather like a man going off to war, or a spy going on his missions, then returning to his normal family life."

"He has a heavy burden."

"The heaviest." Savina sighed, unaccountable tears prickling her eyes. And she was adding to his burden, wasn't she?

A man like Max—a man with brilliant, unique skills and the unwavering drive to destroy evil at any cost, who had a calling that took everything from him: physically, emotionally, mentally, spiritually—had a vocation from which he could not escape, a responsibility to the entire human race.

And loss. Oh, God, he'd suffered such loss—not only of his wife, but of his daughter and her childhood, as well as his own freedom and peace.

What right did she have to demand more from him? What right did she have to expect what he could not give? Was she being a fool? Should she not do her part to eradicate evil by being his love and support so that he could go on?

"Savina?"

She realized Grady was standing there in front of her, holding a handkerchief at her eye level. She hadn't even realized she was crying.

"You love him."

"Incredibly. There is—never will be—anyone else. But…" She dabbed at her eyes with the cloth, feeling like a fool.

How small were her concerns—her mere matters of the heart—when Nicholas Iscariot was in possession of Rasputin's amulet, when he was determined to obtain the Rings of Jubai in order to gain even more power…events that would surely jeopardize hundreds if not thousands of mortals.

Grady sat on the sofa next to her. "It's obvious to any fool the bloke loves you deeply. But surely he's afraid of the same thing happening to you that happened to his wife."

"Of course he is. But it's an entirely different matter. Felicia never fully understood what that world was, what Max's role meant. And he…he kept her insulated from it too. I am—I've been part of the world of the Venators since I was a child. I've staked vampires on my own, in fact. Well over a dozen. You don't have to be a Venator to slay an undead."

"And so you don't." He was almost smiling now; she saw the quirk of his lips.

She couldn't hold back a grin of her own. "They don't call me an adventure photographer for nothing." She reached over and covered his hand, squeezing it. "Thank you so much for listening to me. If I had a brother, I'd want him to be just like you."

At that moment, the front door opened, and in swept Max: dark, wet, and clearly in a mood.

"Well doesn't *this* look cozy." He stood there for no longer than a heartbeat, then turned and walked back out the door, which closed very abruptly behind him.

"Well, bugger that," said Grady.

Max was not happy when he left Woodmore at The Silver Chalice in order to go in search of his daughter—who was not, as it turned out, in her bedroom—and he was even less happy when he returned to the pub several hours later: wet, chilled, and furious beyond belief.

Damned cozy scene, he thought to himself. Fire going, sitting on the sofa together—had they actually been *holding hands?*

He stomped down the steps at Grady's house, then slowed a trifle when he reached the bottom, half waiting for the door to open behind him and for Savina to come rushing after him to explain or apologize…but she didn't.

He didn't wait, but stalked off into the night, brushing too close to a soft arborvitae, which generously deposited all of its collected rain onto the front and side of his coat and down over his trousers. As if he weren't already wet enough.

That's what you get, Denton, you damned wanker. You left her, remember? Savina told you she didn't know if she could ever trust her heart with you again.

He told his conscience to shut the bloody hell up. He didn't have time to deal with personal matters right now—he had other personal matters to attend to. Not to mention a buggering *vampire lord* who was determined to control the world.

Thus, the mood he was in when he slammed open the door of The Silver Chalice was not one that invited reprimand or even comment from those inside—even when the entire damned place shook and rattled, and two glasses fell off the shelves, shattering. Damned Venator strength.

He stepped inside and whipped off his coat—he'd forgotten a hat in his rush to leave—flinging droplets of water everywhere, and hung it on a hook. It was only then that he realized three people were staring at him from their seats at the bar: Woodmore, an elegant Negro woman of about thirty, and Macey.

His daughter.

He faltered, but only for half a step, then continued on his way toward the group of them. This gave him the chance to actually look at her this time. To take in all the details he'd only been able to imagine over the years—for he'd refused to see photographs or read any letters about her for fear his resolve to stay away would falter.

She was slender and petite, like Felicia had been, easily a head shorter than most men. She'd reach only to Max's chin if he ever got close enough to her for an embrace, which at this point seemed unlikely. The thought of that delicate figure taking on a vicious, powerful vampire was enough to make his heart stop.

And yet he knew she had done so.

And won.

A little stroke of pride flitted through him, followed by pain.

His daughter's hair was the color of ripe walnut shells and curly, like his, though she had looser ringlets that were also damp from the rain. So she *had* been out. She had the Pesaro eyes—but of course she'd had them from birth, the large, dark, expressive ones fringed with thick lashes. Her face was chiseled and feminine, with a strong and determined chin, a wide mouth, and graceful brows.

In those moments, he recognized how beautiful, confident, and strong his daughter had come to be—and without an iota of his help. All on her own.

"Ah. The prodigal father has returned," Macey said. "Presumably, you're in Chicago to assist with Iscariot—or were you just passing through?"

Max ignored Woodmore's smothered bark of laughter and slid onto the stool that gave him the best view of his daughter. His blasted knees were actually a trifle weak. He was having unusual difficulty corralling his thoughts. "Macey."

When their eyes met, everything he'd thought he might say fled. His mouth was dry.

"Well, Max? Which is it? Passing through or here to join the club? Oh, no, wait…I know. You stopped in to put the fear of God into Al Capone, not trusting your own daughter to handle things on her own. Like she's been doing for *thirteen years.*" Her brown eyes were spitting *fire.*

"Whatever it is, make up your mind, because we haven't got a moment to lose." She pushed toward him a piece of paper that had been sitting on the counter. "We just received this. It was sent through Aunt Cookie's millinery, and Temple brought it over." She gestured to the other woman, who seemed unable to take her eyes from Max.

Well, at least *one* female appreciated him. And was maybe even a little intimidated.

Max snatched up the paper, glad to have something on which to focus other than the snide greeting from his daughter. He thrust away familial complications and became a Venator as he read the note.

Relinquish the pyramid. For every
hour you delay, a very pretty price
will be paid. One by one by one.

"Of course it's from Iscariot. Flora would have gone right to him with the news—and it's her writing, as I should know."

Max looked at Macey. "How is that?"

"She was my best friend."

He held her gaze for a moment, for there were volumes of unspoken words there. He felt a pang of pain for her grief.

"No details or directions either, about where or how to 'relinquish the pyramid.' The assumption being—we'll know," Woodmore commented. "That doesn't make me very optimistic."

"It's Iscariot. There's nothing optimistic about him," Macey replied flatly. "He is evil personified. We don't know where he's been staying or how to find him, so there's no opportunity to besiege him in his lair."

"And he's recently come into possession of Rasputin's amulet. That's part of the reason I'm here," Max said. "But that's not the only reason."

"So I've heard. Tell me, Max…what are you going to do with the extra *vis bulla* you seem to have acquired?" she asked in a very chilly voice.

It dawned on his that she wasn't pleased he'd spoken with Alphonsus. He frowned, but before he could decide how to respond, Macey moved on.

"What is Rasputin's amulet?"

"It's an emerald the size of a peach pit, set in a gold fitting, worn as a pendant or brooch. It increases the power of its wearer, extends it, and—"

"It glows. Green. In the dark," Macey said. Her eyes were wide and she glanced at Woodmore. "That's how."

"You've seen it?" Any last bit of hope Max might have clung to that Iscariot hadn't learned about the power of the amulet disintegrated.

"Seen it, and been the recipient. That explains my dream," she said, looking at Woodmore. "Iscariot taunted me in a dream, and when I came out of it…I was bleeding. In the same place he'd wounded me months ago. As if he'd just reopened the scars."

Max sucked in his breath. "Bites? Macey, have you been Marked by Nicholas Iscariot?" His heart ceased to beat. *No.*

"No," Woodmore said. "She's not been Marked—at least in the same way Lilith did to Max Pesaro. I made certain of it—the bites he inflicted on her were normal, and healed well with salted holy water. But he'd cut her too, with a dagger, and—"

"And those wounds healed, but…but then they came back," Macey explained.

"In your dream?"

"Yes, but also—when I encountered him in person, a month ago, he caused the cuts to open again—they'd healed but there were still scars. They bled. And also last night the same thing happened."

"Last *night*?" Woodmore turned toward her as Temple made a shocked sound. "You didn't bother to mention that."

Macey's face hardened into stubborn, closed-off lines. "Yes, I had a little encounter with him. It wasn't anything serious—he was across the street from me and he stayed there…until he disappeared. He's just…tormenting me. Trying to, anyway. Nevertheless, he made it clear he wants the rings."

"Not anymore. Now he wants the damned pyramid," Woodmore said grimly.

"You said, 'that's how.' What did you mean?" Max said, fighting back the shocking, startling fear that suddenly threatened to overtake his mind. His daughter and Nicholas Iscariot: face to face? His daughter, marked and scarred by the bastard? His insides turned to ice.

Thank God he'd come. His jaws were tight, his fingers curled into his palms, his body fairly vibrating with the need to *go now* and *find him.*

If only he knew *where.*

"And in your dream, two nights ago," Woodmore continued, causing Max to wonder if the bastard had been there when it happened—he knew where Macey slept, didn't he? "Tell him about that. I find that more concerning than the other."

She looked at Max. Now he saw fear in her eyes, which ratcheted up his own protective instincts. He fought them back, tucking them away for when he needed them. It was imperative he focus on facts, not emotions.

"I had a dream and Iscariot was there, threatening me, demanding the rings, and—and when I woke from the dream, I was bleeding. It was real; it stained my clothing. Chas saw it too."

Her fingers, resting on the bar, trembled slightly. "And I saw him wearing the pendant in my dream—something I'd never seen on him before: a greenish glow emanating from here"—she touched herself in the middle of her breastbone—"as if he were wearing a pendant. It might also have been beneath his coat last night, but I didn't see it."

"Rasputin's amulet," Temple muttered. She had an old book in front of her and began to flip through the brittle pages.

"'A root of malevolence shall marshal such power as never before known. It shall permeate far and deep, and only the dauntless one and his peer shall rise up to it,'" said Woodmore.

A root of malevolence. There could be no better description of Nicholas Iscariot. *Shall marshal such power as never before known.* Max had never liked the sound of that, and he liked it even less now that his daughter was in the midst of it.

Thank God I came, her pride be damned.

"But who is the dauntless one?" asked Temple. "Do you know?" This question was directed at Max, but it seemed as if she were too bashful to look at him for more than a second, let alone address him directly.

"Even if I did," he replied, "it wouldn't matter. It would be beyond foolish to rely on a prophecy to determine how to resolve this matter. We must rely on ourselves."

"Right, of course," Temple murmured, and returned her attention to her book.

"Do you have any way to contact your friend—Flora, is that her name?" Max asked Macey.

She shook her head. "No."

"I suppose we have no choice but to wait for whatever will come," he said. "Unless anyone here has a better idea?"

They shook their heads, each as grim as the next.

He suspected it was going to be a long, unpleasant night—waiting for some message, some further information.

While all the while, dodging cold dagger-eyes from his own flesh and blood.

And wondering what the other woman he loved was doing, cozied up on the sofa in front of a bloody fire.

Bugger it to *hell*.

Eleven

In Which our Heroine Considers the Perfect Right Hook

MACEY AVOIDED HER FATHER'S EYES, as well as his person, for the rest of the dreary Sunday and its evening at The Silver Chalice.

She had nothing to say to Max Denton.

Sure, she was glad he was here—for all she knew, *he* was the dauntless one, and as far as she was concerned, *he* could face down Nicholas Iscariot with whoever his "other half" was. But that didn't mean she had to start buying him ties for Christmas and having Sunday dinner with the man.

There were other things on her mind—things she wished she could erase, and things she knew she was foolish to be upset over. After all, the safety of hundreds, even thousands, of mortals would surely be at risk during the conflict with Iscariot. Her own private matters of the heart were of little concern in the grand picture.

But try as she might to stop them, her thoughts kept going back to the moment when Grady had opened his front door earlier today.

She'd looked up at him from beneath her dripping fedora, ready to speak—to make up some excuse to come into the man's house. She knew Grady, knew he would never turn away a damsel in distress, or anyone in need, for that matter. She hadn't had a plan, she just thought if she gained entrance, if she could spend some time with him…maybe…perhaps…they could start over… differently.

Or something.

She didn't know what. Didn't really know why she'd gone there in the first place.

Macey made a sound of disgust that had Chas glancing over at her. He, like everyone else in the group—which was spread out at separate tables in the pub—was poring over ancient books and writings in search of a way to destroy Rekk's Pyramid.

At least, that was what she was supposed to be doing, instead of tormenting herself with memories of Grady—and the fact that Sabrina Ellison, older woman and adventure photographer, *had been coming down from his bedroom in her dressing robe.*

Even now, the thought of that made her well up with nausea, and her very fertile mind delve into imaginings it had no business going into.

Her first reaction, after the stupefaction of discovery and the blind reeling away into pouring rain after a stammered excuse, was that it had been less than two weeks since she'd asked Wayren to use the special gold disk.

Less than two weeks, and he was already fooling around with someone else? An older woman, too, vastly experienced and worldly—and possibly even a very rich one.

But by the time Macey got to the end of the block and was passing Garrick's Butcher Shop, her tears of frustration were mingled with rain, and she realized how foolish she was being. If Grady had no memory of her, it hadn't been only two weeks since they'd been together. There hadn't even *been* a "together" in his mind.

You did the right thing, she reminded herself as she sloshed through puddles and trudged through mud. Grady deserved his own life.

But you didn't give him a choice. Temple's voice mingled with her own conscience, and Macey glared into the waterlogged day.

It's done, she told herself firmly. *It's over. I'll live with my decision.*

And so Macey returned to the pub late in the afternoon to find the ominous note from Iscariot that had sent them all into a tumult. Yet, in a very small way, she was grateful for the distraction it provided.

Now, it was hours later and she was considering her options: continuing to search for the solution to destroying Rekk's Pyramid, going to bed and resting until the next thing happened with Iscariot, or heading back out into the now-pitch-dark city and see what trouble she could stir up. She didn't want to just *sit here*.

Hmm…maybe she should go back and see what Capone was up to. Terrorize him a little, as he was prone to do to others.

As if reading Macey's mind, Chas stood abruptly and gave a graceful stretch that had her watching him with appreciation. Well, there was another option.

"I'm going to bed," he said, his gaze sliding over hers. "My eyes are burning, I'm beat, and it's—Christ, it's nearly midnight. Who knows when we'll hear more from Iscariot."

"Much as I hate waiting for him to act, I can see no other option at the moment," Max commented. He was wearing glasses to help him see the small, faded print of the book he was reading, and the dark-rimmed spectacles made him look like anything but a fearsome warrior. "However, I suggest at least one of us remain in the pub at all times in case we receive another message."

"But don't you feel like we should be—*doing* something?" Macey said. "Rather than just *waiting*? Who knows what he's doing right now!"

Max removed his spectacles and looked at her, lifting a brow. "I'm all ears, Macey. What do you suggest?"

She gritted her teeth. He was right, and, dammit, she agreed with him, but she *wanted to be doing something*. Instead of brooding and thinking. It felt as if they were at Iscariot's mercy.

"If you want to go on patrol, hunt around, see if we find anything, I'll go with you," her father added.

Not what she had in mind. Not with him, anyway. "The weather's so bad out, I suppose everyone's probably holed up for the night," she muttered. "Even vampires."

"Wait...I think I've found something." Temple spoke suddenly and caught their attention. "It says something here about an evil pyramid stone...it goes on with a description—Yes, that sounds like it: onyx stone, shaped like the ancient pyramids, the base is square and the length of a short finger...yes, this must be it. It says here...hmm...let me translate..." Her voice trailed off, and was followed by the scritch-scratch of a pencil on paper and her mutterings.

Macey felt her father's eyes flicker back to her, but she didn't look at him. She wasn't giving him any openings to start up a friendly parental conversation.

"All right," said Temple after a moment of writing. "Here's what I have. Apparently, the pyramid can be destroyed—get this—'with the curved tongue of the ruby-eyed skull.'"

"What the hell does that mean?" Chas said. "Skulls don't have tongues—or eyes, for that matter. Where is Wayren when you need her?"

Macey couldn't help it—she looked reflexively toward each of the doors, half expecting the mysterious chatelaine to walk through one of them at any moment. Both doors remained closed.

"That's all it says," Temple replied. "And I'm confident the translation is right. I checked it three times. There might be more, but that's all there is in this section." She yawned. "I'm going to bed. It's been a long day, and I didn't get much sleep last night." Despite the dark situation, her face softened into a cat-with-the-cream expression.

"I'll stay here—take the first shift," Max said. "In case something changes."

For some reason, his easy offer made Macey feel slightly guilty—but she wasn't going to give in to that base feeling. Then it evaporated as her father went on, "Woodmore, if you'll relieve me at four." It wasn't a request—and he hadn't included Macey.

"*I'll* relieve you at four," she said flatly. "Chas should rest. He's been badly wounded."

Max merely shrugged, ignoring Chas's outraged scoff that he might need to be coddled. "Very well. I'll be here. Presumably, there will be a place for me to sleep at that time?"

Macey couldn't help but feel a tad deflated at his easy acquiescence. "Yes. I'll show you then."

Thus the group disbanded for the evening, and it was assumed Chas would stay on site instead of going back to his own flat, due to the nature of their predicament.

Macey shot a glance at Max just as she went through the door to the private apartments and saw that he'd settled himself at a table with a short crystal glass, a tall, dark bottle, and a stack of books and papers. He looked...forlorn.

A little shaft of something poked her in the heart as she paused, looking at the dark head bent over his studies, one hand holding a pencil, the drink off to the side. She smothered a startled noise, for in that moment, her father looked just like the man in Sabrina Ellison's photograph. The tableau—the mood, the pose, the resemblance—was astonishing in its familiarity. It was as if she'd been brought into the photograph in real life. Even the shadows seemed the same.

Obviously sensitive to everything in his environment, Max lifted his head and found Macey watching him. From across the room, she saw a flash of something in his eyes—pain? hope? apprehension?—and forced her lips into a small, polite smile.

"Good night, Max. I'll see you in a few hours."

"Macey..."

"I'll see you in a few hours," she said again, then fled, closing the door behind. Her heart was pounding, her palms were damp, her eyes felt gritty—and she didn't really understand why.

He was just a man, just the man who'd caused her to be born. And had caused her to have this vocation of hers—the one that would keep her forever alone and solitary, and always the target of evil.

Now he was a colleague, a peer—a partner. Albeit an interfering one. Nothing more.

She stubbornly shoved away the flicker of a long-lost memory of sliced apples and star-shaped seeds and laughter and—No, she didn't need that taking up space in her mind right now.

Macey turned blindly, blinking rapidly, rushing away from it all, and slammed into Chas.

"Whoa there, lulu," he said, catching her with gentle, firm hands.

She managed to look up at him without showing her confusion and pain—at least, she hoped the emotions were hidden—and completely switched the set of her mind. "I was hoping you wouldn't go home tonight," she said, easing closer as she took hold of him.

Strong as steel, smooth and muscular, his arms acted as anchors in the midst of her turmoil. His warmth and the power of his presence steadied her. But she wanted more. She *needed* it.

"I'm glad you decided to stay here tonight," she said, looking up at him. Her heart was suddenly pounding, and she felt a little queasy with all sorts of nerves and emotions.

Chas's eyes shuttered and he eased back a bit. "It didn't make sense to go home."

She moved in a little closer, her attention wandering over the healing wounds on his neck, the strong beat of pulse thudding there, the darkness of his skin beneath the torn white shirt…then over his stubbled jaw and to his mouth. The beauty of his form and features took her breath away.

"Macey," he said quietly. She felt a little tremor run through his muscles, a tiny shiver beneath his skin. "I don't think… Whatever you're thinking, lulu, it's not a good idea." He sounded a little breathless, a little dusky and rough, and as if the words had been wrung from him.

"Why not?" she asked, shoving away a pang of uncertainty. "You didn't seem to have a problem with it the other night in the alley. You practically tore my—"

He swooped down and covered her mouth with his, smothering the rest of her sentence, dragging her up against his steely body. He was warm and hard, smelled spicy and masculine, and tasted salty and hot. He kissed her forcefully, wildly, with deep penetration and long, sweeping strokes…with desperation and desire and something much darker.

It was Macey who pulled away, to catch her breath—or so she told herself—but then it was ruined when she realized tears had filled her eyes. *Dammit.*

She ignored whatever emotion was trying to destroy the moment, and slid her arms up around his neck, pulling his face to hers once again, fitting her mouth to his in her own desperate bid for escape.

This time, Chas pulled away after only a short while, and when he did, he put a hand on her shoulder to keep her at a distance.

"You're trying too hard, lulu," he said. His voice was matter of fact, but there was heat in his eyes, and she could tell he wasn't at all adverse to her attentions. But he was holding her back—literally holding her back.

"What do you mean by that?" She was outraged, and now there were tears welling in her eyes again, *damn him.* "It's always been like that with us—rough, and wild, and—"

He put a finger to her lips, glancing at the door to the pub.

"What, you're worried about *him*?" That infuriated her even more—now Max Denton was interfering in her *private* life. "I can solve that problem." She grabbed Chas's hand and pulled, ready to tow him off down the hall to the privacy of her own room.

"Macey, stop," he said, and pulled his fingers easily from her grip.

Blind with tears, furious and confused and frustrated, she dashed a hand over her eyes and stalked away before she could embarrass herself further. She'd taken two steps before Chas caught her by the arm, pulling her back relatively gently—for him.

"Leave me alone." She tried to punch him—oh, that would feel *great*, to land a few solid ones right on his torso—but he was too strong, even for her, and he pulled her tight against him, his arms capturing her in an unyielding band.

"There's not too many other things I'd rather do than pull off your clothes and make it all the way with you, lulu," he murmured into the top of her head. "Believe me. Especially after…today. But I'm feeling a bit wrung out myself, you know"—she felt the tremor rush through him—"and being a substitute or an excuse doesn't sit well with me at the moment. You don't want *me* so much as you want something to make you forget everything that's going on—and I can't argue with that. I've done it myself…too often. Far too often. Even…"

"Even with me?" she whispered into his shirt, now damp with her tears.

"Ah, Macey," he said, tightening his arms around her. "My life is so bloody damn fucked up, you can't even take offense to me saying it, because nothing I do means anything. I don't belong here. I don't belong back—home. I don't belong anywhere." He drew in a deep breath. "You don't love me, I *can't* love you, we've been using each other for weeks…and though it's been damned *good*—"

"Well, there is *that*." She laugh-sobbed against him.

He gave a pained chuckle of his own. "Right. Look, I don't know what happened when you went out today—you came back looking worse than when you left, and that's not saying much—but one thing I know is, going to bed with me won't help you feel any better. *Inside*," he added with another bark of laughter when she tensed up to argue. "Mentally."

This time, when she drew back, he allowed her to. "It's been a terrible day," she admitted, still enjoying the comfort of solid arms around her.

"Even worse than when I dragged you out of Iscariot's limousine? *That* was a pretty bad day."

"Almost as bad." Her lips quivered, but inside she still felt as if she was a piece of clothing being run through the wringer.

"Max showing up here was a surprise."

"That's an understatement." She sniffled, and to her surprise, Chas produced a handkerchief from somewhere on his rumpled person. "How does he have the nerve to show up after thirteen years and pretend like nothing happened?"

"I wouldn't say he pretended like nothing happened—" Chas stopped when she turned her most furious glower onto him. "Right. The bastard."

"And then I—" No, she didn't want to talk about Grady. Didn't want to admit even to Chas—whose deepest, darkest secrets she knew—how pathetic she'd been, lurking around Grady's house, and even knocking on the door.

"You went to that Irish bloke, didn't you?" His mouth was flat with anger. "The one you castrated."

"*Castrated?* What the hell—I didn't—"

"Oh, you bloody well did. Not saying I completely blame you, but you did—you took every bit of manhood, of humanity, away from him when you made your decision about his future. *For* him. And what—now you're regretting it?"

"I thought you were on my side," she cried, curling her fingers into a fist. Just one punch, just *one*! "You were the one who told me I couldn't be with anyone."

"I didn't tell you to castrate the man, Macey. Never. It's a damned good thing he can't remember you, because if he ever found out what you did—well, making those kinds of godlike decisions for a man is inexcusable. And cowardly. He'd hate you for it."

"It's just what my father did to *me*," she said.

"He didn't manipulate your memory, Macey. It's a whole different situation." Chas reached out with a gentle hand, wiping away a stream of tears—but he was fighting a losing battle, for they were coming too fast now. "What happened when you went to Grady's, lulu? Did you see him?"

She nodded, closing her eyes, folding her arms over her middle to close herself off. She was so damned furious and incensed and confused and *sad*.

Just *sad*.

And scared. Beneath it all, she was terrified.

Chas waited silently—he was good at that too—and she finally blurted out, "That damned lady photographer was there. In her *dressing robe*. They probably sat around all day and talked about her pictures from—from *Paris* or wherever they were. Notre Dame, and the creepy catacombs with those skulls everywhere, and from the tops of skyscrapers. She probably told him all about her adventures, and now he's going to go with her, and…"

Good grief, she sounded like a lunatic. Like a weak, lovesick lunatic.

Not like a Venator. Not like a woman who was born to fight evil, to throw men across the room, to come face to face with a nightmare with fangs…

She was weak, and foolish, and why was she even here? Why hadn't she just remained a normal woman, with a normal life?

"You know, even Victoria Gardella cried," Chas said. "And she made her own mistakes—a good many, if you'd ever heard Max Pesaro talk about it."

"Did you know them? Back then?" Macey spared a moment to be fascinated in spite of the torrent of emotions inside her.

He shrugged. "In a manner of speaking. Pesaro was there when I went through the Trial to get my *vis bulla*. It's all rather a blur due to the way Wayren manipulated me through time—it was as if we stopped in their London on our way here, skipping a decade here, a few more there… But, yes, I met Victoria, and Pesaro as well. You do have his eyes. And her temperament." He smiled, and her heart fluttered.

"You're too damned attractive for your own good, Chas," she said, stepping away, wiping the last stray tears from her eyes. "If you aren't careful, I might drag you back to my bedroom anyway."

He shook his head, his gaze warm and sad. "Macey, love, there aren't many other things I'd rather do, but it's better that doesn't happen. At least…not until you figure out a few things." He glanced again toward the door that led to the pub—and Max Denton.

"And until I… Well." He shook his head again. "Right, then. Against my better judgment, I'm going to bid you good night. I have a feeling tomorrow is going to be an ugly day."

Twelve

The Dawning of the Vilest of Days

MONDAY MORNING, Grady was in the *Tribune* tower working at his desk. He'd come in before nine o'clock, having left Savina to her own devices at his house. He knew she was going to be at the Chicago Library this morning, supervising the dismantling of her photography display.

Neither of them commented on the fact that Max hadn't returned last night.

It was past ten thirty, and Grady was making notes about a list of potential contacts for a story when he heard someone shouting from the elevators.

"There's a hostage situation," said Earl Perry, a typesetter who'd just rushed off the elevator. His face was pale and drawn and his words fell over themselves as the others gathered around to listen to the news. "Man's got himself locked up with at least two dozen girls at Beedle's."

Grady pushed up so fast his chair crashed to the floor. "Who is it? At Beedle's?" He slammed on his hat as Perry stammered a reply.

"I—no one knows who—it just came in on the telephone, and the colonel told us—yes, that fancy school—"

But Grady hadn't waited for the rest of the details. He'd already reached the elevator—whose dial indicated the car was on the third floor. He was on the twelfth.

"Go get 'em, ace," someone shouted at his back.

Grimly, he eschewed the slow-moving elevator and bounded down the steps, trench coat flapping around his legs, the unnecessary *Go get 'em, ace* reverberating in his head.

Yes, there was a hell of a story. But that wasn't why he was winging himself around the sharp corners of each flight of stairs and leaping down the last three to the landings as he reached them.

Beedle's—formally known as Miss Beedle's Perfect School for Young Ladies—was an elite boarding school, and the building itself was a forbidding mansion surrounded by an iron fence topped with spikes. Though he had never had cause to visit the school, he'd passed by it on numerous occasions. Each time, he'd been struck by its impenetrable, prisonlike appearance: the imposing fence contributed, of course, but there was also a large, treeless yard, and sheer brick walls five stories high, devoid of the popular decorative finishes of most buildings. Windows on the first two levels were covered with ornate but efficient wrought iron grilles similar to those found in New Orleans.

The school was known as a place for the daughters of the wealthiest and most powerful men in Chicago—everyone from gangsters to senators to business moguls. It was clearly an institution meant to protect those delicate beings from all external threats—and, likely, to keep them from seeking them out as well.

Grady tossed up a thanks that he'd not been raised by rich or powerful parents. Being sent to a place like Beedle's would have been worse than prison—and, in his mind, far worse than his own tragic and impoverished beginnings. Nevertheless, apparently Chicago's elite (and those who aspired to join them) felt differently, for the school had a waiting list three years long. And when a family learned of its daughter's acceptance therein, it wasn't unusual to see a notice in the *Tribune* announcing it—as if it were a wedding or engagement.

Whoever the hostage taker was, he'd chosen well: everyone in the city would be on pins and needles until the terror was resolved. Whatever the man wanted—perhaps money, which it surely had to be—would most likely be delivered to him on a silver platter in order to rescue the wealthy and delicate hostages.

Unless Grady could help find a way to abort the perpetrator's plan. With his Houdini-like skills and other expertise he'd acquired back in his street days in Dublin, he was in a unique position to offer help. Since he'd assisted in cornering a counterfeit gang several months back, he'd gained some notoriety and validation with the cops. If Linwood happened to be on site, that would grease the wheels with the authorities even more.

Grady drove as far as he was able, but when he was still two blocks from Beedle's, he was forced to park. Streets had been blocked off in a perimeter around the school, and policemen and onlookers filled the throughways. The rain had ceased late the night before, but the ground was still wet and muddy, and the air was thick with moisture.

He used his press pass as an excuse to push through the barriers, and found Linwood with three other cops known to Grady. They were standing at the gate of the school and had strained expressions on their faces. Other officers stood about in different clusters, and he recognized the chief of police, along with some of his lieutenants. Everyone looked grim and hopeless.

"What's the story?" Grady asked Linwood and his companions without taking the time for a formal greeting.

"Guy's inside, not sure which floor—probably the big dining hall. He's got twenty girls under his control, ages twelve through sixteen. The rest of the students and staff escaped or were released," his uncle explained. "When they came out, they gave us the message that if anyone stepped past the perimeter fence, the hostages would be killed immediately."

"Surely he didn't do this all alone?" Grady asked incredulously. "Does he have a bomb?"

"No bomb we're aware of. He's not alone—got a small army with him. We've counted roughly a dozen others, saw glimpses of them through the windows. Reports from the ones he set free corroborate this estimate," said Officer Donahue.

Grady swore under his breath, looking at the fortress-like school. "Has he been in contact with anyone? Do we know what he wants?"

Linwood shook his head. "Nothing yet. The report came in only about thirty minutes ago—you got here fast, Grady. I was just about to have someone call you."

Just then, there was an exclamation from one of the cops at the gate. "The door's opening!"

So it was—the massive oak door yawned open. A young girl of no more than thirteen, wearing her school uniform, stumbled out onto the porch as if she'd been pushed.

She staggered, trying to run, stumbled again, and then fell down the steps. She lay there, sprawled facedown on the damp green grass.

"Someone help her!" cried a woman—unnecessarily, for Donahue and Linwood had already opened the gate, and their companion, Officer Barnett, pushed through at a run. Linwood and Donahue followed in his wake with their weapons drawn.

At this time, the bystanders gathered around the school were completely hushed, though the crowd tried to surge forward to see better. The encroaching group was held off by the beat cops who'd been erecting barriers along the street.

By now, Barnett had scooped up the girl. With a wary glance at the windows of the school, he dashed back to the gate, accompanied by Linwood and Donahue. This event took no more than thirty or forty seconds, and everyone breathed a sigh of relief when all four of them passed back through the gate safely.

Grady was among those who gathered around when Barnett laid the girl on a pallet next to an ambulance with its rear doors open. Thus, he was one of the first to see the blood pumping from a distinctive type of wound on her throat. The mark had been obscured by her long, dark hair and the navy school uniform.

He breathed in sharply and looked up to exchange horrified glances with Linwood.

"Good God," breathed Donahue as a doctor began to examine the girl, and the chief of police pushed his way closer. "Is she—is she…?"

"She's alive," said the physician, whom Grady knew as Dr. Fintucket. A slight, quiet man who went about his work efficiently and practically, he was the doctor who'd been summoned after Linwood was attacked by vampires a month ago, and it was he who had most likely saved the man's life. He was also likely to be discreet about the cause of the wound, just as he had been with Linwood. "And—"

The doctor stopped speaking, for the girl had begun to stir. Her eyes fluttered open, but instead of looking up at the people gathered around her, they remained blank and appeared unfocused.

"It's all right," said Dr. Fintucket soothingly as he continued to examine and treat her wound. "You're safe now, young lady. You have a nasty cut here."

Her lips began to move, and she began to speak, her gaze still unseeing. The words came out in an eerie monotone voice, as if they'd been rehearsed, or otherwise imprinted upon her mind.

"The others will be released unharmed if his demands are met. He will speak only to the press, and will outline his demands then. One man will be allowed to walk through the gate and approach the school. He must prove he is a reporter for the *Tribune,* at which time he will gain entrance to the building. The reporter must come without weapons, and may wear or carry nothing made of metal. He will be searched. If he is found with any metal or weapons on his person, he will be given back to you in a condition much worse than mine. You have until noon today to send the reporter to speak with him. If the deadline passes, he will begin to release the other hostages…and they will fare much worse than I. One by one…by…one."

The girl's eyes sank closed as she spoke the final words on a weak breath.

Silence fell over the circle of people around the young messenger, while in a horrible contrast, birds chirped happily in the trees above, and a fresh, floral-scented breeze ruffled the leaves. When Grady looked up, he found Linwood's eyes on him. He gave a brief nod, but his uncle would already know his intent. There was no decision to be made.

"Is she…?" Donahue asked again.

The doctor nodded. "She's still alive. Her pulse is weak, and she's lost blood—but not too much. I believe she should recover, God willing—let's get her to the hospital. We've seen wounds like this before." He glanced at Linwood meaningfully, then turned to give instructions to the ambulance drivers.

"Salted holy water will help," Grady muttered to the doctor, who looked at him with respect. "For those types of wounds. Lots of it." Then he turned to the others. "I'm going," he said before Donahue and Barnett could speak, then addressed the police chief. "I'm the best man for the task."

Though Chief Ryan and Linwood didn't see eye to eye when it came to allowing gangsters to have their way in the city as long as their palms were well greased—which was true for a good majority of the policemen in Chicago—in this case the two—and, surely, the rest of the force as well—were aligned in their position.

"Are you quite certain, Grady?" asked the chief, but he looked relieved.

"There's no question as to whether I should do it," Grady replied. "It's only a matter of how quickly I can be prepared. What time is it?"

"Quarter past eleven," replied Linwood. His face was taut and his mouth flat. Clearly he was remembering his own encounter with the undead.

Any fear Grady might have burbling inside him had to be ignored. He focused his thoughts on what must be done instead of what could happen.

"Right, then. I'll need several things." Grady began to list off his requirements, sending Donahue and Barnett off to different destinations in police cars screaming with sirens.

Then he turned to Linwood, but before he could speak, his uncle took him by the arm and pulled him away from the others.

"I have no intention of trying to talk you out of this because you know I'd be doing the same thing in your position."

"I know." Grady smiled and gave the older man's shoulder a squeeze.

"But…just in case…" His words became thick, as if his throat closed up, and he gave his head a little shake as if to clear it. When he looked up, his pale gray eyes glistened. "Damn it, Grady, I can't lose you too. So you'd best be damned careful and do everything they say in there. You and I know better than anyone here what you're going to face inside that school."

"And what those girls are already facing," Grady added quietly.

"I'd give anything to be the one to go in there and drive a damned stake—"

"Shhh," Grady said, glancing around to make certain no one could hear. People were terrified enough—if they thought there were supernatural forces at work, if they knew they were dealing with beings as close to the devil as could be, there'd be no telling how they'd react. A wild, panicked mob would not help the situation.

"Right. I know. He might have those girls in there, but we've got…well, hell, we've got sunshine on our side. They don't like that, do they? Maybe there's a way to blow the damned roof off the place. Let the devils *fry* in their seats."

Grady choked off a laugh. "That is an excellent point, Linwood. Why don't you work on that tactic—it's a good one."

His uncle was trying to smile, but wasn't nearly as successful. "And *this*. Take this." He'd been digging inside his pocket, and he pulled out a rosary. Each bead was made from wood, as was the cross at the end. They were strung together on waxed and knotted string. "It was your aunt's, and her mother's before her. I take it to work every day."

"I know," Grady said, his throat suddenly closing up. "Thank you. They might not allow me in even with this, but I'll try."

Linwood looked at the prayer beads for a moment, then, determination on his face, he snapped off the wooden cross at the end and offered it to Grady. It was half the length of his pinkie finger. "You're a student of Houdini—surely you can hide this somewhere."

"That I can. Thank you, uncle. And I suppose I must give you these." He pulled out the silver cross he wore around his neck tucked beneath his shirt, and pulled it over his head to relinquish. Then he began to work the silver ring off his finger, and dropped that into his uncle's open hand as well.

"I've been meaning to ask—where did you get this?" Linwood was referring to the ring. "I don't remember seeing it before."

"It was given to me," Grady replied. "Speaking of Houdini, I hope Donahue can find what I sent him for. I can go in without my hollow-heeled shoes—damn, I knew I should have worn them today, but they were wet from being polished and shined. There are useful things secreted inside them."

"Grady." Linwood's voice dropped low and serious, and his eyes were intense as he took his nephew's arm. "If…if something happens, and you don't— Well, is there anything you want me to do? Anyone you'll want me to…um, send word to? Give a message to?"

Grady shook his head. "You're my only family left, Linny… there's no one else to tell. I can only assume my boss will hear if things don't work out," he added drily. "As will my friends from the paper. And I suspect Father Cork will know in plenty of time for the funeral."

"No one? No…no special woman friend, perhaps, or… anyone?" Linwood asked.

"No."

Grady looked toward the school, and his insides tightened as he thought of what awaited him: both what he expected, and what he could have no idea about. What he might find inside— those poor, innocent girls—but even more worrisome: what the vampires wanted.

What did they want that they were willing to risk exposing themselves to the city at large?

At that moment, Donahue ran up, carrying a satchel with the items Grady had requested. As Grady pulled out a large bottle of holy water and began to drink from it, Barnett approached from a different direction. He was carrying several copies of the *Tribune* to prove that Grady met the qualifications set forth in the girl's message. Barnett was followed by Colonel McCormick, the *Trib*'s much-admired editor, who rushed up to his ace reporter to wish him well—and, of course, hope for a scoop.

But mostly to wish him well.

By the time Grady was prepared to go in for the meeting, it was ten minutes before noon. Early, but he was ready.

He embraced his uncle, then turned and started toward the tall iron gate. He'd left his hat behind, and carried nothing but the newspapers. In his coat pockets were pencils and a pad of paper. Each of the policemen clustered about the entrance patted him on the shoulder, arm, or back as he passed by—and Grady saw a mixture of admiration, relief, and disappointment in their eyes.

The walk across the lawn from gate to entrance was both too brief and stretched too long, but at last he was climbing up the steps to the school.

The door opened by some unseen hand and Grady stepped inside. As he did so, his first impression was one of pressing silence, followed by cold. He subdued a shiver. Evil pervaded the space. He could fairly smell its dank, pungent essence.

No sooner had he passed through the entrance than the door closed behind him and he found himself facing two people: a man and a woman. He assumed they were undead, but he said nothing, merely stood there as he was searched none too gently.

He'd tucked the small wooden cross inside his mouth, and would palm it out as soon as the search was completed.

"The master will see you now," said the woman once they'd finished patting him down thoroughly. As he'd intended, the most dangerous object they found was a thick pencil and pad of paper.

"How is your master called?" Grady asked, though he suspected he already knew.

"Nicholas Iscariot."

A sharp, cold stab of fear penetrated him, but he gave no indication and made no hesitation. Nevertheless, he'd be lying if he said his knees weren't weak as he walked down the corridor to face the most powerful vampire in the world—according to Max Denton.

Speaking of Max…Grady hoped Savina had received the message he'd sent to her via a boy on a bicycle, since he didn't know how else to contact Denton at this time. Grady had directed the courier to start at the Chicago Library, and if Savina wasn't there, to leave it at Grady's own house. He suspected *the* Venator of all Venators would want to know about this situation as soon as possible.

Grady focused, counting the number of guards—presumably all vampires—he passed or glimpsed as they walked. At least ten, including five in the room where Nicholas Iscariot waited. Surely there were more, watching the other exits and entrances.

"Not even noon, and here you are—darkening my doorway," said Iscariot as they paused on the threshold. "Couldn't wait to get your story, could you, Mr. Grady?"

Grady stepped through the wide entrance and discovered that Linwood was correct: the vampire *had* set up his command central in the large, high-ceilinged dining room. Hmm. Perhaps his uncle's idea of blowing off the roof wasn't such a bad one after all. The four tall windows that lined one side of the rectangular space had been covered with what appeared to be bedsheets, presumably to keep out the sunshine lethal to vampires.

Despite the powerful creature sitting on a large chair on one end of the room, and his cronies scattered around, Grady ignored the undead at first and turned his attention to the hostages.

The girls were huddled together in a far corner. What struck him was how quiet they were. It was eerie—the taut silence, without even the sounds of sobbing or sniffling. Yet they all seemed aware and awake—for many pairs of wide, frightened eyes followed him. But no one made even the quietest sound.

Next Grady turned his attention to the vampire lord. The man was slender and very pale, dressed in dark clothing that made his skin look even whiter. He wore something like a pendant in the center of his vest, and it glowed a soft, nauseating green.

What Grady could see of Iscariot's facial features, for he was half in shadow, were just as slender and delicate as his frame. The vampire had sleek black hair, which was so thick that when it was combed back it rose high off his forehead. His eyes were, at the moment, dark and not glowing, and Grady took care to keep himself from looking directly into the vampire's gaze—or to even skim close to it.

"I saw no reason to delay. And you already know my name—I find that a little surprising." Grady gestured with the newspapers he still held; his undead escorts hadn't had the chance to inform their master of his identity.

Iscariot's eyes widened in genuine surprise. "How could you think you'd escaped my notice? But why do you think I arranged all of this? You are the perfect messenger, and I was certain you would be the one to take on the task. The rest of it"—he gestured to the mass of huddled girls—"is just—what do they say?—ah yes, icing on the cake, no?"

"You arranged this in order to speak to me?" Grady thought he'd been as prepared as possible, but this took him off guard.

"Not merely to speak to you, no—but it's another benefit of the situation. I need something, and you are going to be instrumental in me obtaining it."

"Right, then…your demands. I'm here to learn what they are, and to do my best to help you get what you want—but perhaps, as an act of good faith, you'd release the hostages. I'll take their place." Grady didn't figure the vampire would go for it, but it was worth a try.

Iscariot began to giggle, low and dark. "An act of good faith. You'll take their place. Release the hostages. You sound as if you think *you* are the one in control here." He shook his head. "The only way I'll release any of them—alive, anyway—is when I am in possession of two things: Rekk's Pyramid and your lover, Macey Gardella."

"My *lover*? And a pyramid?" Grady shook his head. "I don't know what you're referring to—in either case. Not that I don't want to help," he added quickly, holding up his hands.

Iscariot's eyes began to burn red, and his fangs protruded from beneath his upper lip. He swept to his feet and stalked toward Grady. "Don't play coy with me, mortal," he snapped, stopping in front of him. A chill in the air, along with the faintest scent of something foul, accompanied his movements. "I've *seen* you with Macey Gardella."

Now that Iscariot had come from the shadowy side of the room, his face was in full view, and Grady saw the crooked scar of a cross that marred one side of it. The vampire must have noticed his attention settling there, for his face twisted into fury.

"Yes, your beloved marked me thus," Iscariot said, his eyes now burning dazzling red, their irises ringed with brilliant blue. "And for that, I will destroy her…but first I'll kill everyone she loves. Though perhaps I might spare…*one*…person. If he were to be helpful."

Grady's heart was in his throat, but he forced his mind to remain clear and strong. His hands were still up in the air, and he allowed them to tremble slightly—enough for the vampire to see. At the same time, he felt a wave of…something…emanating from the creature whose eyes glowed with unadulterated evil. A little tug. A coaxing sensation.

It made him feel murky. And slow. And…

He collected his cascading thoughts with difficulty, suddenly remembering to slide his hand into the right pocket. The smooth strength of the wooden cross therein was an immediate comfort, and he managed to speak.

"Who? I don't know— My beloved?" Grady had to force the words from his lips. The allure was stronger now. "I don't know… and I know nothing…of a pyramid. I…"

"Macey Gardella will pay," hissed Iscariot, very close to him… so very close… The green pendant nearly touched Grady's chest. "She will pay dearly for this." His fangs were fully protruding now, and Grady could smell the rusty scent of blood on his breath.

Someone squeaked fearfully in the corner, and through his soupy mind, he heard the soft rustling of the girls…as if they were packing themselves closer together and deeper into their corner.

Iscariot's eyes, so very close, beckoned to him…those twin spots of burning light…and they moved in, filling his vision with a dark red gleam that seemed to swallow him up, drawing him deeper and deeper unto a smothering, warm blanket.

From a distance, he heard Iscariot's words, twining around him like a serpent. "Macey Gardella…you love her…you'd do anything for her…and she'll do anything to save you…oh, *yessss* you will…"

"No," breathed Grady, concentrating desperately on what he had to say, fighting the nausea and terror that rolled over him, over and over, pulling him under… "I don't…know…Macey… Gardella… You have…the wrong…person. I…can't…help…"

From a distance, Grady heard that slithering voice, sleek and hissing and soft: "Come now…release yourself…come to me, and tell me all of her secrets…Macey Gardella has the pyramid. Where will she keep it?"

"I…don't"—he could hardly force the words, but he *had* to… he must *fight* this…for the girls—"know…"

"Very well, then," continued that insistent voice, filtering through the cloying haze of smoky red, "I have other ways of getting the information I need."

The vampire must have moved back, for the smothering pull eased—but then in the next moment, strong hands were pulling at Grady, grabbing his arms and binding them together tightly. His legs were next, lashed at the ankles with rough, inhumanly strong hands. He blinked, trying to pull himself from the thrall, fighting to clear his mind and prepare himself for whatever was coming…

Everything became a blur of pain and darkness, of burning red eyes and the ugly green glow. He felt himself being lifted off the ground, his body stretched and long as he was suspended from above. The undead were rough in their work: their nails scored his skin, tore his clothing…the ropes stretched him so his muscles screamed…broad fists punched him.

"Tell me," came a voice, "where is Macey Gardella?"

"I…don't…know…her," Grady said, panting the words, his body vibrating with pain. "I…don't."

"Very well, then," whispered the oily voice, very close to his ear. "Now I shall have to get serious."

Fangs plunged into his skin, and Grady managed to smother a cry. His last coherent thought was a lament that the holy water he'd drunk hadn't had time to permeate his blood.

Then he spiraled into a realm of fiery pain, and then… darkness.

Thirteen

Above the Fold

B Y NOON ON MONDAY, there'd been no further messages from Iscariot, and no other hint of what he had planned.

"There must be a safer place to put the pyramid than here in the pub," said Max, looking disgruntled as he set his crossbow and a quiver of bolts on a table. He also looked as if he hadn't had more than an hour or two of sleep, even after being provided a bed at four o'clock in the morning.

"We have the Rings of Jubai, as well as the stake and rosary that belonged to Giulia Pesaro—in the sacristy at St. Patrick's Church," Macey told him. "We could put it with them."

Max nodded. "That's the place it all happened, then? With Sebastian? Yes, I think we should remove the pyramid to that safer location."

Just then, Chas, who'd taken the last shift overnight, came into the pub. He looked only slightly less worn out than he had when Macey saw him last. She couldn't help but wonder if she, too, looked as bad as her two male counterparts did.

"I've figured it out," Chas said, but he didn't sound pleased. "Your 'tongue of the ruby-eyed skull,'" he added, looking at Temple.

"It's not mine, but lay it on us, brother," she replied. "What is it and how can we get it?"

"That's the problem. I don't know that we can. I hope there's another solution."

"Tell us what you've figured out," Max said.

"I went to sleep last night thinking about a—a conversation Macey and I had. She'd mentioned photographs of Paris, and the catacombs under the city, and it reminded me of the time I was there. In the catacombs. I was helping Narcise escape from her brother Cezar Moldavi, and the way we got out from his underground hideaway was through a lesser-known tunnel through the catacombs."

"That makes some sense—and so one of the skulls in the wall had ruby eyes?" asked Macey. "But surely it wouldn't still be there—and what did it mean by its tongue?" Her spark of hope disintegrated.

Chas shook his head. "It's not that simple. The skull wasn't in the catacombs, anyway. Before Narcise and I managed to escape, I was an unwelcome guest of Cezar's for several days. It was not at all pleasant, being the recipient of his so-called hospitality."

His expression hardened and his eyes became haunted. Macey wasn't certain whether it was due to the memories of being— what? tortured? fed on?—by Cezar, or merely the reminder of Narcise, whom he'd loved and apparently lost.

"I was in one of Cezar's private chambers, and I found I needed to…well, to have something to focus on in order to, uh, block out the long, burning needles and skewers he was sliding into my body in exchange for information he required." He tried for a smile, but it came out weak. Macey subdued a shudder.

"As I said, not a pleasant experience. If it weren't for Narcise…" Chas stopped, shook his head, then seemed to collect himself. "But even during that hazy time, I remember: there was a skull, in his chamber. It had two ruby eyes—looked as if there were gemstones set in the sockets. They were easy to stare at and focus on, because one of them glinted in the candlelight. And there was a dagger blade protruding from between the skull's teeth."

"Like a tongue," Macey said.

"Sounds right," Max agreed. "But now we have to put our hands on it—I don't suppose you have any idea where to find it now?"

Chas shook his head once more. "Not a chance. Moldavi's long gone from that hideaway beneath Paris—it was in 1804 when all this happened, just after Napoleon was crowned emperor—and when I…left, Moldavi had been imprisoned by Narcise and Giordan Cale."

"Moldavi was a vampire? They didn't stake him?" asked Macey.

"He was a Dracule vampire—different from the ones spawned through Judas Iscariot, though there are many similarities—and no, Narcise chose not to kill him. She had her reasons. Even so, who knows what happened to the contents of his hideaway. Surely they're long gone, and his underground lair since demolished."

Macey drew in a deep breath. "I suppose we'll have to keep looking for a different way to destroy the pyramid—if there even is another way."

"The only one who might know where to find it is Wayren," Chas said. "And since she doesn't seem to show up when *I* need her, perhaps our vaunted *summas* could put in a request for some assistance?"

Macey glanced at Max to see his reaction to this churlishness, but he was merely looking toward the door with an odd smile.

"Ah, Wayren," he said. "You've arrived just in time to put the grousing Woodmore here out of his misery."

The rest of them turned to see the slender, pale-visaged woman moving across the room. She seemed to glide, but surely that was only because the movements of her feet were hidden by the medieval-style gown she wore, its hem brushing the floor. Her wheat-blond hair hung long and loose except for two narrow braids clasped in decorative metal tubes that hung alongside her beatific face. A delicate chain belt encircled her waist, and suspended from it was a ring of keys that seemed much too heavy for it. She carried a bulky satchel.

"Chas? You're grousing and miserable? Is this something new?" she asked, though there was a subtle twinkle in her eyes.

They all laughed—even Chas—for somehow, despite the gravity of the situation, Wayren's presence always lifted the mood closer to peacefulness and optimism.

"It's good to see you, Wayren," Macey said with emotion. She realized with a start that her eyes were stinging. For the first time in days, she felt as if everything she had to face might be manageable after all.

Wayren seemed to sense that she was deeply unsettled, for she took the seat next to her and closed slender fingers over Macey's hand. Immediately, a flush of warmth and peace shuttled through her.

"It's very good to see you too, Macey. All of you," she added. "Even those whom I've seen very recently."

Her smile seemed directed at Max, who folded his arms over his middle as if to ward off any further comments or questions. "Your timing is impeccable as usual, Wayren." He went on to explain what Chas had learned about the ruby-eyed skull's tongue, and the problem they faced in locating it.

"Not to mention the fact that we're sitting here on our damn—on our arses, waiting for Iscariot to make his next move. It's da—it's bloody frustrating."

"I see." Wayren looked grave—as grave as Macey had ever seen her, and that made some of her optimism and hope cool. "Well, I may be able to assist in the manner of locating the dagger in question. That is, if you're willing, Chas."

"Willing?" he asked warily. Then his face changed into one of horror and chagrin. "You don't mean you'd take me back there. Can you do that?"

Wayren merely looked at him, her expression inscrutable.

"Of course you can do that," he muttered. "You can't tell us who the dauntless one is, you can't destroy Iscariot—or the entire race of vampires, for that matter—but you can bend the rules of time and ship people back and forth through the decades like they're on a da—on a blasted ferry." He sighed and settled his large hands flat on the counter, ready to push to his feet. "I suppose we'd better be off, then. At least I'll be able to get a good Armagnac in 1803 Paris."

"Legally, anyway," Max agreed. He stood, holding up a hand for pause. "Right then, Woodmore. It's not strictly necessary for you to go. There are other options—including putting the pyramid in the church here, and also taking it back to the Consilium. I'll be happy to see to it myself when this is over."

"That's assuming it *is* over—and we all survive whatever 'it' is," Chas replied. "Of course I'll go. It'll be safe in the Consilium, no doubt, but it'll be even safer if it's obliterated. I'm the only one who knows where the 'curved tongue of the ruby-eyed skull' is—or was—and it's the least I can do, since I'm the one who— Well, it's because of me we're in this fix."

"It's because of Sebastian Vioget that we're in this fix," Macey said firmly. "He should have sent it to the Consilium." Even as she said it, she wondered what precisely the Consilium was. It sounded...fascinating.

"As I said," Wayren began, "if you're willing, Chas, you are uniquely qualified to handle this task. How coincidental that you're here, and you alone have the memory of the location of this particular object—precisely at the time it's needed?" She looked at him, and before Macey's eyes, all of his tension and disgruntlement seemed to wilt.

"How coincidental indeed," he murmured. "I suppose one could call it that. Very well, then. Let us be off." He glanced around the table, a wry smile twisting his lips. "I'll bring back a bottle of the good stuff."

"Better make that two—you owe me a replacement," Temple told him.

Chas gave a short bark of laughter, but he did, for the first time in Macey's memory, seem quietly at peace.

"Be safe," she said, standing to give him a kiss.

He slipped his arm around her waist to pull her up for a good, thorough one—mostly just to bother Max, she figured—and then released her.

"I'll be back"—he glanced at Wayren, who, as usual, was noncommittal—"as soon as possible."

Macey had a strange feeling as she watched him follow the chatelaine from the room...as if she might never see him again. Or if she did, that it would be very different when he returned.

When she turned back, she found Max's eyes fastened on her. "Are you in love with Woodmore?" he asked abruptly.

"No. Not that it's any of your business," she replied coolly. "Just like it wasn't any of your business to talk to Capone."

"Good." He set his jaw, shifted it a little, and seemed to be considering what to say next when the interior door slammed open to reveal Aunt Cookie.

She rushed in, her face filled with horror. "The *Trib* just put out a special edition, and you need to see it!"

Max was closest, and he swiped the paper from her hand. He didn't even need to read it aloud, for the headline was so large it took up the entire top half of the front page and they all could see it: *Man Takes Students Hostage, Threatens to Kill if Demands Are Not Met.*

"Dear God," Macey breathed, standing. All warmth drained from her body. "That's it. It has to be."

Temple picked up the note from Flora and read it. "'For every hour you delay, a very pretty price will be paid. One by one by one.'"

"Let's go," Max said, and slung his crossbow over his shoulder.

Grady slowly became aware of his surroundings, yet had the presence of mind to refrain from opening his eyes immediately.

Carefully, he assessed the condition of his body: throbbing with pain, weak, sticky with blood and sweat, yet nevertheless fully intact. That was good.

The ground—a linoleum floor—was hard beneath him. That was very good; he was no longer suspended from the ceiling. And—a bonus—though his wrists were still bound and screaming with rope burns, they were in front of him.

Blood still oozed from wounds on several areas of his body— not so good. The side of his torso and hip that rested on the floor was in agony from the pressure against the injuries there, but he dared not move and draw attention to himself quite yet.

He vaguely remembered hearing Iscariot calling off his minions: "He must stay alive for now." That, too, was fortunate, for they could easily have finished him off. Or worse.

After this initial assessment, Grady waited still longer to open his eyes, taking a moment to listen to everything going on around him, though he was also working on the ropes around his wrists.

There seemed to be indistinct conversation to his left—likely Iscariot and his comrades—and to the right, he thought he discerned soft sobbing and sniffling. His battered body tensed, and horror flooded him as he was reminded precisely what fate awaited the poor young girls if he didn't find a way to get them out of here. They must be terrified.

There were no other sounds to give him a clue as to how much time had passed or any other information, but as he was about to open his eyes just enough to see through a slit, a clock struck from somewhere in the building. One chime.

One o'clock. Good, then. He'd been out for less than an hour.

When he finally opened his eyes, just enough to see, Grady was delighted to discover that he was huddled up, facing the wall on one side of the dining room. That meant he could easily release his ties without anyone noticing—unless someone was standing guard right next to him. The place was lit only by four electric sconces, two at each end of the rectangular space, which left him between the pools of light and somewhat shadowed. Excellent.

Still working the ropes that imprisoned his wrists, he covertly looked around, even slightly lifting his head—oh God, that hurt worse than the morning after too much whiskey—to ensure no one was nearby watching him.

When he moved his head, tilting it back slowly and carefully by sliding it along the floor and twisting ever so slightly to see "above" him, he saw Iscariot with three of his vampires at that end of the room. They were sitting around, talking. He wondered what they were waiting for, then saw the girl slumped on the floor next to them. The dark wound glistened at her throat.

Oh no.

That realization galvanized him to work more efficiently—as if he needed the motivation—and moments later, with the help of his teeth working at the knots, he'd freed his wrists.

The rush of blood to his hands caused familiar, painful prickles, but Grady was used to them, and he was already subtly drawing his knees up close so he could work on his ankles. Constantly vigilant for a change in the conversation or a hint that someone had noticed his movements, he worked as quickly as possible, his movements partially hidden because he faced the wall.

As he freed himself, he considered his options. He'd already half formed a plan, but now that the time had come, the details needed to be worked out. Along the wall he faced, he could see two of the four tall windows that had been covered by bedsheets. One was only a yard away, slightly to his left. The other was in the opposite direction, closer to the hostages—which, he decided, was a very good thing.

He'd have to move quickly—hopefully his battered body would cooperate—and he'd have only one good chance. It was one o'clock, so the sun would be high and bright—thank God the rain had stopped—and as the building had no trees to block its rays, the light would spill into the room like a gift.

He stealthily removed the heel from his right shoe and collected the four vials into his hand, still listening carefully for any change in conversation. The fact that Iscariot and his cohorts seemed to be merely biding time troubled Grady. What were they waiting for?

Several answers came to mind, and he didn't like any of them. So it was time to put his plan into action and hope for the best.

He curled and uncurled his toes and fingers, flexed his feet, wrists, arms—gritting his teeth against the thudding pain—and hoped he wouldn't faint from blood loss when he finally flew to his feet.

All right. Time to move.

He had his eye on the lower edge of the nearest sheet, the one hanging from the window between him and the vampires. It was three feet away, and reached nearly to the floor.

One.

Two.

Three.

Grady launched himself toward the lower hem of the sheet in a sort of low leapfrog movement. When he caught it, just as someone shouted, he huffed with relief and *pulled.*

The sheet caught—stuck—for just a moment, but Grady was strong and fast, and the fabric tore…and the sheet fell away.

A beautiful, long pool of light spilled into the room, making a wide stripe nearly across the full width. But Grady didn't stop there—he clambered to his feet and stumbled toward the hostages, half falling toward them and the sheet that hung on the wall behind the group.

The vampires had reacted immediately, and though there was only a narrow passage, it wouldn't be difficult for them to skirt the far edge of the block of sun—Grady had miscalculated, for he'd hoped the light would have cut completely across the room—but even as he realized this, he was already diving for the other sheet. However, his legs still weren't fully cooperating, and he missed, slamming into the wall as he tried to catch himself.

One of the older girls seemed to realize what was going on, and she lunged over to tear the sheet from the window with the help from another girl. More sunshine streamed into the room, bathing most of the group of hostages—and Grady himself—in a sea of light as he pulled to his feet, using the wall for support.

"Out the window," he ordered the nearest girl as he fumbled with the vials he'd stuck in his pocket. His hands were shaking and his knees could hardly support him, and he leaned against the wall, panting, bleeding, and trembling.

Just as he managed to get one small tube open, an undead launched himself at one of the hostages who was at the edge of the light. She screamed as the vampire grabbed her shadowed leg and dragged her toward him.

Grady whirled, flinging the contents of the vial—holy water, of course—at the vampire as he heard the sound of the window shattering. *Good, yes, good. Go!*

The vampire he'd doused screamed and staggered away as the awful smell of burned, dead flesh sizzled in the room, and the girl he'd grabbed scrambled back into the sanctuary of sunlight. As Grady reached into his pocket to pull out the thick pencil he had in there, he glanced over to see that the students were clambering out the window as quickly as possible.

Lightheaded, he unscrewed the eraser end of his pencil to reveal a sharpened point of wood instead of lead—his version of a stake—and thumbed off the cork from another of the vials.

Three vampires were dragging as many of the girls as they could safely reach into the shadows. Grady splashed holy water on the one nearest him, and when the woman shrieked with pain, he lunged toward her, makeshift stake raised.

They fell to the ground, the vampiress still screaming in pain, and he managed, somehow, to drive the slender but powerful pike into her sternum.

It was easier than he'd imagined, for the bone seemed to just give way as soon as the wooden point hit it, and he forced his protesting muscles to shove it all the way through, into the heart.

The woman froze, her mouth crumpled in horror and eyes wide with shock, then all at once—she was gone. Grady collapsed onto the floor as what was left of her body exploded into his face.

Coughing and spitting out the disgusting ash, half blinded by the gritty dust, he tried to scramble to his feet. Just as he began to push up, a pair of shiny black shoes appeared on the floor in front of his eyes.

"Nicely done," said Nicholas Iscariot as he stepped, hard, onto Grady's left, stake-bearing hand. He pressed all his weight down onto it, and Grady smothered a groan of pain as his fingers released the weapon. Nevertheless, he forced himself to look up at his captor—yet still avoid the enthralling gaze that burned there. "But your efforts were in vain, my brave sir."

"The girls...are...safe," he managed to say, fumbling beneath his belly where he still held two vials of holy water.

"That might be the case...but you are not. And that, as it happens, has been my intent all along."

Grady blinked, trying to focus, but Iscariot's strong, sharp-nailed hands reached down and grabbed him by the shirt, yanking him off the ground—but not before the vampire ground his foot into his hand one last time. Grady felt a sharp, painful *pop!* at his shoulder before his hand slid free from beneath the weight on it, and another one at his wrist, and he bit back a scream of pain. But he'd managed to unleash one more vial of holy water, and he held it close to his body as he was whooshed off the floor.

The world tilted and spun, and the ugly green glow at Iscariot's chest caught his attention: hypnotic and evil. Grady swung his arm out in a wide arc and poured holy water up and over the vampire lord's face.

Iscariot cried out, but did not release him. Instead, his irises burning more vibrantly than ever, the blue ring around them cold and furious, he bared his fangs and said, "By the devil, you are *dead*."

He whipped around fast and hard and slammed Grady into the wall, hand cupping him beneath the chin. Then he drove his lethal nails into his shoulder, ripping downward. Grady felt fabric and flesh tear, and the eruption of blood bursting from his body.

His vision swam, but he managed to glance over at the hostages. He saw that the sunny area was empty. He closed his eyes and let go.

It was over.

Fourteen

Architectural Blind Spots

B Y THE TIME MAX AND MACEY LEARNED the location of the Beedle school and arrived there, it was after one o'clock.

They pushed their way through the crowd, heading toward the front of the fortress-like building.

"I'm going to do a circuit," Max said, his crossbow over his shoulder. "Meet you here in a few." He peeled off and went in one direction as Macey headed toward the cluster of police officers, an ambulance, and what looked like other officials.

Frustratingly, she was stopped at a blockade by two officious-looking cops and was forced to step back to consider their options. Causing a scene and pushing through wouldn't help anything, and could end up with either her or Max in jail, Venator or not—but how to explain that they were uniquely suited to assist with the situation—which was already delicate? Plus, they didn't know what was going on except what had been reported in the special edition—which was not much beyond the startling headline and background about the school itself.

Then Macey saw Detective Linwood standing in the clump of authorities. She called out to him and moved up to the barricade, waving to catch his attention. She didn't know if Grady's uncle would remember her, but it was worth a try.

He turned at the sound of his name and looked surprised, then hurried over to her. The officers at the barricade allowed her to pass through when their colleague gave them a nod, and she hurried toward Grady's uncle.

Macey felt a horrible premonition as Linwood approached, for he looked frighteningly grave—and she didn't think it was because he'd not yet fully recovered from his own attack by the vampires.

"It's you—isn't it? Macey, that's your name. Right?" He looked a little confused and perhaps a bit hopeful.

"Yes. I'm here—we're here. My—er—partner, he went for a walk around the building, but he'll be back in a minute. We know— We think we can assist with this particular situation. We're familiar with the perpetrator, and know how he works."

Linwood was looking at her as if he didn't know what to believe. "Grady's in there."

Macey's belly dropped sharply, and her insides swirled like a typhoon. Linwood gripped her arm. Surely she hadn't actually *swayed*.

Macey listened to Linwood's explanation, but at the same time, all she could think was that her nightmare had come true. Iscariot had Grady, and she knew—she *knew*—the vampire lord would use him to get to her. The images of Mrs. Gutchinson— her elderly landlady—and her friend Chelle, both of whom had been brutalized by Nicholas Iscariot, swam in her mind. She felt lightheaded and sick.

The very thing she'd never wanted to happen, the event she'd tried to prevent all along—from the time she realized who she was and what she had to do—had come to pass.

As it had done to her own father, thirteen years ago.

She turned away, pressing a hand to her mouth to keep from gagging, struggled to pull herself together, to touch the smooth silver of her *vis bulla*.

No.

Iscariot would *not* win.

He was evil personified. He was the root of malevolence.

He *would not win*.

But if she had to make a choice between Grady and giving up Rekk's Pyramid to the vampires—and she *knew* that was what fate awaited her—what would she do?

How could she choose? How could she live with herself either way?

"Macey."

She realized Linwood and another cop were looking at her.

She struggled to draw in a breath. "There's been no word since Grady—since he went in? No further message? How long has he been in there?"

"More than an hour—he went inside just before noon. He gave me these to hold before he went in." Linwood opened his hand—it was trembling—to show them a silver cross on a chain, and a silver ring. "They wouldn't allow any metal on his person."

It's a setup, she thought. *He wanted Grady in there—because he knows I'd come for him.*

She glanced at Linwood, who, fortunately, had been distracted by something beyond the gate of the school.

"Right. Of course. We have to get in there."

"You can't go in," Linwood said, turning back to them. "They'll kill everyone inside—that's what they said. If anyone—"

He stopped and they all looked toward the building. "That sounded like breaking glass," said the other cop—Barnett was his name. "From the back of the school."

Macey didn't wait for permission, or even for Max to return. For all she knew, he was already there. She just ran, weaving between people, pushing through the gate—just as a stream of girls came tearing around from the back of the building.

Max walked quickly around the perimeter of the school, looking for the best place to climb over the fence without being seen by anyone inside.

He was damned if he was going to wait for someone to tell him what to do, when to go in, and how. He'd heard enough from bystanders as he made his way through them to get a general idea of what was going on. By now, Max had no doubt Iscariot was in the school, and he was going to string him up with a wooden crossbow bolt with great pleasure—or die trying.

His circuit took him past the halfway point of the perimeter, following the tall wrought iron fence, before he found the perfect place to climb over. Though there were no trees on the grounds to provide cover, there was a blind spot on the building on one side—where the main, wide chimney rose from ground to roof, and at the bottom was a discreet entrance—likely for staff and deliveries. In fact, there was a large delivery truck parked right there, which would also offer some cover. He assumed that windowless vehicle was how the vampires had been transported and gained access to the building.

There was a width of about four feet on the wall with no windows, and the nearest opening after that was past the edge of the jutting chimney.

It was all he needed—just that sliver of space where no one from the inside could spot him as he got over the fence.

Max studied the angle for a moment, determined exactly where to stand so he couldn't be seen, then removed the crossbow and quiver from his back, shoving it through a gap in the fence.

With an air of determination and relief—finally, he was doing something—Max crouched and sprang up on his powerful legs. He caught the fence more than halfway up, and pulled himself up, hand over hand, his rubber-toed shoes helping to propel and steady him, until he gripped the tops of two pointed iron spikes. He waited, staying there for a moment, balanced against the fence with his toes against the bars, his arms flexed to hold him as close to the top as possible.

Then…one…two…*three.*

With one mighty movement, he lifted himself as he twisted his torso, feet to one side, and whipped his legs up like a gymnast, using that momentum and every bit of strength in his arms and shoulders to vault himself up and over the spikes, shoes first, in a wide, high arc.

Then, with a little more thrust to make sure he cleared the top, he let go and landed, flatfooted and slightly out of breath, on the other side, and scooped up his bow and bolts. But he couldn't take any longer to pause and congratulate himself on not skewering his arse on the top of the fence—he had to get out of sight.

He bolted toward the building, staying in the blind spot as much as he could. He noticed, as he ran toward the indentation of the chimney, that there were four tall windows at ground level, lined up along the back of the school, that seemed to be covered up.

None of the other windows were fully covered—though most of them had drapery of some sort—and that told Max all he needed to know about where the vampires were gathered. He was now flush against the wall, and just as he began to make his way along it toward the closest of those covered-up windows, the covering was pulled away from the third-farthest one.

This galvanized him into immediate action—someone inside knew what they were doing, and he suspected he knew whom— so he bolted toward another of the shrouded windows.

He could hear shouts and screams from inside, and then another of the coverings fluttered and was torn away. By then, Max was there, and he looked inside that window to see a pack of schoolgirls, right on the other side of the glass, now safely bathed in the sunlight.

"Watch out!" he shouted at the girls, for one of them had come up as if to open the window. She stumbled back, taking some of the others with her, and Max swung his crossbow at the glass.

It shattered with a loud, satisfying noise, and he smashed at it again so the shards rained down and fell through, creating a large opening. He used his quiver to push the glass from the edges of the window, then began to help the girls climb out as quickly as possible.

Max couldn't see much of what was going on inside, but there were sounds of screaming and fighting. He itched to get in there, to find Iscariot, but…the girls. They were the first priority.

"Run," he ordered as most of them stood on the grass, blank-eyed and confused. "Run around to the front."

"There's a man inside—he helped us—but he's in a bad way," said one of the older students, who'd also been helping the younger ones climb out from the inside.

"Get a doctor," he said, lifting out another hostage. When at last he got the final, desperate girl safely onto the grass, Max climbed inside himself.

"Iscariot!" he bellowed, eschewing the safety of the pools of sunshine to step fully into the room and look around.

The first thing he saw was an undead with one of the schoolgirls who hadn't gotten away. Max yanked a stake from his boot and leaped across the room to slam it into the creature's heart, even as the vampire tried in vain to hold the girl like a shield.

Glancing around the room to take in the rest of the situation—at least eight more vampires, plus, ah, there was Iscariot, holding the injured man against the wall, and another girl was slumped on the floor—Max ducked into the puff of undead ash and scooped up the student he'd just saved.

He rushed back to the window, and just as he got there, he heard the sound of a great ruckus behind him.

"Iscariot!" cried a female voice. "Show yourself!"

He nearly dropped the girl when he realized it was Macey. Dear God, his *daughter* was here.

He fairly shoved the schoolgirl through the window; fortunately, one of the police officers was there to catch her. He saw several others coming around the corner at a run. "Stay outside," he ordered to the one who took the hostage. "All of you. We'll need a doctor—but stay outside."

Then he turned back around, gripping his stake, just in time to see Iscariot drop the man he'd been attacking. With a jolt, Max recognized him as he slid to the floor, bloody and unconscious—most likely dead, or near enough to it. But damn—it was definitely Grady.

"Well, look what we have here. *Two* Gardella Venators. A father and daughter team, is it?" Iscariot taunted, looking back and forth between them as he stood safely in a shadowy area. "I didn't expect to have both of you as my guests, but you'll hear no complaints from me."

Max counted ten undead that gathered near the vampire lord, and realized he'd left his crossbow and quiver on the ground outside the window. He was still standing in the pool of sunlight, and would be protected if he wanted to step back and get them… but he dared not turn his back now. Not with Macey there.

He looked over at her, and saw that her dark hair glinted with undead ash—so she'd taken care of one already. Well done.

Iscariot gestured to the pile of flesh, blood, and bone that was Grady. "Since my previous guest is no longer useful to me, I'll just have to keep one of you as collateral until the pyramid is delivered. Now which one of you would like to have the honor of staying, and which of you would like to retrieve the pyramid?"

"I'll have the honor of your heart on my stake," Macey said, stepping further into the room. She held her weapon like a professional, Max noted with relief.

Then he saw a movement behind her. His heart surged into his throat as he tried to shout a warning, but before he even got the word out, she'd whirled with a neat up-and-over-the-shoulder blow to the undead who'd had the temerity to creep up behind her. The vampire poofed into dust and Macey walked even closer to Iscariot and his group.

"I'm terribly sorry your little plan didn't work out the way you wanted, Nicky," she said, sashaying a little as she moved toward them, as if she wanted his eyes on her in *that* way.

Max couldn't help but watch with a combination of pride, terror, and enjoyment. It was rather entertaining, really, and it gave him the opportunity to observe and plan for the next assault. He wasn't foolish enough to think for one moment they had the undead trapped and at their mercy. It was, after all, ten— no, nine—versus two; though he figured he counted as at least three fighters himself. And one of the nine was Iscariot, who was a tricky and powerful devil. Literally.

Max couldn't wait to drive a stake into his heart, and watch the creature's face freeze in shock.

"Nice design on your face, there, Nicky," Max drawled. "Is that cross a stamp of where your loyalty now lies? How does your *damned* father feel about that?"

Iscariot's eyes blazed wildly as he turned to Max, and he felt the sudden force of his evil wash over him like an ugly chill. "That decides it. I'll keep *her*. And let you *watch*, Max Denton. Unfortunately, you missed the show the last time I had one of your women for dinner."

"Thank you for the reminder, Nicky—oh, I like that, Macey. Nicky. It's catchy and juvenile, and it suits him." He nodded at his daughter while seeming to be at ease, but his attention was constantly skimming the group of undead and the rest of the room. There would be surprises, he knew. It was just a matter of when. It was clear this whole thing had been planned.

"As I was saying, Iscariot"—his voice became cold as death—"thank you for the reminder of what you did to my wife. Not that I've ever forgotten."

"It took you long enough to come after me, Denton. What has it been…thirteen years? Did it take you that long to build up your courage?"

Max smiled. "Oh, I've been busy during those thirteen years—while you were hiding from me, cowering in caves and secluded cities, afraid to show your face for fear I'd find you. In the meantime, I've destroyed anything and everything you might return to. There is no escape for you now. And I've spent some time learning about all the ways an undead can die. There are more than you might realize."

"Oh, but you've forgotten. We're already dead. Which is more than I can say for you—at least at the moment. And now that you mention it, I've been thinking about keeping your daughter with me…forever. Oh, don't worry, Denton; I'd take excellent care of her…for centuries, at least. She is quite lovely, and— *Now!*"

From nowhere came a heavy black wad of netting—launched directly at him, and ballasted with heavy weights that wrapped around him. Max was immediately trapped in the network of cord, and no sooner had the web been fired than the undead were rushing toward him.

He tried to fling the net away, but it was too heavy, and there were too many openings that caught him up. As he dropped to the floor, he glanced over to see that Macey was being attacked by a trio of vampires while Iscariot watched. He saw her plunge a stake, then the poof of resulting ash—but then another undead lunged into the fray and Macey disappeared beneath a wild mass of limbs and torsos.

Incensed, Max rolled away, heading into a block of sunlight while he fished out the knife he carried in a front pocket. The blade was sharp, and it cut easily through the black rope, but a vampire caught the edge of the net before the last of it went into the sun. Max's half-cocooned body was dragged out of the yellow light as he finished slicing down the front of the net.

As they pulled him upright, Max struck out with the blade, catching them by surprise that he was nearly free. He plunged it into the neck of his nearest assailant, then ripped the blade across his throat. Blood spurted everywhere, startling and distracting the others attacking him. Still partly tangled in the net, he held on to the slippery knife and completed the hack job, bringing the blade back around to finish severing the vampire's head. As he cut through the last vertebra, the undead exploded into dust.

But Max was just getting started.

He flung off the remnants of the net and stabbed out with his stake at another assailant, then tripped a third undead, shoving him so he tumbled into the square of sunlight. The second vampire dodged the blow from Max's stake at the last minute, so it slammed harmlessly into his torso. He grabbed Max, catching him off balance after the missed blow, and threw him into the wall.

Max's head hit hard, and he crashed to the floor as the vampire came after him. But he angled his feet back toward his body and met the undead with a powerful blow, thrusting him up and away with all the strength in his legs. The creature flew through the air and landed in a pool of sunshine, screaming with agony.

Max shook his head and clambered to his feet, out of breath, exhilarated, and filled with fury.

And then he stopped.

Iscariot had Macey. She stood there, panting, fiery-eyed with fury, held in place by a vampire on each side. Her hands were empty of weapons.

Then, from the corner of his eye, Max saw movement at the window. One of the damned policemen—no, two of them!—*were climbing inside.*

Bloody fools. And bugger it—he didn't have time to deal with them now.

"Nice show, Denton," crooned Iscariot, looking at Macey with burning eyes. "But now it's time to get down to business."

"The only business I have with you is dusting your evil soul," Max replied.

"The feeling is quite mutual." The vampire lord turned and flickered a glance at Macey. "Yet death is too simple, isn't it? Too quick—even if I tried to prolong it, which I would certainly do for you, Max Denton. But there are things worse than death. For *you,* anyway." He smiled, his fangs long and sharp. "Are there not?"

Iscariot looked again at Macey, but this time it was more than a glance. This time, he was calling to her with his gaze—coaxing her, lulling her. Max could almost feel the vibration of his thrall as the evil lord lured her to look at him.

He saw the way she stiffened, lifted her face, and seemed to respond. Her body softened from its ready stance, and her knees appeared to give way a little.

"Macey," Max snapped, suddenly nervous, trying to jolt her out of the murk.

She shivered, as if struggling to listen to him, to hear him, and Iscariot made a sharp gesture. The vampire goons holding her arms released them, and Macey actually took a step closer to the evil lord. Then she stopped, fairly vibrating in her place, seeming to fight the urge to move again. Max saw her chest shudder as if she were attempting to draw in a deep breath—or fighting to keep her own breath and heartbeat.

"A life worse than death," Iscariot murmured. "What would be the worst thing that could happen to you, Max Denton? Sending you to your grave—oh, that's far too easy. But destroying someone you love…now there's an idea." He turned from Macey, breaking the thrall, his eyes wild and excited as he turned them onto Max—who managed to avert his own just in time. "Watching you live through yet another loss would be beyond entertaining."

"Just try it, Nicky," Max sneered. His heart was pounding normally again, now that Macey seemed to be free for the moment. Still, she wasn't moving, just stood there. He tried to catch her eye, tried to let her know he was here, to give her strength, to remind her how strong she was—but she was watching Iscariot. An unpleasant tremor rippled through Max and he gripped his stake tighter.

The vampire lord was too smart to stand in a position in which Max could hit him with his stake; no, the creature stood at such an angle that there was no possibility. Not yet, anyway.

"But…wait. I've an even better idea," Iscariot said. "She's much too lovely to be wasted on a mere coffin. And I do get lonely sometimes." He smiled at Macey. "Perhaps you'd like to be my consort."

"I don't think so," she replied, and Max's heart started up again.

"But it would be wonderful. I've always had a soft spot for you, lovely Macey. Ever since the first time I tasted you." Iscariot stilled, his attention focused on her. "I could even learn to forgive you for marking me…because, after all, I've done the same to you." His hand moved sharply, and she looked down, as if her gaze was drawn by a string.

Max saw it too: a stripe of red down the front of her blouse, seeming to connect the buttons that held it together. And another one, around the front of her breast.

"You want the pyramid," Max said in an attempt to distract the vampire lord from his current tack.

"Oh, yes, and I'll have it…have no fear. But I think I'll also have this lovely woman as well. And…I think…she's going to come to me quite willingly…aren't you, Macey, my darling?"

"Yes…yes, I think I shall," she said. And stepped toward him.

Fifteen

Our Summas Miscalculates a Second Time

MACEY DARED NOT LOOK at her father. She kept her eyes directed at Iscariot, but slightly averted—safely focused on the inside edges of his two dark brows, right where they nearly met at the bridge of his nose.

Strangely enough, the fear that had simmered below the surface whenever she thought of Iscariot had evaporated the moment she stepped into this room. It was as if she were somehow charged with purpose, as if she'd somehow realized now was the time to make her stand—and that, powerful as he was, he would lose to her.

Now, as she moved closer to the vampire lord, pretending to be drawn by him, she could smell the excitement wafting off Iscariot. It was tinged with death and darkness, and she wanted nothing more than to sneer at him, and tell him he stank.

But not yet.

Max was looking a little disheveled—though she'd seen the way he hacked off the undead's head with nothing more than a dagger, and had annihilated three vampires with spectacular skill and speed. Macey knew Iscariot wasn't finished with him yet— with either of them.

She'd already managed to have Iscariot make the two brute vampires release her by pretending to consider his offer, and acting as if she were about to collapse. Or, rather, to allow Iscariot to think he was enthralling her enough that she was actually considering it.

She'd also refused to look over at the body lying on the floor near the windows. It had to be Grady, and from what she could tell…it was not good. But she also noticed Linwood and another police officer climbing in through the window. She hoped with every fiber of her being that they would see to Grady, get him out safely, instead of attempting to join the fight against the undead.

Though she no longer had a stake in hand, beneath her shirt, Macey was still well armed. She wore the large silver cross, and had a stake secreted along the side seam of her shirt, one beneath each arm. She just needed the opportunity to use them.

"Macey," Max said. His voice was tight, and she knew he was becoming terrified as she seemed to succumb to Iscariot's will.

She turned slowly toward him, as if pulled by his voice, but kept her expression blank and her eyes unfocused. She couldn't let on, even to him, that she was pretending—mostly pretending, anyway. Iscariot's thrall was wickedly strong, and she had felt herself lulled more than once.

But when she concentrated on the heavy weight of the silver cross, and the tiny spark of energy from the *vis bulla*, she felt their protection wrap around her like a cocoon…and she was able to focus on a pinpoint of clarity in the very center of her mind. She held it there, like a small flame, even when she swayed and trembled and felt as if her knees were to give away.

"Did you hear that, Denton?" Iscariot crowed. "She is coming to me. What a long, lustful life we'll have together. And, my pet, with Rekk's Pyramid, we'll be rulers of more than the underworld." He held out a skeletal hand to her. She took it, forcing herself not to cringe at the feel of his cool, dry flesh.

Max moved sharply, and something whipped through the air. But Iscariot was fast, and he yanked Macey into his arms in a lovers' embrace—and a shield.

She cried out as the stake meant for the vampire's heart plunged into her shoulder, lodging there from behind, then heard

Max's own cry of rage and horror, followed by the mad shuffle of fighting.

"Now see what you've done, Denton. Impaled your own daughter! It's no wonder she chooses me…over you. She chooses immortality over a life doomed to fail…as yours is."

Macey's head swam against the pain—her father was supremely strong, and with impeccable aim—and she realized with a nauseating start that the stake had gone all the way through the soft part of her shoulder…and a shallow wooden point emerged from the front. Now her blouse was blossoming red there as well.

She didn't have much time; her head was light and tremors had begun to take over from deep inside. She sagged against Iscariot, doing her best not to gag at the feel of his stringy muscles—and other parts she preferred not to think of—pressing against her.

"*Macey*," Max called out, desperation in his voice.

She couldn't see him, but the ugly noises coming from behind indicated he was battling for his life—possibly even unarmed at this point. She wished she could somehow give him a look—a sign, hope—to let him know she was all right.

But she wasn't all right, she realized murkily. The blood streamed from both wounds, and Iscariot was holding her upright more than she was standing on her own. Her vision swam, her muscles suddenly protested, and when Iscariot gave a soft chuckle in her ear, she hardly shuddered.

"I don't see any reason to waste more time," the vampire murmured. "Let me welcome you to your new life, Macey Denton."

And he slid his fangs into the side of her neck.

Sixteen
Fear and Regret

MAX FOUGHT LIKE A BERSERKER, trying to free himself from the four undead who now held him, all the while watching in horror as Iscariot gathered his daughter up like a lover—then plunged his fangs into her.

Macey. Dear God, Macey…

How could he have miscalculated?

How could he have thought she'd be strong enough to face Iscariot?

How could he have made such a mistake?

He shouldn't have left her all these years. He should have *been* here when she took the *vis*, when she learned who she was. *He* should have been the one to face Iscariot…not his daughter.

Not his *daughter*.

And now it was too late. Now, he'd fairly sent her to her death—no, not to her death. To her *un*death. Unless he could save her before Iscariot drained her dry and forced his evil, undead blood upon her.

Max had one stake left, only one, and he couldn't quite reach it in his other boot.

His vision had gone red with fury, and he punched and kicked like a wild man. But the four undead were vicious and strong, and they tore at him with long nails—though none had gotten close enough to bite.

He whipped his aching head back into the face of an undead behind him, then pretended to collapse in the grips of the remaining ones, becoming a dead weight in their hands. In that brief, quiet heartbeat of a moment, as one grabbed his head to hold him still for a bite, he drew on every bit of strength and cunning he possessed, every bit of divine assistance that came from the *vis bulla*, and asked for help.

And when it came, it was like a white light, shooting through him, exploding into each of his limbs. All at once, he had the strength to vault upright, to whip himself—and his clinging attackers—in the direction of the sunshine block, forcing them to follow with him, to stumble and fall into the sanctuary of light.

They screamed, releasing him just before—or, in the case of one, just after—the light hit them. That was all he needed; the stake was already in his hand, and Max spun like a dervish, striking out while they still roiled with agony.

Plunge…stab…*shove.*

Poof, poof, *poof.*

Max spun around, dashing the hair and sweat from his eyes, to see Iscariot and Macey, still locked in that horrifying embrace. She was moving, struggling against him, her arms trapped between herself and the vampire—blood streaming from the wound at the back of her shoulder, the wound Max himself had delivered.

He shoved back the guilt and self-loathing—there'd be time for that later—and bolted toward them.

He was almost there when the last vampire, a large, solid one who seemed to come from nowhere, grabbed him. Max swore, twisting and fighting; he'd get there, *by God,* he'd get there—there where he could strike, there where he could plunge the stake into Iscariot's heart. He inched and fought to get closer, closer… fighting all the while.

He bucked and struggled, uncaring that he was held, uncaring that fangs were tearing into his own shoulder. His mind was focused on one thing: the target of Iscariot's back. His vampire attacker had him from behind, strong hands grabbing him by the hair and gripped the arm that held the stake.

Max didn't even try to use his weapon on him. He focused, twisted, turned, until finally, at last he had the target in sight.

Iscariot's back—the stake would go right through to his heart.

In smooth, rapid movements, Max flipped up the stake from his imprisoned limb and caught it with his free one, then jammed it point first backward into the face of the undead behind him to catch the bastard off guard. The vampire screamed, loosened his hold—but not altogether—and Max readied the stake for his last chance.

Just as he saw Macey lift her head from where it sagged to the side—she seemed to be saying something to Iscariot, and the creature drew back his head to respond—Max whipped the pike forward, flinging it in a straight, smooth shot toward the back side of Nicholas Iscariot's heart.

Then he shoved his attacker into a square of sunlight.

Seventeen

Like Father, Like Daughter

DESPITE THE PAIN AND MURKINESS from her wound, Macey had managed to slip a stake from beneath her blouse into one hand.

Iscariot had been so determined to taunt her father, and to sink his fangs into her, that her contortions had been unnoticed—or assumed to be struggles.

Her vision wavered, and she felt the blood draining from her body—though the stake that had impaled her shoulder held off a full stream of it—but she held on to that slender wooden talisman, waiting for the right moment. The right position. The strength to use it.

She heard Max's cry of horror when Iscariot bit into her, and the sounds of his struggle—flesh against flesh. But moments later, the scent of undead ash was strong in the air and she felt a leap of pride and relief.

The stake was in her hand, in position—all she had to do was use it.

"Nicholas, darling," she said in a weak voice—it wasn't difficult to feign a weak voice—"I have a question for you, about all of this."

He withdrew his fangs and pulled back to look down at her, as if he really meant to answer her question. Blood dripped from the corners of his mouth, and his eyes were slitted with lust. He smiled down at her, and that was all she needed.

Macey shifted and gave a little upward thrust…and *plunge*.

In went the point…and right then, Iscariot jolted sharply against her, into her stake—as if he'd been shoved from behind at the very same moment.

And that was when Macey saw her father, just beyond Iscariot's shoulder…and the second spike that had gone into him from the back.

She shoved Iscariot away, stumbling backward as the root of malevolence, the condemned evil, the lord of vampires, froze with shock at being skewered—not once, but twice, simultaneously, by the father-daughter Venator team.

"Goodbye, Nicky," she said, panting, shaking, bleeding…

And then her knees gave out.

Someone caught her—Max, of course—and the next thing she knew, he was holding her tightly, hugging her.

Her father—whom she hadn't touched or embraced for thirteen years—was holding her, and his face was wet with tears— or maybe it was sweat—and the big, powerful man was trembling. Possibly even crying.

Was she dreaming? Was she dead?

"Macey, God, I'm so sorry," he said into the top of her head. "We need a damned doctor!" he shouted, heedless of the proximity of her ear.

"A doctor?" Macey mumbled. "I don't need a doct— *Ugh!*" Her eyes bolted wide and she shrieked as something splashed over her wounds—salted holy water.

And then she fainted.

After dousing her liberally with salted holy water, Max reluctantly relinquished Macey to the surprisingly efficient Dr. Fintucket and his staff.

In so doing, he was also required to brush off the insistence that he be taken off in an ambulance and treated as well.

Bugger that.

If they'd been back in Rome, Macey—and possibly Max himself—would have gone to the Consilium to be treated by the Venator medic—a descendant of the excellent Ylito, who'd saved Victoria Gardella's life, among many others.

As it was, Max would have to rely on so-called modern medicine…at least initially. The bloody stake he'd embedded in his daughter would have to be removed, she'd be stitched up, and Max would make certain to replenish and use his supply of salted holy water and the salve the Venators favored to help their wounds heal even more quickly than usual.

She'd live, thank God.

Thank God.

And, almost as importantly, Nicholas Iscariot was dead. Max could hardly believe it.

"Max!"

He turned to see Savina rushing toward him. She threw herself into his arms, heedless of the blood and sweat plastered all over his skin. "Oh, God, *thank God,* Max! You're safe!"

He squeezed her tightly, inhaling the scent of her hair—clean and fresh, and untainted with the blood and violence in which he'd been immersed for more than an hour.

She was safe too. He drew in a shaky breath.

"And Grady," Savina began—not the best way for their reunion to start, he thought, and eased up on his grip of her— "he's going to make it. They're taking him to the hospital—he's alive."

"That's excellent news," he replied, aware of how stiff his lips felt when he formed the words, how inside him there was a strange, curdling feeling. How he suddenly wondered why he was holding Savina so closely when only last night she'd been so cozy on the sofa with his friend.

But he couldn't let go. For until this moment, he hadn't admitted how terrified he'd been that Iscariot would have targeted her in order to get to him. "And my daughter," he said coolly, "*she's* going to be fine as well. In case you were wondering."

Savina pulled away and looked up at him, brushing a lock of hair from her eyes. "I know, thank God—I heard about it. But what about you? I think you should go to the hospital—"

"Don't be ridiculous." Now he did step back. "I'm barely touched. I have work to do—other work. There are far too many people who saw too much today."

"Right. Of course." She was looking at him curiously. "I didn't realize you had the golden disk. Or *a* golden disk."

"I have something similar." Though he was crumbling with uncertainty inside, he couldn't keep from looking at her, devouring the sight of her. As if it might be the last time he did.

Unlike most everyone else in the area, Savina was not disheveled. In fact, she looked as if she'd just stepped out of a Paris café—except for the streak of blood he'd deposited on her cream-colored blouse. Unless it was from Grady, whom she'd probably embraced with just as much enthusiasm as she'd done Max.

That thought didn't sit well with him at all.

"You're not going to the hospital with Macey?" she asked, frowning.

He drew himself up. "I've got work to do—things to take care of."

She shook her head, her attention falling away, her beautiful lips tightening with disgust. "There's always work to do, Max. But maybe it's time you took a moment to be a father, instead of a Venator. For once in thirteen years."

Max stilled, glancing over to where the ambulance had been a moment ago. He thought about what people had seen, how they'd be telling stories and tales—and what that would do, heightening the fear and paranoia in a city that was already permeated with violent gangsters. Of the dreams the schoolgirls would surely have, the nightmares and terrors.

It was his duty: not only to protect the mortals from the violence of undead, but also from the knowledge and fear of them.

"It won't take long. Macey will understand."

Savina sighed. She looked utterly dejected. So sad, so disappointed. His already worn-out heart thudded like a death knell. "Right, then, Max. You do what you think is best."

He wanted to say something else, but the words simply wouldn't come. They looked at each other for a moment, then Savina reached up to touch his grimy, unshaven face. It felt like a farewell, especially when she said, "I hope you'll find peace, now that Iscariot is gone."

She gave him a small smile, then turned to go, back to— wherever.

"Wait. Savina." He reached for her, and to his great relief, she paused, turning to look at him with big eyes, filled with some emotion he couldn't quite define. Max released her and fumbled for something to say…something that would keep her there for a little longer. "How did you know Iscariot was dead?"

"One of the policemen told me—Grady's uncle. He saw it happen. He…knows. He knew before. The uncle, I mean."

Max tensed a little. "Right."

She swept her gaze over him, her eyes lingering. "You could use a shower. Whether you go to the hospital or try and visit those schoolgirls and whoever else you feel you need to, you can't go looking like you just left a bar fight."

"Right. I— All my things are at Grady's."

"And…?" She tilted her head, looking at him like an inquisitive bird…but with challenge in her eyes.

But what was she challenging him about? He was so bloody weary and confused—and he should be exhilarated, now that Iscariot was gone and Felicia's death was avenged. Now that the root of malevolence was gone, and the last of Judas Iscariot's children had been destroyed. Now perhaps he could rest…a little.

Savina folded her arms across her middle. "Max…honestly. You don't really think there was something going on with me and Grady when you came in last night, do you?" Her eyes were steely, dark as olives, glinting like onyx. Her lips were flat as a signature line.

Max didn't respond immediately, because a welling of hope caused his voice not to work. She was tapping her foot—figuratively, not literally—glaring up at him.

"Grady is young enough to be my *son*!"

"If you'd had him when you were *eight*," he said, finding his voice at last.

She paused, as if to calculate. Then, "Right, whatever. But—God, Max, how dense *are* you?"

His cheeks warmed and he glanced over at a trio of police officers who were looking at them curiously. Christ. Now he had an audience. "I…um…well, hell, Savina. It had been a—well, a difficult day. And it was cold and miserable and rainy, and all I wanted was—well, then I saw you two, all cozy—"

"Grady had just finished telling me how obvious it was you loved me." Were her eyes glittering now? Could it be *tears*?

"I *do*. Savina, I *do*." He snatched up her hand and clasped it very tightly, pulling her close to him again. "You know I love you. I've told you."

"So why are you being an arse?"

"Good God, I don't *know*. I'm not *trying* to be an arse."

That made her laugh. Her eyes crinkled prettily at the corners, and her smile was joyous, and Max's knees just about gave away at the beauty of it…and the hope that maybe at least one of the women in his life might forgive him for being an arse.

"Come back to Grady's with me and get cleaned up. And then…you can decide what to do."

He knew what he wanted to do—hell, what any red-blooded man would want to do, having emerged victorious from battle after having annihilated his archenemy along with half a dozen others, and with a gorgeous woman laughing up at him with delight and love.

But he had a feeling that was going to have to wait.

✝

Going back in time, Chas discovered, was less taxing on the body than going forward. But it sure was hell on the mind and heart.

Though it had been more than ten years in his physical lifespan since he'd been in Paris, it was more than a century earlier as far as the calendar was concerned.

There were no automobiles; he had to remember to watch so he didn't step in horseshit. No electric lights. Definitely no aeroplanes. The female fashions were…well, they were surprisingly similar to the twenties styles in the sense that the skirts were straight, light, and loose, and unencumbered by hoops, crinolines, or much in the way of corsets. Though, of course, in Napoleon's Paris the hems brushed the tops of the shoes instead of the tops of the knees, and few women would be caught dead with bobbed hair.

Not that it mattered. Chas was here, for one thing, and then he was getting the hell out—out of Paris, and out of this century.

Wayren had brought him back to Marais, where Cezar Moldavi had shrouded himself in a large mansion. The vampire lived beneath it in a warren of rooms and tunnels—a collection of apartments not unlike those attached to The Silver Chalice in Chicago. It was a necessity for a vampire to be shielded from the sunlight.

"What day is it?" he asked Wayren as the fiacre cab (surprising that the blond chatelaine would even use public transportation) pulled up in front of Moldavi's house. The building appeared closed up and empty, but that wasn't unusual for an undead's residence. They never used the main floors. "What I want to know is…"

"What will you find inside? This is moments—and I do mean moments after they've left… Do you see that carriage there?" Wayren nodded at a retreating black prison carriage with shaded windows. There was not only a driver with a man sitting next to him, but also a sturdy footman riding on the back. "That carriage is the one taking Cezar Moldavi off to his new accommodations, a secure location in the Pyrenees arranged by Narcise. The interior of the house, and its apartments, has been emptied of people."

The tightness in his chest released, and Chas nodded. He wouldn't see Narcise—or Giordan Cale.

Memories would accost him, but nothing in the flesh.

"Are you coming with me?" he asked.

"Not unless you require my assistance."

"No." He'd rather face those memories alone. "I won't be long."

No, he shouldn't be long. For though the time he'd spent under Cezar Moldavi's "care" and "hospitality" had been filled with pain and anguish, it was nevertheless indelibly imprinted on his mind—down to the most minute of details. Once he obtained entrance to the house, he knew precisely where to go to find the stairs to the subterranean level, and then to breach Cezar's private apartments.

Also known as his torture chamber.

The moment Chas stepped through the entrance to the chamber, he was assaulted by a wave of memories. Not only of the agony that had been foisted upon him by Moldavi, but also of the first time he'd met Narcise—a practiced warrior, with her sword at his throat—and of the times following. The times they'd spent here in Paris, hiding from her brother until Chas was well enough to arrange for their escape.

Those had been among the most beautiful—and difficult— times of his life.

Chas's insides were in turmoil, but to his surprise, it wasn't as difficult as he'd anticipated. The room where he'd been tortured looked hardly any different than he remembered it, and he immediately found the ruby-eyed skull and its so-called tongue.

The dagger that had been positioned inside the skull so that its blade protruded from between two rows of teeth was still, blessedly, there. Chas picked up the skull and saw that the blade had been permanently affixed in place, and so he decided to take the entire thing.

They'd figure out how to use or remove the blade so it could be used to—

"Chas?"

He nearly dropped the skull at the sound of Narcise's voice. *No.* It took him far too long to settle his thudding heart before he turned to see her standing there.

Damn. It wasn't a figment of his imagination. She was truly there, as beautiful and remote as always.

And…*damn.* Wayren had lied to him? Wasn't that against the rules?

"Narcise."

"I thought… I was told you went to America."

"I did." Oh, he sure as hell did. If she only knew how far he'd traveled to and from this damned location. But in her mind, he'd been gone from Paris for only a few weeks since their final escape from Moldavi.

"I was sorry you didn't say goodbye." *But I understand.* Those words were unspoken, but their meaning shivered in the tone of her voice.

"I didn't think— What are you doing here? I thought you were gone. Taking Cezar off to…Spain?"

He couldn't pull his eyes away. She was still as beautiful as ever, with her waterfall of blue-black hair, and the truest, most stunning blue eyes he'd ever seen. Her features were perfect, her figure incredible…and yet—there was something different.

Not about her. But about him. Something different about him.

"I wanted to check on one more thing." She didn't seem able to take her gaze from him either. "I have no intention of ever coming back here."

"I had to come back as well…for something. I hope you don't mind if I take this." He gestured with the skull.

She laughed, but it was tinged with bitterness. "Something of Cezar's? Take your pick. I want nothing to do with any of my brother's belongings."

"Thank you. It's…well, it will come in useful."

"Chas." There was grief and apology in her eyes and in her voice—though why she should apologize for never having stopped loving Giordan Cale, he didn't know.

Love was what it was, he realized suddenly.

She seemed to be struggling for something to say, and he held up a hand to stop her. "Narcise, you know I'll always love you, and I'll never forget our time here in Paris, but…that's done. You'll be happy now—and I've— I'm…all right."

He realized as he spoke those words—words that, only days ago he would have believed were a lie—that they weren't, in fact, dishonest at all.

He was standing there, staring at the most beautiful, bravest, and strongest woman he'd ever known—and an undead—a woman he'd fallen for like he'd never fallen for before or since… and he no longer hurt. He no longer *needed*.

Somehow, sometime over the last ten years—or maybe it *was* a century—he'd let it go. He had moved on, even though he'd clung to his own self-loathing in the meanwhile.

"If it weren't for you, I…" she said, her voice rough and broken. She looked around the chamber, sweeping it with her hand. He knew what she meant to say. *If it weren't for you, I'd still be here.*

He shook his head, suddenly realizing the truth. "No. That's not true. Cale would have come for you."

Her eyes filled with tears, and everything between them suddenly felt right and whole. No longer strained, no longer tinged with pain and regret. No longer awkward and tense.

"Thank you, Chas. Thank you for…that…and for everything." She came into his arms, and he tensed a little, preparing himself, as he pulled her close.

But that old desperate desire to *keep* her, to hold her, was gone. That old rush of possession had dissipated.

Now, he held her and was able to press his face into her hair and drop a kiss onto the top of her head…without wanting more.

He was actually *smiling* when he released her. It was as if a massive load had been removed from his heart and mind.

It was as if he had at last been liberated.

Eighteen
A Waste of Good Brandy

GRADY OPENED HIS EYES to find several people standing over him. None of them were the tall blond woman who wore the clothing of a medieval chatelaine, though he was certain he'd seen her again recently…or perhaps he'd only dreamed her while weaving in and out of painful consciousness.

Rest and heal, she'd said, touching his forehead with a smooth, comforting hand. Warmth and white light had rushed through him.

The people gathered around Grady now weren't angels, nor, thankfully, were they demons. Apparently he was still alive.

But damn, he hurt. Everywhere.

"Nice of you to join us," said Linwood, who owned the face closest to him. "We've been waiting a while."

Grady managed a smile to offset the gruffness in his uncle's voice. "Fashionably late…to the party," he managed to say.

Then he looked around at the others who circled his hospital bed, recognizing them as Linwood's colleagues and peers, all four of them dressed in their police uniforms. Beyond the circle of visitors, he could see other beds in the ward. But none of the ones nearby were in use, so Grady had the entire end section to himself.

"Wanted to make sure you'd come out of everything all right," said Officer Barnett. "You're quite a hero."

"Just trying to get the story," Grady replied, and everyone laughed. He tried to join them, but bloody damned hell, it *hurt*. "Did everyone… Are they all safe?"

"All of the schoolgirls are safe, save one who…well, they're not sure she'll make it. But they're doing what they can for her. Dr. Fintucket is the best at—at treating these sorts of injuries."

Grady sobered. *Damn.*

"It would have been a lot worse if you hadn't gone in there," said Barnett. "How you got them out the window like that—"

Linwood interrupted smoothly before anyone started asking uncomfortable questions. "And all the others—the ones who broke in to help you—they're safe too."

Grady nodded, though the action made his head thud harder. "And the—er—perpetrators?"

"Dead. All of them."

All of them? Even Iscariot? Could that really be true?

"That *was* very strange," Barnett said. "I came in right behind Linwood, and one minute they were there, and the next—"

"Hello, Grady."

Everyone turned to the new arrival—a handsome, well-groomed man with piercing, dark eyes and black hair that was beginning to gray at the temples. He stood at the end of the bed, tall and imposing in a smart pinstriped suit and black trench coat with a fedora in his hand. He looked at the others standing around, then meaningfully at Grady.

"This is Max Denton," Grady said, and went on to briefly introduce his visitors.

"Pleasure to meet you. I need to have a word with Grady here, but after, shall we meet for a pint—oh, blast, I forgot that's illegal here. Bloody hell. How about I buy you each a cup of coffee, then? Sounds like you have some stories to tell, and I'd like to hear them." He smiled pleasantly at the others, and no one denied they had "stories to tell."

Arrangements were made for the cops to meet Max shortly after, and they all took the hint and peeled away.

When Linwood lingered, eyeing Max suspiciously, Grady said, "This is the bloke who sent me the note to meet him at the Gold Coast, Linny. We've got business."

His uncle still didn't seem to want to leave. But after Max met his eyes with a calm, steady look, he acquiesced. "I'll look forward to hearing more about your 'business' over a cup of coffee."

Once they were alone, Max took the seat next to Grady and withdrew several items from his pockets. "Salted holy water," he told him. "Use it liberally—till it makes you want to scream. Then pour on more. Then you know it's working. And this is a jar of unguent that will help you heal more quickly. It smells nice, but it's very sticky. Do you still have the silver ring? That will help as well."

Grady showed him the ring he'd replaced on his finger, as well as the cross necklace Linwood had held for him when he went inside the school. "The doctor put salted holy water on me already. It hurt like a live skinning, but I think the bites and scratches have already begun to heal."

"Did he now?" Max paused from opening the small pot of salve. "And how did the doctor know to do that?"

"I told him. Right, Max, about yesterday, with Savina—"

"Don't." He held up a hand. "It was nothing. I was…well, I—Well, forget about it. I'm only here to bring you this salve—and to let you know, if you didn't, that Iscariot is dead. Double-staked. Poofed into a cloud of dust."

"That's bloody good news. And though it might not matter any longer now that Iscariot's gone, I have this for you." With effort—because damn, he was sore, and everything seemed crunchy and painful whenever he moved, not to mention that his head still felt light—Grady reached for the small box on the bedside table where they'd put his personal belongings.

He was grateful that, though he fumbled with slow fingers and it took him forever to get the box onto his lap, Max showed no impatience, nor seemed inclined to offer assistance in order to move things along. Inside the box were several articles of his own—wallet, keys to his house and automobile—but also other items.

The first thing he withdrew was a square emerald—the item Iscariot was wearing that had emitted a nauseatingly green glow.

Max's eyes widened with shock. "Rasputin's amulet. How the devil did you get *that*?"

Grady couldn't hold back a satisfied grin, though even that action, in the wake of hustling the box onto his lap, made him want to puke. "Snitched it right off his shirt just as he decided I'd be a good snack. It's the simple magician trick of misdirection and distraction—you remember from talking to Harry."

"Right. Well, I was more interested in picking handcuff locks than pockets," Max replied with a wry smile as he took the amulet.

"I'd had holy water to drink before I went inside," Grady added ruefully. "But it must not have permeated my blood soon enough to create an aversion."

Max nodded. "That's going to help with your healing, too. It's an old trick of Max Pesaro—you wouldn't know of him, but he's legendary. I'm named after him, in fact—he's my great-grandfather. Savina had that happen to her once as well—she didn't have enough time to let it get into her blood before she was…bitten. That was…a difficult time."

He looked back down at the emerald. "I don't know how you managed it, but thank you. Surely the loss of this pendant weakened Iscariot, and that only helped us to kill him."

"Us?"

"My daughter. Macey. Perhaps you'll meet her some day. She was… She's here in hospital too. I…uh…" His expression changed to one of pained chagrin, then closed off. "She'll be all right. Right, then. Thank you again, Grady."

"I also emptied his pockets, and that of three of the other goons who got close enough. I'm not sure anything is important." Grady shrugged when Max looked at him with a strange side-eye glance. "Old habits die hard."

Max made a show of patting his own pockets and checking for his timepiece, but his eyes glinted with appreciation. "Glad to have you on my side, then, mate."

Grady pulled out the other items he'd taken from the vampires. He didn't believe there was anything else significant, but Max would be the one to know.

"Keys…some coins…a few scraps of paper," he said, poking through the small pile. "Wouldn't have thought the likes of them would bother to pay for anything, but that looks like a receipt. I'll take them; it might help us find out where the rest of the bastards are holed up. Thank you again."

Grady shrugged. "Not sure why you're thanking me. Anyone would do the same. If they knew."

Max shook his head, his expression sober. "No, they wouldn't. Believe me, I know."

"So, what does this mean now that Iscariot is dead?"

"It means for the first time in thirty years, I might sleep well tonight." Max smiled slightly, then stood. "And now, you should rest. I have to meet up with your copper friends to ensure none of them leave remembering what they saw today."

"Linwood…can you spare him? He's known for a while. He's discreet, and with him being on the police force, it helps that he knows when there are incidents like this."

Max nodded and stood. "Very well. I hope they let you out of here soon."

"Tomorrow. At the latest. I've got a story to write." Grady smiled wanly.

Max replaced his hat and touched his brim, then swept out of the ward just as quickly and silently as he'd come.

Grady took the jar of salve and began to use it. Max hadn't lied—it was sticky as molasses, but it smelled fresh and clean.

The sooner he felt better, the sooner he could get out of this damned place.

✝

Max had delayed as long as he could. Now he was out of time.

Grady had been visited, the cops and young girls had been relieved of any memories related to fangs and bloodsucking, and the surgery to remove the stake and stitch up his daughter had been completed. Max had run out of excuses.

His hands were shamefully clammy as he approached the door to Macey's room. He'd arranged for her to have a private room in the hospital—and willingly paid through the nose for the privilege. St. Joseph's was a Catholic hospital, which meant there were crosses, crucifixes, and other vampire deterrents throughout the building and at every entrance, so she'd be protected from any unwanted visitors until he could get her out.

He stepped into the room and closed the door behind him. Macey's eyes were closed, and she seemed to be breathing normally. He exhaled noiselessly, relief sweeping through him.

She's sleeping.

He could go, and he'd be able to tell Savina truthfully that he'd gone into the room and seen Macey.

Max turned, reaching for the doorknob…then stopped.

What the hell was wrong with him? He had no fear when it came to facing an entire battalion of undead, but his knees were knocking at the thought of being alone with his only child?

Of course, he *had* nearly killed her…

As if he'd sent his thoughts to her, Macey opened her eyes. They were clear and lucid.

"Leaving so soon?" she asked.

Damn. She'd been awake all along.

"No." He stepped closer to the bed and looked down at her. She looked frail and fragile, small and pale, under the blankets and what he could see of the bandages around her injured shoulder. But he knew better. "How do you feel?"

"Iscariot's dead. How do you think I feel?" She managed a wan smile, and Max felt a burst of pride and delight.

She was right: Iscariot was gone.

"Nice work," he said, then glanced at the chair next to the bed.

She saw him look at it. "You can sit down. I'm too sore to be in a vengeful mood."

It took him a moment to realize what she meant. "Christ, Macey, I'm so sorry about that." His half-smile disintegrated and he felt a lump in his throat. "I could have killed you."

Christ. He could have killed *his own daughter.* The thought was simply horrifying, and he couldn't get rid of it.

"I've missed being killed several times now, Max. I guess I'm just lucky." She looked at him, and he was relieved to see compassion in her eyes. "You couldn't have planned for that, and I'd have done the same thing if I were you. But you do have one hell of an arm. Even from that distance, it went right through me."

"I wanted the bastard dusted," he said from between tight jaws.

"You and I both."

"Rather fitting that we did it together," he said with another crooked smile. "Both at the same time. We couldn't have planned it that way."

"What were the chances?" she replied. After a moment she asked, "And what about the others? The girls? Anyone else? Did— How are they all?"

"All but one of the girls is safe. The man who was in there— he was a reporter, name of Grady—he's here at St. Joe's too, and doing all right. He'll live. But the one girl…" His mouth flattened with regret and grief. "We aren't sure yet whether she'll make it."

Macey sighed sadly, and they lapsed into silence.

Max had so many things he knew he should say…things long overdue, things that had been locked away so deeply they hadn't seen the top of his mind for over a decade.

But the words weren't ready to come, and so he dug in his pockets to pull out more salted holy water, and another pot of the sticky salve.

"You'll heal well on your own thanks to the *vis bulla*," he said, offering them to her. "But these will help speed up the process. And take away the pain."

"Thank you." She opened the jar and sniffed. "Hmm. Not bad." Her hands dropped to her lap, the jar and its top still gripped in her fingers. She stared down at them. "I'm glad you were there. I don't...I don't know if I could have done it alone."

A spark of warmth popped inside him. "You were brilliant, Macey. Every bit of it. I...I confess, there was a moment there when I was just waiting, enjoying, watching to see what you were going to do next. You're going to make an excellent *Summa* Gardella."

"Let's not rush things. The current *summas* is still alive and well." Her lips curved, and she looked down shyly. "Thank you. That means a lot, coming from you."

"Macey," he began in a rush—because it felt like now or never, "I want to tell you how sorry I am about—"

She held up her hand. "Please, Max. Let's not talk about that right now. I'm— I...don't want to... Look, I'm glad you're here, because I don't know if I'd have been able to take care of Iscariot myself—especially with Chas being gone, and Sebastian, too. But beyond that...I'm not *ready* to think about...about you being here, you know, in any other capacity. All right?"

His spark of warmth fizzled out. "Right. All right."

Take it slow. That was what Savina had said. Take it slow, but accept responsibility.

Damn. This was just not the sort of thing he was good at. Not the sort of thing he understood how to handle. Women: daughters, lovers, mysterious chatelaines...

All of them—unless they had fangs or were in his bed, and even that wasn't a given—were a source of pain and confusion to him.

"But you should know," he went on stubbornly, "that I regret the last thirteen years."

She looked up at him with liquid brown eyes. "So do I."

Returning to 1926 Chicago only a few hours after he'd left it caused Chas no small headache—literally.

Wayren had warned him, asking if he'd rather spend at least one full day in the Paris of a century earlier, but he'd declined. The sooner he returned with the skull and its tonguelike dagger, the sooner they could destroy the pyramid.

But as he walked along the street, making his way back to The Silver Chalice, his legs felt wobbly and his brain mushy. Nothing a glass of good Armagnac wouldn't cure, he thought with a smile, patting the satchel he wore over one shoulder that contained four bottles of the ambrosia. Temple was going to be very pleased, especially when she learned he'd brought her three instead of two.

He'd considered asking Wayren to borrow her book satchel—the one that seemed to be able to hold an infinite number of volumes, but never bulked out or appeared heavy—so he could bring back an entire case of contraband, but he'd thought better of it.

"Extra! Extra! Special evening edition!" shouted a newspaper boy as Chas walked past. "Read an update on the schoolgirl hostage situation!"

That piqued his interest, and his concern, and Chas easily parted with the nickel being charged for what turned out to be nothing more than a one-page flyer.

The headline, which took up the entire paper above the fold, declared: *Schoolgirls Safe!*

Chas stopped on the street to read it, and the sub-headline said: *Beedle hostage crisis resolved with zero fatalities! Perpetrators dead or in custody!*

Next to it was a photograph of a cluster of police officers—and in the midst of it was Max Denton.

Chas swore and took off at a run the rest of the way to The Silver Chalice, the bottles of brandy clinking noisily against him. Hopefully Temple was at the pub, and would have more information.

He hurried past the Chalice finial and down the steps that took him below the sidewalk, slowing only when he noticed the pub door was ajar.

The back of his neck prickled…but in a wary sort of way, rather than a portent of the undead.

He pushed open the door. The satchel slipped from his fingers and four bottles of exquisite Armagnac brandy shattered.

Nineteen

Wherein our Heroine's Life Spirals Out of Her Control

I'M READY TO GET OUT of this place," Macey said, breaking the awkward silence that had descended over her hospital room.

It had been interrupted by a brief visit from a nurse, who checked her vital signs and changed her bandages. She'd clucked in surprise over the speed at which the wounds were healing ("Are you certain it was only a few hours ago you had surgery? It's quite miraculous!").

But the moment the nurse closed the door behind her, the tension settled back over the small, windowless room.

Max had taken a seat in the chair next to her bed, and though he didn't seem inclined to leave, he also appeared as uncomfortable as a cat in a bathtub. He also didn't seem to have much to say. "If the doctor says it's all right, then I don't see why you couldn't—"

"You heard what the nurse said. She can't believe how fast I'm healing." Macey pushed herself up. "See? I can even move my arm now. My shoulder hardly hurts at all."

Not that Max had any say over what she did or didn't do, Macey reminded herself. He might be her father, but she made her own decisions.

"I'll need new clothes," she suddenly realized. She couldn't walk out of the hospital in the flimsy, gapping gown, and her other clothes had been destroyed. "Damn."

Before Max could respond, the door to the hospital room swung open.

"Chas," Macey said—more warmly than the moment warranted, but it was nice to see a new face. "Did you get the—What's wrong?"

It wasn't until he came fully into the room that she saw his shocked, sober expression.

"I just came from the pub. It's Temple. She's dead."

"What?" Max was on his feet, and Macey bolted upright from her pillows, with a cry of shock and grief. "What happened?"

Chas appeared stunned. Macey took him by the arm and pulled him down to sit on the edge of her bed as she waited for him to tell them what he knew.

"I returned from my trip. Yes, I retrieved the item in question and brought it with me," he said, glancing around as if to ensure no one could hear.

"When I got back to The Silver Chalice, I noticed the door was ajar. I went inside and—" He shook his head and pinched the bridge of his nose. "It was carnage. The likes of which…" He shook his head, looking decidedly green around the gills. "It was Temple—and there was also a man. I didn't recognize him. They were both dead. Shot…and…she was torn to ribbons. It was a *lot* of blood. They looked as if they'd been there for some time. Hours, perhaps." He drew in a deep breath. "And to top it off, Rekk's Pyramid is gone."

"Gone?" Macey whispered.

"The secret door to the safe was wide open. Broken glasses and bottles everywhere."

"Temple was taking the pyramid to the sacristy of the church," Max interrupted. "Perhaps she'd done so, and whoever came in looking for it got angry when they realized it was gone—"

Chas shook his head. "No. That was my first thought—hope. I went to the church and checked. It's not there."

Max swore violently under his breath. His fingers curled into fists. "Who even knew it was at the pub? Iscariot and his minions, of course, but they were a little busy with us—"

"Flora," Macey said in a horrified, gritty voice.

They looked at her, comprehension dawning in their faces.

"She wasn't there, at the school today. I didn't see her anywhere. Let's go," she said, and flung back the bed coverings, heedless of the amount of leg and thigh she revealed. "Give me your coat," she told Max. "I can't walk out of here wearing this."

She froze. "Chas. What about Aunt Cookie?"

He still looked grim. "She's safe. I took her with me to the church, and then I put her in a taxi to the train station. I gave her money to go back to New Orleans, even though she argued about not having time to pack. I told her to buy new clothes when she got down there."

Macey drew in a deep breath. There was no reason for anyone to be after Cookie—Flora had never even met the woman.

Moments later, they were on their way out, rushing down the corridor, when Max said, "I'll meet you at the pub. I have to do something first." And he veered off into a different ward of the hospital.

"Is Temple really dead?" Macey asked, gripping Chas's arm. Tears stung her eyes. How?

He just shook his head, his mouth grim.

By the time they arrived at The Silver Chalice, it was nearly nine o'clock in the evening.

"Watch out when you go inside—there are four broken bottles of brandy in the doorway. And...I didn't call the police," Chas said, unlocking the door. "Not yet. I wanted you and Max to see..."

Macey stepped inside and was assaulted by the strong, pungent smell of blood and death mingling with the scent of brandy. Chas had covered the two bodies with sheets, probably dragged from the apartments in back.

Tears stung Macey's eyes, and cold horror filled her as she knelt next to the smaller body, its sheet completely stained with blood. She pulled it back to view Temple's brutalized body. It hadn't been a simple death: she'd been shot in the chest, but then her flesh was scored in numerous places, her abdomen torn open as if sliced by four matching knives. Even her face bore many sets of deep scratches from long, lethal vampire nails.

There didn't appear to be signs of bites, or of feeding. It was as if the assailant simply wanted to maim and kill—and in the most violent way possible.

"Macey." Chas's low, rough voice called her to the other side of the room.

She rose, but before leaving Temple's side, she covered her up once more and said a brief prayer for her friend and mentor. Her insides twisting like a rope, she made her way over to Chas.

"Oh, God, no." Macey gave a choked cry when she recognized the man lying there in a thick, congealed pool of blood. "Oh, no…Dr. Sevin. Joseph Sevin. He was… He and Temple… *No…*" Her last word came out in little more than a whisper.

She swiped viciously at the tears welling from her eyes. They'd been so happy together, Temple and her dapper, handsome "family friend." Macey had never seen her trainer seem so gay and bright-eyed over the last few days.

"They showed a little more mercy to him," Chas said grimly. "Looks like they just cut his throat after they shot him. Instead of…"

"Temple must have fought back; maybe she tried to protect him. Maybe they used him to get her to tell them where the pyramid was…or maybe it wasn't that simple." Macey felt a sudden, ugly chill down her spine.

If she was right, and Flora had been here… Well, Flora had never liked Temple. She'd been jealous of her friendship with Macey.

The mutilation, especially of her lovely face, seemed to be a personal attack. Macey stepped back, staring blankly around the room.

Could Flora really be capable of such violence? The mischievous carrot-top who'd been so tall and gangly, so fun and goofy…?

Of course she could. She was a vampire now. An undead. A soulless, damned demon.

Macey shook her head, feeling even more ill. *What have I wrought?*

It was because of her decision to join the Venators, to take on this vocation, that she and Flora had grown apart. It was because she'd had a good job at the Harper Library at the university that Macey urged Flora to find something just as exciting and well paid—and made her feel so inadequate that she eventually found a job at the vampire cabaret called The Blood Club.

It was because of Macey that Flora felt lost and alone, and had been so easily seduced by the undead Count Alvisi into becoming an immortal herself…all in the name of competing with, or being as good as, her friend.

"I…" Macey could hardly breathe. Her insides were in knots, her palms clammy, her head suddenly light.

"What is it?" Chas pulled her into his arms, wrapping her tightly in his embrace, as if to protect her from the thoughts and horror that surrounded her.

"She hated Temple," Macey mumbled into his shirt. "Because of me."

The exterior door opened and Max walked in, then halted at the sight of the sheet-covered bodies. "God have mercy," he said, after bending to look beneath Temple's sheet.

"Hell hath no fury," Macey said, lifting her head from Chas's chest.

"You believe your friend Flora did this?"

Macey nodded.

Max gave a bitter curse and shook his head. Carefully replacing the sheet, he stood and surveyed the room, hands on his hips. And swore again.

Then, as if remembering something, he glanced behind and gestured at the door. "I've got a bloke here to join our team, such as it is. I've known him for years, and he has a set of particular skills that could come in handy."

Macey automatically stepped away from Chas, curious about whom her father would have brought on to help. As if Max Denton would need help…would he? Was it another Venator? Someone from Rome, perhaps?

When a familiar figure stepped through the doorway, Macey's mind went utterly blank and all feeling drained from her face.

"Meet my old mate from London, Jameson Grady—goes by Grady," Max said. "Don't say James or Jimmy or even Jameson."

"Unless you're ordering the whiskey," said Grady with a crooked grin. His eyes swept over Macey and Chas as he gave each of them a nod of acknowledgment. "Hello."

Macey was lightheaded, and a hundred questions exploded in her mind. Her father knew Grady? Grady knew her father? How long had they known each other? What was he *doing* here? How could this be happening?

And how could he even be on his feet after the condition he'd been in at the school? He did look pale and drawn, and he was, she noticed, holding himself awkwardly—as if trying to ignore pain. He leaned lightly against the wall.

"…my daughter, Macey," Max was saying.

"Oh, I've met Macey," Grady replied, and her heart stopped, lodging in her throat.

She opened her mouth to speak—though she didn't know what to say, and her heart was pounding so hard she thought she might pass out. What in the world was going on? She felt as if she'd been on a carousel for hours, and just stepped off it to find the world still spinning out of control.

But then Grady continued, "We met at the photography exhibit Saturday night." His smile was charming and yet impersonal— exactly how it should be, meeting his friend's daughter.

The mention of the photography exhibit also reminded Macey of Miss Sabrina Ellison, and her insides twisted and coiled even more tightly. Just what she needed. Grady around *and* the knowledge that he'd already found someone to replace her.

"I'm not sure we need to bring anyone else into this mess, Denton," Chas said, moving closer to Macey. He was the only other person in the room who realized the awkwardness of the situation, and she was grateful for his presence. "Especially a civilian. Who is, from the looks of it, hardly able to stand from his own injuries."

Max's smile turned cool and hard. Clearly, the *summas* would brook no disagreement. "Right. You weren't here when everything happened, were you, Woodmore? As it happens, it was Grady who was instrumental in helping the girls to escape today. And through his entire encounter with Iscariot," Max continued, speaking very deliberately, "he remained *undaunted,* and succeeded in saving many lives."

Macey caught her breath and her attention snapped to Max's gaze. *No.* Surely not. But her father gave a barely perceptible nod. Chas tensed with the same shock and disbelief, but Macey hardly noticed…for it felt as if the floor was disintegrating at her feet.

Everything was falling away. Everything she knew and believed and trusted…was…confused.

How could it be? Grady wasn't even a Venator…was he? No, of course he wasn't—she'd seen him…*everywhere*…and no *vis bulla* in sight.

"May I speak with you for a moment, *Father?*" she said flatly.

Max lifted a sardonic brow—whether it was due to her using the word "father" for the first time, albeit in a sarcastic manner, or the fact that she was daring to question the *summas,* she didn't know. And she didn't bloody care.

Nevertheless, he did acquiesce—a measure of the respect he must have for her.

"Are you loony?" she said the moment they stepped into the back hall of the pub. "Bringing a civilian into something like this? Even if he is the dauntless one, we don't need his help anymore. Iscariot's dead."

"I've known the man for years," Max replied. "He's damned good—"

"And so are you, and so am I, and so is Chas! We don't need him. Did you see what Flora did to Temple?" Tears stung her eyes.

It was madness. All of this was madness. "A man like him isn't equipped—"

"He went into the school today on his own and came out alive—thanks to his own doing." Max held up an imperious hand. "It's better to know what he's doing than chance that he might take matters into his own hands. Aside from that, he's quite skilled in a number of—"

"I thought you said we should ignore the prophecy and just do what we had to do," she said. Her voice was wobbly, blast it, and she could feel the beginning of tears stinging her eyes.

"He'll join us," Max said, his voice flat and final.

Damn, oh *damn!* Here she was, in the very position she'd tried so hard to keep herself (and Grady) out of—and it was even worse, because Grady didn't remember her.

He didn't even know her anymore. Yet here he was, shoulder-deep in danger and the business of killing vampires.

Dammit.

Twenty

Of Family Legends and Swooning

I N MACEY'S ESTIMATION, facing Iscariot again would almost have been preferable to the way things happened in the next few hours.

"No one is going to stay here," Max said, referring to The Silver Chalice and, by extension, its attached apartments. "It's already been breached by the undead—incidentally, I can only assume this Flora was able to enter because Temple didn't know she was an undead, and invited her in."

Macey shook her head glumly. "Temple knew who Flora was. She wouldn't have invited her in."

"I allowed her in," Chas said flatly. "Originally."

"Right, then." Max didn't sound judgmental, but Macey heard Chas's self-recrimination loud and clear.

His inability to stop the female vampire had caused even more damage. She reached over and squeezed his hand, noticing as she did so that Grady was watching.

"She planned it perfectly—it all happened while we were busy with Iscariot at the Beedle school," said Macey.

"A classic example of distraction and misdirection—the same tactic used by illusionists and escape artists," Grady commented, glancing at Max.

"Precisely," the *summas* said. "Now then, no one is going to remain here, for a number of reasons. Grady has offered his place for the time being." When Macey opened her mouth to protest—

oh God, no!—her father gave her brittle look. "I've been staying there myself, and it's not only extremely secure, but large enough for us all. And it has a telephone."

"Macey can sleep at my place," Chas said. "With me. It's secure, and it has a telephone as well."

Max turned to him. "I want Macey near me."

Chas appeared as if he were about to argue, but after another look from Max, he set his jaw and said nothing. But that didn't stop him from giving Max a dark look of his own.

"Excuse me…don't I have a say in where I stay?" Macey said, hardly able to keep the anger from her voice. "I—"

"Not right now. There are too many factors at play, and it's important that we're all together as much as possible." Max looked at her, clearly speaking as the *Summas* Gardella and not as her father, trying to interfere in her love life (not that she actually had one).

At least, she hoped that was the case.

It was nearly midnight by the time the four of them arrived at Grady's house.

Macey was overwhelmed by a range of memories and emotions as she stepped over the threshold into the neat and cozy duplex, and it was all she could do to keep from looking at Grady…just in the vain hope that he might also remember.

But she knew better than that—and that point was driven home even more strongly a moment later when she walked into the living room.

Macey's belly twisted painfully when she saw Sabrina Ellison, looking utterly lovely with her hair loose and face devoid of makeup. She was curled up on the sofa in a terrycloth housecoat with a magazine and a pot of tea—as if she lived there.

She probably did.

Oh God.

Macey lingered at the edge of the room, torn between not wanting the woman to recognize and greet her—because then she'd have to make nice and talk to the *older* female photographer—and definitely not wanting to see the warmth and greeting between her and Grady.

She didn't want to think about the two of them going upstairs to the same bed she'd shared with Grady…and Macey having to sleep on the sofa. Right below them.

Her stomach pitched more violently at the images that thought produced, and she had to swallow hard to keep the bile back. Hadn't her day been bad enough?

She should have stayed at the damned hospital.

Or anywhere other than here.

Pretty much anywhere. Even back in the hell of Iscariot's presence would be preferable to this, because at least then, she could fight back.

She could do something about that.

"Macey." Max's voice jolted her from her thoughts. He sounded strange—almost strained.

She glanced toward him and realized Sabrina had risen to her feet. The photographer was looking at her with a strange expression—something between uncertainty and eagerness.

"This is my—er—this is Savina Eleaisa," Max said.

And that was when Macey realized *he was holding the woman's hand.*

She couldn't help it—she glanced at Grady to see his reaction, and saw that he was in the kitchen, pulling out the bottle of whiskey he kept hidden beneath the floorboards. He either didn't notice, or didn't mind.

"You know me as Sabrina Ellison," said the woman, stepping toward Macey with a tentative smile. "It's a pleasure to meet you—again."

"So you *have* met," Max said, looking between the two of them. He seemed as uncomfortable as Macey felt confused.

"At the exhibit, of course," Sabrina—or was her name Savina?—said. She gave him a knowing look, and patted his hand as if to comfort him. "That's all right, Max, darling—we didn't talk about you at all. Yet."

Macey's brain was beginning to catch up, albeit slowly. She blinked as comprehension began to dawn, and then was startled when Grady suddenly appeared next to her, thrusting a small glass of whiskey into her hand.

Before she could thank him, he turned and gave another drink to Chas, then returned to the kitchen to retrieve two more glasses for Max and the photographer.

"After today, I thought something stronger than tea was in order," Grady said, unnecessarily.

Macey sipped the strong amber liquor, grateful for the excuse not to speak. Things made much more sense now. Max said he'd been staying here—then presumably so had Sabrina, or whatever her name was. Which could easily explain why she'd been in a robe coming down from the upstairs when Macey knocked on the door yesterday.

Good grief…had it only been yesterday afternoon?

It felt as if a decade had gone by since then.

"Not to your liking, there, mate?" Grady said, and Macey looked over to see that Chas had set his glass down on the counter.

"It's not that. I'm not in the mood for a drink at the moment."

Macey looked at him sharply. She'd never known Chas not to be in the mood for a drink—or for that matter, never to be the first one who needed his glass refilled.

"I see no reason for me to stay. Obliged for the offer, Grady, but quarters are cramped here and I have a perfectly fine place of my own." Chas looked at Max as if to challenge him to argue.

Max, who was standing next to his…whatever Sabrina was, merely shrugged. "Suit yourself."

Apparently he didn't care so much whether they were *all* together, or whether just *Macey* was with him. She gritted her teeth. She would *not* be treated like his daughter, or like a weak female.

"Have a seat," Grady said, gesturing to the sofa as Chas retrieved his coat and hat.

"Actually, I think I'd rather go to sleep," Macey said, and finished off her whiskey. At least now she wouldn't have to worry about hearing—or thinking about—Grady and Sabrina (Savina?) together.

Except that now she was going to have to *not* think about the older woman and her father together. Though she didn't really think of Max as her father, he still was.

Ugh.

"I hope you don't mind me breaking up the party," she added, glancing at the sofa while trying at the same time to appear as if she had no idea where she'd be sleeping because she'd never been at this place before.

Why in the world had Max thought it was such a great idea to have them all stay here?

"Of *course* you need rest," Sabrina said, handing her glass to Max. "After what you've been through today! All of you." She smiled up at him, but there was a hint of steel in her expression. "I'll take Macey up and get her settled."

She looked at Macey. "We'll share a room—I hope you don't mind, but there's only one bedroom here. Max can sleep on the floor—he's used to doing that." She slanted a meaningful look at Max, and he closed his mouth on what looked like a protest and finished off her drink with a big gulp. "And Grady, you need to rest as well, so it's still the sofa for you. You're looking quite pale there, my dear."

Before she knew it, Macey was upstairs—still pretending she had no idea where she was going or even where the lavatory was—and Sabrina was fussing around with the bed coverings and pillows.

"Excuse me," Macey said, causing the other woman to stop and straighten abruptly.

"Yes?" She looked at her with that same expectant but wary expression, her hands clutching a pillow.

"I'm…er— Well, we're going to be sharing a bed, and I'm—uh—not sure what to *call* you. Miss Ellison or Miss Elee—I didn't quite catch your name."

She broke into a beautiful smile. "Oh, no, you must call me Savina. That's my real name. I only use Sabrina Ellison professionally—it's my cover for when I'm out doing…well, work for the Venators."

"Work for the Venators? *You're* a Venator?" Macey sank onto a chair in the corner.

That was unexpected. The only female Venators she knew of—though, granted, her knowledge of their history was spotty at best—were directly descended from her family line, and were long dead. In other words, if Savina were a born Venator, she would be Macey's aunt or close cousin.

"No, I'm not a Venator. But I was raised with them. I've known your father since I was a young girl, for my father worked for the Venators at the Consilium in Rome before he—before he died." A shadow crossed her face, then was gone.

"Right." Macey was doing her best to keep up with all of this interesting and surprising information, but she had had a grueling day. Between that and the glass of whiskey, her brain was turning to mush.

Savina plopped the pillow onto the bed and fluffed it. "Why don't you wash up—I see you brought some nightclothes—and then I can change your bandages while we talk more. I'm sure you have many questions. I'll be happy to answer as many of them as I can."

It wasn't until Macey was toweling off her face in the bathroom that she remembered the photograph that had so captivated her attention at the exhibit. What had Savina said about it the night they'd met?

Taking that photo was very nearly as life-threatening as shooting the one of the cobra. This subject is far more dangerous, and he didn't know I was taking the shot.

Macey stilled. Savina had been talking about Max.

Staring into space, Macey hung up the towel on its rung in the bathroom. Savina had gone on to ask her a very telling question. *Have you ever loved a man it was safer not to?*

Clearly she'd been talking about her father.

Had Savina known then that Macey was Max's daughter? Surely if she and Max were…whatever they were…Savina had known about Macey. Was that why she'd sought her out, and why she'd started such a private conversation?

Macey sighed. The only way to get the answers to these questions was to ask them—and Savina seemed willing to answer.

"Let me check those bandages," Savina said as Macey came back into the bedroom—the bedroom where she'd made love with Grady. She tried not to think about that day, but it was impossible not to. Just being in the room, seeing his things, remembering how he'd laid her on the bed and knelt in front of her...

She'd miscalculated, that day. Or maybe she hadn't.

Macey had asked herself many times since: had she known, in the back of her mind, that the moment Grady saw her without her clothes, all of his suspicions about her being a vampire hunter— and the existence of the undead—would be confirmed?

That she would irrevocably change things between them— allowing him to know her most precious secret?

She decided that, yes, she had known. And she'd consciously allowed it to happen.

His reaction when he discovered she was wearing a *vis bulla* pierced through her navel: so beautiful. So...right. He'd been awed, and yet not the least bit intimidated—even when he asked her how strong the amulet made her, and she replied: *I could throw you across the room.*

Instead of being shocked, he'd smiled, long and slow and sweet. Grinned with absolutely delicious delight...and then knelt and went down on her, kissing her, making love to her... delighting in her—to show her how much he loved her. *All* of her.

Oh, *dammit.* What a fool she was!

"Am I hurting you?" Savina stopped what she was doing, looking at Macey in alarm.

"No—oh no. I'm only a little sore, which is quite miraculous, considering. Thank you for doing that," she added, blinking quickly to rid herself of the tears.

"Max told me what happened. He was horrified. He knows how close he came to— Well, thankfully, you're going to be fine.

But wouldn't that have been terrible: the day after he finds you—after thirteen years—and he stakes his own daughter?"

Macey couldn't help it: despite her maudlin emotions, she laughed. "That would have been one for the Venator history books, wouldn't it? Poor Max…he would have gone down in history in quite a different way than his namesake Max Pesaro."

Savina smiled too, then became dreamy-eyed. "Ah…Max Pesaro. All you have to do is mention his name in the presence of any female who knows of the Venators, and she tends to swoon and get all fluttery."

Macey laughed again. "Really?"

"Oh, he was quite something. Arrogant as hell, always had to be right about everything—though I understand Victoria was good at demonstrating otherwise—rigidly black and white, and as true and loyal and fierce as they came. And he was a brilliant Venator. He could even glide through the air!"

"No…that must be an exaggeration." But Macey was intrigued.

"Not at all. It's an old Chinese fighting technique called *qingongg*, and he mastered it." Savina looked bashful for a moment. "I grew up listening to stories about him—and Victoria and Sebastian Vioget, and Lady Cat and Andreas, too—but I was always simply enthralled by anything related to Max Pesaro. He was like my…my Noel Chavasse, I guess. A perfect hero."

"Yet he was harsh and arrogant." Macey had heard Sebastian complain about her great-great-grandfather often enough to know of his faults and foibles, but it certainly was enlightening hearing about him from a different perspective. "And who were Lady Cat and Andreas?"

"Oh, yes, Max Pesaro had his faults—no one denied that. But inside, he had a heart as soft as cotton candy—especially when it came to his wife and girls. He never had a son, you know. Only daughters. I once heard Bellitano—he's the acting *summas* at the Consilium, because your father…well, he's been…doing his own thing. Anyway, I once heard Bellitano telling someone that according to Victoria Gardella, it served him—Max Pesaro—

right to have only daughters, since he needed lots of practice in dealing with strong women."

Macey could only blink and stare at Savina, and wish desperately that she wasn't as exhausted as she was. This was *fascinating*—and a side of her family and the world of the Venators she'd never heard about. Savina certainly brought a different— and more interesting—perspective than the cynical Sebastian and sarcastic Chas.

Temple—God rest her soul—had mostly been interested in teaching Macey how to fight and defend herself, and everything she knew about the undead and their strengths and vulnerabilities. Not gossipy stories about her family.

"Who were Lady Cat and Andreas?" she asked again, quite willing to be distracted from reality for the moment. She'd had enough reality for the day.

Having finished her work with Macey's bandages, Savina settled back onto the bed near the foot, drawing her feet up next to her and reclining on a pile of pillows. "Lady Catherine Gardella. She's where the red hair in your family comes from—Isabella Pesaro had red hair too, you know. Max's youngest daughter? Anyway, Cat lived in the Tudor court of Queen Elizabeth. I have no idea how she managed to fight vampires while wearing ruffs, stomachers, and panniers—let alone *walk* in them, or get through a doorway, for that matter—but she was just as fierce and fiery as her hair would suggest. And Andreas…" She sighed. "He's my second favorite Venator to swoon over. Very mysterious. In fact, Lady Cat didn't even know his true identity at first."

Macey leaned up against the headboard, more pillows propped beneath her, desperately trying to stay awake to hear all of Savina's stories. "Andreas. Was he a Venator too?"

"After a fashion," Savina replied with a crafty smile. "Apparently, their story—Cat's and Andreas's—is quite dramatic, taking place mostly in the Elizabethan court. I'll have to get Paolo to tell you—" She stopped abruptly. "You're getting tired. I should let you sleep."

Macey didn't argue. Her eyelids were drooping. Her body was sore and exhausted.

But just as she was about to lie down and allow herself to drift off, her eyes popped open. "That photograph. At the exhibit. That's my father, isn't it?"

Savina didn't hesitate. "You must have realized it somehow, don't you think? That was why you found it so compelling."

Macey nodded. Then she looked up. "Was it…well, it's titled *A Letter Long Due*. Why?"

"I think you know why."

She nodded again, her head scrubbing against the pillow. Yes, she'd discerned enough of what was written to know that it could have been—it *was*—her name.

Dear Macey…

"I never received a letter from him, you know." Macey felt a prickling of the old anger again. "He never sent it."

"He sent it. Several of them. But…they weren't delivered. I should let him explain. I really should— But since we're talking about it…it was Al Capone. He never gave them to you."

"What did Capone have to do with any of this?" Macey was suddenly wide awake and outraged. "Why would my father trust him with anything?"

"Alphonse is—was—a Venator. Max is the *summas*. Why shouldn't he have trusted him?"

Macey sagged back against the pillows. She certainly knew Capone well enough to understand where things had gone wrong. And now she understood why her father might have paid a visit to the man. If Capone had, for some foolish reason, decided not to do something the *summas* had requested—like deliver a letter to his daughter—that could be a reason for a severe talking-to. Or worse.

"I'm not trying to defend your father, Macey. I've told him numerous times what a terrible parent he is. How cowardly he is"— Macey huffed an appreciative laugh at that— "and what an arse he can be. But he's the bravest, most dangerous and brilliant vampire hunter in the world. He's given his life—and more—to protect mortals and to keep the undead at bay. Without him…well, the world would be a much more dangerous place. But he's not perfect. None of us are." Savina seemed to be speaking to herself as much as to Macey.

"Are you married to my father?"

Savina gave a pained laugh. "No." She rose from her place at the foot of the bed and brought her pillows up to the other end, clearly ready to go to sleep herself—or perhaps simply to avoid answering. "I don't think a second marriage is in his future. And I don't mind. He has enough to attend to in his life."

But Macey didn't think that was true. There was something in her voice, something in her eyes, that bespoke some great pain.

"At the photo exhibit when you asked me whether I'd ever loved someone it was safer not to love…you were talking about him, I suppose."

Savina sighed and paused, then flung back the bedcovers on her side and climbed abed. "Yes, of course." Then she looked at Macey keenly. "And you answered yes."

Macey suddenly found the French knot design on the coverlet extremely fascinating. "Right."

"Chas Woodmore?" Savina asked.

Macey looked up. "No. Not him."

Savina seemed satisfied. "That's probably just as well. He seems as if he has as much junk stuffed in his figurative suitcase as Max Denton."

"He does. But we're…close. At least, as close as one can get to Chas." She gave a sad laugh.

"Right. He seems a sad sort of chap." Savina pulled the covers up over her as she turned toward Macey. "It's very nice of Grady to give up his bed to guests. He's an exceptional man."

Macey nodded, then realized she wasn't supposed to know him well enough to know whether that was true or not. "I… Well, when I saw you at the photo exhibit with him, I thought you two were…uh…" She shrugged and gave a half-smile.

"You weren't the only one," Savina said wryly, shaking her head. "But no. Not at all. It's your father for me, Macey. There won't be anyone else, ever again. No matter what happens."

A shaft of pain and remorse caught Macey by surprise, and Savina looked over at her. "Are you in pain? Do you want more of that sticky salve?"

"No. It's not that. It's…"

Macey closed her eyes. She'd been just about to confess everything to Savina. But no. Not a good idea.

The woman was kind and funny, and she seemed genuine… but what would the benefit be if Macey told her about Grady?

"Good night, Savina. Thank you. It's been…nice talking to you."

"Same here, Macey. I'm very, very glad to have met you. Finally."

Macey closed her eyes, her thoughts in more turmoil than her healing body.

Tomorrow, she would once more face the reality of a world in which her former best friend had brutally murdered two people… and that she had possession of one of the most powerful objects of evil in the world.

Sweet dreams, Macey, she told herself.

Twenty-One

Wherein the Summas is Given a Set-down

MACEY AND SAVINA went upstairs and Woodmore bade them good night while Max and Grady finished their whiskey.

The Irish bloke was looking pale and sickly, and Max realized what a fool he'd been to expect as much from him as he would from a *vis bullaed* Venator, or even a Comitator. The man wasn't equipped in the same way, and he'd nearly died earlier today.

"I'm going out," Max told him abruptly. If he was quick enough, he could catch up with Woodmore. With all the horror at The Silver Chalice, he'd temporarily put aside the message he had to deliver. "I may not be back until morning."

Before Grady could ask more, Max slipped out the door and started off in the direction Woodmore would have gone—assuming he was, in fact, returning to his own place.

He hadn't gone far before he caught sight of the broad-shouldered figure, for the man was ambling along as if deep in thought, rather than walking with a purpose.

"Woodmore," Max called out as he approached. After the day he'd had, he didn't feel like having to defend himself from a surprised Venator.

"Denton. I thought you were in for the night. Wanted everyone to stay *together*."

There was a definite sneer in the man's voice, and Max bristled. "I have a message for you. If you want it."

"I don't know. Do I?"

Max gritted his teeth. He'd half a mind to start a brawl, right here and now with the bastard. The man had no right to be putting his hands on his daughter the way he had—and he sure as *hell* had no right to be snide and cutting simply because Max had done the *fatherly* thing and interrupted their plans for a cozy little love-nest tonight. Macey needed her rest, goddammit.

And Chas Woodmore was simply bad news—for anyone… at least, as far as women went. He was too damned handsome and far too arresting for his own good. It hadn't escaped Max's attention that Savina had *noticed* Woodmore. Really noticed him, if the way her eyes traveled up and down over the dark and muscular Romanian were any indication.

Why couldn't Macey be attracted to someone like Grady, for example? Nice chap, funny, talented, and relatively polite—a little quick with the hands dipping in the pockets, but at least Max and Grady generally saw things the same way.

"Well, what is it?" Woodmore asked.

He hadn't stopped, and had actually sped up to a faster pace. Thus, Max was forced to walk abreast with him along the edge of a sidewalk that wasn't wide enough for two people, which in turn required him to dodge bushes, trees, mailboxes, and other obstacles along the way. That didn't make him feel any friendlier toward the man, especially when he tripped on a tree root in the dark and nearly took a header.

Bugger it.

"First things first," Max said, suddenly out of patience. "Are you in love with my daughter?"

Woodmore snorted. "Why do you care?"

"Just answer the bloody question—and without commentary, if you please. You might not like it—hell, *she* might not like it— but I'm not only her father, but also the *summas*. I need to know these things. She is the heir apparent to the Venators."

"No. I'm not."

Max felt a wave of relief, then a burst of fury. "Then why the bloody hell did you have your hands up her buggering dress?"

Woodmore cast him a glance. "I don't see how it's any of your business, father or *summas*-in-name-only notwithstanding."

Max felt a definite *crack* in his jaw, and hoped he hadn't actually broken a tooth. Damned Venator strength. "Look, you might have a problem with me and my decisions, but I don't give a devil about that. All I want is my daughter to be safe and happy—"

"Then where the hell have you been for thirteen years? She thought—we *all* thought—you were dead. And why in the *hell* did you make her go to Grady's house tonight?" Woodmore stopped at last, swinging to face Max.

He halted just before he slammed into the other man. "What do you mean?"

"She's in love with Grady, you pompous arse. *That* is why I wanted her to go to my place tonight. Not for any other reason. She doesn't need any other pain in her life tonight."

"What the devil are you talking about? She and Grady have never even met—except at the exhibit."

Woodmore was shaking his head. "That's where you're wrong. They've met. But she asked Wayren to use the golden disk to erase herself from his memory. Like father, like daughter," he added snidely. "Making godlike decisions for everyone else just to make it easier for themselves."

Max wanted nothing more than to take a swing at him—and he just might have done so if he hadn't thought he might need the man who'd obtained the tongue of the ruby-eyed skull.

"I'll overlook your disrespect this time," Max said, causing Woodmore to snort again. He gritted his teeth—damn, he might have broken a tooth after all—and continued, "Because I appreciate the information."

And as he said those words, the meaning sank in. Now he was going to have to object to Grady—and dammit, he was rather fond of the bloke.

Oh…but Macey had had the man's memory altered, and so he didn't know their history.

That was good.

"The message, Denton. What is it?" Woodmore had started walking again.

"Right. It's from Bell, at the Consilium. Cezar Moldavi has escaped from his prison in Siberia, and no one knows where he's gone."

Now it was Woodmore's turn to stumble. "Impossible. Narcise and Cale and I designed it ourselves. It's impenetrable. Moldavi's been there for more than a century—how could he have escaped?"

"I would agree, but there's no disputing the facts. Moldavi is gone. And since you're the one most familiar with the creature, you should be the one tasked with finding him."

Woodmore swore under his breath, but nodded. "Very well. I'll head to Siberia."

"Not until we're done here," Max told him, and he was admittedly relieved when the other man agreed.

He wanted every bit of help possible until the threat from Macey's best friend was over.

Macey dragged herself out of the dream and lay there, heart pounding wildly, body clammy and weak.

It took her a moment to realize where she was, who was sleeping next to her…then the terror of the dream seceded and was replaced by grief.

It should be Grady beside her in his bed.

Macey stared at the ceiling for a moment, aware of the aches and twinges from a body that had been brutally abused less than twenty-four hours earlier. She found it easier to think about that pain than the emotional strain of knowing her former best friend had destroyed two people—at least—and that her former lover was sleeping one floor below her.

Along with the myriad of emotions that kept her miserable and confused, she found that her belly was very insistent on being fed. Macey couldn't remember the last time she'd had anything to eat—maybe some sort of soup in the hospital?—and when her stomach snarled for a second time, she slid from beneath the blankets and put her feet on the floor.

Savina was sleeping soundly and she didn't stir as Macey padded silently down the stairs. A glance at the sofa told her Grady still slumbered there—a long, lumpy figure beneath a blanket. She didn't see her father in a chair or on the floor, and allowed a moment to wonder where he'd bunked down, then shrugged.

He knew what he was doing. At least, when it came to hunting vampires.

Making her way through darkness broken only by a streetlight glancing through the window, Macey found a box of crackers. She winced when the packaging crinkled, then winced again when her glass made a soft clink as she pulled it from the cabinet. The water pump thunked on and went into a low hum when she turned on the tap, and to her ears it sounded like an elephant lumbering around the room.

But the house remained silent and still, and after a moment, she breathed more easily. Standing at the kitchen window, she looked out over the park in the next lot. The swings hung empty and straight, and the trees were just beginning to show their leaves against a dark gray sky. Dawn threatened, and with it would come a new day of challenge and conflict.

Macey's fingers traced the silver crosses embedded in the sill as she chewed the crackers—which tasted as dry as sawdust and only went down when she forced them by drinking water. But her gnawing belly didn't seem to mind.

"Did you find what you needed?"

Macey held on to her glass—just barely—and turned to Grady. "Yes. I'm sorry…I didn't mean to wake you." Her heart was in her throat—forget swallowing any more crackers—and her insides were doing the Charleston.

Bathed in a shaft of light from the street, he appeared rumpled from sleep. His dark hair was every which way, and a thick curl had tumbled over his forehead. His eyes were in shadow; his chin and jaw were dusted with stubble that glinted in the dusky light. He wore a flimsy undershirt that outlined the sleek muscles of his chest and broad shoulders, as well as the bulky bandages that telegraphed the locations of his worst injuries. His feet—long and elegant—were bare beneath loose sleep pants.

"You didn't wake me."

That was all he said, and Macey couldn't help but try to meet his eyes in the dark, hoping for something…some sort of connection, recognition, *something* that told her…

Well, what? That she hadn't done a terrible thing to the man? That somehow Wayren's golden disk hadn't worked?

That he still loved her?

She swallowed hard and gestured with the package of crackers. "I hope you don't mind. I was hungry."

"Not at all."

"Well, then…good night." When he didn't immediately shift for her to pass by, she swallowed hard and said, "Pardon me," and went to move past him.

"No," he said, closing strong fingers around her wrist, halting her abruptly in the narrow space, right next to him. He was close… *so* close…so warm, and delicious smelling, and familiar. Her heart galloped like a runaway horse, her belly filled with fluttery wings.

"I can't do that, Macey," he said in a low voice that had gone cold and hard. "I can't pardon you. I can't *forgive* you."

Macey jolted, her belly dropping to her knees, and looked up at him. Rage and accusation blazed in eyes illuminated by a slice of streetlight, and his expression was harsh and set.

He knew her.

He knew.

Oh God… She felt light-headed and nauseated.

Oh, Grady.

Macey tried to swallow, tried to speak, but he released her roughly, turning away to present her with broad, rigid shoulders as he faced the window.

Devastated, she stepped closer, reaching to touch him. Her hand settled lightly on the top of his shoulder. He stiffened sharply, and she sensed the faintest tremor beneath her fingers, felt the heat and firmness of his skin…and discovered that rage and pain could, in fact, vibrate from a person's body.

"I'm here—*you're* here—because Max asked me," he said, still in that cold, awful tone, his body rigid as steel. "That's the *only* reason."

Macey recoiled, her hand falling away to land at her side. Her gut churned more violently.

"Never fear—when he no longer has need of me," Grady continued, "it'll be just as you intended. As if you never knew me."

"Grady…" she whispered, holding on to the edge of the counter as her knees wavered.

"Good night, Macey."

But she knew he really meant *Goodbye*.

Throat burning, eyes stinging with hot, horrible tears, she spun and fairly ran back up the stairs.

She'd made her bed, and now she must lie in it.

Twenty-Two

Wherein the Expectations of Friendship are Enumerated

SAVINA WAS IN POSSESSION of a secret that she knew would cause no small upheaval to certain people. She didn't know when it would be revealed, or how, or even if it would, and so she could do nothing but sit on it like a hen waiting for an egg to hatch.

Which, in light of the fact that Rekk's Pyramid was now in the hands of the undead, was a much more tenable eventuality to wait upon—rather than whatever terror and evil the vampires would visit upon Chicago.

When Savina awoke, Macey was still sleeping soundly next to her. Sunlight streamed into the room and she checked the clock—nearly eleven. Late for Savina to rise as well, but that was good—the poor girl had gotten some much-needed rest. Along with her Venator genes and the treatments Max had given her, Macey would likely be nearly as good as new by tomorrow.

Savina slid out of bed carefully so as not to wake her bedmate, and even remembered to drag on a robe over her flimsy nightgown before leaving the bedroom. When she came out into the hall, she nearly ran into Max—who was coming from the bathroom.

Freshly showered, but unshaven.

Wrapped only in a towel.

She was still put out with him, still keeping her distance— besides all of the other issues between them, how could he even imagine for *one minute* that she and Grady had been…well, whatever he'd thought?

But seeing him there in the short, narrow hallway, all clean and wet and muscular and smelling yummy and fresh…with that air of triumph and arrogance, and yet a charming undercurrent of diffidence…

Even wrapped in a towel and with weariness in his eyes and dark circles under them, scars and bites scattered on his shoulders and arms, he looked ready to take on the world. One-handed.

But hell—that was part of why she'd fallen in love with the idiot, wasn't it? *What* he did, *how* he did it—and the fact that he was so blasted charming and good-looking while doing it.

"Good morning," he rumbled, his dark eyes sweeping over her with interest.

All the feminine parts of her body sprang to attention, warm and quivering with delight. Drat it.

"I trust you slept well," he added…with a definite undercurrent of *You'd have slept better with me.*

Damn right, but she wasn't about to admit it.

It was all she could do to keep from throwing herself at him right then and feasting on that warm, sleek, damp skin, and having his strong arms around her, and feel his lips everywhere…

"Eventually, I did," she replied with a warm smile, her voice still rough with slumber. "After your daughter and I had a thorough chat."

His arrogance slipped a little at that. "Ah."

But he recovered quickly and reached for her with a certain look in his eyes. "I couldn't sleep last night myself," he said, moving closer. "Spent a lot of time walking the streets. Didn't get back till after dawn."

She inhaled a breath of Max mingled with the soap he'd just used, and her knees weakened as he reached for her. "Macey and I talked quite late," she said, a little more breathlessly than she would have liked. "About all sorts of things."

But her taunt didn't work this time, for he'd moved close enough that she could feel the warmth from his body, and now he was pulling her closer so that she bumped against his damp chest.

"Max," she said, evading him as he bent to cover her mouth with hers. "Your daughter is sleeping *right there*."

He eased back, glancing toward the bedroom door. "Did I tell you what I walked in on *her* doing?" he muttered, his fingers lingering on her shoulder, touching the ends of her hair. "With that devil Woodmore?"

Savina pushed him back, her hands landing on that broad, warm, taut chest…and stayed there. *Weak woman*, she told herself, then made her palms drop away. "No, you didn't. But that doesn't mean I want her to see *me* in a—in a compromising position."

"But *I* want to see you in a compromising position," he murmured, swooping down again.

"*Max*," she said, but it was more like a moan than a protest. He'd found that tender spot on the side of her neck, just above her shoulder…and when he kissed her there, with his soft, hot mouth, all sorts of hot sensations trammeled through her body. Her knees were threatening to give out. "Not here," she managed to say.

"No problem," he said, and the next thing Savina knew, they were in Grady's tiny, steamy bathroom and the tile wall was against her spine. Condensation seeped through the back of her robe as Max kissed the hell out of her—and she kissed him back, sliding her hands down over the solid muscles of his shoulders and chest.

He'd released his grip on the towel at some point, and now she could feel every bit of him pressed up against her: hard, sleek, and damp.

He muttered something low and intense, and yanked the robe from her shoulders, slid the straps of her nightgown down, and uncovered her breasts. Savina had one foot propped up against the side of the bathtub to keep her from sliding down the damp wall as he bent to kiss one of her nipples.

His mouth felt so good…sensual and warm, his tongue delicate as he slid it around, tasting her sleepy skin, his lips tight and strong as he sucked and licked while she tunneled her fingers into his damp hair, holding on for dear life.

"Savina," he whispered, lifting away then burying his face in her neck as he backed her fully against the wall, pushing his hips up against hers, "I'm going to tear this if you don't get rid of it."

She gave a short laugh, and pushed his hands away from the delicate lace of her shift. "Better not," she said. "It's the only one I have with me."

"You can sleep without it," he said, his hands sliding up her torso then cupping her breasts as she shimmied out of the nightgown. It had barely joined her robe on the floor, tangling around their feet in a pool, when Max lifted her up.

She wrapped her legs around his waist as he found her with his fingers, all wet and swollen and hot. *Oh, yes,* she thought as her head tipped back against the wall as he gave a soft sigh of his own. *Yes.*

Then he shifted, and her eyes flew open as he drove up inside her. They both groaned with pleasure—it had been too long—and Savina tightened her legs around his waist, burying her face in his hair, gripping his shoulders as he moved with powerful strokes.

As she came, Savina bit her lip, smothering a cry that would surely alert the household otherwise. She arched against him, eagerly taking the full force of his last thrust as he groaned his release.

She rested there, head back against the wall, panting and damp, smiling and sated. He still held her up against the slippery tile with an arm around her waist. Max was breathing heavily too, and he helped ease her legs from around his waist, settling her back onto the floor.

"Well, then," she breathed, suddenly feeling *really* good. Her hand slipped down the front of him, traveling over solid pecs and a ridged belly, then slipped around to pat his arse. "I'm definitely awake now."

He grinned down at her, terribly pleased with himself, and brushed the hair from her eyes. "And I find I'm not as weary as I thought I was."

Then he stepped back, his expression changing from hubristic to something closed and wary. "You and Macey talked last night."

Savina picked up her nightgown and slithered back into it. "We did."

"Did she…did she say anything about me?"

Her heart gave a pang at the mix of emotion in his face. "Not very much, to be honest."

"She hates me, doesn't she? I'm gone for thirteen years, then the minute I show up, I stake her." He looked miserable. No wonder he hadn't been able to sleep last night.

But Savina resisted the urge to smooth away all of his pain and uncertainty. Only Max could do that, with the help of Macey— and surely that would happen in its own time.

After all, Savina herself had mixed emotions about her relationship with him. She was besotted with the man, and he loved *and* respected her…even if he was an idiot sometimes. He was simply afraid.

The big, bad, fierce *Summas* Gardella was afraid of feeling too much…for he knew how easily it could be taken away. He knew how it could be used against him as well—and that, Savina had to admit, was a compelling reason for his reluctance to become attached or committed to anyone.

His decision to see Macey—though it had actually been forced upon him when he realized Nicholas Iscariot had Rasputin's amulet—was a step in the right direction.

"You have to give Macey time," Savina replied, touching his face. "After all, she thought you were *dead* for thirteen years. What do you expect—for her to run up to you and call you Daddy while she hugs you and cries with joy?"

He shook his head. "Of course not. But…she won't even— She calls me Max. And she won't even talk to me. All she does is give me angry looks."

"Give her time. I did warn you, didn't I, that you needed to take things slow and expect some anger and coldness? What happened the first time you saw her?"

He looked away. Pursed his lips. Sighed. "I…uh…walked in on her with—kissing Woodmore."

Savina couldn't control a burst of laughter. "And you're surprised she wasn't happy to see you? Max…" She shook her head. "And I'm sure you took it well, didn't you—walking in on them. I'm sure you were polite and warm and expressed your delight at seeing your daughter for the first time since she was eight."

"Well, Christ, Woodmore looked like he was… Well, hell. She's my *daughter*." Max ground his teeth. "Right. Give it time. I just hope we both live through these next few days."

The warrior was back, the lover had gone…but Savina was used to that, and she didn't mind. He wouldn't be who he was if he didn't have that dedication to his life's work.

She stood on tiptoes and gave him a kiss. "How about I get a shower now."

He kissed her back, but didn't move. His expression had changed again. He seemed ready to speak, but wasn't able to.

"Max?"

All at once, his face seemed to crumble. He snatched her up, gathering her into a suffocating embrace. "Oh God, Savina," he whispered against her hair. "Don't…ever…leave me."

Her eyes flew open wide with utter shock, her lashes brushing against his neck. Had she heard him correctly? She tried to pull away, but he was holding her too tightly. And he was *trembling* a little.

"Max," she said, realizing that *he'd* realized he needed something from her…something he was articulating for the first time. Something that terrified him. Something that turned her insides upside down with tentative joy and happiness.

"I've never done the leaving," she said. *It's been you who couldn't stay.*

But she didn't need to speak that part.

She eased back enough to look up at him, taking his beloved face in her hands. "I would never leave you, Max Denton. You know that. You'd be a mess without me."

He nodded, a flicker of humor gracing his face. Then his eyes turned sober and wary, and as he looked down at her, they softened. "Marry me, Savina."

She stilled, tamped down the rush of surprise and delight and became realistic. "I—I don't know, Max…look at where we are—"

"Yes, we're in a bathroom—not exactly the best place for a proposal, I know, but—"

"No, I mean…where we *are*. You're feeling vulnerable because of Macey, and—"

"And because of the way you were looking at Woodmore," he said in a steely voice.

"Woodmore?" she scoffed. "Don't be silly. He's as beautiful as a dark angel, but he's not for me. Though I *would* like to photograph him—anyway, besides, that is *not* a good reason to get married. Because you think I was looking at Woodmore. Hell, Max, I look at other men all the time, but it doesn't mean—"

"Christ. You do?" He looked utterly flummoxed. "When?"

Savina laughed. What a lunatic. The man had such an ego he thought he was the only creature she noticed. So she wasn't about to tell him he was the only man she'd ever looked at twice.

"Max, we can talk about this later. We're in a bathroom. I have an appointment at two. And you've got to go off and save the world." Her smile faltered a little. Yes, it would always be that way—him going off to save the world, nearly dying at least once a week.

"Right. All right. But…this isn't an impetuous thing, Savina. I've been thinking about it for a while. And last night…well, I had a lot to mull over. And I realized I'm a terrible father, and a cowardly lover, and…" He shrugged. "Aren't you going to argue with me?" he asked hopefully.

"Max." She laughed again, shaking her head. "You've *been* a terrible father—I've told you that before. But you're trying to fix that. And as far as a lover…well, I'm smiling, aren't I?" She pecked him on the cheek, shoved his towel back at him, and said, "I love you, Max," then flung open the bathroom door and shoved him out—right into the path of Macey.

Oh dear. That was awkward.

Savina grinned and closed the bathroom door before he could bolt back inside.

Let him handle it. That would be a nice father-daughter interlude.

She chuckled and turned on the shower.

Max felt his face go hot as his daughter's eyes flashed from the closed bathroom door to him, then skittered away from his unclothed torso.

Thanks a lot, Savina.

"Good morning," he said, managing somehow to recover from the fact that he'd just: one, had his marriage proposal shot down; two, exited from a lavatory where it was obvious he'd just been in there, naked, with a woman; three, was clutching a towel to the front of him.

In front of his daughter.

Thanks again, Savina.

Macey just looked at him. Then, her face blossoming red, she spun and marched back to the bedroom she was sharing with Savina—which was the same room *he'd* been sharing with Savina.

Usurped by his own daughter. Bloody hell.

More than an hour later, however, Max had forgotten—or at least was pretending to have forgotten—that awkward moment as he and the others, including Woodmore, were gathered around Grady's kitchen table.

"I have to go into the *Trib's* office this morning," Grady said. He didn't look all that hale and hearty and he had circles under his eyes, but he wasn't moving nearly as slowly as he had been yesterday. He glanced at the clock and frowned. "Well, hell. It's well past morning, so I have to get there as soon as possible. I have an exclusive to write, after all." He smiled broadly.

"There's not much to be done at the moment," Max said grimly. "I want to go back to The Silver Chalice and see if we can find anything that might help. Macey, do you have any idea where this Flora might be hiding out?"

"I would guess the same place Iscariot was, but we weren't able to find his hideout." She looked disgusted with the situation. Or maybe she was just remembering seeing her father in the buff.

Max forced himself to ignore that incident. "To get to the school yesterday without being exposed to sunlight, they had to be transported under some sort of cover. I suspect the white truck that was parked near the servants' entrance was the vehicle. I'm going to check that as well and try to determine where it came from. Maybe we can trace them that way."

"I'll go to the Chalice," Woodmore said. "See if I can find anything."

"Where is the crooked tongue knife?" Max asked suddenly. "If we find Flora, we'll need it when we get in. And do we know what to do with it when we get Rekk's Pyramid?"

"I'll look at Temple's notes while I'm there," Woodmore replied. "See if she had more information. If not, maybe Wayren will help." There seemed to be less of a combative nature beneath his words today. Perhaps the thought of going to Siberia after Cezar Moldavi had cooled his ire. "And I have the knife with me. I'll keep it on my person at all times."

Max nodded. "Brilliant." He noticed Woodmore's face relaxed a bit at that show of trust and support, and he was glad for it. The man was an asset. He just needed to keep his hands off Macey.

That brought his attention to Grady, and then casually over to Macey.

Was Woodmore right? Was Macey in love with the Irish bloke? If so, Max sure as hell couldn't tell.

And why on earth was he so interested in who was in love with or sleeping with whom all of a sudden? They had work to do.

He looked at his daughter. If possible, she appeared even more strained and exhausted than she had yesterday. As if she hadn't slept a bit last night.

"Macey, I know you're going to argue with me, but I would appreciate it if you would stay here just for a while today. Let yourself heal, *and*"—he rushed on before she could speak her outrage—"be here in the event one of us learns something and needs assistance. Like a home base—there's a telephone in case we need to use it and someone should be here to answer it. Only for a few hours, while Savina is gone."

"Where is Savina going?" Macey asked, mutiny blazing in her eyes. Max had a feeling he was going to regret this, but as a father and as the *summas*—but mostly the former—he really wanted her to take a little more time to rest and heal before whatever terrible challenge they were going to face next.

For he knew it would happen, and he greatly feared how ugly it would be.

"I have a late lunch meeting with the mayor," Savina replied, entering the room at that moment. "In fact, I'm off right now. We're meeting at two, and it's after one."

"A meeting with Dever? Why?" Macey asked, still a little belligerent but curious nonetheless.

Savina, who looked good enough to eat in a pink suit that made her arse look spectacular and a pair of shoes that showed off her gams, was charmingly bashful. "I'm being considered for the honor of receiving a key to the city. It's just an initial meeting—I suppose to see whether I qualify."

"Good luck," Max told her, his eyes lingering. Damn…that interlude in the lavatory had been something.

She glanced at him, and he swore he saw her cheeks flush slightly more pink. "I can't imagine I'll be more than two or three hours, at the most. It's only lunch."

Macey reluctantly agreed to stay at Grady's for the time being, though Max was most definitely the recipient of an icy glare.

Just another to add to the list.

✝

As she rode in a taxi to her meeting, Savina quivered a little at the memory of the steamy—literally—interlude in the bathroom that morning.

Then she exhaled a long sigh when she thought about Max asking her to marry him. She was a modern woman, and marriage wasn't a requirement for her. She'd never really thought about it with Max. She figured he'd already had one marriage, and he wasn't about to try it again.

But he'd surprised her this morning, and she'd had plenty of time to think about it while getting ready for her luncheon. Maybe marriage was the only way *he* could prove his commitment to her—for his own sake. Maybe it was his way of letting her know that he really never would leave her again.

If that was the case, she'd happily agree.

She smiled, suddenly flushed with excitement as she climbed out of the cab. She was going to get married!

Savina put all thoughts of Max and their upcoming nuptials (she'd insist they marry somewhere in Rome) out of her mind as she walked into La Petite Café, a small restaurant inside Marshall Field's department store. She'd been surprised and delighted when a messenger from Mayor Dever's office had found her yesterday morning at the Chicago Library while she was supervising the breakdown of her part of the photography exhibit.

She'd dressed smartly in a pencil-slim skirt and matching jacket of pale pink, a white blouse with a large silk flower pinned at the throat, and a splendid cream and navy hat she'd bought in Paris. Her gloves were pristine and white, and her kitten-heeled shoes had been polished for the occasion and gleamed navy. Max had certainly seemed to approve, if the look in his eyes was any indication.

Savina walked into the café, which was just as elegant as the Sainte Antoine in Paris—with its cloth-covered tables, single red roses in black bud vases, and fabric-swathed chairs. A print by Alphonse Mucha hung on the wall, along with other Art Deco decor echoed in vases, trim, and furnishings.

A woman at a table near the corner gave a little wave, and Savina recognized her from the photography exhibit Saturday night. That must be Miss McGillicut, who'd sent the message. Savina had seen the woman with Mayor Dever at the show, and any last bit of nervousness that she'd somehow been mistaken or fooled about the honor of being gifted with the key to the city faded.

Savina made her way across the room and greeted the woman as she approached the table. "And here I thought I'd be early," she said with a smile, then offered her gloved hand to shake.

"I've only just arrived myself," replied Miss McGillicut. "Please, sit here—it's such a lovely view to watch the street."

Savina took the seat next to her hostess and removed her gloves, setting them on the table next to her pocketbook. "I must say, I was quite surprised to receive your message yesterday."

The woman smiled. "I was very happy that my messenger found you at the library. Mayor Dever wasn't aware of where you were staying while in Chicago, but I told him I was certain you'd be present while they were packing up your lovely photographs. Of course you wouldn't take the chance some damage might be done to them."

"Most certainly not. And will the mayor be joining us?" Savina asked, glancing toward the door. She'd *thought* the message indicated Dever would be present, but maybe she'd misunderstood. "Or is it to be just the two of us gals?" she added, not wanting to sound as if Miss McGillicut wasn't worth her time.

"The mayor wanted me to get to know you a bit first. I do hope you don't mind." She flashed a broad smile and tucked her bright red hair behind an ear.

"Of course not," Savina said, then glanced around the café. "What a lovely place. It reminds me of a little slice of Paris, right here in the middle of America."

"It is, isn't it? I am particularly fond of that print over there— do you see it?" Miss McGillicut pointed to the Mucha lithograph Savina had noticed. "Do you know what the name of it is?"

"Why, no, I don't," Savina replied as a waitress brought over a tray with coffee set up for two and began to pour their drinks.

"It's called *Friendship*. What a lovely thing, a friendship. Do you have any close friends, Miss Ellison?"

Savina was momentarily startled at the reminder that her companion and the mayor both knew her by her professional name. Would the key to the city be engraved with her real name, or her professional name? Would she have a choice?

"Do you mean female friends? Girl friends? I'm afraid in my line of work, I don't have much of a chance to…cultivate many of them. I…er…travel quite a lot," Savina replied as she added two lumps of sugar to her coffee.

But she hoped, in the deepest part of her heart, that perhaps someday she and Macey might be friends. It would be refreshing and freeing to have a close friend—who wasn't her lover—who understood what sort of life she and Max lived.

It would be so fun to have a female friend with whom she could talk about things like where to hide a stake on her person, or how to use a garter belt to secret vials of holy water, whether silver cross earrings would be effective at repelling vampires…or even to simply talk about what an idiot her lover could be. Even though the man in question would be Macey's father.

And at the moment, she suspected Macey *might* just agree with her assessment. She smiled to herself as she stirred the sugar, then looked up to find Miss McGillicut watching her closely.

"And you?" Savina asked, quickly remembering the thread of the conversation—though how it had anything to do with getting the key to the city, she didn't know. Unless the mayor was just trying to find out what sort of person she was before he made a decision, and had sent his assistant to evaluate her. "Do you have many close female friends? I should think so, living in a city like Chicago. You probably go to the cabarets and jazz clubs and dance all the time, don't you?"

To her surprise, Miss McGillicut's expression hardened. "I used to have a very close friend. And then she…changed. She became a different person, and no longer had time for me. She made different friends and began to do different things. She had a good job, and I couldn't even find one that wasn't working as a seamstress in a sweat shop."

Savina didn't know what to say. "I'm so very sorry. It's difficult to lose a friend."

"Especially since we'd been friends since we were young girls. We even moved to the city within months of each other. And then she just…left me. Left me behind." Miss McGillicut shifted, digging in her pocketbook.

"That must have been very upsetting for you," Savina replied.

"Very. But now, I'm in a much better position than she is. Look at me now," Miss McGillicut said, a hard smile on her face. "She has no idea what she is missing."

"I see." Savina felt wildly uncomfortable with the turn of conversation. Surely the mayor hadn't intended for this assessment meeting to deteriorate into a personal diatribe. "So, tell me about your work in the mayor's office."

"My work in the— Yes, right," her companion replied. "My work is quite rewarding. Very rewarding. My dear, *dear* friend should be envious of me. She should even be frightened of me, really. I hold so much more power now."

By now, Savina was acutely uncomfortable. "Right, then," she said, seeking a way to permanently change the topic—or, better yet, to escape the situation—without also losing her chance with the mayor.

"She'll regret what she's done to me. She'll realize she should have—"

"Uhm, Miss McGillicut, I really appreciate your time. But I'm afraid I'm going to have to cut our meeting short." She gathered up her gloves and began to pull them on. Even a key to the city wasn't worth this sort of awkwardness.

The woman next to her was smiling again, and she shifted closer to Savina. Something hard pressed into her side, and Savina looked down to find the nose of a small derringer making an ominous dent in the fabric of her skirt.

"Oh, no, that would never do. We have much, much more to talk about, Sabrina. I hope you don't mind if I call you Sabrina. And please…you must call me Flora."

Twenty-Three
A Cryptic Call

MACEY WOULD NEVER ADMIT IT, even if someone held a gun to her head, but having a few hours alone to rest and relax was exactly what she needed.

Especially since she hadn't slept very well last night, after the great, awful revelation in the kitchen.

Grady knew her.

And he knew what she'd done—or tried to do.

How he'd hid the fury and loathing he clearly felt was a mystery—though she did remember that flash of irritation she'd noticed when they'd first seen each other at the photography exhibit. He'd disguised it well after that, but it had been there at first. She just hadn't known what it was.

The thought made Macey feel even more disconsolate. He hated her.

But perhaps not as much as she hated herself.

Now, with everyone gone and herself alone at Grady's place, she found it spectacularly painful to sit on the sofa and smell his scent on the pillow there, to see the photos strewn over his fireplace mantel and know she'd likely never see Linwood again, to see the selection of books about vampires—which they'd discussed the first night they'd met. There was no chance of getting past this.

Remembering the cold rage in his face made her stomach churn. *You've emasculated him. Castrated him.*

It must be just as hellish for him to have her here as for her to be here. Yet here he was—putting himself in danger to help the Venators. To help her father.

But the thing that stuck in her mind, the fact she couldn't keep from gnawing over, was how could he be the dauntless one? What made him dauntless? What made him special, and who was his "half"?

Max? Herself?

Oh, wouldn't that be a bitter realization, a terrible irony, if Macey had destroyed their love—only to discover that it had been written that they were to be partners.

She closed her eyes and tipped her head back against the arm of the sofa. Tears leaked from the corners of her eyes as she considered the selfish, foolish choices she'd made.

"But I was doing it for *him*," she said aloud. "I didn't want the same thing that happened to my mother to happen to Grady!"

Or the same thing that happened to my father to happen to me.

And yet it already had.

Macey lay there, stretched out on the sofa, miserable and grieving and furious with herself and the choices she'd made.

I can make decisions for no one but myself.

But it was too late now.

Grady—the man she'd known and loved—was gone. It was over.

And sometime in the next few days, she had to find and kill her best friend.

Macey must have slept, for the telephone woke her. She opened her eyes, and the first thing she noticed in the darkening room was the clock on the mantel.

It was after seven o'clock.

She sat up quickly and looked around. Savina had said she'd be back in two or three hours, and she'd left just after one. The lunch had either gone far better than expected, or she'd ended up shopping at Marshall Field's.

And where were Chas and Max? Neither had called all day?

Macey climbed off the sofa and stumbled to the telephone, which was still ringing shrilly. Maybe it was Savina, explaining why she was late. Or some news from Chas or Max.

"Hello?" she said.

"Grady?" said a strained female voice.

"No, it's not—"

"Hi, Grady, it's Sabrina Ellison." The voice spoke over Macey's correction, loudly and rapidly.

"He's not here—" Macey stopped. *Sabrina Ellison?* It was definitely Savina's voice, Grady knew her real name…what was going on?

"Listen, I'm in a bit of a pickle, and I know you're just the one to help me out." The tension in Savina's voice vibrated over the telephone, and Macey went very still.

"What can I do?" she asked, her heart beating hard.

"I need you to come…come and help me." Her voice, though tense, was steady. She rattled off an address that had Macey fumbling for a pencil and paper to write it down. Fortunately, newshawk Grady had plenty of both next to the phone. "I… It's a little embarrassing what happened, but I ran into an old friend of—of someone named Macey—"

She stopped suddenly and there was a struggling sound and muffled voices from the other end. When Savina spoke again, her voice was a little unsteady—and angry. Underneath, Macey heard anger.

"Just come. Come alone. You must come alone, or… I need your help…I only have until half past eight before— Please help me—"

The phone line was cut off before the last word was out of Savina's mouth. Macey stared at the silent instrument for a second before dropping it back onto its receiver.

That left her hardly more than an hour.

She swung into action, dashing upstairs to change and to equip herself with supplies and weapons.

She was racing down the stairs when the front door opened—good, reinforcements—but when she got to the bottom, her heart sank when she nearly ran into Grady.

"What is it? What's happened?" he demanded.

"I have to go," she said, rushing into the living room for her pocketbook. "It's Savina. She's in trouble. I've got to get there by half past eight."

"What's happened?" He dumped his satchel on the ground and strode over to block her way out of the living room. "You aren't going to be going off without telling me—or anyone else—what's going on. Unless Max and Woodmore already know?" He sounded really annoyed, and very determined.

Macey knew she could easily get past Grady—but that would entail putting her hands on him…and that might not be a good idea. Yet he was right. Of course she couldn't go off without telling anyone what was happening or where she was going—and of course she had been planning to write a note.

She quickly told him about the phone call.

"Savina was calling for *me*?" he said, beginning to add a variety of objects—some innocent-looking, some clearly dangerous—in various place on his person. "Why would she be calling for me in particular?"

"I don't know. But she knew she wasn't talking to you—that was clear. I *think* she was supposed to be giving you a message, but the person with her didn't know someone else answered the phone. Which means the message wasn't really specifically for you. It was for—"

"I'm going," he said flatly. "So we might as well be making a plan together and take advantage of the fact that we know more than the person on the other end of the phone line."

Macey hesitated, but then she nodded. She had to put her personal feelings aside—and anyway, he was right. He'd already proven how "dauntless" he was.

"Savina said to come alone," Macey warned.

Grady began to pack a large duffel bag. "There are ways around that, lass. Where did you say this place was?"

She tried to ignore the little offbeat thump of her heart when he called her "lass," and told him the address. He called everyone "lass." Even Savina.

"I know the place." He smiled. It was a grim one, steely and yet satisfied. "Just give me a minute while I check something." He went over to the massive wall map of Chicago that hung on the wall and stared at it for a few minutes, tracing streets with his fingers, while Macey wrote a note to Max and Chas.

When he was finished, Grady came over and scrawled a few sentences at the bottom of her note—"Telling them exactly where to find us"—and then she did something she never thought she'd do again: she drove off with Grady in his car.

"This isn't the address she gave," Macey said when Grady parked.

In fact, the place they'd stopped was nowhere near the address Savina had given them. They were at a train yard that was long abandoned. Rusted-out locomotives and their cars sat unused on overgrown railways. A few decrepit buildings looked just as worse for wear. As Macey looked around, she saw two separate figures— tramps?—scuttling into the shadows.

Her panic was growing. It was past seven thirty, and they weren't anywhere near the place. She had to have time to get in, figure out what was going on…who even knew whether Flora would keep to the timeframe Savina had given. They didn't have time to spare.

"I know. But they'll be watching the place, won't they now? They'll be making sure I come alone. We need to get you secretly inside before I make an appearance."

"Right."

That was the plan they'd agreed upon—well, that he'd insisted upon, and she hadn't been able to argue him out of because it made sense. Grady would go in as if he'd received the message. But in the meantime, Macey would sneak in a different way and then… Well, they'd go from there. She'd find a way to take care of Flora once she saw what the woman had planned.

"But we're more than six blocks away, and on the other side of the street." She looked around unhappily.

Grady grinned as he yanked on the parking brake, and Macey's heart did that sweet little *ka-thump*. For that instant, she saw the old Grady—the one who looked at her with laughing eyes. The one who knew her and loved her.

Then the memory was gone—for the grin wasn't directed at her. It was for the adventure about to come.

"When you're wanting to get into a building unnoticed," he said coolly, "you have to look at it very differently than your average bloke. Even the architects who design the buildings… they don't look at it the same way."

"All right." She climbed out of the car and met him on the other side. "So…we're approaching on foot, and going to sneak in somehow through a rear window?"

"No." He pointed to an old train tunnel as he slung a heavy bag over his shoulder. "We go in there."

"Ah." She was beginning to see. "So we follow that underground…to where? There aren't any train lines that run toward Delancey Street."

He was already walking across the street toward the building, his long legs leaving her behind. "You're right about that. But there's an underground creek that cuts across the block next to it. You see, the first rule of housebreaking is—you're not using doors or windows. That's for bloody pansies. And a sure way to find yourself apprehended."

His brogue had suddenly appeared, and he wore a crafty, intense expression Macey had never seen before. It was almost as if he'd become a different person, or taken on a different personality.

"Housebreaking? So you have some experience with that, do you?" she asked, intrigued in spite of herself as she followed him into the musty old building.

"Grew up making m'way into any number of fancy buildings that preferred to keep out the likes o'me."

He had a flashlight and turned it on to illuminate their way, and she saw a variety of creatures—from rats to spiders to a man dressed in ragged clothes—slinking into the darkness.

To her surprise, Grady stopped and spoke to the man in ragged clothing. She saw their hands meet briefly as if Grady had handed him something, and she tried hard not to chafe at the delay.

"Savina is in danger," she reminded him. "We don't have any time to waste."

"I'm not about wasting time," he told her, continuing on his way down a ramp that led below the ground. "He's doing me a favor. And we've got more than fifty-five minutes. Plenty of time."

Macey couldn't argue with that, and she followed him along at a good clip. She had no difficulty keeping up with him, for she was wearing low-heeled shoes, dark trousers, and a dark sweater. Tellingly, he didn't wait for her or even offer to help her along by taking her arm. He didn't speak unnecessarily, or even look at her other than impersonally when he had something to say.

True to his word, they followed the train tunnel only a few yards in before it became shorter and narrower.

"I never would have known this existed," she said when he led her deeper into the darkness where the passage became a more natural tunnel, with dirt ceiling and walls instead of brick.

"I wasn't completely certain until now," he admitted, ducking a little. The contents in the bag over his shoulder made soft clinking and clanging noises as he shifted. "But the signs were there. You ever see a place on the street that always stays misty for longer than the areas around it, especially when there's been no rain? It's because there's a creek running beneath it. If you're knowing where the creeks and sewers are under a city, you're already halfway into any building you want to be into."

Fascinating. Macey filed that bit of information away into the back of her mind. Venators tended to rely on brute strength, speed, and exemplary fighting skills—not to mention mundane things such as doors and windows—to make their way into a place with undead.

They made their way along the creek quickly and efficiently, with both of them having to duck often, as well as brush away the occasional dangling root. Unlike sewers, or even underground railway tunnels, this passage smelled pleasant—like moist earth and vegetation. There were occasional twists and turns of the creek, and therefore of their route, due to man-made obstructions like the brick walls of random building foundations.

It wasn't long before Grady paused, checked his compass (which had appeared from the bag over his shoulder), and grunted something that sounded like "Here."

He'd stopped at a grimy, moss-covered wall and slung the bag from his back. Moments later, he'd withdrawn what looked like *a stick of dynamite.*

"Is that what I think it is?" Macey asked.

"If you're thinking it's an explosive, you'd be correct. Now step back around that corner if you want to keep those pretty legs of yours attached to the rest of you." The way he spoke wasn't a compliment; it was grim and flat and cold. Still underscored with loathing and rage.

She did as he told her, and after a minute or two, he rushed back to join her, hustling her even further backward through the tunnel. She heard him counting under his breath, and at *ten!*, he pushed her up against the wall and huddled around her. Macey didn't have time to appreciate or regret the familiar, painful feel of Grady's solid body around hers, for—

Boom!

The explosion wasn't as loud as she'd feared, but it sent a cloud of dust rolling through the tunnel.

"Let's go." He released her and darted back through, holding a sleeve over his nose and mouth.

Macey followed and discovered he had indeed blown a hole into the brick wall.

"So this is the building they're in?" she asked. "You don't think they might have heard the explosion and been warned?"

He shook his head pityingly in the dim light. "Two doors down, we are. And who's going to think twice about a muffled boom in Chicago? There's gunfire and cars backfiring all the time."

"So now what?" Macey was beginning to get nervous about the amount of time that had passed, but when she checked her timepiece, she saw it had been less than an hour since they left Grady's house.

"This is the easy part."

He gestured to the hole and shined the flashlight on it. She climbed through quickly, and Grady followed then paused to check his compass while Macey looked at her timepiece.

Thirty minutes. Her heart began to beat faster. She was just about to nag him again when Grady muttered, "Brilliant," then started off on a route only he knew.

She followed—up a set of iron stairs, into what appeared to be the back room of a store. Macey froze when she heard voices coming from nearby—as in, from the *front* of the store. But Grady didn't pause, and they went on. She wondered how he knew where he was going.

I know the building, he'd said. All right, she trusted him.

At last, he stopped at a wall in the next building over, presumably attached to the one where Flora was keeping Savina. "Here we are." He began to knock lightly on the wall, pressing his ear to it as if listening.

"Normally, I'd be coming in from the ceiling in a case like this," he commented, "but for the likes of you, we'll do it this way."

Macey wanted to bristle at his implication, but she kept quiet. So far, he knew what he was doing, and she was only concerned about getting to Savina in time.

She was *not* thinking about the fact that Flora had made Savina call for Grady. Why would she do that? Was it just chance? Had Savina just phoned Grady's house knowing one of them would answer? Or had Flora forced her to do so?

"Hold this there." Grady shoved the flashlight at her, and she saw it was directed at the wall and that he'd drawn a rectangle on it flush to the ground. "There's your entrance to the building. I'll get you through, and see you on the other side, then."

While she held the flashlight, he used a saw to cut through the wall. Though she offered to help, he declined and kept at it. "Got a rhythm going."

It was incredibly, surprisingly easy to create a new passage from one building to another. He was right—most people didn't think about going through walls or ceilings or even floors to break into buildings.

Yet it was startlingly simple. And when he carefully kicked through the pieces he'd cut, Macey looked into a boiler room. By this time, the back of her neck was frigid and she knew there were plenty of undead in the vicinity.

"Time?" Grady asked, swiping an arm over his perspiring forehead. A hank of dark hair, now frosted white from the drywall dust, fell back into his eyes.

"Eight *twenty*." Macey's heart surged.

But he nodded. "Good. Took far less time than I thought." Then he handed her the flashlight. "I'm off, then. You're on your own."

And before she could say another word—wish him well, say goodbye—he turned and loped back the way they'd come, leaving his bag of tools on the ground and her heart in pieces.

Not a goodbye. Not a good luck. Not even a softened glance.

So this is what it feels like to have destroyed a man.

Blinking back tears, Macey checked her pockets, pulled out a stake, and went to battle.

Twenty-Four

Of Memories, Expectations, and Blame

WHEN MAX RETURNED to Grady's house with Woodmore and found it empty and still, at first he didn't think much of it.

Yes, it was far later than he'd imagined returning—and after two dead ends of tracing the white truck at the Beedle school, between comparing notes with Woodmore at the pub. They'd taken their time, both of them implicitly agreeing that it wouldn't hurt for Macey to rest as much as possible.

Now it was closing in on eight o'clock, and the house was silent. Surely Savina had returned, and she and Macey were likely sitting upstairs and gossiping—although that thought made his hair stand on end.

But the house was too quiet.

"Denton." Woodmore was standing by the telephone, staring at a piece of paper. The tone of his voice had Max going on full alert.

"What is it?"

"A note from Macey—and Grady." He thrust the paper at Max, and immediately began to check his pockets for weapons.

Max's heart plummeted to his knees when he read the letter. Terror exploded through him as the realization penetrated.

Savina.

No. Not again.

Not again.

He read the letter a second time and managed to get past the part about "Flora has Savina" and actually comprehend the words. It took him a little longer to decipher Grady's scrawl at the bottom, which directed them to an old train yard in order to get access to the building where Flora was.

After that, he pushed every bit of emotion out of his thoughts and turned his brain to cold and lethal.

Things would end differently this time.

Now that Macey was inside, she realized the place she and Grady had broken into was nothing more than a three-story building that had burned at some point. At least two sections were attached, like row houses—which explained the wall through which Grady had cut—and that gave her a blueprint of the layout of the building where Savina was, for the row houses had identical floor plans.

The part in which Flora was keeping her hostage had suffered fire damage. The windows were broken and boarded up, which was probably part of the reason it had been abandoned and taken over by vampires. The scent of smoke and must still lingered, and cobwebs and dust clung to many surfaces.

Macey could hear voices, and she crept through the building toward them, stake in hand, flashlight turned off. There were several undead posted at doors and watching through cracks at the boarded windows—so it had been the right plan to break in the way they had.

Macey dusted two vampires, easily and without fanfare. Brushing the ash from her arm and shoulder, she at last came close enough to discern the voices.

They were coming from a room on the first floor, and Macey knew there were stairs on the back part of the building that led to the second floor...which in turn had a balcony that overlooked a large foyer. From the sound of the voices, that was where she suspected Flora was stationed.

As Macey drew near, she heard the sound of a door opening and closing, and then a familiar voice through the oak-paneled wall.

"Well, you've made it just in the nick of time, Grady." Flora's tones were high and triumphant, and from the sound of it, they were in the large, high-ceilinged dining room. "The deadline is only one minute from now."

"What is all this?" Grady asked. His voice carried easily through the walls, as if he wanted to make certain Macey could hear him.

"Welcome, my dear. Welcome."

By now, Macey had crept down the back hall and was approaching via the kitchen, of which there was nothing left but burned-out appliances and a rusted sink. She paused just beyond the entrance to the dining room and carefully peered around the corner to look inside.

Flora was standing by a large chair that had clearly been brought quite recently to this location, for it was clean and new, padded with floral upholstery. It made the vampiress look as if she were about to be seated on a throne, for she stood next to it—tall, slender, and regal, with the glow of a lamp illuminating her bright red hair from behind.

But instead of a scepter, she was holding a gun.

Macey drew in a deep, silent breath.

"Yes, indeed. Most undead don't think to use a firearm," Flora said—speaking to Grady. "They tend to rely on their brute strength and the effect of their thrall…but I say, why not use the sure thing that can stop a man in his tracks? Even a Venator cannot withstand a bullet. And it works quite well from a distance—much more effective than fangs."

Cold settled over Macey. Flora was correct. This had just become a much more tenuous situation than she'd expected.

"What is going on here?" Grady asked. "Sabrina, are you all right?"

Good for him—remembering to use the wrong name until they determined what Flora's intentions were.

"What have you done to her?" Grady's taut voice had Macey tensing even further. She couldn't see far enough into the room to know what had happened, but nor did she see any sign of Savina.

Yet the scent of blood lingered in the air, mingled with dust and the mustiness of old wood.

"Step away, if you please."

"What is going on here?" Grady asked. His voice was extraordinarily calm. Perhaps too calm. "Your people can take their hands off me anytime. And there's no need for guns."

But Flora didn't seem to notice his calmness. "What is going on here is a very simple prelude to someone—that would be yours truly—taking control of a very powerful object. The object is there—on the table. It looks quite innocent, doesn't it? Hardly worth noticing. It's not even particularly beautiful.

"But from what I understand, Rekk's Pyramid gives its master—or in this case, mistress"—she gave a delighted titter—"vast and far-reaching control over her…what did you call them? My people? Yes, over my people."

Macey, crouched and still peering around the corner, could see only a small slice of the room. But she heard Flora's movements, and could tell the vampiress was walking about as she spoke.

"But let me start at the beginning. Poor Miss Ellison…how are you doing over there, my dear? *Tsk, tsk.* That does look like it hurts. Well, you needn't worry too much longer, for the pain will soon be gone."

"At least let me stanch the blood a bit," Grady said.

Flora gave a great sigh. "Very well. I might have need of her later. You may help her, but make it quick. As I was saying, this entire situation began when my best friend betrayed me. We'd been close chums for years. Even had the same piano teacher—who we were both terrified of—and we grew up in the same small town. And then we moved to Chicago, the big city, and everything changed.

"At first I thought things would change for the better. We had our own flats, and there were cabarets and jazz clubs, and my brother knew some of the owners of the speakeasies, and he said he'd get us in one sometime—though he never did." Her voice turned bitter and hard. "Another person who betrayed me.

"But through it all, Macey and I were best friends. We had other chums, but it was the two of us who shared secrets, and talked about men and what we wanted to do with our lives, and everything. I loved her. She didn't make fun of my red hair and freckles and long, gangly arms and legs—even when we were younger and the other kids did. She introduced me to all of the men—they gathered around her like flies. And some of them even liked me, too. Though I was their second choice, at least they liked me. She even tried to help me find a job that was as good as hers—she worked at the library at the university, you see, and she was a professional and made good money.

"And that's when I realized…perhaps she didn't think I was good enough for her after all. I tried to get a job working as a secretary, or in a typing pool, and none of those options worked out. She laughed and pretended to sympathize and encourage me when I told her how I spilled ink on the woman who interviewed me at the secretarial pool, but I started to think she was laughing *at* me and not with me. And when I told her I was going to try and get a job working as a seamstress in one of the clothing factories, she looked down her nose at me, as if I would no longer be good enough to be her friend if I did.

"And then she met a Negro woman named Temple. And she and that nigger bitch became friends, and Macey didn't have time for me anymore. She even quit her job at the library. She was never home when I called her or came by to see her."

By now, Macey's eyes were welling with tears and she needed to blow her nose. *Oh, Flora!* How terrible that her best friend believed all of those things, and how ill it made her feel.

And yet…Flora was right about some things. Once Macey had become a Venator, she *didn't* have as much time to spend with Flora or Chelle or Dottie as she wanted.

And to make things worse, she hadn't been able to tell them about her new life and why she wasn't available.

"But that was when my life changed. I met a very charming man named Count Alvisi who owned a cabaret called The Blood Club. And he introduced me to a secret society called the Tutela, and told me that if I played my cards right, I could become *immortal.* I'd be strong, and have power that surpassed what any human could have. And for once, I'd be *better* than Macey Denton. And maybe *I'd* be the one helping her.

"And so I was very careful and very good—and for the first time, I was doing something *well.* I was successful at it. I worked at The Blood Club, and I made friends with many of the—what did you call them, dear Grady? People?" Flora tittered again, then cut off her laugh abruptly. "You've been near her for too long. Get away."

"What happened at The Blood Club?" Grady asked, and Macey heard him move away from Savina.

"Oh, yes...that." Flora's voice hardened. "A most unusual thing happened there. It turned out to be the best thing, but at the time, it made me quite angry. You see, once Alvisi learned I was best friends with Macey Denton, he was suddenly *extremely* interested in my...in me. And he turned me immortal almost right away, because he wanted to *use me* to get to Macey. So once again, the only reason anyone wanted anything to do with me was because of *her.*"

Flora had moved into view now, and Macey eased back from the edge of the doorway to ensure she wasn't seen. At any moment, she could expose herself, but she wanted to know more of what Flora had planned, and whether there were any surprises.

Yet she was acutely aware that any delay could cost the injured Savina her life.

And if that happened, what would she tell Max?

Her chest felt tight. Hopefully Grady had been able to help her somehow, but Macey could delay no longer.

She gripped her stake and eased further around the corner, crouching low to the ground so it was less likely she'd be seen.

"And then I realized something: how valuable *I* was to the— *people,* as you call them," Flora continued in that triumphant voice. "But let's call a spade a spade, shall we, Grady dear? They're vampires, and so am I. And I *am* getting to the point of my story, so do bear with me. Once I realized how important I was to the vampires—being the best friend and confidante of the famous Macey Gardella Denton"—bitterness took over her words—"I began to use it to my advantage. Especially when I discovered that Macey simply *won't kill me*. She's had several chances to do it, you know, and she hasn't been able to bring herself to do so. The first time, she *missed*. She just missed me—like a baseball player striking out. What sort of Venator *is* she?"

Flora was laughing by now. "And there have been other times since. Even if she were to walk into the room at this moment, and I gave her my heart, she wouldn't be able to drive in that stake. It's because she still believes she can save me. That things can go back to the way they were. She even believed me when I pretended to be weakened by your presence, dear Grady, at the photography exhibit Saturday night. She's believed *everything* I've ever told her. That I wanted to go back to being mortal—as if *that* were likely— and that I missed her.

"But things can *never* go back the way they were…and it's *Macey* who's going to need to be saved. Her entire life is going to be ruined…as soon as she gets the message that you're here and she sees what I'm about to do to you, Grady dear. And what a waste that will be, you handsome Irish devil."

"But I am here. And you didn't even need to send a message." Macey stepped into view as Flora spun. Her eyes were wide, and she still held the gun in one of her hands.

In that instant, Macey took in the details of the room: Grady under control of two undead, who gripped him by the arms and back of the neck. Savina lying on the floor unmoving, her clothing stained with blood, her dark hair spread around her. A small, tall table next to the throne-like chair holding the squat black pyramid. On a different table: the silvery glint of two knives, a bronze dish, and several books and tools. At least six other vampires lurking near the main doorway to the room—

probably where Flora expected Macey to enter, had she sent a message.

"Well," Flora said, her eyes flaming red, "so you are. And thus I won't need to repeat the entire story for you. Just the ending, Macey, my girl."

"And what ending would that be? In your fairytale world?" Macey tried to catch Grady's eye, but he wasn't looking at her. He seemed to be looking at Savina instead. To Macey's relief, the inert woman seemed to show some sign of life, shifting slightly.

Flora was still ranting, her fangs exposed and her eyes wild with fanaticism and fire. "You've destroyed my entire life…and yet here I am, like that bird that rises from the ashes…what is it called? Ah, it doesn't matter. But that's what I am: better and more powerful than I've ever been when we were friends.

"And now I'm going to destroy your life, and let you see what it feels like. No, I have no intention of killing you, my dear friend. None at all. You see, I feel the same way: I could never kill you. I could never live in a world without you." Flora wandered over to the table and picked up Rekk's Pyramid, hefting it in the hand not holding the gun. "This is one thing I didn't lie to you about, you know. And what a happy accident that I should happen to discover it before Iscariot did!"

She held it flat on the palm of her hand and looked at the small onyx object as if it were a diamond. The lamplight caught on the shiny edge and glinted brilliant blue and green.

"You see…it's ready for a new master. For me to take over as its mistress. All it needs is to be awakened."

Macey was waiting for the right moment to strike—when she could send her stake winging across the room and directly into Flora's heart.

She'd show her who wasn't able to kill whom.

"And how do you intend to do that?" she asked, stepping further into the room. One of the undead started to move toward her, and Macey gave him an encouraging look.

He stepped back, edging toward his comrades near the door.

Flora saw the interplay, and her smile became harder. But she spoke to Macey. "There is one thing in the world you care for above all things—and he's right there. You tried so hard to keep this very moment from happening…but, alas, like your father, you couldn't prevent it."

"Why are you doing this?" Macey asked, still waiting for her chance to act.

"You've taken so much from me that I simply have to return the favor." Flora smiled, and her fangs were a stunning reminder that no, things *would* never be the same.

"I see." Macey needed to buy more time so she could move closer in hopes of a better shot. Then all at once, she realized exactly how she could pull this off. "But I seem to have missed something. Why is she here?" She looked toward Savina.

"Why, *she* was simply a handy way to get Mr. Grady here, who in turn was meant to be the bait which brought *you* here. But I see that didn't happen quite the way I anticipated. Still…" Flora's smile was cold. "You're here, and I'm the one holding the gun. Even a Venator cannot withstand a bullet.

"Thus, I don't see anything changing from my plans. In just a moment, Mr. Grady here is going to help me awaken Rekk's Pyramid. And you'll be able to watch it all happen…very slowly and painfully."

"When did you decide to steal the pyramid?" Macey took a half step closer. She held the stake partially behind her in hopes that Flora wouldn't notice while she was so busy prattling on about her accomplishments and plans.

"Iscariot didn't even know that it was here in Chicago until I told him. He'd already planned that sweet little episode at the girls' school, but at the time, he meant to bargain for the Rings of Jubai. When I told him he no longer needed them, he simply changed the purpose of the hostage taking. But I had other plans. While he was so busy luring you to the school to save those girls, I was helping myself to the pyramid. I had no intention of giving it to Iscariot, and I was quite certain you wouldn't either—and I was hopeful you'd take care of him for me as well. It was a winning situation for me in either case."

"Nevertheless, you must have been very valuable to Iscariot." Macey started to move forward again, but Flora's eyes fixed on her sharply and she raised the gun.

"Not another inch closer. I see what you're doing. I will use this." She held the firearm like she meant it, and Macey knew what a good shot Flora was. They'd grown up using milk cans during target practice for shooting crows away from Flora's family's cornfield.

"Oh yes, Iscariot did find me very valuable. In fact, he did something for me he hasn't done for another in more than two centuries." Her smile was frighteningly wicked.

"What was that?" Macey was still trying to capture Grady's attention, but she had to keep her eyes on Flora at all times, as well as the other six vampires waiting at the door. If Max and Chas ever made it here, she hoped they found a different way into the room.

"He fed on me and drained most of my blood one night… and then he allowed me to drink from him. I was already undead, but now I have Iscariot blood mingling with my own immortal blood, Macey…which makes me nearly as powerful as Nicholas himself! And when the pyramid recognizes me as its mistress, I'll be even more powerful than he was." Her pale lips twisted into an ugly smile. "I suppose I should thank you for ridding me of him—it might have been a battle between us for the pyramid after all."

Then Flora turned and looked toward Grady. Speculation blazed in her fiery eyes, and she set the pyramid down on the table. "I think the time for talking is long past. You know everything you need to know, and I'm ready to have some fun."

Still holding the pistol, as if for insurance, she picked up one of the knives. Its long blade glinted wickedly in the lamplight, and Macey tensed.

She was going to have to act now…but she wasn't quite close enough, and Flora was standing in such a way that she didn't have a good enough angle to whip her stake forward. And that form of attack happened to be one of Macey's weaker tactics—as Temple had always reminded her.

Temple.

Macey remembered her friend and mentor with a sudden heave of grief, and she stepped forward determinedly. That knife was not going to touch Grady, and Temple would be avenged.

"I don't think you planned any of this very well. You never were very smart about things like this," Macey said in a sneering voice. Though it was painful to speak those words—even to someone bent on destroying her life—she kept on. She knew Flora better than anyone, and it wouldn't take much to rile her red-haired temper.

"What are you talking about?" Flora turned, her voice icy, the knife trembling in one hand, the gun in the other. She raised the gun and pointed it at Grady, who hadn't moved. He was still held by the vampires. "Say that again."

"That would be you—shooting a helpless man. A coward *and* a failure. The only reason you have the pyramid is because I killed Iscariot for you. Otherwise, you'd be nothing more but his lackey. Vampire blood or no vampire blood." Macey lifted her chin, still holding the stake, staring Flora down.

The vampiress's eyes blazed, and Macey felt the tremor of its power. It shuttled through her like a lightning bolt, and she focused with difficulty to keep it from owning her.

Flora would not control her.

But the vampiress was strong. And she had Iscariot's blood. Macey shuddered deep inside as she felt the thrall connecting with her…tugging at her breath, her heartbeat.

"How dare you say such things!" Flora's voice was high and tight, and now the gun was pointed at Macey. And though it trembled a little in her hand, Flora held it firmly.

"You were never better than me, Macey, but you always thought you were. Just because you were small and delicate, and I was a tall, ungainly *horse*…that didn't mean you had to treat me that way. And I'm *not* a coward. I'm braver than you could ever imagine—giving up my soul for *this*. You'd never do that, would you?"

Flora stepped closer, the gun still pointed at Macey, her eyes blazing wildly red…their alluring thrall coaxing, and teasing, at the edge of Macey's vision. She felt herself softening, felt the edges of her gaze become murky. Felt the pull on her pulse.

She adjusted her grip on the stake, focusing on the center of Flora's chest. She was still much too far away to hit her accurately, and the vampire knew it.

So Macey had to do this just right. She had to calculate perfectly: the right time, the right angle, the right words.

"That's not brave," she taunted. "None of this is brave. You're only here because it was an accident that you discovered the pyramid, Flora. Everything you've done has been an accident. Even shooting Temple—and yes, she was my *best* friend. And you took her from me. You were probably standing right next to her, so you couldn't miss…and that was the only way you could overpower her—a mere mortal—in order to tear her apart. You can't even be a good *vampire*." Macey forced the words out, forced herself to say the hateful things even though she knew how deeply they pained Flora.

For her friend was still inside that damned, soulless body. The friend she'd loved as a sister for so many years was still there…she still hurt.

But there was nothing to be done for it. Flora had made her decision. Her soul was no longer her own.

"We could have been friends together. Forever. We should have been," Flora said, her words coming faster, tighter, more desperate. "But you had to betray me—"

Just as Macey saw a movement at the doorway, she let the stake fly, whipping it sharply through the air toward Flora.

The vampiress shrieked when it winged harmlessly past her. "How dare you!" she cried. "You tried to kill me!" She dropped the knife, aimed the gun with two hands, and pulled the trigger.

Macey was looking toward the doorway when the bullet struck her in the chest with great, shocking force. Pain shot through her, and she whipped back and onto the ground.

Twenty-Five

A Man of Clear Heart

MAX HAD JUST REACHED THE DOORWAY when he saw the bullet slam into Macey's chest, and watched her tumble to the ground, stake falling from her lifeless hand.

"*Noo!*" he cried, and plunged into the room, Woodmore at his heels.

But as they breached the threshold, a swarm of undead surged onto them. Max lost sight of the red-headed vampiress as he thrust his stake at the closest undead, then spun and ducked in order to evade the next one. They came after him, one by one, as he kicked, dove, scrambled, and knocked them to the ground, finishing them off with well-aimed strokes to the heart.

He and Woodmore were shoulder to shoulder, then back to back for several minutes in a melee of undead before they emerged from the cloud of dust and vampire remains, and he saw Flora, on the ground, bending over Macey's body.

"No." Flora was sobbing, rocking back and forth a little. "I didn't mean to do that." She'd dropped the gun, and Grady had lunged forward to snatch it up—not that it would do any good against an undead. "I never meant to kill you…Macey, I didn't mean it. You have to believe me…I didn't mean to!"

Wild and mindless, Max leaped toward the red-headed vampire, only to be caught midair and snatched backward by none other than Woodmore.

He whirled, his vision red with fury, fist raised—but Woodmore blocked it, grabbed him by the arm, and said, "Look."

That was when Max saw the hand that had lifted from Macey's inert body and now grasped Flora by the front of her shirt.

"You didn't mean to kill me," Macey said, lifting her head from the ground. "And you didn't. But now, at long last, I'm going to kill you, Flora. I'm sorry…and I pray you'll somehow be at peace…but it's over."

"Are you really going to do it…this time?" Flora whispered. Max saw a tear fall from her and plop onto Macey's face.

"Yes. I really am." Her voice was soft and rough.

"I loved you."

"I loved you too."

"Do it fast, Macey."

Macey's other arm shifted sharply, and Max saw Flora jolt from behind…freeze…and then explode into a silvery cloud of dust.

And then everything was quiet and still.

He looked around. Grady, who was holding Flora's gun, as well as a stake that he'd likely put to use, was helping Savina to her feet—she was bloody, but standing on her own—and she was holding a stake as well. She looked over at Max, and when their gazes connected, he felt a rush of relief shuttle through him so violently he visibly shook. *She was alive.*

He was damned well going to marry her, too.

Macey was pulling herself slowly to her feet, shaky and grim-faced, holding up a hand to ward off Woodmore when he tried to help. A tear trickled down her cheek and she turned away to wipe it, her shoulders shaking, her head bent.

Woodmore glanced at Max, then went over to the table on which Rekk's Pyramid sat, innocent and quiet in its evil.

Max hesitated for the breadth of a second, then he went to Macey and, before she could move away or protest, he pulled her into an embrace.

A long-overdue embrace.

"How did you do it?" he said. "You're not even bleeding. I saw the bullet hit you."

"The one and only asset I took from my time with Al Capone—a special bulletproof corset."

He closed his eyes, ignoring the way they burned, and squeezed her tighter. Maybe he owed Alphonse another visit. This time, as a thank you.

Macey heaved a long sigh, then exhaled, sinking deeper into his arms, trembling as she wrapped her arms around him and hung on for dear life.

And for the first time in thirteen years, Max felt like a father again.

✝

"Are you going to do it here, Woodmore?" Max asked after a moment.

His arms were still tight around Macey—so tight she could hardly breathe—but she didn't care. She hadn't been held by her daddy in a long time, and she discovered she needed it.

"I'm not sure," Chas replied. "There are…considerations."

Macey pulled away to see what they were talking about, and her attention couldn't help but skim over Grady. He seemed unhurt, and was standing next to Chas, who appeared to be ready to apply the curved-tongue blade to Rekk's Pyramid.

It struck her sharply then that this was it. Their work here was done—Grady's work for Max—and it was over.

It was really, truly over. Her eyes burned again and she swallowed hard.

No sooner had Macey released herself from her father's hug than Savina was there, rushing into his arms, heedless of the blood staining the front of her pretty pink suit. The embrace Max gave her was markedly different than the one he'd given Macey, and she turned away, fighting both tears and a smile.

"What sort of considerations?" she asked Chas, forcing herself to keep her emotions under control. She would not look at Grady. She simply would not.

Of course he'd heard everything Flora had said during her ranting—about him being the most important thing to Macey—and she wasn't certain what he believed or how he felt about it. She hoped he'd just…forget about it.

And return to his regular life.

When Max no longer has need of me, it'll be just as you intended.

Macey drew in a deep, shaky breath. Maybe she'd go back to Rome with Max and Savina, and see the Consilium. There was no longer any real purpose for her in Chicago, and Chas could stay and keep an eye on things.

"Temple's notes said to penetrate the pyramid with the ruby-eyed skull's crooked tongue by a man—"

"A man?" Macey asked.

Chas shrugged. "I'm just repeating what Temple wrote, lulu."

"All right, then. By what sort of man…?"

"By a man clear of heart." He paused and looked around, a sardonic smile on his face. "That wouldn't be me."

She looked up at him, placing a hand on his arm and squeezing. "You've never stopped loving Narcise Moldavi—for more than a century. I'd say that means you're clear of heart."

He blinked rapidly and looked down at the knife in his hand. "Perhaps. But…" He shrugged. "I suppose it can't hurt for me to try."

"I can't help but notice you didn't suggest I try it," Max said drily. Macey looked at him in shock, then saw that he was grinning, his arm tight around Savina's waist, his face relaxed and handsome.

She laughed with the others.

They gathered around, Max and Savina fairly glued to each other's side and her father's arm slung around Macey's shoulders.

Chas took a long in-breath and rested the point of the dagger at the pyramid's point. He gripped the hilt in two hands, preparing to force the weapon straight down into the stone, when it began to slide in…all on its own.

They gave a soft, collective gasp of surprise as the blade penetrated the center of the pyramid—as easily as if it had been soft butter. And then, the onyx split, falling apart into two pieces…and then shattered, exploding into dust—just as Lilith the Dark, its creator, had done a hundred years earlier.

Macey looked up at Chas. His eyes were bright and shining. Clearer than she'd ever seen them.

She whispered, "Clear of heart."

Twenty-Six

In Which the Lady Photographer's Secret is Revealed

WITH REKK'S PYRAMID nothing but tiny flakes of shiny black onyx, and the undead put to rest—for the time being—the five of them agreed there was no reason to linger in the old house.

Yet Macey lingered.

She stood there, staring at the place Flora had been turned to dust. Her eyes stung with tears as she remembered those last moments: opening her eyes after the shock of the bullet's impact to find Flora bending over her.

The glow had gone from the vampire gaze, and her blue eyes were filled with tears and pain.

Macey had looked up at her, tears clouding her own vision, and pulled the stake from her pocket. This time, she had no hesitation, no uncertainty, and she grabbed her friend's blouse.

Are you really going to do it this time?

Yes. I really am.

I loved you.

I loved you too.

Do it fast, Macey.

She said a prayer, asking for forgiveness—for the hurt she'd caused Flora, for some chance that her friend might in some way be redeemed—and rammed the stake up into her heart.

Flora's eyes bolted wide at the force, and she stilled. Then she smiled, as if released from some great pain…and she was gone.

Now it was time to leave, and Macey wiped her eyes once more, sniffling like a child, wishing for a handkerchief.

Suddenly, someone was there, offering her one.

Macey recognized his hand: Grady. Her body gave a little tremor and she took the offering, then quickly wiped her eyes and nose—all the while hiding her expression from him and avoiding the fury in his eyes.

"Thank you," she said, stuffing it into her pocket, and looked around the room one last time—as if to make certain she wasn't forgetting anything—then started for the door. Escape. That was all she wanted now: escape.

"Macey?" Max's voice penetrated the murky pool of her emotions. "Are you ready?" His voice was unusually gentle.

"I'm coming," she said, crumpling the handkerchief in a fist and starting toward her father. She was startled to realize she wanted another hug from him.

Grady slipped ahead with Chas, and Macey, Max, and Savina followed as they made their way back the way they'd come—through the makeshift door cut in the wall, the dynamite-blasted entrance, and the subterranean creek-path.

When they emerged from the old railway station, they discovered it was well into the night. Wispy clouds covered the moon and stars, and in the distance a trio of colored spotlights scored the dark sky.

The five piled into Grady's car: Chas in front, Max and the two women in the back. Macey chose to sit directly behind Grady so she wouldn't be tempted to try and see his profile. The sooner she got away from him, the sooner she could begin to rebuild her life—and her heart.

"You did do that on purpose, right, lulu?" Chas asked from the front seat. "Goaded her into shooting you?"

"Of course," Macey replied. "Flora was an excellent markswoman, and she also was smart enough not to give me a good target for the stake. I just didn't expect the force to be such that it would knock me on my behind!"

"You did that purposely? You made her shoot you *on purpose?*" Max's voice was tight. "What if she'd aimed for your bloody *head?* What if the bulletproof corset hadn't worked? Did it ever occur to you—"

Macey interrupted, patting his hand. "She wasn't going to shoot me in the head—it's a smaller target, and besides, she hadn't shot either Temple nor Dr. Sevin in the head. Only in the chest. I thought my chances were pretty damned good."

"*Pretty* damned good? That's not good enough—" Max grumbled, then stopped abruptly.

Macey got the impression Savina had kicked him, and she smiled to herself. She really did like Savina.

"Al Capone—Alphonsus—wears a vest like that some of the time," Macey went on. "He'd had the corset made for me when I was—when we were working together." She glanced at the back of Grady's head as a swath of streetlight passed through the car, knowing he despised the gangster and his ilk. But there was nothing to indicate whether he was listening or not. "It's not very comfortable, but I thought it would be a good idea to wear it, since Flora had already demonstrated her propensity for using bullets as well as her fangs."

They pulled up in front of Grady's house, and Macey climbed out quickly, her stomach in knots. Almost over. *Just get your things and get the hell out of here.*

Chas paused on the sidewalk in front of the porch. "This is where I take my leave," he said.

Macey embraced him, and he planted a quick, smacking kiss on her lips. "Be strong, lulu," he murmured into her ear, giving her a crushing, one-armed hug.

"I'll see you soon?" she asked, clutching his arm. Suddenly, she didn't want him to go.

"I'm off to Siberia in short order," he replied, "but I have some things to attend to here before I go."

Then he turned to shake hands with Grady, followed by Savina and Max. They stood there talking as Grady unlocked the door.

"I'll just get my things," Macey said, going through the door as soon as Grady pushed it open. She ran up the stairs, leaving them all to say goodbye to Chas. She wanted to get out of here, and go somewhere private where she could begin to deal with everything that had happened in the last few days.

She was stuffing things into her satchel as quickly as possible when Macey heard Savina come into the bedroom.

"I've got an extra—" Her heart stopped. It wasn't Savina standing in the doorway, bathed in light from the hallway. It was Grady.

She recovered quickly and returned to shoving lingerie, stakes, and vials of holy water into her bag. "I'll be finished here in a second."

"I thought you were dead." His voice, low and tight, cut through the room.

Macey stilled and looked up, looking at him fully for the first time. His face was a mask of pain and anger as he stood, blocking the doorway.

"I stood there and I watched her put a bullet into you. I thought you were *dead*."

She swallowed, though it was difficult with a dry throat and the lump clogging it. "I..."

Leaning against the doorjamb, he bowed his head, rubbing his forehead with jerky movements. "I thought I'd lost you—that you were really gone. And I realized I...couldn't... I was..." He was shaking his head, his expression tortured with misery, anger, and regret.

"I'm sorry," she said, finally able to force out the words. "I didn't mean to upset anyone—well, except for Flora," she added with a tense laugh...for the grief still lingered in her heart. And now it was expanding even more, painfully swelling inside her chest as she saw the agony playing out on her beloved's face. "It was the only way I could—"

"Macey, my God—what you asked of Wayren was wrong. *So* incredibly wrong..."

"Oh, God, Grady, I *know*, I was…" Her voice broke. How could she ever apologize, explain…ever be worthy of his forgiveness?

"But the simple truth is—despite it all—despite the—the enormity of what you did…Macey, I don't want to live my life without you. Dammit." His voice was raw, and he was barely grinding out the words.

Tears trickled down her cheeks, and she wanted to go to him…but she dared not. "I love you. So much. I know what I did was an abomination, an unforgivable decision. It was as good as—as destroying you. I was wrong."

He lifted his face finally, and the look in his eyes stabbed her low in the belly. They were dark, brilliant blue—like clear and bold sapphires, tormented and desperate…yet there was a flicker of hope in them.

"In spite of that, oh, dammit, Macey…I want you by my side—and I want to be by your side—through all of this: whatever hell or fury you might face. Whatever wars or grief or loss we might have, I want to face them together. With you. And I find I…I can't change that."

He stepped away from the door, into the room, holding her with that intense gaze. "In spite of it all, *a rún*, I love you more than anything. I always will."

Macey didn't remember moving, but the next thing she knew, she was in his arms and they were kissing as if they needed it to breathe. His face was wet, and the saltiness from her own tears mingled with the sensual warmth of his lips as she devoured him, pulling his face closer to hers.

She couldn't control a delicate tremor, and pressed closer into his embrace—for it was like coming home and having a great weight lifted from her shoulders and arriving in heaven—all at once.

He sighed her name as he tightened his arms around her, burying his face in her hair then trailing soft kisses along her jaw and along the front of her ear. She shivered with pleasure, her body coming alive as it evolved from intense pain and grief to sweet, sudden passion.

"Macey, do you need— Oh."

She pulled away to see her father standing in the doorway. Savina was right behind him, and she tugged at his arm—which, of course, did little to move him. "I told you that everything was fine. Now, leave them be. I've been sitting on this secret since Sunday, wondering when it was going to come out."

Savina gave Macey and Grady a smile. "I know you have much to—er—talk about, so Max and I will be leaving now." She tugged at his arm again. "Right, darling?"

But Max seemed unwilling to move as his eyes went from Macey's face to Grady's face…then to the locations of his hands. His expression darkened.

"I suppose I'm going to have to learn to dislike you intensely now," he muttered. "Which is a damned shame, because I was rather fond of you, you bloody mick."

Then he turned and walked away.

Twenty-Seven

A Lot of Talking & Some Other Activities Too

THE DOOR CLOSED behind Savina, leaving them alone once more.

"Grady," Macey began, now that she'd settled abruptly back to earth. "I can't imagine how—"

"Don't," he said, and pressed a light kiss to her puffy lips, then coming back for more: a long, slick one that had her head spinning. He licked the inside of her mouth with slow, sensual strokes, teased her tongue with his, sucked and nibbled on her lips as desire rolled through her like an approaching storm.

He pulled away and spoke, his voice soft and rough. "We can talk later. Right now…I just want to make love to you, Macey. I need to put all of that aside for a little while…and—and feel again."

She blinked back tears of guilt and pain. "Oh, Grady, yes… please," she whispered as she lifted her face to kiss him, then moved along to taste the saltiness of his warm skin along a jaw gritty with stubble, and to the long, strong tendon of his neck.

He vibrated a little, giving a soft groan as she kissed and licked and nibbled there—all the while, he was pulling up her sweater to slide his hands over her back, his hands caressing her bare skin.

It wasn't long before he had her over to the bed, leaving a trail of shoes and trousers and stockings along the way. But he paused when she flung off her sweater and began to unhook the special corset.

"This," he said, moving his hands over the stiff, uncomfortable girdle, "is what saved my life…because it saved yours. I'm thinking I should be kissing Al Capone's damned feet."

Macey gusted out a laugh—because otherwise she would cry—and replied, "I don't think that would be very pleasant— *Oh!*" She squeaked in surprise, for he'd slipped his hand, not beneath the corset as she'd expected, but down into her drawers.

He muttered something bordering on profane when he touched her there and discovered how slick and full she was, and looked up at her with hot eyes.

"Macey," he whispered.

She realized at that moment, in a blinding rush of shock, that he hadn't been certain she'd want him the way she had before. That something might have changed between them.

What a fool. What fools they both were.

"Help me get out of this thing," she said, matching his look with her own avid, promising one. "I need to feel you against me…and inside of me. Please, Grady."

That was all he needed—and his clever, clever fingers made short work of the Capone contraption as she yanked his shirt apart. Buttons flew, bouncing everywhere, and as the prison of her corset fell away, she had the pleasure of sliding her hands up over his taut, lightly haired chest, carefully avoiding the scores and cuts from his vampire battles.

At last they were completely naked, sliding and easing against the other—muscle to curve, rough hair to smooth skin, legs twined, mouths engaged, hands everywhere. Grady breathed something in Irish against her lips as she guided him between her legs, raising herself to take him in.

Oh, yes. Macey closed her eyes and held him, lifting her hips in easy, slow movements to match his, reveling in the beauty of this age-old rhythm that could bespeak such love and passion. It was enough to bring tears to her eyes—tears of grief and joy, tears of pleasure and comfort.

And when their movements became more urgent—deeper and harder and faster—she forgot the tears and the grief, and settled into the joy and pleasure building inside her. Macey cried out, arching up into him, pulling him close and hard as she came. He groaned her name with his final stroke, and she dragged her hands through his thick, wild hair, looking up at her love as his face went slack with pleasure and release.

Then, swimming back to reality, her body still humming and hot, her mouth settled on the warm, salty skin of his shoulder, tasting Grady…feeling at last as if she was no longer alone, and would never be alone again. He lowered himself so their damp bodies touched, then eased off to the side, pulling her close with him.

Some time later…much later, after another hot, passionate interlude and another doze…Macey realized sunlight was pouring into the room.

It was morning. And, for the first time in weeks, she'd slept beautifully.

Out of habit, she dragged on a robe and slipped down the hall to the bathroom to freshen up, then down to the kitchen to find something to eat. All of a sudden, she was hungrier than she'd been for a long time.

She was in the kitchen, making a tray of food from the slim pickings in Grady's fridge—a boiled egg, some good Irish cheddar, some apples, and a half loaf of bread that was almost stale—when she heard the stairs creaking.

"There you are," he said, coming into the kitchen. When she saw his face, she realized with a sharp pain that he'd been afraid she was gone.

It wouldn't have been the first time.

"Grady," she said, setting the tray aside and walking into his arms. He folded her against his strong, naked body and she sighed, bumping her nose gently against his skin as she drew in a deep breath of his scent. "I'm not going to leave—unless you want me to."

His arms tightened, and he dropped a kiss on the top of her head. "Not until I'm quite finished with you," he replied, a smile in his voice. "And I'm thinking that will be a while, *a rún*."

"What does that mean? *A rún*?" She looked up at him.

"It means, literally, my secret…as in, the secret of my heart. The deepest, truest secret of my heart."

"Oh. But…you called me that…before."

His expression took her breath away more effectively than even the kisses they'd shared. "Yes. But now it's even truer, is it not?"

"You never forgot me, then, did you?" She shook her head. "Your memory wasn't…well…" She couldn't even put into words the travesty of what she'd tried to do. Her stomach felt like a lead balloon had settled in it, and suddenly she was no longer ravenous.

"Wayren gave me the choice."

"I see."

He nodded gravely and stepped back a little. His eyes changed, turning to wintry Lake Michigan instead of warm blue sky. "She gave me the choice of living in oblivion—and safety—or staying as I was. When she told me you'd— Well. It wasn't a difficult decision—I didn't hesitate. But I've been unspeakably angry with you, Macey. I don't deny it."

"As well you should be." Her heart gave a little awkward *ka-thump* at the thought that he might still, and always, deep inside be unspeakably angry with her. That he might never trust her again. That, despite the last hours of the most beautiful and passionate lovemaking she'd ever had, they might never be the way they once were…or could have been. That it could be the last time they were together thus.

"I tried to understand, but how could I? After what we'd been through?" His voice was hard and he looked away, curling his fingers over the edge of the kitchen counter. "After all of that, you'd still rejected me."

Macey's throat closed up and she couldn't speak. Tears obliterated her vision and she found she needed a damned handkerchief again.

He sighed and groped in a drawer, then handed her a kitchen towel. "For a lethal Venator, you're certainly unprepared at times."

"What I did was inexcusable. I know that. I-I was just trying to protect—"

"Me?" His voice was like flint.

"No," she whispered. "*Me.* I was trying to protect myself from having to go through what my father did. From—from being in a situation where I'd have to make a choice about whether to save you or to save the world. From having to live every moment in fear that it might happen, that someone would take you from me. From doing what Victoria Gardella did, when she married Philip de Lacey."

He was silent for a moment, but his strong, dark hand moved to touch hers in a brief squeeze. "Savina said the same thing." He looked at the tray and picked it up. "I'm hungry. Let's sit down."

Macey released her breath. Now she understood how he felt, walking into the kitchen to find her there—discovering that their passionate interlude was not just a flash in the pan, not just a short, false interval. That they were going to talk, and hopefully heal what had gone between them.

"Savina knew?" Macey asked as she sat on the sofa. He'd set the tray of food on the table next to them.

"She figured it out. We spent a lot of time talking on Sunday—that horrible rainy day. That day you came here." He looked at her, and Macey blushed, turning away.

"Savina didn't recognize you, but I did. Why did you come? It made me— It disturbed me. I'd been doing…all right. Even after seeing you at the photo exhibit the night before. That was… impossible. I hadn't expected you to be there, and there you were. And you looked…" He shook his head. "I thought I was never going to recover."

Macey needed a handkerchief again. What a damned fool she'd been. Was there any way to turn time backward? To fix this somehow?

"But I made it through that night—I was glad you left the photo show early, you know. I might not have been able to… And then there you were, showing up here the next day, in the rain, looking so forlorn and lost and sad under that blasted hat you were wearing. And after that, after you were gone…well, I said too much, asked too many questions of Savina about your father, and their relationship…and she figured out that you and I had… that we'd been together."

"She's quite clever."

"Your father is mad about her, you know. I suspect very soon she's going to be your stepmother."

Macey smiled. "I think I'd like that." She settled back against a pillow, nibbling on a piece of cheese. Her appetite was slowly recovering. "About that…about my father. Obviously, you know him…but how? When?"

"During the war. We met through Houdini. I was good friends with him, and your father was taking some of the training he did for the soldiers in England. I hadn't moved from London to Chicago yet, and that's how we met."

"Is that how you learned about vampires? Because you've always known, ever since I met you."

He nodded. "Right. I didn't know for certain for many years, but I suspected after I saw Max stake one in an alley once. I wasn't really certain what I'd seen, and he wouldn't answer any questions—but I'd read enough literature about the undead that I was suspicious. And then when I moved here and Linwood and I started talking about some of the injuries on bodies they found…well, it became a certainty. Once I read *The Venators*, my suspicions were confirmed."

"Max and Savina were staying here…so it wasn't an accident that you were involved at the Beedle school?"

"That part *was* an accident, though I would of course have helped if I hadn't been involved otherwise. Max needed a place to stay when he came to Chicago, and he didn't want to take the chance of being seen or recognized by any undead. Though he never mentioned anything about you at first, I guessed you were his daughter—I'd suspected that since I saw the photograph you had in your flat of him and your mother. I never had the chance to ask you about it, because—well—you weren't really talking much to me, were you? About all of this?"

"No. But that's how it's supposed to be," she said weakly. "With non-Venators."

He snorted. "It might have saved some grief if you'd been more forthcoming, Macey, lass."

"But you never told Max that we—that we knew each other."

"By the time he got here and contacted me, we *weren't* supposed to know each other. And so I… Well, you'd made your choice. Who was I to go against your decision?" The bitterness was back, and Macey's belly pitched down once more.

Could they ever get past this?

"And then, all indications were that you and Woodmore were together," he added in that same voice.

Right. Because she'd told him that. "Chas and I are…friends. Good friends… We've been… We have a lot in common. Nothing more."

"Nothing more." He lifted his brows.

She shook her head. "I don't *love* him, Grady. I've only ever loved you…and I hope some day you can truly forgive me for what I've done." She wiped her eyes once more, silently damning herself for being such a waterworks.

"When Flora shot you—right in the chest, right *there*—and I thought you were dead, I realized right then that I'd forgiven you, *a rún*. And I thought I was too late." His voice was rough and broken. "Savina…well, she'd helped me to look at things in a different way.

"It wasn't that she was trying to convince me of anything. I think she was actually trying to convince *herself* that she and I don't really…that we can't fully understand what sort of life, what sacrifices you and your family are required to make."

He sighed, looked her, took her hands. "What you did was horrible, Macey, but I understand now it wasn't out of malice or selfishness—well, maybe a little bit of that, of protecting yourself," he added with a harsh laugh, "but it was mostly for love. And that, my heart, is a very noble cause."

She smiled at him through watery eyes. "Thank you. I'm so glad Wayren didn't do what I asked. And that she gave you a choice."

"There is one thing you're going to have to do for me, though, lass. To help me get past all of this angst." The quirk of a smile—the first real hint of humor and teasing she'd seen in days—curved his lips.

She held back a relieved grin of her own. She thought she knew what he was going to say—he was a man, after all. And make-up sex was particularly satisfying, as she'd so recently discovered.

But he surprised her.

"St. Patrick's," he replied, reaching for a slice of apple.

"What?"

"We're getting married at St. Patrick's. Where you spent an awful lot of your time—and Sebastian Vioget too."

"But I'm not Catholic," she protested...yet she loved the idea. To be married—*married?*—in the same church where she'd lost Sebastian, where he'd found his salvation and completed the long promise with his own beloved Giulia. She couldn't think of anything more fitting.

"I know a priest," Grady said with a little chuckle, then pulled her over to cover her mouth with his. He tasted like apple, but she didn't mind. "I'll take care of it. As long as you promise to be there, in a lacy dress and with a flower in your hair—like you wore that first night at The Gyro. You will make an honest man out of me, won't you?"

"Nothing would make me happier," she told him. "*A rún.*"

Epilogue
Endings & Beginnings

Thirty days later

SANTO QUIRINUS was a tiny, unassuming church in a very old part of Rome. Hardly noticed by passersby and completely ignored by tourists, the minuscule cathedral nevertheless acted as the threshold of a very special location.

If one walked through the tiny worship space—which was stark and simple in comparison to the other architectural wonders of Rome—and found a certain confessional booth, and pushed a certain lever…the screen between the priest and confessor opened to reveal a secret staircase.

And if one descended those curving steps—taking care to avoid certain ones that would set off an alarm below—one would soon find oneself in an underground chamber quite different from the other catacombs of Rome.

In the center of the entry chamber was a large fountain that gently bubbled from a center spire, with water that spilled over in a constant stream. In the bottom of the pool, if one looked closely, one would see not coins, but tiny silver crosses fastened to the small hoops that had once been pierced through the flesh of some fearsome Venator.

From this main chamber, several entryways led off into a warren of corridors, saferooms, and laboratories.

This was the Consilium, the heart and center of the Gardella family of Venators—and all those who wore the *vis bulla* or fought alongside them in an effort to eradicate the evil of Judas Iscariot's vampire race, as well as other forces of malevolence.

On this day in particular, the usually quiet and empty church of Santo Quirinus was filled with a small crowd of people. But today was an unusual day, for the *Summas* Gardella was getting married for the second time…and everyone was rejoicing that he had at last found love again.

Macey stood by, holding Savina's bouquet as the lovely woman vowed to always love and honor and respect (but not necessarily obey) her husband, the fierce, intense, and charming *summas*.

Standing across from Macey was her own deliciously handsome husband, looking slightly harassed as he fumbled through his pockets for the rings with which Max had entrusted him.

As planned, Macey and Grady had been married at St. Patrick's a little more than two weeks earlier, with the affable priest in attendance—as well as Max Denton, Savina Eleaisa, Jameson Linwood, and others. The bride had worn a silver-gilded white rose in her hair and a silvery-pink frock, and her wedding ring had belonged to the groom's Aunt Camilla.

Now, as the former groom and current best man to the *Summas* Gardella looked up in dismay at the couple currently being married, he saw that the groom, with a broad, cocky grin, was holding the two rings *he'd* pickpocketed from Grady.

"I've been practicing," Max murmured to his best man before turning back to the incandescently beautiful woman who was becoming his wife.

Once the vows were exchanged and the wedding ceremony was over, the guests made their way down to the main chamber of the Consilium to celebrate the nuptials, as well as a memorialization of Temple Deveraux and Sebastian Vioget.

Macey, who knew both of the fallen better than anyone present, spoke briefly about them.

"Sebastian acted as both a father and a mentor to me during the year I knew him," she said. "And when he was reunited with his Giulia, it was one of the most beautiful scenes I've ever witnessed. It came after a terrifying, horrible event, and through it all, he remained strong and cognizant—even when tested to his limits. Even then, I could see the Venator strength burning in his eyes. Though an undead himself, he has always had a place reserved in the gallery in the library, to have his likeness hung there, along with Max Pesaro, the famous Brim, and, of course, Kritanu." She'd boned up quite a bit on her Venator history in preparation for the visit to the Consilium.

"Temple Deveraux was one of my closest friends during a most unsettling year. From the first time I met her—when she dragged me out of a dance club during a vampire raid—I was impressed by her strength of body as well as her heart and mind. She taught me everything I know about how to wield a stake, and what to do with my arms and legs, and even my forehead, when faced with a vampire—or anyone else trying to back me into a corner.

"She was filled with advice on everything, from how to wear a fascinator to how to perfectly clean the bar counter of every bit of sticky ale, to where my strengths and weaknesses are when training in the *kalari*. She showed me how to read texts that seemed too faded to see, and she always had a wise comment when I needed to be brought back to reality." She glanced at Grady and her vision began to swim. "I'm going to miss her so much, and I'm mostly saddened that she was cut down in the midst of a great love affair—the only time I ever saw her truly happy. I hope the sister of my heart and her Dr. Joseph are happily together in the same place Sebastian and Giulia are."

Everyone clapped, and when Macey went back to her seat, Grady had a handkerchief ready for her. But this one had her initials—MDG—embroidered on it, along with a delicate shamrock design in ivory. A set of them had been one of her wedding presents from him, and he'd stashed them all over the house and always carried one on his person.

Max rose and moved toward a pair of shrouded paintings. He whisked away the coverings to reveal Temple's and Sebastian's portraits, which would hang in the library.

"In honor of two of our own," he said, standing tall and handsome in his dark suit, "let us have a final moment of silence."

After that, the somber mood of the guests broke up into one of celebration. After all, Nicholas Iscariot was dead, Rekk's Pyramid was destroyed, Rasputin's amulet was safely locked away…and their *summas* was back in Rome…along with the daughter most of them had never met. Thus, as the heir apparent to the Gardella legacy, the new Mrs. Jameson Grady was even more popular than the bride and groom.

Macey, who had only arrived in Rome two days earlier, and was visiting the Consilium for the first time, was fairly giddy with excitement as she and Grady selected glasses of champagne— delightfully legal in Italy—and visited with the other Venators, Comitators, weapons masters, medics, and others who helped in the battle against evil. She met Bellitano and the elderly Paolo, and the handsome and clever Liam Stoker—who wanted to know all about the bulletproof corset that had saved her life.

But it wasn't until Max, still glowing with happiness from his nuptials and pride over his daughter, took Macey into the main corridor that angled off from the fountain room that she was truly overcome by her family's calling.

"Who are all these paintings of, Papa?" she asked, slipping her hand through the crook of his arm. "I thought all of the Venators' photos were hung in the Great Hall. These are much larger and fancier than the others."

He looked down at her fingers settled on his arm, then back up at her with a surprisingly misty look. It seemed he still found it unbelievable that she was there, and with him—and that she no longer called him Max.

"Your family. Those who have come before us. All of these in this hallway are from the direct line of Gardeleus, and each of them were the *summas* at one time. Someday, after I'm gone, my portrait will hang there, and yours as well."

"I hope that's a long time from now," Macey told him. "Because I think I'm going to be a little busy for a few decades."

Max looked down at her in astonishment, and she replied, "Grady wants four children. I'm trying to negotiate him down to two, but he's pretty insistent." She laughed, so incredibly lighthearted and happy—and so relieved that she was, at last, no longer alone. With a father, a stepmother, and a husband—and now Bell and Paolo and Liam and the others—she no longer had to face all of her nightmares and challenges alone.

"But you aren't… You can't be… Not yet," Max replied. "You're not with child *yet*, are you?"

"Not yet…but we're doing our best." She grinned cheekily up at him and was delighted when his face turned ruddy.

"Damned mick. I knew I was going to have to learn to detest him," he replied, laughing uncomfortably. "I don't think I need any more details, Macey. Just let me know when…there's something to know."

She grinned up at him and bumped against his side affectionately. It had taken a while for her to get to this point, but she'd realized rather quickly that Grady's forgiveness and understanding of her actions should translate into compassion of her own toward her father.

"You'll be the first to know," she told him. Then stopped at the portrait of a beautiful dark-haired woman. Though she'd never seen pictures of any of her ancestors, she didn't even need to look at the nameplate. "Victoria."

"Yes." Max's voice grew solemn, and was filled with awe. "Did you know she wore two *vis bullae*?"

"Two? How could that be?"

"It's quite an interesting story. You'll have to ask Paolo about it."

"Does Max Pesaro figure in it much? I understand he's quite worth a swooning over," she said, still staring at the portrait.

"You must have been talking to Savina," Max replied with a sigh. "She's quite fixated on my great-grandfather for some bloody reason."

"I'm certain that's the only reason she agreed to marry you," Macey said gravely. "So she could say she was wed to a descendent of Max Pesaro."

Her father actually stopped short and looked down at her.

Macey burst into laughter. "I'm teasing," she said.

He grinned at that. "Well, his shoes are damned hard to fill."

"You've succeeded in one-upping him in at least one way," Macey told him, moving further along the corridor. This time she stopped in front of a red-headed woman with whiskey-colored eyes that sparkled with sassy delight. "Oh, this one looks like an interesting person. Lady Catherine—oh yes, Savina told me about her as well. But Paolo has promised to give me more details."

She looked up to find her father looking at her speculatively. "What is it, Papa?"

"I'm just trying to figure out how I've one-upped Pesaro," he muttered.

Macey hooted with laughter, then she realized he was quite serious. "You don't know? What did you do today?" When he still looked blank, she said, "Max Pesaro only married once, didn't he? See, you've overshot him by taking a second wife. And thank God you have," she added under her breath. "From what I've heard from Bellitano and Paolo, you definitely needed to do it."

He was still watching her. "You truly don't mind that I've married again? That you have a stepmother? You know I've never forgotten your mother, that I'll always love her…"

"Of course not, Papa. Truly. I've come to love Savina, and I am so happy for you, and for her. You deserve to have something good in your life after…after everything that happened."

He was blinking a little too fast for it to be normal, and Macey realized he was tearing up. She turned back to the portraits to give him a moment, then mused aloud, "All of these seem to have been done by the same artist. Yet didn't you tell me the portraits are finished shortly after each *summas* dies? How can that be, when so many of them are centuries old?"

"It's quite a mystery, isn't it, Max?" came a familiar voice.

Macey spun to see Wayren standing there, with a bemused smile on her face. "You're here," she said breathlessly. "We— I wasn't certain you'd come."

"I wouldn't have missed it for anything." Wayren's beatific smile fairly lit up the corridor. "I had things to attend to, and so I slipped into the church at the back so as not to disturb the ceremony. I heard your lovely speeches about Sebastian and Temple. They would have been very touched—as was I."

"Could I…could I speak to you alone for a moment?" Macey asked.

For some reason, her heart was thudding wildly. This woman before her…she was such an enigma, and unaccountably powerful…and yet she was so peaceful. And seemed to carry no judgment.

But Macey was determined to unburden herself, and take whatever punishment or reprimand she might face.

"I would like that. I have to speak with Chas as well, but I would like also to talk to you, Macey." Wayren glanced at Max, who nodded and stepped aside, walking off to rejoin the rest of the festivities.

Macey hesitated, then plunged in. "I wanted to ask you—to tell you—that I completely regret that I asked you to…what I asked you to do to Grady. It was wrong. I was wrong. But I have to know…why did you even offer me the option?"

Wayren took her hand, and at once Macey's heart rate settled and her churning insides calmed.

"It was part of your education," she told her. "With such great power wielded by the Venators, there comes with it temptations and choices with which mere mortals are never faced. You've learned a great lesson, and I trust you'll remember this should you be faced with any similar situation. And, most importantly, I suspected that some day, you might be on the receiving end of a similar situation…and might need to make a decision for compassion and forgiveness yourself."

Macey felt a shiver of comprehension. "Of course. My father."

Wayren simply nodded.

Macey continued. "You gave Grady the choice, and he…"

"He chose *you*. That's all you need to know about our conversation." Wayren's lovely smile and warm eyes took away any sting her words might have carried.

"Is he really the dauntless one?" Macey asked.

Wayren merely smiled in that enigmatic way of hers. "Whatever he is, he loves you very much, and he is more than worthy of a Venator wife." She looked behind Macey. "And now…I see that Chas is approaching. I need to deliver some news to him."

"Thank you, Wayren. I'm so thankful Grady chose the way he did, and that my father is back in my life."

"And soon you'll be quite busy," she replied, her eyes crinkling a bit at the corners. "In…I would say, eight months and two days."

Macey gasped, her eyes going wide. "Truly?"

"Truly. And your father…he's going to be a most gentle, loving grandfather. Now, go be with your husband and tell him the news—with my blessing."

Macey almost lunged up to kiss the woman on the cheek, but caught herself at the last minute. Wayren just didn't seem like the kissing-recipient type.

"Chas," she said as she came upon him. He wasn't, she noticed, holding a glass of the champagne—or any drink at all. "Thank you for coming. I know you're leaving for Siberia, and I hope to see you again soon. Godspeed."

"Thank you, lulu," he said. His face was more relaxed and his eyes brighter than she'd ever noticed. She didn't know precisely what had changed him, but it seemed to have happened after he went back to Paris to retrieve the curved-tongue dagger. He pulled her close for a brief kiss on the lips, then released her and said, "Go back there and find your husband. He's having too much fun showing off, picking everyone's pockets."

"I guess he wants to prove himself after what happened with Papa picking his at the wedding." She hurried off to find Grady, leaving Chas and Wayren alone.

✝

"You have news about Cezar Moldavi," Chas said as soon as Macey was out of earshot.

"Yes," Wayren replied, looking up at him with a cryptic smile. "You aren't going to need to go to Siberia after all."

"I'm not?" Chas had no complaints about that—he certainly hadn't had any interest in going to the cold, remote region, ever.

"No. He's…resurfaced, and I've managed to learn where—and that's where I'd like to send you. If you'll agree to go."

"Of course I will," he replied. "I'm finished here, am I not?"

"You are indeed. You've done well, and—"

He didn't know whether it was permissible to interrupt an angel, but he did it anyway. "And I've changed quite a bit. Especially since I saw, and spoke to, Narcise."

"Indeed." Her smiled was so warm it threatened to bring tears to his eyes. "Chas, if you agree to go this time, it will be your last journey. That I promise you."

"I can't argue with that," he said, feeling a wave of relief. He was ready to be done, to find a home. A place. A permanent state of being. "So where are you sending me? Where has Cezar Moldavi escaped to?"

"Hollywood, California. In the year 2016."

Colleen Gleason is an award-winning, *New York Times* and *USA Today* best-selling author with more than twenty novels in print. Her international bestselling series, the Gardella Vampire Chronicles, is a historical urban fantasy about a female vampire hunter who lives during the time of Jane Austen. Her first novel, *The Rest Falls Away*, was released to acclaim in 2007.

Since then, she has published more than twenty novels with New American Library, MIRA Books, Chronicle Books, and HarperCollins (writing as Joss Ware). Her books have been translated into more than seven languages and are available worldwide.

Visit Colleen at:
colleengleason.com
facebook.com/colleen.gleason.author

Or sign up for new book release information from
Colleen Gleason here: **http://cgbks.com/news**